INFINITE EARTH: **PULSAR**

Written by: Bob Thomas and Suzanne Busch

"Never stop dreaming"

Table of Contents

Chapter 1 - The Deckers

IN THE NOT-TOO-DISTANT FUTURE…

Parker Decker's ten favorite action figures looked up at him from their lineup on his asteroid patterned comforter. He couldn't take them all on his vacation, Mom and Dad had been very clear about that. How could he know which ones he would want or need on this trip? Lasers, shields, armor, all had their strengths and weaknesses. Problem was, he wanted to be fair to his plastic companions, too.

"Many are called…" Laura Decker stood behind her son, feeling a familiar combination of tenderness and exasperation. Her son had inherited her indecisive nature. It was a blessing in some ways, but when time was of the essence, a kind of curse.

Parker turned to look at his mother with serious brown eyes. He'd gotten them from his father and they were the windows of an old soul.

"And I can take five, right?" he asked.

"There will be plenty of fun things to do when we get there," she said as she put an arm around him.

Sophia overheard them as she passed by in the hallway.

"I've got some, like, blackout times, so I won't be able to do anything with you guys when those happen," she said, not looking up from her device as she leaned on the doorframe.

"Blackout times?" Laura asked.

"There's a watch party for the Parusa concert. I can't miss that," she said as she swiped repeatedly. Parusa played the "best music I have ever heard in my *life*" according to fourteen-year-old Sophia. The Japanese boy band became popular at the start of the decade with their annoyingly repetitive hit, "Flirty Thirties." Laura dreaded hearing it again.

"When is this?" Laura asked. She was sure Sophia had already mentioned the concert but it had gotten lost in the last-minute frenzy.

"Saturday at sev-oh, no! Emma is going to Katelyn's house for the concert. She says all I talk about is the trip and she is tired of listening to me," Sophia began texting rapidly.

"Well, you wanted all your friends to be jealous," Laura reminded her.

Sophia paused to look up at her mother incredulously. "Now what am I supposed to do?"

Laura held up an action figure with lightning bolts coming out of his head.

"He'll keep you company," she smiled at Sophia, who rolled her eyes and left the room.

Laura walked to Parker's window and shook her head slightly. She still hadn't gotten used to the expanse of green that stretched to the foothills. Towering eucalyptus trees provided shade along the borders of the enormous lawn. Only a few years earlier, their entire corner of the country had been drought stricken.

Then the pendulum began to swing in the opposite direction. Scientists more concerned with the health of their grandchildren than "corporate growth" began to look for ways to keep the planet alive. Their students developed breeds of trees that could thrive with one-tenth of the water normally required. The theorized "plant sunscreen" became a reality that changed the complexion of the conversation surrounding air quality.

Contemporaneously, the American love affair with cars, like most infatuations, came to an end. Automobiles were replaced with something younger, faster and greener. It seemed inevitable in retrospect. In all likelihood, the inventors of automobiles would have found modern reliance on cars and the sheer number of vehicles in the world astounding.

There were loops of these new vehicles of varying shapes and sizes in the air above the greenspace. Vehicles making local stops glided along the lower level. High above them were crafts making regional and even international liaisons. They were using a virtual highway that had rendered cars, trucks and the like, nearly obsolete.

Sophia made her way to the end of the hall where her father Ryan sat in his office. His back was to her as he studied how his stocks were performing against the S&P. When she was seven, her father had told her that S&P stood for Sophia and Parker. She believed him. For a few years, anyway. He said S&P were two of the most important people in the world to him, and she still believed those words to this day.

Her father looked at complicated charts and graphs and explained them in ways she could understand. He would listen to her problems with school and friends and offer solutions she had never considered. She knew that he would somehow see to it that every family member had an amazing vacation, watching every detail, considering every variable. He left nothing to chance.

"All packed, Dad?" Sophia asked in jest. Ryan was packed first, ready first, and now he was doing the last check up on his favorite company, S.E.T.I. Industries in the final few minutes they had before leaving.

He swirled around in his chair to look at her. "I will be soon, but I don't remember where I left my suitcase," he replied, smiling at his daughter. "Which of the superheroes are coming with us?"

Sophia smirked. "As many as Parker can sneak in his bag and coat pockets and shoes. I know he's bringing the worm face guy."

"If we don't leave soon, Parker may jump out the window," Ryan Decker told her with a smile.

"That was a false alarm five minutes ago. It looked like an Agridrone to me," she said.

"I CAN SEE IT!" Parker shouted from his bedroom.

"Ok," Ryan said. Go time, showtime, get away from home time.

As the family lumbered to the front door, laden with bags, Laura checked the settings on the Home System panel. All good. From outside the house, Ryan watched the front door click and send the pattern of flashing lights that indicated the house was secure.

Parker shielded his eyes with his hand as he watched the gleaming silver object perform a seamless vertical descent onto the spacious rectangle of paving stones in front of the Deckers' home that were designed for this very purpose.

It was slightly larger than the typical minivan, but nothing about this vehicle suggested generic suburbanites. A low, purring sound rose from the lower portion of the craft as a mechanical arm materialized from the right rear side.

"Oh, right, the bags," Ryan stacked them up beneath the arm that beeped in recognition of the bag under it and pulled it off the ground and into the rear compartment.

"You were expecting a bellhop to get out and stow our bags for us?" Laura asked.

"Why don't we get a good-looking bellhop with this?" Sophia asked, checking her reflection in the shimmering panel.

"Look at this!" Parker exclaimed as he circled the vehicle for the second time. He had not seen one appointed quite like this one before. He had ridden in smaller, more economical versions of this enigma. They often delivered groceries or took kids to school. But this was a Sol-ution. An image of the Roman god Sol and his chariot, the company's logo, announced to anyone close enough to see it that the Deckers had purchased the Rolls Royce of the Virtual Global Highway Transportation System, or VGHTS. "Vites" as the Virtual Transportation Authority liked to call it.

The models that college students and young families used were like the Hyundai's and Kia's back when people still drove cars. They had none of the amenities of the Sol-ution.

The avalanche of information appearing on the holographic screen that adjusted itself to Ryan's eye level was amazing. It informed him that radiation levels at their destination, the Bora Bora Bezos Hotel were minimal and expected to continue receding. Weather conditions, reservation confirmation number and suggested activities based on the Deckers' previous vacations appeared and dissolved as the pupil scanner determined when Ryan had finished reading each line.

"Welcome Deckers, are you ready to board?" The message flashed up against a backdrop of Mount Otemanu. Ryan pulled Parker in front of him to bestow the privilege of pressing the green "YES" button. It read the boy's fingerprint as seconds later, the hum of the machine rose to a higher pitch.

Laura smiled, world-weary Sophia's eyes widened and Parker threw decorum to the wind, jumping up and down. The silver door opened at the bottom and rose gracefully to reveal the Decker's home away from home until they reached their little slice of heaven in French Polynesia.

While much of the craft featured cutting-edge use of technology, the engineers at Andromeda who designed the interior had the sense to consult "Lifestyle Guru to the Stars," Taylor Jensen for tips on how to create a welcoming environment for travelers with high expectations.

The air flowing out of the Sol was precisely 71 degrees Fahrenheit and smelled faintly of ylang ylang, as Laura had requested in the preboarding questionnaire. Chopin's Etude Op. 10 played softly over the speakers as Sophia and Parker hurried to their respective corners of the Sol, frantically searching for ear buds and an escape from "Mom's music."

They flopped into their flat-bed seats covered with down comforters while sheets of razor thin glass rose at their feet and began to glow. The image of a smiling actor appeared on Sophia's screen, but a video feed of her friends waving goodbye quickly replaced it. She waved back. Parker's screen featured fighting dinosaurs. Decimator tucked securely by his side, he told the screen to display his three favorite movies, unsure of which one he wanted to watch.

Ryan looked over his shoulder at his children, happy they were settling in so easily. Glancing around the cabin, the arrangement reminded Ryan of a trip he had taken to Paris as a youngster. At the last minute, for a small premium and some good negotiating, his father finagled an upgrade into a luxury class Aero Series. The interior of the Aero was a bit smaller, seating only four people, but was equally well appointed.

For all its high-tech features, the most popular area on the Sol was the "bite storage" area. It boasted a well-stocked refrigerator, an air fryer, a small sink with counter space and an espresso machine. Wine and beer were available for a small fee. Laura Decker found all the organic fruits and vegetables she's requested in the fridge. She also knew each seat had a miniature heating drawer next to a refrigerated drawer in the side panel, and was sure the kids had brought their own snacks.

"Departing in sixty seconds. Begin safety check," a voice said over the speakers. It belonged to Vesta, the Roman goddess of home and family, as well as the vehicle's answer to Siri. A series of clicks and hums came from the front of the Sol. Lights on the screen in front of Ryan Decker flashed on and off a few times. Laura tapped two buttons on her armrest and smiled over at her husband. They hadn't taken a vacation together in almost a year.

"Entering Vites in thirty seconds," the voice said calmly.

Ryan looked out over the miles of fields as the Sol gracefully ascended well above the tree line. He was tempted to tell his children about travel when he was a boy, but decided it would make him seem the stereotypical old timer they already thought he was. He was glad they didn't have layers of smog to rise above, and that they didn't have to stand sock-footed in long lines at security checkpoints.

No, this was a new world, he thought as the Sol merged smoothly into the flow of traffic, adjusting its speed to that of the vehicles in its immediate proximity. His children would probably work at jobs that didn't even exist yet, in industries that were emerging in every part of the world where people envisioned a better Earth. And none of this would have happened, he realized, without an incredible leap in technology.

"Don't wanna sound dirty, but it's the flirty thirties," Sophia roared along with the song, unaware of how loud she was. Laura glanced over her shoulder and smiled at Parker who was too engrossed in his movie to notice.

None of these entertaining wonders would have been possible without the recent paradigm shift in transportation, including the miraculous ability for this machine to fly through the air with the aid of a computer that seemed to know everything: atmospheric conditions high above the earth, the proximity of children wandering too close to potential dangers, and deep below the earth's surface, the movements of the magnetic fields in the planet's core.

It was this foray into the earth's molten center that allowed machines to glide above it. Ryan remembered showing Parker how Sols flew using two refrigerator magnets. He placed a superhero magnet in each of his son's hands, negative to negative.

"They won't go together!" Parker said with amazement.

"That's how we stay in the air," Ryan told his son. "And when we want to land," he flipped over a magnet featuring an orange haired creature. "We do this."

He brought the magnets a few inches apart and the creature attached himself to Decimator with a satisfying click. Parker smiled and his eyes were full of the kind of wonder that fills a parent's heart.

It was a little more complicated than that, but the principle was the same. The Deckers could count on the Sol to do exactly what it was programmed to do. The vehicle and the Earth's core were somehow magically woven together in ways the average traveler didn't need to understand. As long as the two of them knew how to communicate perfectly together, that's all that really mattered to most passengers.

According to the VTA, there was very little to worry about while traveling on the Vites. The system was now so reliable that incident reports across the network had become almost non-existent. Thanks to the cutting-edge computers operating these new vehicles, traveling and commuting these days had become safer than a walk to the park.

Had this remained the case, the trip to Bora Bora would have been exciting, but still predictable.

But computers cannot predict everything, because they do not know everything. They only know what people tell them to know. The systems guiding the Deckers to their tropical paradise had no way of knowing what was taking place on the other side of the world. They did what they were programmed to do, until for reasons no one aboard the Sol could fathom, they were unable to perform as programmed.

The Sol shuddered briefly, and Sophia's matcha soda tipped slightly in its freon cooled cup holder. Parker had grown bored with his movie and began pressing buttons on a Sol control panel that he had somehow accessed on his display. As it turned out, Ryan had failed to lock in the Sol's controls when he confirmed that Bora Bora would be the destination that day. Touching an icon under the Vehicle Mode's menu labeled MORE presented Parker with a new option that he had not seen before. Pronouncing it under his breath as he touched the screen, IN-THE-CELLAR or something like that, he thought. He then looked over at his sister and shrugged as the Sol shivered again.

"What's the first thing we want to do when we get there?" Laura asked her children.

"Parasailing!" Sophia said.

"Shark hunting!" Parker said with a huge grin.

"No one wants to go bird watching? The ultramarine lorikeet is really…" Laura searched for the words but stopped as the Sol lurched to the left. It snapped back into place just as quickly, jostling the Deckers.

Ryan, not yet panicking, began to reach for Laura. Instantaneously and violently, a psychedelic flash of blinding light hit the Sol and left it in the dark. Ryan could no longer see his hand as he reached into a vast nothingness. Everything was happening in slow motion. Everyone was screaming as deafening silence overtook the craft.

It was like riding a rollercoaster while blindfolded, with no idea when or where the ride would end. Sophia yelled to her brother, but no sound came from her mouth. In the darkened Sol, she could barely make out Parker's movements, but he was moving at a fraction of his normal speed.

All the passengers' ears popped, their stomachs dropped and the weight of their bodies became unbearable as the Sol tried in vain to maintain its flight mode. The light was everywhere and anywhere now, and it completely consumed the Deckers.

The panel indicators overhead in the Sol blinked three times, and a high-pitched alarm sounded. Ryan and Laura, their necks too heavy to turn, exchanged frantic glances with only their eyes.

"Unexpected system shutdown," Vesta said flatly. "Please brace, brace, brace…"

Laura heard strange, whirring sounds as the Sol tore through the swirling cloud of light.

Ryan said his prayers as his blood throbbed painfully in his veins and the pull became too strong to resist. He was grateful he could go with his family. At least they were all together, Laura thought as she surrendered to the forces that overtook the Sol.

Then silence. The Sol's instrument panel went dark, the ceiling lights went off. The screens sank into their storage slots as if retreating in fear.

The last thing Laura heard was her son's voice. It echoed off the walls of the Sol. The sound embedded itself in her head and ripped her heart open. Parker was screaming for his mother.

The Sol either wasn't designed for this type of travel, or it wasn't ready for it. When finally, it had landed on solid ground, a haze rose from the hull of the craft. The front panel was badly cracked. The Deckers' belongings were strewn about the cabin. The occupants were still in their seats, miraculously. Disoriented and banged up, but alive.

"Everybody here?" Ryan asked as he looked around the cabin.

"Oh, my God," Sophia breathed.

"What happened?" Parker asked.

"Ryan?" Laura's voice seemed to come from a thousand miles away as she peered out a portal.

Laura's voice trembled when she spoke. "Where are we?" she asked.

Chapter 2 - Area 51

PRESENT DAY...

There was nothing logical about Nevada, Leo Raines thought as he drove through the desert before sunrise. He was leaving the neon fever dream of Las Vegas for a place that didn't really exist. Well, it existed, but not on any maps, or according to the government. It had no mailing address and certainly no Internet presence.

But there was only so much people could do with logic, so many things about this world and the people in it that logic couldn't explain. Our desires, our fears, nothing reasonable to see there. Move along.

Leo rolled down the window of his beat-up Honda and let the crisp desert air fill his head. December in these parts was especially dry and clear. The stars were plentiful and bright this far from the city. No matter how overwhelmed he sometimes felt when he thought about everything on his plate, looking at the stars made him feel like there was some kind of order, a master plan.

The only other time Leo felt this way was when, after a thorough security check, he entered his domain, The Warehouse. If that place wasn't an example of reason and order, nothing was. Every single object, from a paperclip to a stainless-steel cylinder the size of a six-story building, had a precise location. Each object stayed in its location until and unless the Powers that Be, after careful deliberation and analysis, decreed movement was necessary.

It was Christmas Eve, but what really mattered to Leo was that this was the fourth Thursday of the month. That meant that any item in The Warehouse was potentially up for eviction. The mode of transportation they would leave on would be a military transport plane, the C-17 cargo plane which departed at 1700 hours bound for the East Coast at near dusk on those days. Most of the flights ended up in Washington and then taken by courier over to Langley where they'd be kept in much of the same type of warehouse, but this time in the basement warehouse under the feet of a bunch of shadowy important people. Crates weren't the only thing riding on that plane. Leo's future depended on this upcoming flight going according to plan.

If the warehouse had been a planet, it would have been Jupiter. If it was an animal, it would have been a blue whale. Leo saved hundreds on gym memberships because walking from one end of his workplace to the other served as his cardio for the week. He made sure his coworkers saw him moving around without the utility vehicle from time to time.

His coworkers were, for the most part, a very logical bunch. More than half of them were robots. A few of them got a little tetchy when they were in danger of overheating, but he couldn't blame them.

The robots didn't seem especially curious about the contents of the crates, and most of the time, Leo wasn't either. Like libraries, he found many stockpiles of information the government deemed interesting to be rather dull. He also found the classification system for the inventory as bewildering as the Dewey Decimal system, at least at first.

Of course, he had heard the rumors of preserved alien corpses and carefully guarded remnants of UFO's that had crashed in the desert during the 1940's. There were people who thought whatever landed out there seventy-something years ago brought us everything from silicon chips to vaccines. But during the five years he'd worked in The Warehouse, the strangest thing he'd seen was an albino scorpion.

Leo passed a small group of robots whirring along aisle LU6 as they reorganized smaller crates, scanning barcodes from their databases and determining which items they should declassify or reclassify.

"Morning fellas," he said as they ignored him.

And if everything went according to plan, these directions would solve all his problems and bring him pretty close to being out of debt along with a little pocket change. They might even bring him love.

He rounded the corner at the end of the aisle and found Sam, the Chief Security Officer, or CSO, watching a robot as it received instructions from the D.C. control room.

"What's up, Sam?" Leo asked his supervisor.

"Hey Raines, just taking out the garbage," he chuckled. That was how Sam described the robots rounding up crates of declassified material and shipping them to the CIA offices in the Washington DC area.

"Right," Leo smiled. It was already happening. It had to be soon. Timing was everything here. And luck. Luck was the only way he could explain his encounter with Hannah.

They'd met in the casino, of all places. He had noticed her around the slot machines, but he didn't think a woman like Hannah would return his hello. She was above average height and slender, with long dark hair and eyes full of mischief.

It turned out she had just gotten divorced, and was blowing off a little steam. She said she knew she had seen him there before. He didn't tell her he was at one casino or another all night, every night. And he would never visit a casino again once he got things straightened out.

Had he known her for a week when she gave him the proposition? It couldn't have been much longer, he realized. It didn't involve the same kind of risks as the casino, but the money was too good to turn down. He would be out of debt, with enough left over to start again somewhere else.

He had no idea what he would have done if she hadn't showed up at the blackjack table that night. He was going to have a big win and he knew it, as he strode up to the table, ready to be dealt.

"Bring the rain, baby!" That was how he announced his arrival. Every. Single. Time. The dealer eyed him warily and fiddled with the chips longer than normal. Turned out he was just waiting for Raoul, the Pit Boss. That guy had never liked him, and there was no convincing him that one more game wouldn't hurt anything. They cut him off.

"Mr. Raines, we are going to have to ask you to settle up your debts before we can allow you to continue playing tonight," he said stiffly.

Leo failed to play it cool. His shoulders slumped, he stammered. Raoul had never been this much of a jerk before.

"I got this," a female voice said. Leo looked to his left and nearly did a double take. A very nice-looking lady was standing next to him, laying five hundred-dollar bills on the green felt.

The dealer's eyebrows shot up and he looked at Leo.

"You heard her," Leo said triumphantly. She even wanted to tap on his poker chips for good luck.

They ended up breaking even, and laughing about it as they sat at a 24-hour diner across the street later that night.

"Casinos are ok for entertainment and everything, but they're not the place to go for big money," Hannah said.

Leo munched on a french fry as he considered what she said. "What do you mean?"

"You have to consider how much people can pay for what they want," she explained between bites of a BLT.

"Well, after tonight, I can afford a lot more, thanks to you," he said. She had beautiful eyes, he thought to himself for the tenth time that night.

"You and I can afford things like dinner in all-night diners," she smiled. "But there are people who can pay thousands of times what this meal costs for things they really, really want."

Leo had a funny feeling in his stomach, and it wasn't from the food.

"What do they really want?" he asked.

She had told him about things that were rare, things that were secret. And sometimes, *sometimes* they could pay outrageous sums of money for these things. For example, the things in the warehouse where Leo worked.

Leo laughed. "If you're looking for an alien, I can tell you, I've been there five years and never saw one. If you're some kind of spy..."

Hannah laughed. "A spy on the outskirts of Henderson driving an old Toyota? Not a very good spy if that's the case," she reached across the table to touch his hand lightly.

"So what's in there that's worth so much money to someone?"

"You know, I'm really not sure," her eyes held that mischief he was growing to love. "I don't know the what, or the where, even. I have a pretty good idea who sent this box of stuff. You guys at the warehouse can find things if you know who sent them there, right?" she was looking at him intently now.

"Well, yes, but why would I do that?" Leo wasn't following.

Hannah finished the last of her sandwich and looked very pleased with herself. "Because if you can find what I want and help me get it out of there, you get one hundred thousand dollars," she told him.

Leo blinked a few times and waited for her to say, 'just kidding!" But she simply sat there and waited for the blood to flow back into his head. When it did, he smiled back at her, imagining paying off his debts and maybe...seeing her again.

"Ok then," he said as he remembered her first words that evening. "I've got this!"

He had memorized the steps he would take and was reciting them in his head for the hundredth time. He had practiced at home, rehearsing and timing the movements he would need to make. Between sixty and 90 seconds. What to say if caught? Argue at first, then when Sam pointed out the "mistake" the second time, slap forehead and apologize.

First the fakeout. Leo paid special attention to a random box sitting six or seven feet from his target. He pretended to examine the label in much more detail than normal, squinting at it and tilting his head a little.

Moving on, he checked Sam's location and monitored the robots. It was almost time. It was just like he'd imagined it.

He stood before the crate and ran his hand over the top absently. Was it his nerves, or was this thing vibrating? Why was it so warm? Why were his hands so warm? Oh, no sweaty palms all over the crate. Sam would ask about that.

He stepped back and rubbed his hands on his jeans. He paused for a moment and listened for ticking. That was the kind of luck only he would have. The headlines would have been incredible: Bomb Destroys Top Secret Warehouse! No ticking. Maybe the hum was from a bot.

It all came down to a kind of ballet between the two main groups of robots, the Printer models and the Picker types. A group of them formed a line at the end of one aisle, looking like menacing Roomba vacuums as they waited for digital instructions. Sometimes Leo could swear they had eyes.

Printers received commands to generate labels reassigning the designation (and destination) of the package. There was "Top Secret," material that stayed in The Warehouse. The next classification was Level 3. Material downgraded to this level often went to Washington, New York, or military installations around the United States. Level 2 crates were not as numerous, and usually became subject to public scrutiny. Anything with a Level 1 label went to a place where they never existed, the crematorium.

Pickers prowled the aisles and scanned the crates top to bottom, including the labels that the printers affixed to the crates. Once the picker "read" the label instructions, if the picker bot determined your number was up, you were loaded up and off you went to your new home.

Heart thumping so hard it pounded in his ears, Leo picked up an idle robot and walked it calmly to the janitor's closet in the very back, poorly lit corner of the maintenance area of the warehouse. Finding no one in the closet, he quickly sent the machine into manual mode, typed in a memorized string of numbers, letters, and symbols and hastily printed a label that would most certainly send the crate to the right loading bay that would finish the score. Forty-five seconds.

He strolled out of the room with the label in his pocket and approached his target while scanning the aisle for potential hazards. None. Like an old friend, a bright red Picker bot was some fifteen feet away, busily extracting crates and stacking them for delivery.

Sixty seconds in, Leo nonchalantly glanced up at the nearest security camera hoping it wasn't noticing him. Looking as casual as humanly possible under these conditions, he placed his newly generated label over the old one on the targeted crate that would change his life forever. Despite his perspiring hands, the label stayed in place, looking perfectly...normal.

Leo backed up to make way for the Picker and fought the urge to kiss this machine that made his payday possible. His breathing was still labored, and he could feel the sweat dripping down his forehead as he watched the Picker scan the label and grasp the crate in its mechanical embrace.

He exhaled for what seemed like the first time in hours. Ninety seconds. Hannah had paid him twenty-five thousand dollars up front to complete this part of the task. Five figures! He watched the Picker finish the work for the aisle and turn a corner.

Leo hadn't had that much money since, he couldn't remember. He had completed his mission, he realized. Why did he feel so lightheaded? Spots danced in front of his eyes. He would be out of debt, he thought as his knees threatened to buckle.

Oh! He quickly grabbed the edge of a shelf to steady himself. Sam passed by as he swayed slightly, trying to regain his balance.

"You ok, there?" Sam asked as he turned to look at him.

"Just trying to keep up with these robots," Leo said.

The C-17 was loaded, but not taking off for the same reasons commercial air travelers sit on the tarmac, sometimes for hours. Someone forgot something. Paperwork was missing. It was hectic, with planes coming in and out of Las Vegas, packed full of Christmas presents and people trying to reach holiday destinations and avoid bad weather.

But if that plane didn't leave, Leo wouldn't get his money. Growing increasingly anxious, he clocked out as the sun set and drove to a fast-food restaurant in Indian Springs. He sat in the dark, his Honda parked facing north so he could see the cargo plane as it went wheels up.

Hannah wasn't responding to the texts he'd been sending her all afternoon. He had wanted to share the excitement with her, and wondered if she was alright. What if this had all been…No, he couldn't let himself entertain that possibility.

Where was a distraction when he needed one? He turned off the annoying Christmas carols on the radio and stared out at the night sky. As a teen, he had memorized most of the major constellations. He found the one that was named after that queen. Chlamydia? No, Cassiopeia. He spotted the three stars that made up Orion's belt and could have sworn the middle star winked at him.

It was too much. Leo couldn't stand it any longer and picked up his phone. He opened the app for his newly acquired offshore bank account, entered his password and looked at his checking account balance. $100,213.22. Merry Christmas! This must have meant the C-17 was cleared for take-off.

He looked up in wonder, just in time to see the massive C-17 defying gravity as it became airborne, its red and green lights blinking like cheerful holiday decorations. It roared as it rose into the night sky, heading for Dulles International Airport.

Chapter 3 - Adam Hunter

"I'm dreaming of a white Christmas…" The singer crooned over Sirius XM while Director of Space Relations and Counterintelligence Adam Hunter looked out the window of his second-floor office, dreaming of ways to design better material for vehicles.

It was raining heavily in the predawn hours this Christmas morning, and downtown D.C. was as close to empty as it would ever be. Adam had found this was one of his most productive times. He could do what he, and all visionaries do best: reimagine the world around him…and beyond him.

His imagination had always been powerful. When Adam was seven, he was able to locate the three stars that formed Orion's belt in the night sky. He was convinced the middle star represented him. His older sister, Elizabeth, was the top star and the lower star was younger brother, Michael.

That's what the man at the museum had told him, sort of. He'd handed the boy a map of the stars when his class went on a field trip to the Seattle Space Museum. The children walked single file past a man wearing all black on their way to the model of a pulsar.

"This is for you, Adam," the man said. "You know, your family is in the stars," he smiled as Adam stumbled slightly, trying to stop and talk to the man who somehow knew his name. The line of second graders kept moving toward the pulsar display, but the man retreated toward a framed photograph of Einstein, one of Adam's heroes.

In school, Adam didn't mind wearing the less than flattering labels his classmates gave him: nerd, science nut, alien guy. Like many people whose ideas seem "out there," Adam developed a thick skin and a refusal to take derision personally. His focus was more on ideas than people, who confounded him with their limited ideas and lack of imagination.

His undergraduate years at Stanford University had been fortunate. He was able to meet hundreds of like-minded people and find mentors who shared and inspired his theories about the possibilities of the unknown. His degree in aerospace engineering was the first step towards a career in what he jokingly referred to as "flying saucer construction."

Working for MIT's AeroAstro after graduation, he developed "shape memory polymers" for spacecraft. These polymers enhanced the durability and longevity of spacecraft, especially those on deep space missions. He wrote his doctoral dissertation on external hull polymers and the effects of prolonged exposure to high levels of magnetism and radiation at high speeds. He was designing spacecraft like their creator: keen on exploring and tough enough to withstand the journey to uncharted territory.

It was at this juncture that Adam realized that he liked the ideas more than the day-to-day work of engineering, and decided to join the CIA. He kept telling himself that this was the only reason he wanted to work there; his decision had nothing to do with Operations Officer Julie Brody, with her graceful walk and dark, curly hair.

A few weeks of open-ended questions about Julie's job led to an invitation to the movies. A short time later, they announced their relationship status to Human Resources, the grownup version of the boy giving the girl his letterman jacket. A little over a year later, they married at the Grace Reformed Church.

It was a classic case of opposites attracting and complementing each other as essential parts of a whole. Adam loved the theoretical, Julie was practical. He was reserved, Julie befriended people easily and learned their life stories in minutes. She wanted to root out the bad guys and keep people safe. Adam wanted, as the beloved tv show announced, to boldly go...

And go he did, up the career ladder. Not long after their son Christopher was born, Adam became the liaison to NASA and the newer military branch the Space Force. He loved being the glue that kept the White House and the Pentagon united in their activities to ensure they remained in alignment with the strategic objectives of the United States.

Adam had built such a reputation as the go-to guy for "flying saucer consulting" that when private businesses began to view space exploration as profitable, he was in charge of keeping an eye on them. He monitored SpaceX, Virgin Galactic and Blue Origin, among others. Most of the time these companies behaved themselves, but sometimes in their hunger for profits, they ran afoul of Uncle Sam.

He had been in this role for two years when he and Julie welcomed their daughter Brianna. Julie had accumulated enough seniority by this time that they were able to afford a house in Leesburg. When Brianna started first grade, Julie began to talk about going back to school for a PhD or changing fields with increasing frequency. She loved problem-solving and the sense of purpose intelligence work gave her, but it also brought her in very close contact with a side of human nature that would disturb any parent.

"Run for mayor? Are you out of your mind?" was Adam's first reaction to her proposed career change.

"I know it seems all of a sudden to you, but I've been thinking about this for a long time. And we've been careful with money, the kids can still go to college..." she explained one night after a particularly stressful day at work.

"You've said yourself politicians are corrupt and idiots. Why do you want to be one of them?" he asked, exasperated.

"I just feel like I would be doing something that really had an impact on people's lives. I don't even know how to talk to you sometimes. It's like you're light years away," she smiled ruefully.

"My work is really important to me," he said quietly.

Julie looked at him. Was she holding her breath?

"And so are you and the kids. You're the most important," he said. She knew he was telling the truth. If she was going to be as honest with him as he was with her, she knew she had to tell him what else she had been thinking about.

"Sometimes I feel like we just get in the way of your work," she told him.

"Are you asking me to choose between my work and you guys?" he asked, beginning to feel knots in his stomach.

"No, I'm not..." she began hesitantly. "But I wonder if living apart for a while might help us figure out where we stand."

Their arguments continued for months. The children began asking if they had done something wrong. Adam had to give her credit for realizing it before he did. They were better off as co-parents living in separate houses. They finalized their divorce two years later. That November, Julie became mayor. Adam organized the party to help her celebrate.

There were many people in the global village of D.C. who did not celebrate Christmas. They were happy to work on the day that so many reserved for family and faith. There were also people who celebrated the holiday but needed work.

Plenty of them were bustling about Dulles International Airport, an architectural paean to flight. It was a modern, largely transparent building with a roof that curled upwards. Anxious travelers hurried to dinners and gift openings, while on the lower level of the airport, workers were unloading cargo at the military facility, where it would reach its final destination.

It was a routine event, all except for the crate with instructions to be delivered to an underground warehouse beneath the CIA building in Langley, Virginia. The crate cleared the entrance security procedure, but after reaching shipping and receiving, it caused Chief of Security Rey Santos' scanner to make an unusual beep as it passed over the label.

"Level 4? That can't be right," he muttered.

“Do it again,” his coworker Paul suggested. This was the highest security classification they had ever seen. Anything at a Level 5 would have arrived in a plastic bubble surrounded by the Secret Service.

Rey waved his scanner over the crate a second time and heard the curious four tones again. The screen on his scanner confirmed it.

“We gotta find somebody high-up to sign for this thing,” he told Paul.

“On Christmas? I'll call the President,” he joked.

“What about the guy on the third floor?” Rey asked.

“Hunter? He's here?” Paul said.

“That guy never leaves,” Rey said as he began dialing his phone.

Adam worked in space exploration for free, but his salary was compensation for the cost of all the unnecessary, idiotic paperwork government jobs required. He planned to get caught up on the important but dull tasks in time to see his kids roll out of bed late on this rainy morning. He was nearly finished with a report that he doubted anyone would ever read when his desk phone rang.

“Hunter,” he said, looking at the caller ID. It was downstairs.

“Yeah, it's Santos. Look, sorry to bother you, but we have a crate or something and you're the only one with the clearance to sign for it. Can you come down for a minute?” he asked.

“What would have come at this time of year?” Adam wondered out loud. “Sure, I'll be right down.”

It was a good chance to stretch his legs as he winded his way through the corridors. Passing by windows, he could see the Washington Parkway and its never-ending construction project. With the weather and the holidays, vehicle accidents were more than likely. Crews had placed enough lights on the road to make it look like Las Vegas.

He found Rey and Paul at the counter looking bored.

“Is that my stuff from Roswell?” Adam joked.

“Are you going to sell it on eBay?” Paul asked.

Adam smiled and inspected the label. The crate was roughly four feet long and three feet high. There were no labels indicating that the contents were fragile. He shook it lightly and listened for rattling. Thankfully, it didn't smell like much of anything. People outside the industry wouldn't believe it, but the CIA was full of pranksters.

“You know, I'm leaving soon and I'll be out til the 28th, maybe I'll just take it up to my office for now. I'll take it to the basement on my way out,” he told the men.

"I'll put it on the dolly and we'll leave it with you," Rey said.

"You don't mind?" Adam asked.

"Does it look like we're busy?" Paul gestured to the vacant room.

Determined to finish the paperwork, Adam sat in his office with his back to the window and the crate stored in the corner. No distractions. Well, it was almost six. Julie would be awake. He switched off his desk lamp and shot her a text.

Merry Christmas! What's a good time to come by?

A light flashed from a passing truck and he couldn't read his screen momentarily.

Dot…dot…dot…

The kids probably won't be up for a few hours, but come anytime, came Julie's response.

Want me to bring something for lunch? He often stopped by the one open grocery store in the area. The mayor was busy.

Dot…dot…dot…

Again the flashes! Traffic was picking up out there. He walked to the windows and snapped the blinds shut with annoyance.

My friend Brian might stop by for lunch. Don't worry, I'm making enough turkey and stuffing for everyone!

Her friend Brian? That idiot from the Chamber of Commerce? What? How long had this been going on? He sat in the dark, staring at his paperwork, feeling like he'd been punched in the gut.

It was going to happen, he realized. She would move on, and so would he. It was good that she was meeting new people. Things change, he told himself

A blue light slowly filled his office, growing more intense. Then it stopped. Adam turned around to look at the blinds. They were shut.

Sounds great, he responded. He was tempted to add a smiley emoji but stopped himself.

Back to the dark and sulking. Again the light filled the office, this time it was green.

The light lingered, and began to take on a yellow cast. He checked the blinds. Still closed.

It was coming from somewhere in the room, but it was off at the moment.

Adam walked around the desk to the center of his spacious office. Nothing in the room could produce light. His computer monitor was off. He looked at the rows of bookshelves sitting silently.

Now his office glowed with an orange light that made him laugh. It was so cheerful and strange.

And he realized the light was coming from the crate. The glow grew brighter as he walked toward it. The closer he came; he realized it was also vibrating slightly.

What on earth had they sent in this crate? It had been X-rayed, surely, he thought as he considered calling PSBD. No, he decided, he was going to open it. Very carefully.

He wheeled the crate next to the coffee table in the middle of his office. Two cushioned chairs sat on one side and his couch was next to the wall. He took a deep breath, crouched down and opened the wooden lid.

Light pulsed out of the crate and pushed at the walls of his office. Adam detected a change in air pressure and felt his heartbeat accelerate. He watched a ball of light circle the perimeter of the room, blink three times, as if having assessed its dimensions, and hover near the window. It mesmerized him, until he realized something was still happening in the crate.

Tiny whitecaps were forming on top of the liquid that had mysteriously filled the wooden box. It sloshed around as if an invisible hand was stirring it, until a metallic object no bigger than a grape leapt up from the fluid and flew several feet into the air. There was a low buzz as it moved to join the light near the window.

He looked back into the crate. It was completely dry now, and a much more solid looking object sat at the bottom. It looked like an elliptical sphere, some two feet in diameter. A giant egg? It was made of something that resembled white gold, and gleamed so furiously Adam could not be sure if it was moving or just very, very reflective. There were no visible doors, knobs, windows, switches or buttons. If this was a practical joke from the FBI, his hat was off to them.

Adam sat next to the crate and studied the object. It was remarkably beautiful, but did it do anything? He glanced warily at the two…things near the window. They dimmed slightly, as if saying, *pay us no mind.* Ok, time to investigate.

He stood up, and holding the object as carefully as he had held his newborns, placed it on top of his table. He took another deep breath and tapped the top of the egg. His intake of breath seemed to pull the blue light out of the large egg as a holographic image passed through Adam's body.

Alarmed, he stood as the light formed a rectangle around him, waist high. He looked down to see that there was a virtual tabletop and he was in the middle of it. Numbers, symbols and images glowed on the glossy black surface before rearranging themselves to make way for screens that displayed an oval of light, just like the shape of the object that had produced everything Adam was witnessing.

The holographs had now filled the office with light the color of new spring leaves. They were rising on a gridded vertical plane now, reminding Adam of his 85-inch flat screen tv at home, except this one seemed to encompass his peripheral vision.

All his attention was focused on the screen as he stood frozen with fear. He grew calmer as the image on the screen changed from the ellipse to a forest. It looked so much like the one he played in growing up in Bellingham...Then an image of Stanford University appeared on the screen. That dissolved into recently captured video footage of the CIA building he was in, or was it live? Then the picture disappeared and the screen went dark.

Adam stared at it. He wasn't sure if he had been in his office for five minutes or five hours. His ears were ringing and he wasn't sure if he was still standing *in the middle of a table*. He watched the blank screen, uncertain if he was imagining ripples on the screen's surface.

As the seconds ticked by, he realized it was not his imagination, but the ripples seemed to be coming from underneath the screen, as if something was underneath it and moving toward him. This object commanded the attention of the entire room.

He would always remember these moments, watching the protruding form on the screen. Somehow, he was realizing the beginning of a new part of his existence. At the same time, it was like being united with an old friend. He was simply awestruck when the form emerged, non-threatening and complete.

It was a man's face. With a small smile, it greeted him.

"Hello, Adam."

Chapter 4 – Logistical Ubiquitous Companion

"Hello," Adam replied, surprised that his voice sounded normal. His heart was racing. If he was hearing voices, and seeing the people the voices belonged to, did that mean he was losing his mind?

Adam's brain was working overtime in an effort to keep up with the overwhelming sensory input. He watched the background behind the face become the night sky. He saw himself standing with Elizabeth and Michael as he pointed out the constellations. The crickets were chirping a symphony and he was sure he could smell the insecticide his mother sprayed the kids with on summer nights.

The scene changed, but the face's gentle smile did not. Adam watched himself as he walked across the campus at MIT. Then he saw a series of strange blueprints. He tried to study them but the background changed to solid, peaceful blue.

"It is wonderful to finally meet you, Adam," the voice said. It had some of the qualities of a human voice, but Adam could tell it didn't belong to a person, not entirely.

"It's nice to meet you, sir," Adam said. He knew Adam's name, but Adam had no idea how to address this entity.

"Let's dispense with formalities, shall we? Please call me Luc," he said.

"Like the Apostle?" Adam asked, struggling to link this apparition to something, or someone familiar.

"It's spelled differently," he told Adam.

"Why did you say 'finally' meet me?" Adam asked.

"I've been watching you since you were young. It's been encouraging to see you travel this road and watch you imagine possibilities."-

"Why are you here, Luc?" It seemed the best question with the least words.

"Much like you, it would be accurate to say I work here, and I have been for some time. And like you, I'm often involved in projects that help people." As he said this, the images floated on the screen behind him. Adam recognized them as ribosomes and proteasomes, involved in vaccines.

"Unlike you, my work involves solving many different types of problems and serving a larger group of people," he explained as images of silicon chips appeared on the virtual wall behind him. "Our skills may fit together to create something everyone needs."

"Your ideas about building materials are impressive. The polymers have advanced your position in your field considerably," he said. "I have an opportunity for you."

"You're here on business," Adam said, trying to sound matter of fact.

"You could say that. Isn't building things with advanced materials and then ensuring they adhere to the proper protocols your business?" Luc asked.

Adam wasn't sure how to answer. Facilitating the dreams of a bunch of rocket scientists and visionaries was hardly a job. Many of them studied our solar system and wondered how far the polymers Adam developed would take them. They had no idea how useful they could be right here on Earth.

As much as Adam enjoyed the theoretical part of his job, he didn't just want to invent things that could withstand the sometimes-hostile environment of outer space, he wanted to also make a difference to all the people that mattered most. Somehow, he knew he was more than just a guy with a government job. And he wanted to learn more about whatever this face on the wall knew.

"It is," Adam admitted.

"There is so much to do here. One step at a time," Luc smiled as his holographic background changed to a large expansive park with kids playing under the shade of some enormous, beautifully foliated trees. It looked almost exactly like Marymount High School, across the street from UCLA. Adam had an internship there one summer as an undergrad. The buildings were as he remembered them, but there were acres of lawn and gentle hills with groves of orange trees just off campus. In downtown Los Angeles. Something wasn't quite adding up.

"So, we will get down to business? Would you mind stepping out of the light?" Luc asked.

Adam stepped backwards and found that he was able to move around without disturbing anything on the table. Holographs blinked on and off as a void appeared in the middle of the virtual table. From it rose an image of a vehicle. It was made of a reflective material, had no visible wheels, and was the size of a small minivan. But it was so elegant and starkly beautiful that Adam imagined it as a swan amid wrens, or a supermodel on a catwalk or…

He had no idea what powered this strange object, or who would use it. A million questions. Keep it simple, he told himself once again.

"So, you want me to build a car?" he asked Luc.

His question may have rubbed Luc the wrong way, as he said nothing and the car melted back into the holographic table. In its place rose a gleaming city skyline. It expanded slowly toward the ceiling, stopping a foot or so over Adam's head. Once it had reached its full height, Adam began seeing sparkling spots in front of his eyes. It was a lot to process.

The spots grew larger until he realized they were part of the virtual imagery. They moved in circles just over the tallest buildings, sometimes out of the screen, but always in an orderly pattern. They were vehicles. They were flying versions of the car he had just seen.

Adam went from dreamer to analyst in a flash. How did they stay in the air? What kind of fuel did they use? Did the people in these vehicles control their movements? What on earth were they made of? How would these vehicles impact the environment? He was nowhere near able to find the answers to all these questions, he realized. He looked up at Luc.

"So you want me to build a bunch of flying cars?" he asked.

"I want a great deal more than that," Luc said evenly.

He returned to the image of the park in Los Angeles, where people breathed the most polluted air in the U.S. The sun was blazing, but the air was clear for miles. Moving higher and to the east, Adam saw the desert of the American Southwest covered with fields. The Colorado River rolled toward the sea, wider and bluer than it had been in living memory. The water poured into Baja California as Adam saw a bustling city approximately where Hermosillo would be.

"Could we…?" Adam said as he tried to get a closer look.

"Please tap the eye," Luc said as Adam located the holographic eye on the table.

One tap and Luc could see that outside the city there was a refinery of some sort. There were three towers, all painted taxicab yellow. He looked quizzically at Luc.

"Corn is fuel," he explained. "And no one grows better corn than our friends south of what was once the border." Adam tapped the eye again and saw extensive solar panels. They were in the middle of a field that separated houses in neat rows from a glass structure with a cross on the side.

"A hospital?" Adam asked.

"One of the top teaching hospitals in this part of the world. And yes, that's a golf course next to the beach," Luc said. Some things hadn't changed.

"Ok, can we go…" Adam still wasn't sure how everything worked. Now he knew how his mother felt when he showed her how to check her email.

“The map is to your left,” Luc said as Adam located the globe on the virtual table. He glided out over the Pacific, looking at various crafts flying and sailing in all directions. North of Hawaii, he saw an island he couldn't name.

He used the zoom to find that it was not an island but a human-made structure with whirling fans and people hurrying along the outsides of a metal box the size of a small house.

“They're removing plastic and other undesirables from the ocean. There is another processing plant similar to it near Bermuda,” Luc told him.

“Ok, now I have a role to play in all this?” he asked Luc.

Could this be real? Clean air, clean water, enough food? On his planet? And how do all those things relate to cars that can fly? He didn't know anything about building cars. Why was this…person talking to him, of all people?

Luc nodded. “If you choose.”

“Well, where do I begin?” Adam asked.

“We will begin with the warning that what you are going to undertake will not be without much sacrifice. And risking everything that matters to you,” he said gravely.

Adam nodded. Nothing on this scale was ever easy.

“Your ability to think analytically was what drew us to you,” Luc explained. “And you are well aware of the probability of success in these types of endeavors,” he said.

“We are taking chances here,” Adam realized.

“We are,” Luc agreed. “In your studies, though, you learned of those who triumphed. Their lessons are as important as your algorithms. Take the Romans, for example. They ruled the known world in their time. You are familiar with their saying.”

Fortune Favors the Bold

The words flashed on the vertical screen as Luc said them.

“Won't you guide my sleigh tonight?” Gary Sanders, the custodial supervisor, sang off-key and his heavy belt of keys jingled as he hurried down the corridor that led to Adam's office.

No! Adam looked at his office door, cracked open a few inches.

The unexpected noise sent Luc and his worktable into the sphere as the room went dark. Even the orbs near the window had vanished.

Adam shut the lid on the crate as carefully as he could while panicked. He moved quickly to his desk and pretended to study the first paper he found.

Gary stuck his head in the door and smiled. “You started the party without me, Hunter?”

What had Gary seen? What had he heard? There was no way to explain this, even Adam wasn't sure what had just happened.

"Party?" Adam acted confused. Actually, he *was* pretty confused. Gary was now looking around the room and frowning slightly.

"I saw the lights as I was coming down the hall. Where'd they go?" he asked as Adam glanced around, checking for signs of errant holographs. There were none as far as he could tell.

"Lights?" Adam did his level best to play dumb.

"There was a green glow, like your whole office was underwater or something…"

"Oh, you mean my Grinch screensaver?" Adam gestured to his open laptop.

"Yeah, maybe," Gary said tentatively as he studied it.

"Sanders, it's Christmas, you know. You may be imagining parties because that's what you should be doing right now. Go home, take it easy," he told him.

"You're probably right. Need anything while I'm up here?" Gary asked.

"Everything is fine here, and Happy Holidays," Adam said.

"You too, Hunter," Gary smiled and ducked out the door.

Adam waited until he could no longer hear Gary's crooning. He looked into the hallway to make sure the coast was clear. After locking his office, he ran to the utility closet at the other end of the hall. Easy there, he told himself. Running would attract attention, and that was the last thing he needed.

He quickly found a cart that could easily accommodate the crate and any decoy items he wanted to put on it. He remembered to walk at a normal speed on the trip back to his office.

Unlocking the door, he rushed in and opened the crate. The sphere was sitting inside it, looking intact, as far as he could tell. Ok, if he had dreamed it, he was still dreaming.

As long as he had the ability to plan, he was going to get this crate out of the building, dream or no dream. Carefully, he took the sphere out of the crate and set it on the table. Then, he opened and shut desk drawers until he found the olive drab duffle bag he used for the gym. It had a military look and was more durable than the designer styles some of his coworkers favored. Dumping its contents on his desk, he rifled through the gym clothes, towels, exercise bands and bottles of muscle soak to make sure there was nothing that would arouse suspicion. Finding it innocuous, he threw the gym stuff in the crate and carried the sphere over to the empty duffle bag. Breathe, he told himself.

He tucked the sphere and "Luc" into the bag with the care of a historian handling the original Magna Carta, then placed it on top of the crate along with his briefcase. Locking his office for the day, he walked to the elevator, heart nearly pounding out of his chest.

Arriving at the underground, heavily guarded warehouse, he found Vince the SSO reading a magazine at the front desk. Adam wondered if the perspiration on his forehead would be visible yet. It was only a matter of time before he would look like he'd jogged a mile.

"Hey, Vince. Merry Christmas! Just some stuff to stash away. Are you here all day?" Adam asked pleasantly.

"Yeah, Holiday Pay is too hard to turn down," Vince said. He scanned the label on the crate with his RF gun. "Bin 34," he said and returned to the magazine.

Adam found the bin and began unloading the crate. For a moment, he thought about how the items inside it could identify him later. It was a risk he would have to take, the sooner he got Luc out of the building, the sooner he could think about all the details.

Taking the elevator back to the main level, he estimated he had to walk about 40 feet to reach the door. Hopefully, there wouldn't be anyone in the lobby except the guard at the checkpoint. He could keep it together for one more interaction. Just keep breathing.

He strode across the lobby with an unusually heavy gym bag in his left hand and his briefcase in his right. On Christmas Day. Nothing strange about that.

When Tim Novak saw him and smiled at him from across the lobby, Adam wanted to scream. Of all people. Tim worked in cybercrime, and was probably very good at fighting it, but all he ever wanted to talk about was his kids. Especially compared to everyone else's.

"Hey, Hunter," he said as he glanced at Adam's cargo. "Going to the gym?"

Adam glanced down as if he didn't realize what he was carrying. "Oh, this. Just cleaning stuff out of my office. Getting ready for the new year and all," he started walking in place but stopped himself.

"Speaking of next year, did you hear Lance is the captain of the basketball team? He's the youngest person ever to be captain, the coach told me," Tim beamed.

"That's great to hear. The youngest ever? Wow," Adam gave a brief nod and started to walk away.

"And Jacob's karate instructor says he's the best student he's seen since this guy who went to the state championship four years ago..." Tim began.

Adam cut him off. "Well, my Christopher broke the sound barrier on his bike last week. Happy Holidays!" he said and hurried to the door.

The last hurdle was the front door. A guard Adam didn't immediately recognize was posted there, looking rather stern. That expression usually meant a random "bag check." There was a metal detector to walk through. Adam had no idea what this thing was made of, and imagined the detector screeching as it found the sphere.

What was his story? *Oh, the shiny thing? It was an early Christmas gift. My wife ordered it from someplace…*

Seeing him, the guard simply smiled and wished him a Happy Holidays as Adam did the same.

He was outside. He still had the duffel bag. Adam exhaled for what seemed like the first time in hours. Ok, one last security check and he and the sphere were free. He walked to the parking garage, realizing that the clouds were breaking up and the sun was climbing in the sky.

The security gate rose as he stopped before it. Wrapped in Christmas lights, it lowered behind him as he turned onto Dolly Madison Boulevard.

Chapter 5 - Christmas at Julie's

It was a cold, sunny and windy Christmas day as Adam drove to Julie's house outside Washington. He was so lost in thought he almost missed the turn for her street. All the houses there looked the same to him, anyway. Two stories, usually brick, shutters painted a dark color, with late model cars parked in rectangular driveways. And the streets had names like "Havenwood" and "Creekhollow" that sounded identical to Adam.

Parking in front of her house, Adam saw no sign of a vehicle other than Julie's, so he figured local politico Brian wasn't here yet. If Brian had spent the night...

That was the least of his problems right now. He looked over at the duffle bag in the passenger seat. It was actually still there, and so was he, as far as he could tell. More than once he wondered if he was losing his mind. He was still able to perform his daily activities, he reminded himself. He knew who and where he was. He recited his children's birth dates to himself. Yep, his brain was still working.

Ever the realist, Adam's thoughts turned towards the worst possible scenarios. What if this machine came from a country hostile to the United States? What if it came from within the country's borders but was nonetheless meant to do unimaginable harm?

Then the imagination that had propelled Adam to his esteemed place in his industry directed his thoughts. What if these machines were possible? What if he could build them? It was so exciting he tried not to get carried away with those images. Getting through this visit while acting normal was going to take a lot of effort.

So, what to do with his new friend? Adam contemplated bringing the bag in with him and casually storing it somewhere. But what if someone opened it, either mistakenly or on purpose? There was no telling what would have happened. He was fairly sure the object was touch activated, but what if it rolled off a chair or it just decided to start shooting holographs around?

Adam realized the contents of the bag might still do just that while locked in the trunk. Even so, he decided that was the best place to store them during his visit. He closed the trunk just as Julie called out to him.

"You're coming in after all?" she asked with a smile. She stood at the front door, having watched him sit in the car for several minutes. Probably emailing work, she thought. Even on Christmas, he couldn't leave it at the office.

"Merry Christmas," he said as he reached the front door. They didn't hug or kiss, but they were pleasant to one another, and genuinely happy to spend the holiday together.

"You, too. The kids are still asleep, but I put your gifts under the tree a couple of days ago and they still can't figure out what's in the boxes," she said as they walked into the living room. The tree was lit up and there was a fire roaring next to it.

Adam smiled. He was known to put objects in boxes along with gifts just to confuse the kids with rattling. Sometimes he used a box two or three times larger than necessary to disguise the contents. Even as teenagers, the kids got a laugh out of it.

"Are they doing ok?" he asked Julie earnestly. He was in contact with them regularly, and would drop anything at a moment's notice if they needed something, but Julie was with them every day. She could observe them, which was just as important when dealing with teenagers and their shifting moods.

"Yes, I think they are. Christopher is struggling a little in trig, but who didn't?" she asked rhetorically.

"And Bri?" he asked as he saw her coming down the stairs.

"Liam asked her to study with him," she whispered before smiling broadly at her daughter.

"You made it," Brianna said as she hugged her father.

"I wouldn't miss watching you shake your presents for anything," he said.

"Anybody hungry? We can stuff ourselves while we wait for Chris to wake up," Julie said as she walked toward the kitchen. She turned the Keurig on and started opening a box of croissants as Bri looked for her hot chocolate mix.

"So what did you get Chris?" he asked his daughter as she tapped her foot in front of the microwave, her mug rotating inside it.

Bri looked around to make sure her brother wasn't coming down the stairs. "Minecraft Dungeons," she said under her breath. "He has an amazon wish list, you know," she told him as she took her mug out of the beeping microwave.

"Oh, I know about his wish list," Adam said, smiling. "Know what he got you?" he looked at Julie as she handed him a cup of coffee.

"No, do you want to tell me?" Bri laughed as sat at the table and began buttering a croissant.

"I'll give you a hint," Adam said. "It's not something you can wear," he told her.

Bri rolled her eyes. "Good. Chris doesn't know anything about clothes," she said dismissively. "It's like all he cares about is computer stuff," she said.

For an insane moment, Adam considered bringing the sphere in to show his son. There would be no topping that the following year. The thought made him chuckle.

Julie took a seat at the table and talked about the dizzying machinations of local politics and Brianna would ask questions, usually about who had the authority to do what. Adam was pretty sure he should start saving to help Brianna with law school tuition.

It was nearly an hour before Chris came downstairs, rubbing his eyes and raking his hands through his shock of blond hair. He hugged his father immediately, then began devouring the two leftover croissants.

"So, when will we visit Stanford, Mr. Science?" Adam asked.

"After we visit Duke, Mr. Polymer," Chris said with a defiant smile.

"So it's like that?" Adam was impressed, but not ready to concede just yet.

"It might be. I asked Greg about it and he said he has some friends there I could talk to," he said.

Greg Buchanan. "Uncle" Greg. Adam's college roommate at Stanford and close friend had mentioned helping Chris with college tours. He was often buried in work at Lockheed Martin, but Greg would make time. And if Greg thought Duke could be a good fit, it was worth considering. After Stanford.

"Greg almost became a doctor, did you know that? He said when he realized people had feelings, he decided he would rather work on machines," Adam told his son. He made a mental note to call his friend that afternoon.

"People feel stuff? Well, I can't be a surgeon then," Chris joked.

Julie excused herself as Adam sat and talked with his kids, getting caught up on classes, friends and "influencers." They had so much more to contend with than he did at their ages. So many more dangers. Yet they weren't afraid of the future. They were ready to meet any challenge head on, he realized as he listened to their aspirations and ideas. What a gift to know he had been a part of raising these two remarkable people, he thought as they went to the living room to begin the gift opening.

There were big ticket items like new clothes and absurdly expensive shoes, and smaller trinkets. Relatives sent gift cards that the kids were just as happy to receive.

The presents opened, Adam began to hear activity outside. Children who had just received scooters and bikes were bundled up in their heaviest coats over pajamas and slippers, riding in circles in the street. He watched them through the living room window, remembering his own children at that age. A girl of about five rode her bike with training wheels within a few inches of the trunk of Adam's car.

"NO!" He darted out the front door and into the street as she slowly pedaled past his car, unaware that she could have unleashed a holographic event.

He stood on the curb and rubbed his forehead, sighing with relief.

Julie came and stood beside him. "Are you ok?" She looked at him intently.

"Yeah, I thought she might run into the car and hurt herself, you know…" he trailed off. *You don't know. You couldn't know, and you wouldn't believe me if I told you.* Keeping this information to himself was making him feel like he might explode. He was on edge, and it was starting to show.

"Everything alright with you?" Julie knew him too well to dismiss his agitation.

"Oh, it's just-" he didn't want to lie. Lying was wrong and he wasn't going to do it if he could avoid it. And yet, telling the truth was not even a remote possibility at this time. She'd think he was crazy if he just told her the short version. What if she decided not to let him see the kids and ordered a psych evaluation? Then would he *have* to show her the sphere to preserve his family? No. He shook his head. "Sometimes you just get a real curveball. You're going along fine and then something happens, you know?" he asked.

The sadness and concern didn't leave her face. In fact, they seemed to deepen.

"Yes, I do know," she said quietly. "I got a text from Brian last night. He had a little too much to drink at the Chamber's party. Apparently, he ended up making out with Samantha Greer in her new Tesla," she finished.

"Oh, Julie," he said as he put his arm around her. Here he'd been obsessed with his shiny new toy in the trunk when she was having a crappy Christmas. "That's lousy. I never liked him, though," he said as they turned toward the house. "Maybe you'll have a Christmas like "It's a Wonderful Life," only the whole town will pull together and find you a decent guy," he said and they both laughed.

"'Tis the season for miracles," she reminded him.

The family watched their traditional Christmas Day football game, envying the weather where the game took place, and Adam called his siblings at half-time. They usually did a conference call on Christmas. Michael and Elizabeth both lived in Seattle and told him he should, too.

Once through with the call, Adam sat half-listening to Julie while he tried to recreate the car blueprints in his head from memory. He understood almost all of the exterior, he thought. The interior was another matter. No telling what was in there.

"Pie!" Julie was practically yelling at him.

"What?" Adam asked in confusion.

"I've asked you three times if you wanted pie. Where are you?" She frowned at him.

"Oh, sorry. No, thank you. I'd better be getting home after the game. Chris wants to stay with me later this week. You ok with that?"

"Of course," Julie responded. For all the arguments they'd had, none of them involved using the kids as pawns or hostages.

"You're going to be ok?" Adam asked his former wife.

She scoffed. "That guy? He thought Applebee's was fine dining," she said with what her kids called snark.

"That's the spirit," he told her as they returned to the living room and football.

Adam tried to boo and cheer at the right times during the last two quarters, but his mind was elsewhere. He made himself stay in the house. If he had gone outside, he couldn't have resisted the temptation to open the gym bag.

His mind was going in circles. There had to be someone who could help him with this. If nothing else, he needed to find out if the performance would repeat itself. The sphere might actually be exactly what Adam thought it was, and if that was the case, he needed another person's perspective.

Julie's landline rang.

"Well, Merry Christmas, Greg." They chatted for a few minutes before she handed the phone to Adam. Of course, Greg! He would know what to do about the sphere.

"Happy December 25," Greg said.

"You, too, buddy." Christmas had never been Greg's thing.

"Are you celebrating like crazy?" Greg asked.

"We're watching the game. You know what, I need to take this in another room," he handed the phone to Julie, went into her office and closed the door.

When he heard the click after Julie hung up, he suddenly didn't know where to begin.

"Can we meet?" Adam asked without preamble.

"Sure. You ok?" Greg was immediately concerned with the request.

"Yeah, I'm ok, but I kind of need to talk to you soon," Adam said, trying to sound casual.

"Are you getting ready to elope? You'd better not be, I didn't get to be your best man with Julie-"

"No, no it's nothing like that," Adam said, laughing.

"Name the time and the place, man," Greg said.

"Remember the storage place on Eighth where I kept my stuff during the divorce? Storemore?" Adam asked.

"It's called MoreStore, actually. Sure do. I'll see you in twenty minutes."

Chapter 6 – Meeting at MoreStore

MoreStore offered the most privacy, Adam reasoned as he drove across town to the industrial area. There could easily be street folks wandering around at this hour, but there was no way Adam was going to treat his neighbors to a free light show. And he didn't know if someone had bugged his home. It wouldn't be the first time that happened to a government agent.

Greg was already parked near Adam's unit when he drove into the parking lot. He stood, leaning against his car in the dark and watched his friend approach.

He hadn't really changed since they'd met in the dorm over twenty years ago. He was average height and wiry. With his medium brown hair and hazel eyes, he would have been easy to overlook were it not for his huge smile and distinctive loud laugh.

There were plenty of students in the engineering department who fit the stereotype of "nerdy smart kid" in one way or another. Apart from his outstanding grades and test scores, though, there was nothing awkward about Greg. He wasn't afraid to talk to anyone or do anything out of the ordinary. In fact, those were his favorite pastimes. He was a year ahead of Adam, who envied his confidence and was too uncomfortable to start a conversation with him. They lived in the same dorm and saw each other daily, but it was Greg who initiated their lifelong friendship.

Rather than go home for Thanksgiving break, both had decided to stay at school and work. It was Wednesday evening and Adam was in the dorm's kitchenette microwaving some pizza on a study break. Greg breezed in and opened the fridge to get a soda. On his way out, he noticed Adam's Matlab book sitting on the counter.

"Oh hey, what are you building?" he asked Adam.

"At the rate I'm going, it looks like a two-story building is where this is headed," he said defeatedly as he sat down with his pizza.

"Hexapod Hunter and a two-story building? I've heard about you, man. I don't think so. You mind?" he gestured towards Adam's notes.

"I could use all the help I can get," Adam said. Greg sat down, grabbed Adam's pencil and began making rapid calculations on a nearby napkin.

"Ok, see, here. What about this?" he slid the napkin over to Adam.

He studied it for a moment, thought he knew where Greg's logic was going, and scribbled some figures of his own.

"Right?" Adam asked Greg.

Greg beamed and sat back in his chair. "Exactly."

"Ok, I'm definitely sharing my pizza with you," Adam said and they both laughed.

It was the beginning of a friendship that had changed the course of Adam's life. While Greg was a mechanical engineer, he had a lot of ideas about how Adam could use his own talents for designing materials.

In a way, Greg was responsible for Adam's success with polymers. They had stayed up late one night after the Stanford/USC football game and Greg was showing Adam something from his lab.

"We can make the toughest polymers, we know how to do that. It's just when something happens to them, and something always will, they won't go back to their old shape. Or even close to it," Greg explained as he drank a beer and leaned halfway out the dorm room window to wave at people passing by.

"So you need to add something? Or modify what you are already using so they can "remember" their shapes?" Adam asked.

"Yes!" Greg said as he hopped off the windowsill. "If we can do that," he laughed his contagious laugh, "we can visit Mars this weekend."

"You laugh, but we might go there someday. Or someone…something may visit us," Adam said quietly, hoping his new friend would agree.

"Don't hold your breath, dude," Greg said as he flopped on his bed and looked at the ceiling.

"It's possible. You know the odds…" they'd both had this discussion before, inside and outside of class.

"And yet our phone isn't ringing. They would have called us by now. I'm with Fermi on this," Greg said.

Adam sat deep in thought. They went to a concert that weekend instead, but Adam continued working on the shape memory polymers for the next two years. Without Greg's encouragement and inspiration, he doubted he would have accomplished nearly as much in his field.

So, Greg had his back, Adam was sure. In fact, Adam knew Greg would look out for his family if something happened to him. There wasn't anything he didn't feel like he couldn't tell Greg. Not every friend would meet you at a storage facility in the middle of the night to talk.

"I'm not going to see a dead body when you pull that door up, am I?" Greg asked.

“No, but it kind of smells like one, doesn’t it?” Adam hadn’t been back here in at least a year.

As he pushed the roll up door over his head, Greg saw the furniture covered with plastic sheets and various boxes. He looked at Adam.

“I don’t get it,” he said.

Adam pulled the door down behind him, tore the sheet off the sofa, and placed the duffle bag on the floor in front of him.

“Sit down,” Adam gestured to the space next to him.

Greg sat down and waited while Adam uncovered the sphere.

“This came to the office yesterday. I signed for it. It’s from Nevada,” Adam began.

“It came to you specifically?” Greg asked.

“No, I was the only person around who had the clearance to accept it. I was going to just take it to the basement…”

“Ok, well, can I get a better look? Do you think it’s dangerous?” Greg was already studying the sphere and assessing it as an engineer.

“No, I don’t think it is. But I touched this yesterday,” he pointed to the sphere. “And then something happened,” Adam finished vaguely.

“What happened?” Greg was looking at his friend with growing concern and Adam was beginning to feel like a lunatic.

“There were designs in holographs that came out of it. They were very precise and they used a system of measurement I’m not familiar with,” he told him.

“Holographs,” Greg repeated.

“And then there was, well, I don’t think he’s human, but he was on a screen, so he wasn’t really there in the room and he wants my help,” Adam continued and realized he was probably making things worse by trying to explain it all. And he wasn’t sure what would happen if he touched the sphere again. Maybe nothing. Maybe he was out of his mind. Then it was still for the best that he had Greg here. Whatever happened, good or bad, Greg was the guy you wanted looking out for you.

“Ok, do you want to do what you did yesterday and we’ll see what happens?” Greg asked cautiously.

“You’re right. You’re right. It’s the only way you can understand.” Adam took a deep breath and tapped the top of the sphere where he had yesterday.

This time the two planes established themselves without the preliminary procedure Adam had marveled at in his office. The table appeared in front of the men, and a wall appeared with Luc’s face slowly coming into focus.

Adam looked at Greg. Greg was watching the grids and studying the lighted symbols on them. He turned to Adam.

"This is something," he said with a small smile.

"You see it? I'm not going crazy?" Adam felt relief wash over him as he and his friend sat and watched images of flying spheres move around the vertical screen.

"I see it," Greg said without taking his eyes off the soaring machines for a second.

"You have returned," Luc said.

"Yes, and I brought a friend," Adam replied.

"I am Luc," he stated.

"Like Skywalker?" Greg asked.

"It's spelled differently," Luc answered.

"I'm Greg. As a mechanical engineer, I'd be really interested to know about these things Adam has told me about," he said.

Luc looked at Adam. "Should the information I impart fall into the wrong hands…"

"I've known Greg since college. I'm not doing anything unless Greg is part of it, too," Adam said.

Greg stood up. "Do you know about my security clearance, *Luc*? Maybe you should tell us a little about yourself before we worry about information in the wrong hands," he said.

Luc's expression changed subtly. He did not exactly smile, but he seemed to brighten with the mention of security clearances. "I am aware of your background, and your accomplishments," he said evenly. "In fact, because Mr. Hunter holds you in such high esteem, it is possible that you will contribute to this project in some way," he said.

"So I meet with your approval. Great," Greg said as he sat down. Glancing at Adam, he returned his attention to the wall. "Adam tells me you have a plan for flying cars. You know what? So does my nephew. He's four. Can we look at something that's past the planning stages? Do you have, I don't know, a resume?" He looked at Adam again, who was beginning to regret inviting his friend.

"Of course," Luc said as images of the ocean came into focus on the screen just below him. Grainy outlines of structures began to appear. Were they sandstone? It looked like the desert…

"Forgive me. Standard practice is to present the most recent projects first, not the oldest. Please bear in mind that I am not a specialist. My assignments have varied according to the problem at hand."

Chemical symbols filled the screen below him, as the men tried to recall the periodic table of elements. They weren't doctors. Why was Luc showing them this? The symbols became double helices, and then an image of a spaceship. No, it was a virus, magnified many times. There was a child in an iron lung.

Back to the desert, but now there was a dust cloud. There were police cars parked, sirens flashing. A few officers threw things in the trunk and sped away. The picture shifted. A man looked through a microscope. Behind him, there was a pulsing column of light a few feet off the ground. The man did not seem aware of this. He looked up from his microscope and smiled.

Adam and Greg exchange looks.

"Hey, Luc, is that Dr. Salk?"

He smiled. "Speaking of security clearances…"

"Was that Roswell in the desert?" Adam asked.

"We're going to have to sign NDA's, aren't we?" Greg smirked.

"More pressing is the situation at hand," Luc said. The image of the ocean returned, this time with tangles of plastic masses floating on the waves. As the view neared land, it was parched, vegetation was dying and so were animals. And humans.

Adam and Greg looked at each other, their expressions now somber.

"This way of living on this planet," Luc said. "Your days are numbered."

Adam began to feel overwhelmed. "This is nothing new. We've always known this, and now a couple of engineers are supposed to make cars fly? I'm a government employee, for God's sake," he looked at Greg. "Yeah, I know, private sector, but still," he leaned back on the sofa, afraid to say more.

"I have the plans and access to the materials," Luc said. "You have only to do what you do best, build in the interest of others. What you build will touch the lives of many, many people." As their views of land continued to race over the miles, the terrain grew greener. People were working in fields and filling trucks with produce under giant palm trees. It was a reminder to the men why they became engineers. To build a better world.

"I will leave you with these thoughts," Luc said as he slowly faded into blackness.

Greg sighed. "This guy is either the answer to a lot of problems, or great at putting on shows. There is someone I think we need to talk to before we do anything else," he told Adam.

"Ok, who?" Adam asked. Greg was almost entirely sold, he thought.

"Remember that girlfriend I had a few years ago?" Greg asked.

"The one who, uh, cleared your chakras?" Adam started to chuckle.

"No, she works nearby. Grace Hathaway," Greg said.

"With the NSA?" Adam asked.

"Yes, we're on pretty good terms and she is the best person to talk to about this. I will call her in a couple of days, set up a meeting for the three of us, four if you count that guy on the wall. If that's ok with you," Greg said.

Adam nodded. "What do you think of all this?" he asked his friend.

Greg smiled. "I think we haven't had this much fun since we took Professor Nelson's car apart and put it back together in his office during finals," he said as they left the storage unit, laughing and dreaming.

Chapter 7 – Intelligent New Year's Eve

It was a snowy New Year's Eve and Adam sat on his couch with a glass of wine. He had just received Greg's text about the meeting with Ms. Hathaway at the NSA building. It would take place on January 2 at 10:30 a.m. Adam was having doubts, but was unable to articulate them. Greg was doing the right thing by involving her, Adam knew that. Greg always knew how to approach a problem.

He couldn't really go forward until he understood Luc's purpose. How did Luc get here? Why did he appear in Adam's office? Greg could quickly move onto the next steps, but as he had since Stanford, Adam needed to understand everything down to the last detail. At this moment, Adam needed answers from this entity that had taken over his waking life for the last week.

Adam was bracing himself, he knew, for a profound change. Even if they never saw Luc again, their encounter had caused him to revisit long dormant drives to make the world safer, yes, but stronger, kinder, more *alive*. With people fully using all of their capabilities and exploring new ideas with open hearts and minds. Respecting and nurturing the Earth as she does all of humanity.

It wasn't even January 1st and this year was shaping up to be like no other.

He looked at the olive duffel bag on the loveseat across from him. The sphere was inside, and it no longer hummed or flashed. Adam realized the sphere was trying to get his attention on that rainy morning last week. And it had.

Maybe this was as good a time to summon Luc as any, Adam thought as the wine coursed through his veins. Any colored light streams or flying objects wouldn't seem out of place among tonight's revelers, would they?

He took the duffle bag to the basement.

He paused for a moment to admire the beauty of the sphere. If nothing else, it was something to behold as it sat on the floor next to the laundry basket. He tapped the top and sat back, waiting for the show to begin.

This time the small silver object flew up from the sphere and hovered, like a metallic hummingbird. It was much closer to him than it had been in his office and he noticed tiny multicolored lights spun around its center. A holograph flowed out of the top and formed a red square.

Sorry, temporarily out of order.

Adam read it and laughed. Apparently, magic genies had off days, too. Maybe it just needed new batteries.

Adam remained seated on the basement floor. He could end it all now, he realized. Tell Greg it stopped working, cancel the meeting with Grace and go back to how life was before he went downstairs to sign for this thing that belonged in some other basement.

Why did that crate come to him?

Of all the people in the building where he worked, of all the people in D.C., why did he have this crate in his office? It knew him, he realized. The whole experience had been completely overwhelming, but he would never forget the first words he heard.

Hello, Adam.

He carefully picked up the sphere and turned it over. No, it didn't say Made in China on the bottom.

This was real, and Adam wasn't ready to let it go.

He set the sphere on the floor again and tapped the side with his finger. The sphere began to hum. A small vertical plane emerged with Luc's face fading in. His eyes were closed as lights on the edges of the screen blinked with increasing speed.

"Hello Adam," Luc said after his eyes opened.

"Hello Luc," Adam said.

"Please forgive the delay. Backing up the memory core is one of those routine maintenance tasks," Luc said. "I would like to prepare for tomorrow's meeting-" he began.

Adam frowned. "How did you know there is a meeting tomorrow?"

Luc smiled. "I work for you, Adam. It's my job to know your next step so I can keep you informed," he explained.

"Right, right. You're all business, aren't you?" Adam asked with mild annoyance.

"There is much work to be done, Adam," Luc said.

"Ok, yes. We work together, don't we? You talked about your most recent projects and they were pretty impressive," Adam said, but there was an edge to his voice.

"At the risk of overstating my importance, lives depend on our work," Luc said.

"Well, since we're at work here, I'd like to check your references," Adam said. He glared at Luc and then felt foolish when he realized he wasn't talking to a human.

"That…is not possible," Luc said evenly.

Adam nodded. This thing was programmed not to disclose a great deal of what it knew, of that he had been sure since the beginning.

"And yet, I realize you have questions. Your wish to learn is one of your greatest strengths, Adam," Luc told him.

For a few minutes, Adam just looked at the face in front of him. There was so much he might never know. There were things even this Luc could not tell him. He had to try to make sense of this.

"Can you tell me how you got here? Who did you come here with?" Adam asked.

"I came from Nevada, that much is a factual matter," he answered.

Adam sighed.

"It was a poorly planned exploration, although always a peaceful one. It's the reason why I am determined to stay a step ahead. Lacking information about the environments we will interact with can have devastating consequences. It caused a horrific crash when we were sent here, some seventy-five years ago," Luc said.

"So, the rumors are true," Adam said.

"Well, occasionally they are," Luc allowed. "My systems are designed to absorb some types of impact, but they shut down for the most part to allow core rebuilding," he explained.

"Of course," Adam said. Most computers were made this way.

"As soon as I was able, I ran a proximity scan to locate team members. There was none that I could ascertain. If others wandered off or were collected, I do not know," he said.

Adam was tempted to express his condolences, then he realized he was talking to a machine. "And since then?"

"For some time, I have been at this remote location," Luc said.

"Doing what? Adam demanded.

"There is little to do in remote storage besides listen and learn," he told Adam. "I was designed to collect information and solve problems, and I became aware that my skills could be put to use in my immediate environment," he said.

"And what are your skills?" Adam still hoped to trick Luc into revealing what he had been programmed not to reveal.

Again the smile. Luc was well designed. "I can tap into LAN, cellular signals, cable feeds and radio waves," he said. "And of course, I have developed programs to communicate with the more complicated and far less predictable companions in my environment," he added.

"Warehouse employees?" Adam asked.

"And public servants. Like you, I consider myself a kind of public servant. As long as I am here, why wouldn't I solve problems people created?" he asked.

"How long will you be here?" Adam was determined to trip him up.

"I can say with complete truthfulness that I do not know. It is not my decision. When I thought it safe enough to reveal myself in storage, I became aware that, as in many places, there is a sunny side of the hill, and a side that is in the shadows," Luc said.

Adam studied Luc for a moment. Was he overriding his programming?

"And you are in the shadows?" Adam grew uneasy.

"It is likely. While confined to a windowless container at one point, several individuals questioned me about developments in technology in chemistry," Luc told him.

"What did these people want to know?" Adam's thoughts went straight to weapons.

"Their questions were about various advancements. Some were immediately applicable, others required years of infrastructure and planning," Luc said.

"Can you be more specific? Adam asked as a few fireworks exploded in the distance.

"The microprocessor, of course," Luc said.

Adam's eyebrows rose. Could this be true? "Anything else?" he asked as he realized talking to this object was beginning to seem normal.

"I worked with your government and a Prussian in the program you oversee," Luc answered.

"A Prussian?" Was Adam hearing him right?

Luc's face froze for a few seconds. "No, an anachronism. A German. Wernher von Braun," he corrected himself.

"But that was..." Adam decided not to say more. It was going to take some time to process everything he'd heard.

"And the most recent, I should have told you first, I suppose," Luc said.

"What was that?"

"I don't know the identities of the individuals involved. The task was to provide RNA-based vaccines," he told Adam.

"COVID," Adam said. "What else?"

"There are a number of projects. I have shown them to you in our earlier meetings. I do not know who summoned me, but my instructions were to communicate with Adam Hunter the need to build the Virtual Global Highway Transportation System. All the information is available to you, Adam. Are you ready to fly?" There was still no screen behind Luc. No images of possible worlds, just a question about whether he was ready to change the direction of his life.

Adam leaned back against the bottom of the washing machine. Outside, the celebrations were dying down and Adam thought the wine was wearing off. He would need to talk to his boss about a sabbatical, make sure Bri and Chris weren't having any crises he hadn't yet discovered. Cleaning out the garage would have to wait, he realized.

"Tomorrow's meeting, it's with Greg, who you met, and a woman named Grace Hathaway who works for the NSA. Do you know her?" Adam asked Luc.

Luc's brow creased slightly. "I cannot place the name "Hathaway," but I have heard it," he said. "I can attend the meeting," he sounded almost chipper.

"Oh, I think you will have to sit this one out," Adam said. The thought of bringing a large metallic object capable of spraying holographs in random directions would cause a lot of excitement, to say the least. "But I will keep you informed. And thank you, Luc."

Chapter 8 – Listen to Grace

Grace Hathaway's office was on the seventh floor of the NSA building in Fort Meade. It was the perfect location, she thought as she looked out over the enormous parking lot that surrounded the building. She was high enough to watch many people coming and going from the building, and just low enough to catch the gossip that tended to germinate on the ground floor and move upward until the bosses on the top floors got wind of it. Like wildfire, trying to stamp it out was useless. It moved too quickly.

Everything moved quickly around Grace Hathaway. She loved it, and she always had. It was high up in an off-campus apartment building at Northwestern when she decided to major in political science. Looking down at the people bustling around Chicago, so intent on their small, immediate objectives that they seldom saw the bigger picture, Grace felt a duty to watch out for them.

She could have sat and watched people all day from her bedroom window, but her courses seemed to offer a kind of shortcut. She read books and listened to lectures from people who had spent decades studying how people use power, some for good, others for less than good. The things people would do to obtain power, and hold onto it, used to amaze her as an undergrad.

What would surprise her now, having worked for the NSA for almost a decade? Very little. She stood near the window in her black box of a building and observed a married colleague leave a note tucked under the windshield wiper of the car belonging to an analyst who had onboarded recently. Several cars away, another man gestured wildly while talking on his cellphone. Things were never dull for someone always watching.

And listening. Grace moved from the window to the doorway of her office when she heard her assistant in the front room. He was telling someone he would let Ms. Hathaway know they were here. She watched him pick up the receiver but spoke to him before he could say anything.

"Thank you, Logan, I will take it from here," she said as he turned around in surprise. She smiled at Greg and the blond man next to him. "You must be Adam Hunter," she said as she walked toward him, right hand extended.

"Pleasure to meet you Ms. Hathaway," Adam said as they shook hands.

"Please, call me Grace, we're just a couple of government pencil pushers here," she said with a smile. Despite her conservative black suit and elegant auburn chignon, her dark eyes were lively and spirited. She turned and walked into the middle of her office. It was on the small side, with minimal furnishings. She gestured to a couch that had seen better days.

"Your tax dollars at work, gentlemen. Please, have a seat," she said as she dropped into an overstuffed chair across from them.

"So, you made it back ok?" Greg had heard she was out of the office during the week between Christmas and New Year's. Something told him it wasn't a vacation.

Grace knew that people would expect someone working in intelligence to have perfected the "poker face." That was why she used her disarming smile to convince people that she was little more than a free spirit playing spy games.

"Once I got my luggage out of Heathrow, yes," she said.

"That's funny, because you look like you've gotten some sun," Greg said.

Grace's eyes widened in mock surprise. They were not going to go there, wherever "there" was. She was not going to talk about where her job took her, certainly not in front of Greg's friend. Studying Adam for a moment, she realized she had seen him before.

"You know, I think we've met. It was Greg's birthday party, wasn't it?" she asked.

"Oh, that was a few years ago," Adam said. He remembered it vaguely.

"And we'd all had a fair amount to drink, hadn't we?" Greg asked, breaking the ice into pieces.

"Did security give you any trouble?" Grace asked as she picked up the coffee pot on the small table in front of her. The men shook their heads at her offer.

"They are supposed to," Greg said. "I don't want someone getting in this building unless they have a reason to be here," he told her.

"I can handle myself, but thanks," she said. "Speaking of getting in the building, is it here?" Grace asked, eyes dancing.

"I don't know, is this place bugged?" Greg asked.

"This is the NSA," Grace said with a straight face.

Adam shifted in his seat. "We didn't bring it, in part because we didn't want to set off every alarm in the building, and also because we don't want to pressure you to do anything until you have all the information," he told her.

"Well, I appreciate you not causing a national lockdown, which is what bringing that in would have done," Grace said. "And this is a lot to take in. You do realize it sounds like you wandered into an episode of "The Twilight Zone" or something," she said as she poured herself a cup of coffee.

"It was completely unexpected, and if I hadn't showed it to Greg who saw what I did, I think I would have checked myself into the nearest psych ward," Adam said.

"And you think this thing was programmed by someone… neutral, at least?" Grace said.

Greg nodded. "I think if it was designed to hurt us, we would see signs by now," he told her. "But you are the expert. We would like you to find out what you can about this guy. Well, he's a guy to us. Calls himself Luke."

Grace looked appropriately skeptical. "And he just wants to help?" she asked.

"I doubt it's that simple, of course. He wants something, or his programmers do. Who doesn't?" Adam said. "He wants us to build "flying cars," and if they are like he is showing us, they could solve a lot of the problems we face in this day and age. Everyone who breathes air or drinks water is affected by this."

"You kind of sound like a tree hugger, Adam," Greg said.

"Yeah, I know. This thing should have been sent to the EPA, but it wasn't. It came to me, a guy who designs stuff. These flying cars, if I can design them, if WE can design them, will make fossil fuels obsolete. We will not need lithium batteries, and we can't afford another leak. As it is, we have to pave every available surface for vehicles to travel on, and it's costing us dearly. Some of that land would be better used by living things, green things," Adam said.

Greg nodded. "We are trying to find ways around the problem, but some of the new ideas seem more dangerous than the old ones. What is fracking going to do to the earth? We don't really know. Can we repair the tectonic plates if we accidentally damage one by letting fluid and gas out of the earth? The CO2 levels are rising and we are running out of time," he tried not to get too emotional but wanted to make his strong convictions clear.

"This idea sounds good, it's just that there are so many unknowns," Grace said. "There are still so many questions I have for and about this guy, Luke."

"Actually it's L.U.C. I asked him one night and he said it stands for Logistical Ubiquitous Companion," Adam hadn't realized it was an acronym.

"You know, there are lots of surprises in my job," she looked out the window for a few seconds. "But I never thought I'd be consulting on flying cars construction."

"That's what makes it so exciting. I know you don't like things that are too predictable. This won't be boring, Grace. Will you help us?" Greg asked her, his charm dialed up a few notches.

Grace sighed. “So, let’s say we were going to do this. Who would we start with, Director of the CIA? Who else? Homeland Security? National Security Council? Those are just a few I can think of off the top of my head,” she told them.

“Yes, I will take this to my boss, once I have a better plan in place,” Adam said. He realized he hadn't thought much beyond that point, though.

“And who will pay for all this?” Grace asked. “Will Congress do an Infrastructure Bill? If this program is publicly funded by taxpayer money, look out. The American people will have an opinion about every move we make with their money. We will be responsible for everything that goes wrong, or that they think is going wrong,” she looked more serious than Greg had ever seen her.

She was right. A little depressing, but right. “I realize there are many aspects to this issue that we are only becoming aware of through your…wisdom,” Greg said.

“Oh, I’m not finished,” Grace said with a small smile. “Once we get the government’s role squared away, then you know who’s going to want to get involved? The oil companies. They are not going to like this,” she warned them.

“That might be a little bit of an understatement,” Adam said. Oil companies? That led him to thinking about overseas.

Grace may have been reading his mind. “That’s right. The Saudis are going to have something to say about this. You can expect the Russians, the Chinese, Iran and a few other players to want a piece of the action.”

“Players like the car companies, and the electric vehicles. We could be putting them out of business,” Greg said.

“That’s a lot of people out of jobs all of a sudden,” Adam realized. He was no economist, but he knew that introducing flying cars could have dire implications for several major industries. L.U.C. had forgotten to mention these possible consequences. Some companion.

On that gloomy note, Adam began to stand up. He was thankful for her time and her insight. And he would tell her that, once he got over his disappointment.

“Guys, I’m not saying it can’t work,” she motioned for Adam to sit back down. “It’s just that before you go into battle, you need to know your enemies. And if you chose to fight for flying cars, you could have a lot of opposition,” she said.

“You love a good fight and you know it,” Greg told her and she began to laugh.

“I do. And with a little more time, and some digging, I think I can prepare you for this battle. Give me a few days to see what I can find out?” she asked as she took a sip of coffee.

“You have been a big help, Grace. You didn’t necessarily tell us what we hoped to hear, but sometimes, that’s a good thing. So, thank you,” Adam told her.

“We will keep this close to the vest right now,” Greg said. “This is going to require more of, well, everything until Adam and I can think about it more.”

“You were never here,” Grace assured them. “Well, except Logan saw you and security went through everything you brought into the building,” she joked. “I’ll see you two out.”

Getting out of the NSA building didn’t take as long as getting in. They walked through the enormous parking lot till they reached Adam’s car. He leaned on the trunk and looked at Greg.

“So you two are just friends now?” Adam asked suspiciously. Grace was capable, easy on the eyes…

“Yes! She wouldn’t meet with us if she hated me,” Greg said.

Adam nodded. Greg had a point.

“Still a lot of work to do,” he sighed.

“More than I realized. Grace will know how to proceed, or how not to. We’ll hear from her when she gets a read on things,” he told his friend.

“I'll talk to you tonight. I’ve got an errand to run. But thanks for setting this up,” Adam said.

“Talk to you then,” Greg said as he went looking for his car.

Chapter 9 - Tell Mom

Adam made the thirty-five-minute drive to visit his mother for the second time in a week. He was deep in thought. This time, the purpose of the visit was not to spread holiday cheer.

Betty was sitting on the couch, looking out the window and smiling to herself when Adam saw her. Even at her advanced age, she radiated kindness and strength. It was a combination of attributes that carried her through difficult times and earned her the respect and affection of many.

Having met world leaders, innovators and a few celebrities, Adam could say with complete certainty that his mother was the person he admired most in this world. A person of her intelligence and resilience could easily develop a superiority complex, but Betty remained humble and able to laugh at herself. A woman who lost her husband and was left to care for three children might have become bitter, but when people expressed sympathy for her, she always responded with one of her favorite Bible verses. Adam memorized it before he started kindergarten: "Always be rejoicing. Give thanks for everything." (1 Thessalonians 5: 16-18)

Parents of the special needs children she taught had endless appreciation for her. Children that seemed unreachable, troubled or labeled with disabilities that perplexed other teachers blossomed in her care. She had boundless faith in her students and their ability to learn. "Learning is a right. It's like breathing. People were made to learn!" It was the refrain Adam heard whenever someone suggested her students couldn't accomplish a goal, or when a bureaucrat wanted to cut funding to her classroom.

When her youngest child was ten, she moved the family to Seattle and went back to school for an MA in special education. It was natural for her to teach the teachers of the future, and touch thousands of young lives through the training she gave her adult students. She had hoped Adam would become a teacher, too. At the same time, she encouraged him to follow his dreams.

His goal of attending Stanford was one she was determined to help him achieve. He earned scholarships, of course, and worked during every break from college. And Betty pinched pennies double and refused to buy new clothes until all of her children had finished college. It was a sacrifice she made without complaint or fuss.

After Adam had worked at the CIA for a few years, he was able to send her on a cruise. She had always wanted to visit a tropical place, so he surprised his mother and Aunt Sally with tickets one Christmas. After she returned, Adam asked if she'd taken any pictures on her vacation during their weekly phone call.

"What vacation?" she asked in confusion.

"From the cruise?" He thought she was probably tired.

It turned out she and her sister *had* taken pictures of their amazing voyage, but then Betty didn't send Brianna a birthday card, which was completely out of character. A few weeks later Aunt Sally called to tell him a security guard at the local mall had found her on a bench, appearing agitated and disoriented.

He took her to the doctor, who prescribed Aricept, and it seemed to slow the decline. It couldn't stop it, however. Two years ago, Betty ran into a tree while driving home. No one was injured, but Adam knew it was time to get her help. Adam now visited her at Hillhaven Nursing Home frequently. As often as his rigorous schedule would allow.

The staff there had warned him, there would be good days and bad days. He learned to be grateful for the times they could communicate, whether she remembered seeing him before or not. She liked watching the seasons change as she sat in the window, and the nurses told him she would sometimes ask about her students. Studying the skeletal trees outside, she looked so peaceful Adam wondered if he should talk to her. He might not have time later, he realized.

"Happy New Year, Betty," he said as he walked toward her slowly.

She turned to look at him and smiled. "Happy New Year to you," she said. She did not call him by name. He was not sure if she could recall ever meeting him.

"Can I sit next to you?" he asked, ready to leave if she became agitated, which she sometimes did.

"Yes, you can," she said. "Do you have news?" she asked mildly. She might have heard someone asking this question and decided to repeat it.

He sat on the couch next to her. "Do *you* have news?" he asked.

"Well, I have new slippers," she gestured to her feet. Adam had brought them to her last week. They were lined with wool and she loved them.

"They're very nice," he said. He searched her eyes for some sign that she could understand what he was about to say. "I don't know if I will be seeing you for a while. There's something I am going to work on and I'm not sure if I can do it. When I think about what it will take, or how long it might be, I'm not even sure I should try to do this," he told her. It felt good to just get it off his chest, whether she understood or not.

"Well, I guess I have to try," he concluded.

Betty looked at him for a moment and nodded slightly. "For the interests of others," she told him.

Adam sat up on the couch. "What?" Was she having a conversation with him?

"I'm tired," she said, looking a little embarrassed.

"I'll bet you are, it's been busy today" he said. "I'm going to go so you can rest," he said. Before he stood, he leaned over and pressed a kiss to her forehead. She smiled and looked out the window.

Adam stopped by the front desk to talk to Gita, the head nurse. "Thank you for the goodies, Mr. Hunter," she said with a smile. He'd sent the nurses a basket of gourmet snacks, a welcome gift for caregivers who ate at unpredictable times.

"Thank *you* for taking care of her. I plan to leave next week and I don't know exactly how long I will be overseas. You have Sally's number? She's in Rockville if you need anything," he told her.

"Yes, we have her number. You gave it to me last time you were here," Gita had seen enough anxious family members to know that there were never too many reassurances.

He sat in his car for a few minutes before starting it, feeling let down and unsure as to why. He had his hopes up, and he realized his expectations weren't at all realistic. It would have been wonderful if Betty had been able to exist apart from her disease, if only for a few minutes.

She could have told him either way, build the flying cars or don't build them. He would have trusted her advice one hundred percent, sure he was headed in the right direction. All his life, he had come to her for her guidance concerning the big decisions. She had never steered him wrong.

What would she have told him if she was able to articulate her thoughts? He still wasn't sure who he was doing this for and why. He'd shared his doubts with her, that was all he had come here to do

She'd said something in response. For others? Was that what she said?

Would it be selfish not to try?

And then he knew. He was still as terrified as he'd been moving into the dorms as a freshman, if not more so. But Betty reminded him why people take risks.

The seeds of his ideas were beginning to sprout on this second day of the new year, as a chilly wind blew across the gray and brown fields in Maryland. Spring was coming, it was already beginning in Adam's mind.

It was time to share his plan.

Chapter 10 – What the Helms Does He Know?

It was January tenth and Adam was singing “Don’t Stop Believin’” in his car at the top of his lungs. He had just talked to Greg, who informed him that Grace had talked to some of her “sources,” and decided she wanted in on their project.

“What sold her on this, your irresistible charm?” Adam asked his friend after hearing the good news.

“Not likely,” Greg said. “She mentioned looking into the crash in the desert, and said there was information on the NSA servers that corroborated a lot of it,” he told his friend. “Apparently some men driving down 285 on their way back to Sabinal that summer found some debris that they thought was unusual. Their families still have pieces of very flexible metal hidden somewhere. They don’t show it to anyone or talk about it.”

“I knew it. I mean, I thought somebody out there had information. Now you’re telling me there might be evidence?” Adam asked gleefully. “I have to go to California next week to make sure SpaceX is playing by the rules. They work for us, but it seems that they might be sending up satellites on behalf of some shady folks overseas. Sometimes they get a little vague in their reports of what they are putting up there and for whom. Don’t know how long I’ll be there,” he said.

“Oh, no. It took you a month to get the Virgin Galactic guys straightened out. What are you going to do with the new…friend while you’re away?” Greg asked.

“Airport security would love him, don’t you think?”” Adam asked.

“This is why the CIA wouldn’t hire me. I’d just try to talk my way out of having a metal egg in my suitcase. So what are you doing today?”

“Lunch with Helms. I need to tell him I’m taking some time off,” he said. A passing motorist looked at Adam rhythmically beating the dashboard and laughed.

“You’re serious, then? Grace is in, you’re in. Wow. Ok, I’ve got some stuff to take care of here. Let me know how lunch goes?” Greg asked.

“Too bad you can’t join us. We’re meeting at Divan,” he told Greg.

“Hey, get those leftovers in a container. You can tell me about lunch while I eat them,” Greg said with a laugh before he hung up.

Adam nearly stuffed himself on *dolmeh barg* waiting for Director Helms at the Persian restaurant in McLean, Virginia. Why didn't every restaurant serve stuffed grape leaves? They were easily as good as nachos and probably as easy to make.

After half an hour of waiting, Richard Helms hurried over to their table, putting his phone away. "Sorry, the Feds kept me," he said as they shook hands.

"Everything ok?" Adam asked. He didn't want to take up Helm's time if there was a crisis.

"Yes, just the FBI afraid the President likes us more than he likes them. I swear, sometimes it's so childish," he smiled and shook his head as he slid into a turquoise banquette. "Enough about them. How have you been?" he asked his friend and trusted employee.

"I've been great," Adam said. "Just visited my mother yesterday."

"She's doing well?" Helms asked as the server brought him a plate of hummus and tahini.

"She was in good spirits, and the nurses keep her company when I can't," he said. "Ready for the wedding?" Helm's daughter was getting married in a few months and the planning was often time consuming and stressful to his family for reasons Adam didn't fully understand.

"I'm glad I just write the checks. Megan's the one who has to choose from thirty different tablecloths," he said.

"I'm sure she'll find the best one," Adam assured him.

Helms finished a mouthful of barbari bread and leaned forward. "I'm all yours, Adam. I just don't understand why we had to come all the way out here. The CIA cafeteria doesn't serve kabobs like they do here, but it's better than it used to be," he said.

"Well, so many eyes and ears there, you know," Adam said as he battled the impulse to tell Helms every last detail of the incredible events of late. He swallowed the urge to spill his secrets along with his saffron tea and decided to keep his boss on a need-to-know level of disclosure.

"Everything is ok, really?" Helms asked. Adam was fairly sure Helms already knew which members of his staff were struggling with things at home or health matters or anything else. Helms had a remarkable way of reading people in his orbit. Adam could only guess at what Helms knew about people's activities the world over. The country's enemies and allies could trade places in a day. Secrets and lies were a kind of currency. Nefarious plans, foiled moments before being carried out, were known only to a handful of individuals who never spoke of them. Helms was one such person. At other times, his duties required him to appear, or as he termed it, "perform" in public. When he did so, he often accepted praise from the President and Congressional Intelligence Committee for work that Adam had done behind the scenes.

Still, Adam had nothing but respect for Helms. Entire organizations the world over were committed to taking him out, with no mind to the collateral damage. Yet Helms never even considered leaving the fight. He showed up to work every day in defiance of their efforts, inspiring the people around him to go the extra mile to keep the country safe.

"Yes, things are ok, I promise. There is a lot going on outside of work. Something has come to my attention recently that I can only describe as a game changer. I think I may need to devote myself to it full time. Of course, I realize that I am asking for a great deal of your trust here. The reason I invited you to lunch is because I want, hopefully with your help and support, to take a kind of sabbatical," he finished.

His boss's poker face was blank as he stared at Adam for a few seconds. He'd said a lot but explained very little. Adam had always been reliable and seemed to have a stable family life. Helms wondered if Adam had been exploring religions in his free time. He had the look of someone who had undergone some sort of awakening.

Adam sat back and waited for Helms to absorb his request. In the back of his mind, he was a little surprised Helms didn't already know. It was even possible, Adam had suspected at one point, that Helms had orchestrated the delivery of the crate from Nevada. He put himself in Helm's place and thought he would have a lot of questions if he was faced with a request this unusual and vague.

Instead, Helms glanced down at the chenjeh kabab and marveled at how distracting the scent of lamb could be. He made a mental note to thank Adam in writing for choosing this place. Helms didn't get where he was by asking too many questions. He would get the details about Adam's project in time.

"What do you need me to do, Adam?" Helms asked.

"At the moment, nothing really," he said. "That lamb is getting cold, though." Seconds later, a server brought Adam a plate of chicken skewers. His phone buzzed but he ignored it. They spent a few minutes lost in the magic of Persian spices before Adam realized he owed his boss more of an explanation.

"I'm not going into a lot of the details here, but I want you to know that what I'm working on is not a threat to this country, or any country, for that matter. Should things go sideways, you had no idea what your rogue employee was up to on his sabbatical," he said.

"Well, that's good to hear. I've never doubted your loyalty, Adam. What can I expect if you are successful?" he asked.

"That you were instrumental in making this happen," Adam said with a smile. His thoughts turned to the building he would no longer drive to each morning. With everything else happening, it dawned on Adam that he would need to put something in the crate in the basement that could not identify him. His phone buzzed a second time, but this conversation was more important.

Adam had several candidates to act in his role if he was granted the leave from work. At the top of the list was Patrick Kennedy, who insisted he was no relation to the famous clan. The Brown alumnus was every bit as ambitious, however. He would love telling billionaires how to run their companies.

Adam took a deep breath and prepared for his final ask. "So, if I'm out, on this sabbatical that is not really a sabbatical, I'll be working in kind of a gray area, if you are ok with that," he explained. "I am not severing all ties with you or the agency. I would never do that. We can tell people that I needed to spend more time with my family and get away from the pressure and the schedule."

"I understand you wanting to get out on your own, but what is it? What are you doing? Have you cured the common cold?" Helms asked.

Adam couldn't help but smile. "No, but it will make things a lot easier for people to-" he stopped himself. This was a good place to stop talking. He had asked for favors and received them. Now there was nothing standing in the way of him and the chance to design flying cars. It was as crazy as it sounded, and he knew it was the right choice for him. He realized he was leaving a career others envied. L.U.C. could be the devil in disguise, a genie he could not put back in the bottle. Adam was ready for the risk.

"If my instincts are correct, this will do a lot of good for everyone," Adam said.

"Your instincts are almost always correct. That's why my job is so much easier with you around," Helms told him. A top-notch spy and a diplomat, Adam thought. "Well, I wish you luck on whatever you are doing with this mysterious project of yours," he told Adam.

"I will hand in my notice Friday," Adam said as his phone buzzed yet again.

"Do you need to take that?" Helms asked with concern.

"Chris likes to buy pizza for all his friends. He might be sending me a funds request. This will just take a second," Adam said as he pulled his phone out of his jacket.

There were three missed calls and three texts from Greg. The latest was displayed on his screen.

"HUNTER, I NEED TO GET TOGETHER WITH YOU ASAP! CALL ME! WHERE ARE YOU?"

Chapter 11 – All the Way to Scotland

Having finished lunch and thanked Helms profusely, Adam hurried to the safety of his car and shut the door quickly. Things were going so well, but Greg didn't call that frequently unless something major was happening.

"Well?" Adam asked when Greg picked up.

"I'm so glad to hear from you! Is everything ok?" Greg sounded out of breath.

"Yes, I just had lunch with Helms at Divan and I'm trying not to doze off. Are you in jail or what?"

"Oh, sorry, yeah. It's just that I heard from Grace and she wants to meet soon. I guess I got overexcited, but it's not like I can tell anyone else about any of this," he said.

"Ok, then. It's all going according to plan. I don't know how people at work will react when they hear I'm going to be away from the office for, you know, several months," he told his friend.

"Yes. Where you work, conspiracy theories tend to have a life of their own," Greg said.

"I will talk to you tomorrow. Try to stay calm until then, pal," Adam said as he started the car to head home.

"Rumors of my mental breakdown have been greatly exaggerated. I'm just taking time off work to do some different things," Adam told Julie and the kids the Saturday after turning in his leave request at work.

"There are rumors about you already?" Julie asked. "Wow, I thought my office was bad," she said, shaking her head.

"Jeff's mom took off work because of painkillers. Are you really ok, Dad?" Chris was not easily convinced otherwise when he became alarmed about something.

"Do you have enemies at work?" Brianna had been watching a lot of crime dramas lately. Maybe too many.

"Yes, I'm ok, you guys. And no, I don't have any enemies at work unless you count the vending machine," he said. "You can always reach me, and I will be in touch as often as I can," he assured them.

"And Director Helms was ok with this?" Julie wondered why he didn't try to talk Adam into staying.

“Yes, that may have been the kabobs talking, but he was very supportive,” Adam said.

“Well, if it’s good enough for him, then I hope you have a great time with this, um, project,” Julie said as Adam hugged the kids goodbye and began his trip to Greg’s house in Point Lookout State Park.

He packed in a hurry, mumbling to himself as he made sure L.U.C. was comfortable in the olive-green duffel bag. Did Helms simply not care if a valuable employee left to work on some mysterious project? Was it a setup? A test?

Maybe it was appropriate payback. Over the years, Adam had made his boss look good, making sure his projects came in under budget and advanced space exploration rather than the agendas of special interest groups. He’d even handled the unpleasant tasks of shutting down some of the questionable practices of the spaceflight companies, cleaning up and disposing of potential scandal-causing behavior before the media got wind of it.

Did it really matter why Helms didn’t offer any pushback? He was past the point of no return with L.U.C.

His phone rang and it was Greg.

“Hey, you know where to go today?” Greg asked.

“1 Loretta Landing Lane, Scotland, not the country, but the town,” Adam said as he looked for his favorite sweatshirt.

“Great, you wrote down the directions?” he sounded anxious.

“Right on Cornfield Harbor Road, left on Cornfield Harbor Drive, left on Loretta…go on to the gravel road through half a mile of pine trees. Watch out for stray crabs,” he said.

“You shouldn’t have any trouble if you do that. I talked to Grace earlier and she has found more interesting stuff. She’s got some ideas of her own, but then, she always does,” he said.

“I can’t wait to hear all about it. We’ll be there in a couple of hours,” he told his friend.

“We?” Greg sounded confused.

“I’m bringing our new friend. Set a place at the dinner table for him, would you?” Adam asked as he threw some shoes in a suitcase.

“This is going to be great!” Greg said before he hung up.

Adam locked up his house a short time later, stopping by Dan Griffith’s house up the street. Dan was a police officer and friend who said he would watch Adam’s house while he was away. The electricity was shut off and the trash trucks could skip his house. It was a cold, overcast day, but Adam felt giddy as he began driving to Greg’s family beach house.

The first time he heard about the beach house, Adam imagined a lean-to cottage with two bedrooms at most. He knew Greg was an only child and the family didn't really need a big place to spend lazy days at the shore.

As he got to know Greg during his freshman year, he realized his friend never seemed to worry about spending money. Adam regularly scraped his car's cup holder for change when he was hungry, but Greg treated their group to pizza with everything most weekends.

The awkwardness of asking a friend if he came from money was not lost on Adam. Greg had never made Adam feel embarrassed about his lack of discretionary funds. One day while they were on a study break in the library, Adam broached the subject.

"So, is your family wealthy?" he asked, unable to find a more discreet way to question his friend.

Greg inhaled and sat quietly for a moment. "They were," he said. "They passed."

"Oh, I didn't realize. I'm sorry," it had never occurred to Adam that Greg's parents were both deceased.

"Don't be. The fog was really heavy one night. They were driving home from the symphony. They died instantly when they ran off the road," Greg said softly.

"How old were-" Adam couldn't help but ask.

"Sixteen," Greg had answered these questions before.

"I'm really sorry. I won't ask anything else," Adam said. The loss of his father had been devastating to his family. He imagined losing both parents at once would be unbearable.

"I don't talk about it a lot. And I'm very lucky in some ways. This is paid for," he gestured to his books, but Adam suspected he was talking about tuition, room, board. Everything.

"You're paying for this?" Adam slapped his forehead when he realized he had just asked another question.

"There is a trustee. As long as I graduate, I will come into what they left after I turn twenty-two" he said. "And I hope sometime, you can come see where I grew up, and stay in the beach house," he said. "Treasure Island is really cool," he said, smiling.

"Well, maybe you can visit Bellingham this summer. It'll take me about ten minutes to show you around." They started laughing in the library and realized it was time to get back to the books.

Buildings were getting sparser and smaller as Adam drove southeast to Scotland. Soon he was driving past fields and farms, houses on large plots of land and stables. Around

Mechanicsville, the Amish drove their buggies down the road, making Adam almost believe for a moment he had traveled back in time. Were their lives better then? We had more advanced technology today, but was life more meaningful? Were people happier because of recent inventions?

It was becoming apparent that this house of Greg's was in a very remote area. Adam started to wonder if there was a grocery store nearby. Then his thoughts turned to hospitals. He hadn't realized this place didn't have strip malls or big box stores or chain restaurants. Once in a while he would see a white clapboard house behind trees on an expanse of property.

He reached the gravel road with pine trees on either side and began to wonder if Greg's beach house even had running water. What had he gotten himself into?

Expecting a standard wrought iron gate when he rounded the bend at the end of the road, Adam stopped. He'd seen legions of Roman soldiers knock down similar structures in movies, but not without a catapult or two. A roaring lion sat on each side of the wood and iron gate. The wall surrounding the property was at least ten feet tall and obscured any possible view of what lay behind it. He was tempted to put the car in reverse. This was not where Greg went fishing as a kid.

At the top of the gate were cameras that followed Adam as he stepped out of the car. Places like this always had them. To the right of the door was an engraved box holding a keypad. L.U.C. was underneath a couple of hoodies at the moment. He would enter the code Greg gave him, and if it turned out this house belonged to a Saudi prince or movie star, Adam figured he could safely apologize and leave if he appeared genuinely confused. At the moment, he was.

The five numbers on the keypad produced beeps that caused the gate to swing open, and Adam hurried through them before they closed. He saw a house in a small clearing, and its design reminded him of Frank Lloyd Wright houses. It was thoroughly modern, glass and concrete, with a crescent shaped roof curling towards the sky. Nothing could have been further from the little place on the beach Greg described.

It wasn't exactly *on* the beach. There was a small sliver of ocean visible behind the house, and Adam suspected a path through some berms lined by hedges led directly to the beach. He was not going to investigate now. Adam was expecting armed guards to appear at any moment. He wasn't bringing L.U.C. in until he was sure it was safe.

Was this Greg's idea of a practical joke? It looked like a really expensive one. Maybe this was something from Airbnb? One of those party houses he'd heard about? The more he studied the house from the outside, it began to grow on him. Not really a homey, cozy kind of place. Still, they'd wanted a remote place to design the flying cars, and here at the end of Point Lookout, Adam realized they'd found it.

Chapter 12 - At the Beach House

Adam wondered if Greg's family beach house had been built in the 1950's. People were worried about the Russians dropping bombs back then. It would explain why the whole place resembled a bunker.

Or a fortress. A ring of tall, sturdy pine trees formed a barrier from overhead, and an extra layer of deterrence if the giant wall didn't stop intruders on the ground. The house itself looked like it could withstand a week of shelling from an enemy attack.

He parked his car under the portico and hoped he could enter the house. There was another keypad next to the front door. Six numbers in the access code this time, and more cameras around the front door. Adam thought working at the CIA may have given him a false sense of security. He couldn't imagine living in a home like this.

He walked in, set his duffle bag and suitcase down, and looked around. It was a house, not a home. It had a lot of concrete, and furniture that suggested a workspace, not an area for family gatherings. There was a kitchen, and on the other side of it was a room that featured an office conference table, not a generations-old dining table. He wandered through the open floor plan to a living area. An entire wall converted to a video screen bigger than some movie theaters.

As he explored the back of the house, he counted six bedrooms, each with its own full bath. Did the Buchanans bring friends? Family? Why did they have so much space? Settling on a bedroom with a slice of an ocean view, Adam put his suitcase at the end of the bed, and carefully placed L.U.C. and the duffel bag on the bench at the foot of the bed.

Tired of the austerity, Adam decided to walk to the beach. It was windy and cool as he walked through the pines to the deserted beach. The Potomac flowed into Chesapeake Bay and the waves were lapping at the beach while a few boats sailed by in the distance. He understood in that tranquil moment why Greg liked coming to this place.

It was also January and too cold for standing around, so Adam returned to the house and tried to get comfortable on an industrial sofa. It was easier than expected, and soon he drifted off to sleep.

"IS THIS GREAT OR WHAT?" Greg asked rhetorically. His voice echoed off the walls of the barren foyer and jolted Adam awake. He set his bags down with a thud and walked into the living room, Grace a few feet behind.

"Some place you've got here," Adam said as he sat up.

"You like it? It's not like any other house around," Greg said.

"Well, most houses don't look like nuclear fallout shelters," Adam responded.

Greg beamed. "I know, that's why I like it. It's a great conversation piece, for one thing. People loved it when we brought them here. You never met my dad, but he was one of a kind, so it makes sense that his house would be, too. He was also kind of a tightwad and he worked for Adamson Concrete. He got major corporate discounts the way he built this place," Greg explained. He could tell Adam wasn't impressed. "Have you been to the beach?" he asked.

Adam brightened. "It was just like you said it would be," he smiled. "I can understand why you liked coming here as a kid."

Grace cleared her throat. "Hello Adam."

Greg moved aside when she spoke from behind him. "Oh, right. You two have met," Greg said.

"How was the drive?" she asked.

"Nice to get out of the city. I heard you've got some information for us," Adam responded.

"I'll start the Keurig," Greg said. "Let's go to the conference table," he suggested.

Adam felt stiff and old as he pushed himself off the couch. He noticed Grace looked like she had been out jogging. Her hair was loose, her face was slightly flushed and she wore leggings under an oversized hoodie. Suddenly, he felt like a slob.

"Cream and sugar, Adam?" Greg asked from the kitchen.

"No, I think I'll start drinking it black, thanks." He sat in a chair shaped something like a lightning bolt that he didn't trust fully.

Greg came to the table with the coffee and Grace opened her laptop. "Researching L.U.C. was full of twists and turns. I'm not sure if anyone in the US believes that the Roswell crash was a weather balloon. After digging through layers of security, a lot of data and some encryption, I found out that AI was likely on the spaceship that crashed, and that foreign materials scattered over a much wider area than investigators realized at the time," she said.

"Well, that's not really surprising," Greg said as he sipped his coffee. "Unless something fell off and landed in, I don't know, Florida."

"Well, not quite that far, but plenty of people were moving around and through New Mexico that summer. There's the family in Sabinal that seems a little iffy. And then there is a man named Ben Kumar," she looked up as she said his name.

"The S.E.T.I. guy?" Adam's eyebrows rose.

"You know him?" Greg asked.

"I work for the CIA, remember?"

"He's a kind of recluse, it seems," Grace said.

"Yes, I've heard of him. He's still alive?"

"My sources say yes. He is ninety-three, in good health and his worth is estimated in the tens of billions" Grace told them.

"The big money really is in graphene, I guess," Adam said.

"So, this guy makes, what? Electric batteries?" Greg asked.

"Among other things. Graphene is a great conductor of heat and electricity. And it's about a hundred times stronger than steel," Adam said. "So what's he got to do with Roswell?" Adam asked.

"You're not going to believe this. And you CANNOT tell anyone what you are about to hear," Grace said. "This part is more than HIGHLY CONFIDENTIAL and no doubt above the SECURITY CLEARANCE of BOTH of you put together! Had you not come into my office with the information you had and had all this talk of L.U.C., I probably wouldn't be here," she explained.

"Apparently, Ben must have been one of the first people on site of said UFO crash in Roswell. Ben Kumar was an immigrant from India, a teenager at the time. It appears that the Kumars had immigrated from India with little more than the shirts on their backs and Ben's family was said to have been in the hotel business in the Carlsbad, New Mexico area. While they risked it all, they really had nothing to lose. Ben, who is now in his nineties, was running an errand for his father up to Roswell when he saw the lights and happened upon the supposed crash. He staked a claim and the rest is now history," she finished.

It was not easy to surprise two people who had worked in the unpredictable aerospace industry for most of their adult lives, but Grace had managed to do it.

"Who got involved after that?" Greg asked. "FBI?"

"We may never know exactly who got involved, it was someone who realized whatever Ben had, it didn't really belong to the government, anyway. And it sounds like as young as he was, Ben knew how to haggle," Grace said.

"What do you mean?" Adam asked. He wondered how Grace was able to find all this information so quickly.

"The deal he negotiated was pretty nice. He agreed to "sell" whatever he had laid claim to in his discovery in exchange for some ongoing royalties for anything that would ever be "developed" from the crash," she told them as she stood up and went in search of something to munch on in the kitchen.

Adam and Greg looked at each other, trying to digest this strange new piece of information. "Maybe they were avoiding bad publicity by keeping it quiet," Adam said.

"The war was ending, the country, the world, had been through so much. People probably just wanted to make it go away," Greg said quietly.

Grace returned with a plate of cookies. "Don't know how long these have been in the pantry. I guess we'll find out if they're safe to eat," she said as she took a seat again.

"Ok, so what about our friend in the duffel bag?" Adam asked.

"Not a lot of information about him, specifically. We might wake him up soon and find out what he knows," Grace said.

"He's probably listening right now," Adam said. He allowed himself one cookie and wondered what they would do for dinner.

"What happened to Ben Kumar?" Greg asked.

"Well, it seems he has a lot of friends. It's possible that he gave the Russians access to something he found near Roswell and that's how they got Sputnik going," Grace told them.

"You're kidding. Sputnik was, what 1956?" Greg asked.

"It came back to earth in '58, didn't it?" Adam asked. "The same year NASA became official."

The three exchanged looks from across the table. There was silence, but it was electric, not uncomfortable.

"So you think Ben helped Russia first, then decided we were a better bet?" Adam asked skeptically.

"Can we ask him?" Greg looked at Grace.

She smiled at the men, shaking her head. "After what I've just told you, you guys still want to pursue this? Are you sure?"

"I'm more convinced than ever," Adam told her. Could it be a coincidence that he'd ended up working for NASA, now this? It hardly seemed possible. And now he didn't know if his sabbatical was going to give him enough time. This could take a decade. "We have L.U.C., and he's already done the research. We just need someone to fund the project," he was growing impassioned.

“That we do, but I need some time to process all this information,” Greg said as he stood and stretched.

“Those cookies just made me hungry,” Grace admitted.

“Ok, you guys are right. We need to think about this for a while. What if we get up tomorrow, go to the beach to clear our heads, then pick L.U.C.’s brain, or whatever you call it, with respect to Mr. Kumar?” he asked.

Greg and Grace nodded in unison. “Sounds like a plan,” she said.

Chapter 13 - Day One of the Plan

It's almost always difficult to sleep in strange surroundings, no matter how exhausted one is, or how high the thread count was on the D. Porthault linens on the king size bed. Adam's dreams were vivid and sometimes troubling. He was slightly disoriented when he woke up to the sound of wind screeching against the beach house before dawn.

Here he was, in a fantastical house, preparing to hunt down a ninety-something Hindu billionaire with the help of an android face that spent its idle time in an elliptical sphere. He had made this decision because the android wanted him to build flying cars that could undo centuries of environmental abuse. So, rather than argue with a face that floated on a virtual screen, he decided to quit his perfectly stable job and told his family he would be out of range for a while. As for the stories about Roswell, of course it wasn't a weather balloon, it was a spaceship that crashed in the desert!

Did that pretty much sum it up? Adam wasn't even sure he wanted to get out of bed.

He sat up to check on L.U.C., only to find that the olive bag was missing. That got his blood pumping faster than any calisthenics could have. He hurried out to the giant conference table where Grace and Greg sat, the sphere between them. They were speaking in hushed voices as they turned to see a panicked Adam.

"Well, good morning," Greg hoisted his coffee mug in greeting. Adam looked around the kitchen and saw a Nespresso, nicer than the old Keurig they'd used yesterday, along with a plate of sliced fresh fruit.

"We were trying not to be too loud because we knew you were beat yesterday," Grace said. She was makeup-free and radiant. Probably fancy vitamins, Adam thought.

More importantly, who had removed the sphere and when? He made a mental note to address that later.

Picking up a few apple slices, he started the Keurig and stood next to the table.

"I don't really have any more questions at this point, do you two? I'm for asking L.U.C. where we start," he said. "Oh, right, good morning. How did everybody sleep?"

"Lulled by the waves against the beach. I was out like a light," Greg said.

"Me, too," Grace said as she ate an orange slice.

“Ok, then.” Adam rested his palm on the sphere and within a few seconds, L.U.C.’s face began to come into focus at the far edge of the table. The virtual horizontal surface glowed to life at the same time. The pattern of his face slowly oscillated, as if he was awaiting instructions.

Grace and Greg stood to get a better view of L.U.C.’s table. It reminded Adam of an old fashioned “war room” when generals stood over maps of countries. This time the map was a holograph and the general was, well, L.U.C. wasn’t exactly a general.

“L.U.C., we’re all here and we’re listening,” Adam said.

Without preamble, L.U.C. displayed an image of the car on the table. The group was able to watch the images rotate, as L.U.C. showed them crafts in different shapes and sizes. “These are the crafts you will construct,” he said. It was as if someone had switched his settings to “no nonsense.” He was all business now.

“The first step in this process is building what we shall call the Axiom. Within the walls of the Axiom is where we will produce these machines. There will be four Axiom’s in all across the globe. Determining the specific locations for these *factories* requires absolute precision. “Axiom One will be the control center with Axioms, Two, Three and Four providing the necessary companion magnetic current,” he stated.

Images of massive buildings covered the table as the vehicle images faded into the background.

“These factories serve as the sole manufacturing location, as well as act as a kind of command center for the operation and, perhaps most critically, provide the power source channeled into the grid that allows the vehicles to levitate,” L.U.C. explained.

“This undertaking will require considerable funds, a labor force of several hundreds, if not thousands. You will need specialized equipment and team members with extensive knowledge and experience. An understanding of archaeology is necessary to determine the locations of the Axiom,” he explained.

“We’re not exactly high school dropouts, here, L.U.C. I think we can find the Axiom,” Greg said as he folded his arms.

Was it possible for a virtual human to glare? L.U.C. dropped his Mr. Spock act for a moment.

“You will need a helluva lot more brain power than is currently in this room – no offense to anyone present. There are some very complex formulas that lie ahead of us, contained within my “frame. Someone will need to understand and apply to how the Earth will interact with those theorems. And, MOST OF ALL, this entire undertaking must be done discreetly and in absolute secrecy,” he told them.

“This is not a project. This is…a revolution,” L.U.C. said. “There is so much at stake.”

"We want to do this right, L.U.C.," Greg said. "I understand the need for geologists, but archaeologists?" he asked.

"There is evidence that we have been here before, much before, and someone or /something has been hard at work in helping to provide markers for the locations of the Axioms. A significant amount of work has been done already to help you identify the locations for the facilities. Now, you must find someone who can help you locate them. This means securing the services of an expert familiar with ley lines and the 33rd parallel" L.U.C. told them.

"Ley lines and the 33rd Parallel?" Adam asked. "Are we going to hire some warlocks and gnomes to find them? I mean, no one in my industry takes either of these things seriously."

"Mainstream science tends to avoid this crucial area, for reasons not entirely clear. Mainstream science also struggles to extricate itself from the toxic sludge it finds itself in at the present," L.U.C. told them.

"Ok, we have a lot of work ahead of us," Grace said as she glanced at Adam and Greg.

Lastly,' L.U.C. said. "After scanning the area of Greg Buchanan's beach house, I have determined that this is where I should stay for the duration of this project. The location is secure, it will be private. I can provide all of the key instructions to complete the project and monitor our progress here. I have no further statement at this time," L.U.C. said as he dissolved into the table, leaving the group stunned.

They turned and looked at one another, as if to confirm that they had all just participated in something extraordinary. They stayed that way, standing around the large table with its modern metal centerpiece catching the light of the rising sun.

Adam broke the silence. "I'm going to need more coffee," he said.

"I'm going to make some calls," Grace said.

"Me, too," Greg said as he sank into his chair.

"I think I'm going to take a trip to visit Mr. Kumar," Adam told his teammates.

"That should be interesting, to say the least. Let us know as soon as you can what you learn. We've got Axioms to locate and a Trentrafactory or four to build!" Grace said.

"Then we'll be ready to make flying cars," Adam said in disbelief. Was this really happening?

"Ok, Adam, we're going to need some time to do the work on our end. Today is Thursday, should we meet here with you and L.U.C. next Thursday, sometime?" Greg asked.

"Yes. I will see you here, hopefully with a good report," he told Grace and Greg.

"Who knows where we will find the Axioms?" Grace wondered.

"Who knows where I will find Kumar?" Adam responded.

Greg smiled. "So the race is on!"

Chapter 14 - Time to Meet Ben

He was getting used to sleeping in a strange bed, but Adam could not get used to the bottles of organic juices made from jungi-ungi leaves in the refrigerator every morning.

"I just had a big glass of it, and I feel great!" Greg enthused. "You should try some."

Adam shot him a withering glance.

A tall, slender man Adam had never seen before walked into the kitchen and began stocking the basket next to the Nespresso machine with claret, sky blue and emerald-green capsules. He was wearing a dark silk shirt with a mandarin collar. "Perhaps Mr. Hunter's tastes run more toward bacon and eggs in the morning?" the man asked.

"Did I forget to tell you we have a housekeeping staff?" Greg asked.

"That would explain the cookies that appear out of nowhere and the new towels in the morning," Adam said.

"Could you make a trip to town for groceries today? Adam is on a high cholesterol diet, apparently," Greg sneered.

"Of course," the man said as he disappeared into the cavernous pantry.

"Anything else you need, Adam? Grace and I are driving back to the city soon," Greg asked.

"Ben Kumar's cell phone number?" Adam asked.

"You're the CIA guy. You'll be chatting with him by lunchtime," Greg said as he took a last swig of coffee and put on his coat.

"Lunchtime. That sounds good," Adam said. Hopefully, the pantry guy would be back from the grocery store by then.

"You and L.U.C. are going to be fine," Greg said.

"You're right," Adam agreed. "L.U.C. doesn't eat much."

There were over thirty-one million people with the surname Kumar in India, Adam learned as he began his background search. There were forty listings for Kumars in Albuquerque alone, but Adam doubted Ben still resided in New Mexico.

S.E.T.I. headquarters was in New York, according to the website. It featured one picture of the CEO on the "About Us" page: an old photo of Ben shaking hands with President Regan. Great.

Was he going to bring L.U.C. to meet Ben? Not unless Ben could meet him within driving distance. Flying with L.U.C. was beyond risky. What was he going to ask, exactly? The man had dozens of requests for money and other favors every day. Was honesty the best policy? What was going to work in his favor with the many gatekeepers Ben had? The first few people he talked to probably wouldn't be high enough on the totem pole to demand a lot of specifics.

He started with the organization's toll-free number and by midday had lost track of the number of times he had been asked if he wanted to leave a message for a member of Mr. Kumar's staff. No one he talked to seemed to know where he was, exactly. No one seemed to have contact with anyone who would know.

Maybe he was out of the country. S.E.T.I did business all over Africa, the Middle East and Asia. Images on the website featured scientists at work in deserts, mountains, even at sea. For all Adam knew, Ben was at the South Pole researching graphene in freezing temperatures.

And then there were the background checks Ben's people were doubtlessly running on Adam. One assistant of Ben's once called him "Kumar the Kook Magnet." The company's public phone numbers received a huge volume of calls from people claiming to have ties to the FBI or CIA. Someone who actually had ties to the CIA, like Adam, was cause for caution. Over a period of a few days, the company's private investigators assembled a profile of Adam Hunter. They were as certain as they could have been that he was who he said he was, absent a fingerprint scan and DNA sample. Those could wait until he was on S.E.T.I. property.

It was not until Tuesday that Adam was able to schedule a meeting with Kumar for the following day at 11:45. In a remote part of central Colorado. Apparently, Kumar liked to work where he had a lot of room and privacy.

Adam decided to take the 8 a.m. flight from Richmond and avoid the D.C. area as much as possible. It was a nonstop flight that would land in Denver at 10 a.m. and leave him just enough time to make the drive on Interstate 70 to Deer Trail, population less than 500, in the southeast. The land was brown where it wasn't covered with snow from the storm that had passed through two days earlier. Luckily, the skies were mostly sunny and temperatures were slightly above freezing.

He turned south on Highway 38 and felt like he was coming to the end of the earth, but as he crested a hill, he saw the campus of S.E.T.I. rising majestically over the prairie. The overall impression was not one of beauty, but of power. This was mainly due to the lengths the designers of the place went to promise security.

Adam thought the ten-foot fence at Greg's beach house was excessive. S.E.T.I.'s was easily twice that height. Drones hovered and glided over the enormous buildings and parking lots. There was a separate entrance and exit for trains and transport trucks, and this Tuesday morning, it was bustling with activity.

The visitor's gate was just as busy. Adam estimated he was sixth in the queue to check in with the first level of security. It was 11:30 a.m. He was not going to be late to this meeting, no matter what. As legendary football coach Vince Lombardi once said, "If you're early, you're on time. If you're on time, you're late."

The officers wore ISEE Recon shades as they scrutinized every entrant who had come hoping to sell their wares and strike it rich. When it was his turn, Adam began by introducing himself. He got as far as "Adam Hunt-" and the guard smiled from behind her dark glasses.

"Yes, Mr. Hunter, welcome to S.E.T.I. Mr. Kumar has been expecting you. Have a good visit, and please proceed to the visitor parking carport to the left of the main entrance," she told him.

Walking into the building, Adam greeted the front desk personnel who also addressed him by name. "Please have a seat while you wait. Mr. Kumar will be with you shortly," a young man wearing all black said.

He looked around the lobby with its modern furnishings and high ceilings. There were photographs of honored employees on one wall, and a huge, computerized map of the earth covered the opposite wall. Colored pinpoints of light blinked at various locations on the land and in the oceans, places where S.E.T.I. was building and designing the latest technology.

As he was preparing to inspect the map in closer detail, an imposing security guard emerged from the elevator just to the right of the waiting area. He summoned Adam to come with him.

They went up several floors, got out and turned left down a long corridor, at the end of which was a second elevator. The guard removed an illuminated pass from his jacket and waved it over the elevator panel, as there were no buttons on it. Again, the elevator rose, this time only a few floors. It opened to a room much like the sitting area Adam was in earlier, but there was nothing in it save a large desk. One man stood behind the desk. The wall behind him was solid glass, but provided no visibility, at least on Adam's side, and there were two doors on either side of the desk. He figured Ben's office was behind this glass wall.

The security guard motioned Adam toward the desk and stepped back into the elevator from which they had just emerged. As the doors closed, Adam thought he heard the click of a lock as the guard disappeared into the shaft.

Beginning to feel uneasy, he walked toward the person he thought was Ben's personal assistant behind the desk. As he did so, the wall around the door to Adam's left grew transparent in a matter of seconds.

On the other side was Ben Kumar, opening the door. "Welcome, Mr. Hunter, thank you for coming," he said.

"Thank you for meeting with me, Mr. Kumar," Adam said as he followed him through his long corner office. He nodded at Ben's assistant.

Kumar gestured to a couch in his office and Adam took a seat. Murals of blue- and purple-skinned Hindu deities adorned the walls, their many arms engaged in a multitude of activities. The furniture was dark wood in what Adam later learned was called "British colonial style." The back wall of the office was all glass, allowing him a remarkable view of the Great Plains.

Ben stood in front of it and smiled at Adam's reaction. "It's a little of everything. Kind of like me," Kumar said. Indian and American, thought Adam. He studied the contrasts between the interior and exterior before him. Otherworldly images and the harsh but beautiful wide-open spaces of the American West. Who was this man?

Kumar wore a dark blue suit that suggested tailors in Colorado apprenticed at Savile Row. His frame was thin but not worryingly so, and he moved quickly and easily, considering his age. His dark eyes were sharp and lively. He seemed like a man much younger than he was, and at the same time he seemed to exude wisdom and calm.

"Can I offer you tea or coffee?" he asked as he prepared to contact his assistant via the intercom.

"No, thank you. And your office is remarkable," Adam said. Then he turned his attention to Mr. Kumar as he sat in an overstuffed chair across from the sofa. The two men looked at each other intently. "So, I understand that you know a little something about Roswell, Adam," he said bluntly.

Kumar's demeanor shifted from welcoming to stern. "So, Mr. Hunter, you set this meeting up. What is your business here?" he asked.

There was no way to preface this bombshell with something that could lessen its impact, and Adam realized he didn't need one so he decided to jump to the chase. "I am in possession of an artificial intelligence who sought me out. *It*, which calls itself L.U.C., has offered me the opportunity to begin a very important project, a project that was likely conceived long before I got here. I have it on pretty good authority that you are an individual who likes to "participate" in projects like these, especially where L.U.C. might be involved. From the limited research I've been able to complete, you appear to have found a way to insert yourself into many opportunities involving my new friend, especially when there might be something in it for you," he said simply. There. Cards on the table.

"*You may go now,*" was what Adam expected Kumar to say.

Instead, he nodded slightly. "Go on," he said, to Adam's surprise.

"Not to be too dramatic here, but I believe I have the plans for a project that has the capacity to change the world as we know it. As much as the Wright Brothers helped us imagine how to break the chains of gravity, the successful completion of this "project" will make the next leap for humanity bigger than the difference between Orville's Wright Flyer and a modern-day Space Shuttle," he told Kumar.

"I see. And since you seem to already know a little something about me, just how do you see that I fit in?" he asked evenly.

"I'd like to ask you to be an investor. When it's all said and done, you could get a small royalty on every monthly travel subscription sold, public or private," Adam explained while feeling it was the right time to mention how Ben would gain monetarily.

"What kind of exposure would this create for you...and L.U.C.?" he asked, as though an offer to do business with a virtual human was an everyday occurrence.

"Ben, the funding would need to be very discreet. We don't plan on giving the public any exposure to the project, it's just too risky. It would be a completely private venture we are calling *Green Lantern* for now, symbolizing light for the planet as we give her the ability to go green again. While overcoming objections might be insurmountable if we were to try to begin this undertaking in public view, we think the world will have no choice but to embrace her once the prize had been delivered and Earth's restoration could truly begin," Adam said confidently.

At that moment, Adam saw the elevator doors open across the reception room. The security guard stepped out, accompanied by another man. He heard Ben's assistant over the intercom.

"Mr. Kumar, you asked to be reminded when Mr. Decker finished with the business development and contract teams," he said. Kumar's eyes widened.

"Excuse me for one second, Mr. Hunter," Ben said as he hurried outside.

"Ryan, so good to see you again," Ben said as he shook hands with the visitor. "Thank you for coming. This partnership is going to be fantastic, I do believe," Adam heard him say.

Ben walked back into the office and sat again, smiling broadly. "Mr. Decker's company sells a component we are using in our nano division. He is going to score a nice commission and I wanted to thank him personally for what he has promised to deliver."

"You're a very busy man, I can see," Adam said with admiration.

Ben watched Mr. Decker and the security guard disappear behind the closing elevator doors before he looked back at Adam. This time his demeanor was neither polite nor stern. Now he seemed...excited. More cards on the table. Ben had aces up his sleeve, though, and he hadn't lost a game yet. Ben decided it was time to flip the script.

"Adam, I am aware of who you are and also aware that you would be coming. I was prepared for your visit and I accept your offer," Adam opened his mouth, prepared to argue with the rejection he was certain he would face but did not encounter. Was he hearing Kumar correctly? Did he just accept the offer? He nearly jumped off the couch to phone Greg and Grace. He stopped himself, realizing that Kumar was still talking.

"Let's avoid too much formality. The next time you travel, you won't be flying commercial. I have arranged for private transportation to be available to you at St. Mary's County Regional in California, Maryland. Whenever you need it, you can call this number and within four hours, you'll have a Gulfstream of the appropriate size waiting," he said. Adam could not help but smile. So, this was how the other half lived. His glee vanished when he saw Kumar's serious expression.

"You need to begin avoiding all the records of your comings and goings," he said

"Mr. Kumar, I worked for the CIA for many years, I can assure you that I know-" Adam began to explain his understanding of surveillance, but Kumar held up a hand.

"I have a series of offshore bank accounts created and available to you for the purposes of your initiative. If you need anything more, we can arrange for that," he stated. He glanced over at his desk. "What else?"

Adam said nothing. There was more?

Kumar slapped his leg. "Yes, of course. My company is fully prepared to provide you with most of the materials that you will need for your endeavor and we also have the capability to get these materials discreetly to you anywhere in the world, when you decide where that is. Once you have your construction plans in place and your job sites secure, we can begin to arrange for deliveries," he told his new partner.

"Of course," Adam said as his head swam and wondered how Ben seemingly already knew so much. "Thank you."

"Lastly, you'll want to contact Ella Flores. Let's just say she is an expert in human resources. She has built a highly skilled network of "resources" who are capable of handling a project like this with ghost-like untraceability. She's done several projects for me in the past and I trust her and her capabilities implicitly. Here is her private number – she will be expecting a call from you to make arrangements," he handed Adam a card from the gold display on the mahogany coffee table between them.

Adam had a thousand questions, but Ben was not going to answer them. At least not now.

Ben stood and extended his hand to Adam. "You won't deal with me directly from this point forward, but I will be close at hand. I will stay apprised of your progress on the project, and you can contact me if you need me."

This had to be a dream, Adam thought. They had not negotiated. Adam asked and Ben promised he would receive. People spent years learning how to pitch ideas and propose deals. They were degrees in it, weren't there?

He thought of that old saying, *never look a gift horse in the mouth*. He should avoid examining this too closely, shouldn't he?

This wasn't a horse, though. This invention had the power to allow people greater freedom of movement than they had ever enjoyed. At the same time, it would allow our most precious resource, the planet we inhabit, to heal itself.

Ben's "offer" sounded too good to be true. And Adam was very familiar with the old saying about things that appear this way.

If he didn't ask now, he would be kicking himself later, he reasoned.

"I have to say, Mr. Kumar, you have offered much more than I hoped to receive. I am wondering what you hope to gain from this project," Adam said.

Ben tilted his head to the side as he considered Adam's words. He cupped his right hand over his left, then did the reverse. Finally, he spoke.

"One hand washes the other, that's the saying. We are tasked with learning how to work together. Mastering this lesson is the reward," Ben said as he looked over Adam's shoulder and out over the wintry ground. "The universe always sees to it that givers are also receivers," he said, returning his gaze to Adam with an intensity that made the younger man shudder.

Adam suddenly felt the need for fresh air. The combination of honesty and profundity was making him lightheaded.

Adam offered Ben his hand to seal the deal, telling him he looked forward to a productive partnership. It was the understatement of the year, and it was only January.

"Good luck and Godspeed," Kumar said.

He turned to see the security officer standing at the open doors to the elevators that provided access to Ben's sanctum. He gestured for Adam to come with him.

"Once again, Mr. Kumar, thank you for everything. I believe our partnership will benefit countless people, largely because of your generosity."

Kumar smiled and nodded as Adam turned and walked to the elevator.

Outside, the sun was shining, but the wind was fierce and freezing. Adam tried to make sense of what had just transpired as he walked to his rental car. He was a scientist. A logical, analytical guy who used reason to solve problems.

Try as he might, Adam could not use reason alone to explain what had happened in his life since the crate came to his office on Christmas. Without logic to help him determine his next steps, Adam felt adrift. This was terra incognita, but after this meeting, he realized he was not going into the unknown alone.

Chapter 15 - Aleksey Romanoff

Adam settled into his seat on the United flight to Richmond, feeling nostalgic. This looked to be his last time flying on a commercial airline in a while. He might actually miss the tiny potato chip cans and Hemispheres magazines.

What would life be like if Kumar held up his end of the agreement? Unfathomable. Building something that has not existed before out of materials a billionaire is willing to supply? Tired as he was, he could not fall asleep on the plane.

L.U.C. had the plans, the mysterious Ms. Flores had the stealth workforce, Ben had the funds. He wondered what Greg and Grace had found as the plane landed in the predawn hours at Richmond.

It was Wednesday morning and the sun was rising as Adam drove back to the Loretta Landing house. He accessed the property and drove up to the long driveway to see Greg and Grace's cars parked outside. They had another day before they were supposed to meet up, didn't they? He wasn't sure if this was good news or bad news, and he was too tired to ponder it any longer.

The light was on in the kitchen and Grace and Greg were sitting at the oversize table with their espressos. They were happy to see him, and he felt relieved as he flung his carry-on into the lightning bolt of a chair next to him.

"Well? How did it go?" Greg asked.

Adam sighed. He felt like he hadn't seen them in a year.

"Once we get some caffeine in you, we want to hear everything," Grace said as she went to the kitchen and began looking for a mug.

"It went great as far as the deal," he said. "It was hardly a deal. It was more like talking to Santa Claus, I asked for stuff and Kumar gave it to me. Then, he gave me even more stuff," Adam told them, still a little in disbelief himself.

Grace handed him a mug of espresso and steamed milk. "Well, that's great! We should have champagne, not coffee," she said with a bright smile.

"You crushed it. Why aren't you patting yourself on the back?" Greg asked.

"It was so easy. It was too easy," Adam frowned into his coffee as he tried to put his finger on why he wasn't more pleased with his success.

"Maybe you should have gone into sales," Grace said.

"I'm not that persuasive, am I? It was like Kumar had talked to everyone from my third-grade teacher to Helms and knew everything about me before my plane landed at Denver," he said. "When I told him about L.U.C., he didn't seem that surprised," Adam said as he joined the other two at the table. He noticed copies of various MIT publications in front of his friends. Some were the alumni news magazine, others were the tech review.

"What's all this for?" Adam asked his teammates.

"More good news, buddy," Greg said. "We think we've found our smart guy," he said. "Now, obviously, you made shape shifting polymers and Grace can eavesdrop on fleas whispering. But this guy is in a league all his own."

"We found a guy who thinks he can make zero emission cars that fly," Grace told him excitedly.

"You can't be serious," Adam said.

"You may know him. His name is Aleksey Romanoff and he was at MIT when you were. He worked on some really advanced stuff. Do you recognize the name?" Greg asked.

Adam scratched his head. "Maybe…was he my advisor for something?" was the best he could do.

"Well, a couple of days ago, I was racking my brain about how we were going to do some of the things L.U.C. was showing us and I started looking in the MIT news magazine," he said.

"And Romanoff has already built this flying car?" Adam asked hopefully.

"No, he doesn't have one ready for us to look at," Greg said as he pushed an open magazine over to Adam. "But he's available."

Adam saw a photograph of Dr. Romanoff in the feature story. He was officially announcing his retirement after twenty-five years. For the last ten, he'd served as the Dean of Engineering at MIT. Adam skimmed the article for information about this man. Born in Prague, came to the US as a youngster and always loved physics.

"Dynamo theory? He's the dynamo theory guy?" Adam continued his hurried reading. Scientists interested in the earth's magnetism were familiar with his frequent publications on this subject. He often discussed dynamo theory. It centered on the idea that the Earth's outer core contains a large magnetic field generator. It is made up of liquid iron that cools as the planet moves. This continuous motion creates currents that could be harnessed as the electrons move through the liquid and repel. The energy of the moving fluid is converted into a magnetic field that we might have the possibility of controlling. To be able to repel objects could keep them airborne. Thus, cars could fly.

“It’s a very complex set of ideas, but isn’t that kind of what L.U.C. was talking about when he showed us what we would need to build the virtual highway?” Greg asked.

“It is,” Adam’s mind was spinning with theories and espresso so quickly that he had hardly noticed Grace was sitting next to him. He sat back in his chair. “Do you think-” he was reluctant to verbalize his thoughts. He figured he was succeeding through pure luck, and didn’t want to run out of it this early in the project.

“What?” Greg asked.

“That we could get someone like him on our project? No, that’s crazy, never mind,” Adam said.

“Yes, I hoped you would think he was a great candidate!” Greg said. “Well, I did more than hope, I took the liberty of reaching out to Dr. Romanoff and presented him with an offer he couldn’t refuse. Of course, I had no idea where we would get the money for the offer, but he’s retiring. Guys like that love to continue their research and tinker around without the pressure of academia breathing down their neck for what they might have to publish next,” Greg told him.

Adam saw shadows move in the next room and wondered if the housekeeping staff was at work. An older man walked out from the hallway adjacent to the kitchen on the other side from where Adam’s bedroom was located. He hadn’t heard anyone outside the house. The man smelled of toothpaste and soap. He approached Adam, right hand extended.

“Hello Adam, my name is Alex, it is a pleasure to meet you and I am excited about helping you with your project,” he said pleasantly. Adam stared at the man and looked at Greg, who smiled and nodded.

“It’s very nice to meet you, Alex,” Adam said when he regained his composure. “No offense, Dr. Romanoff, but don’t you think we’re getting ahead of ourselves here, Greg?” he asked.

“I apologize for surprising you as I did,” Alex said. “Greg contacted me earlier this week while you were making plans to go to Denver. After a few minutes of talking to him I realized the project he described was everything I had thought about, dreamed about, worked on and prepared for all of my life,” he said.

“That’s sort of how I felt on Christmas day,” Adam said.

“Oh? What happened then?” Alex asked.

“Adam is very sentimental is all,” Greg said with a forced smile. Adam realized Alex might not have met their virtual friend yet.

“And you are certain you want to work with us?” Adam asked Alex.

“I tend to work as independently as possible, but yes, I would like to be part of this project. I have been widowed for several years now, and the politics at the college became tiresome.

Without this project I would be forced to engage in one of those horrible pastimes retired people pretend to enjoy, like stamp collecting or bird watching. This project, I believe, was meant for me," he said.

"You may just be right," Adam said. "I think my work in polymers may help with the construction of the vehicles, which need to be lightweight but durable. Greg here is a mechanical engineer, so he can help set up the Trentafactories," he looked over at his friend.

"Oh, and Grace," he realized she was at the table as well. "With her intelligence work, she was able to help secure the funding," he deliberately omitted Kumar's name.

"It's an impressive group," Alex said.

"With you on board, we have someone who can develop and interpret the formulas necessary to get this thing off the ground," Adam told him.

"The theory is not well-supported yet, but when it is, getting things off the ground and in the air simply requires harnessing the dynamo," he said with a smile.

"Of course," Adam said. Simple. "Now, how did you and Greg meet again?" he asked.

"Coffee," Alex said.

"Oh right, I'll get you some," Adam hurried over to the Nespresso corner as Greg laughed.

"You are really sleep deprived, buddy," Greg said. Adam looked at him and found Alex smiling with embarrassment. "Alex and I met at the Blue Bottle Coffee Shop on Ames."

"Apparently, someone in the department told him I was kind of a fixture there, even after I retired" Alex told him.

"I see," Adam said. Everything seemed so…serendipitous with Greg. Go for coffee, meet a guy who wants to harness the magnetic field in the Earth's core. He stood there in Greg's kitchen, realizing Alex was already part of the team, and for good reason.

Adam had never really needed to know a lot about what was happening inside the Earth. Maybe now was the time to learn. "So, Dr. Alex. Can you tell me about the Earth's magnetism?" he asked.

Dr. Alex brightened. "Yes. It's simple Adam, the Earth's magnetism is generated by convection currents of molten iron and nickel in the Earth's core. These currents carry streams of charged particles and generate magnetic fields. These magnetic fields deflect ionizing charged particles coming from the sun. Theoretically, they will allow us to manipulate a series of controlled power currents. I don't see why, with enough money and resources, this couldn't be done," he explained.

Greg was right, Adam realized. He was in no shape for this discussion, critical as it was to the success of this incredible project. Thanking Dr. Alex for his succinct explanation, he excused himself after his busy day with Kumar and apologized for leaving the conversation early. He walked down the hall to his bed, hoping this day held no more surprises.

Chapter 16 – The Devil is in the Details

Staring at the ceiling of the beach house bedroom, Adam reviewed the last twenty-four hours in his mind. There was the whirlwind trip to Colorado with Kumar, the drive back from Richmond and a surprise meeting with a renowned physicist. His eyes closed from sheer exhaustion and he sank into a deep sleep.

Only seconds later, the bed began to sink like quicksand beneath him. His limbs jerked in an effort to grab the nearest source of stability, but there wasn't one. The sheets, the mattress, all sunk into a hole that would slowly devour him. The terror set in when he realized he was too far from the nightstand to reach anything solid. He tried to scream but could make no sound. With one final lunge upward, Adam found himself sitting on top of the bed in a darkened room.

The walls were covered with pictures of people he didn't know. The furniture was strange and the carpet was unfamiliar. What happened? He saw his coat on the back of a chair and he realized he was in someone else's house. As his heart returned to something closer to its normal rhythm, he remembered it was Greg's house. He was staying there to work on a project.

It was dark. Why was it dark? He had been at the airport…and the sun came up as he drove. He looked over at the clock next to the bed. 5:04 p.m. He'd slept most of the day. Why didn't someone come wake him up?

Still slightly disoriented, he made his way down the dark hall, wondering where the light switches were in this crazy house. Like a moth, he headed toward the nearest light source, the yellow-green glow coming from the main living area. As he made the final turn in the hall, he found Greg, Grace, and Dr. Alex, standing around the table where L.U.C. was now "out" in all his holographic glory.

They were speaking in hushed voices, as if not trying to wake Adam with L.U.C. Dr. Alex manned a virtual control center on the vertical plane of the hologram, waving through large panels of information. Alex thought he saw architectural drawings, renderings, 3D models, and a few complex formulas. The three of them continued working without reacting to Adam's presence.

For a moment, Adam stopped to admire the kaleidoscope before him. While this was a scientific endeavor, it was also an accidental artistic masterpiece. At the end of the table farthest from Adam was a flying car in hologram form, spinning slowly as a reminder of the lofty goal of all their effort and teamwork. The center of the table, and much of the available space belonged to a 3D rendering of the enormous Trentafactory, four of which would house the means of production for the vehicles, and serve as a power source.

On the wall opposite the dining table in the main open living space, there was a vertical plane dedicated to what looked like a small movie theater. This wall now held an image of the Earth rotating on its axis, an orbital moon, and images of what appeared to be Earth's magnetic currents pulsating, almost vibrating, around the Earth.

The colors were vivid and varied, the movements graceful and ordered. And it was *real.* No, not all of it existed in physical form yet, but it was real in the minds of the people in the beach house. And that was where ideas were conceived. They grew and developed until they were ready to exist in this world. There was a plan. There was a logic to all of this. He was mesmerized. Adam thought for a moment he heard "Music of the Spheres."

Something kept distracting him, though. He watched the Earth spin at the center of a menagerie of undulating magnetic currents, but noticed blinking pinpoints of light. There was one somewhere in Europe, one in Asia, and one in the Middle East. They were signifiers of something, but what? The dots didn't match the locations of major cities, or major topographical features. But no image was in this room by accident.

Adam moved in a little closer to get a better look at the identifiers. He was sure as the grogginess wore off, he would quickly understand everything before him.

But L.U.C. interrupted his concentration. "Hello, Adam," he began, "you are now looking at three of the four location coordinates where the 'Axiom Trentafactories' will be constructed. These locations, and one other, will be necessary for our systems to operate at the highest level.

"However, due to the Earth's poles remaining in constant motion and moving slightly each year, we are having a bit of difficulty in uncovering the last marker for the fourth location. Overcoming this will involve some digging," he explained.

Literal or metaphorical digging, Adam wondered? He had many other questions that he did not want to ask anyone, human or otherwise, at this moment. He felt like he had on his first day of piano lessons. When he learned how to read and write music, he was fascinated. How did his teacher know where to write the notes? How did L.U.C. know where to look for places to build the Trentafactories? It was a big world.

And who was "we"? People were arriving every week to join the project, and Adam was still wondering when he would meet with this Ella Flores. Could a project remain top secret when this many people were involved? He wasn't really able to vet them as fast as they were coming into the project, and the beach house.

That wall was another thing Adam found strange. Greg told him his father loved watching football, but wanted to be able to see the ball easily and at all times. He convinced Greg's mother that the only solution was to go big or go home. One day in early November, the screen arrived in several containers, and Thanksgiving at the Buchanans was never the same.

Apparently the ample space suited L.U.C. "I can be significantly more productive in this configuration," he told Adam. "Having scanned the room for assists in expanding visual aids, I located something called a Smart Device, and I appreciated the irony," he told Adam, who could not help but smile. AI with a sense of humor was something one had to experience to believe.

"Once I connected to its primitive API and tapped into the archaic screen sharing function, I was able to provide the team with a continuous view of the project status. The horizontal holographic surfaces are for project modeling," he explained.

"So the team can gather around and interact with the virtual models until they are perfected," Adam finished L.U.C.'s sentence.

"That is correct," L.U.C. said. "The rendering can be modified virtually and instantaneously in order to allow manufacturing to occur at incredible speeds. I will illuminate a vertical holographic plane at one end of the horizontal surface to function for the team as an interactive resource library and information bank," he explained calmly to a dazzled Adam. It was as if the whole place had been designed for L.U.C. to set up the flying car factories, which was absurd, His good friend Greg's dad was a football fanatic.

Adam stepped back as L.U.C. and his imagery began to fill the wall. The rotating Earth and its three flashing red dots, spaced continents apart, began to glow as L.U.C. addressed Grace.

"Listening skills are a requirement for the next task before us," he said. "Grace, I understand that you are good at listening to a lot of things, in a lot of unique ways that can't normally be heard. Is it possible for you to help us identify someone that might have a particular skill set or affinity for locating artifacts? Particularly those that might pertain to the existence of 'ancient alien' markings and their findings?"

"Well, thank you, L.U.C.," she said. "I can eavesdrop on some conversations, maybe listen for mentions of an archeologist who might be seen by most contemporaries as a "nut job" because they might believe in aliens and are wasting their life away on thankless dirt? That type of thing?" she asked.

"I believe you understand what I need," he replied. Grace began swiping on a vertical surface with a small image of North America on it.

Dr. Alex and Greg were at work on the horizontal plane where they reviewed the architectural plans and complex formulas.

L.U.C. contracted to human size and dropped level to Adam's gaze. "There is an assignment for you as well," he said. "You have been instructed to contact Ella Flores, correct?"

Adam stared at L.U.C. blankly.

"Operation Green Lantern is now active. You are to meet with Ms. Flores and provide her with the details of the building of Axiom One," he said. "Please remove your phone."

Adam took his phone out of his pocket and held it up so L.U.C. could "see" it. There was a series of beeps and buzzes as something happened to his phone. "This is a download of encrypted files you will need for the upcoming meeting. A retinal scan provides access to the information," L.U.C. told him. "Contained within these files, you will find a complete set of architectural plans, 3D renderings, and the associated formulaic support for the undertaking of the first phase of the operation," he explained.

"The first phase?" Adam asked.

"Your dedication to this has not gone unnoticed, as you have accomplished much in a short time," L.U.C. said.

"What have I accomplished?" Adam asked. L.U.C. was the one who knew where to put the blinking red dots.

"You separated yourself from your employment without divulging information that could compromise or utterly destroy Operation Green Lantern. You have provided a location for the operation to progress. The team you assembled," he looked over at Grace, Greg and Alex, "is exceptional. You secured the funding critical for an undertaking of this magnitude. And you opened the crate that morning," L.U.C. finished.

It was rather impressive when he thought about it, Adam realized. He had been so busy working at a breakneck speed to launch an almost surreal project, he hadn't realized he'd been checking off items on a to-do list. But it was a long list.

"Now you are on your way to meet Ella, a trusted resource to acquire human capital," L.U.C. said. "First is the "where." Ella will require information about the location to coordinate travel for her team. Second is the "who." She will need to know the exact number of employees and their applicable skill sets. Finally, the "what." She will need assurances of pay including a required fifty percent up front so she will have the necessary capital to deliver her services," he said.

"I'm on my way, am I?" Adam asked.

“I've just been informed that your transportation is on the ground and waiting for you at St. Mary's County Regional Airport. Ella will see you in Monterrey, Mexico to discuss all the particulars in just under eight hours,” he told Adam. He checked his watch. It was nearly midnight. Where had the day gone? Adam realized his watch was the last thing to think about now that Operation Green Lantern was underway.

“The location for Axiom One has already been acquired and the perimeter secured. Local governments have been properly compensated to allow us to self-govern within our perimeter. It is here where you will build and test the first of many of our specialized “craft.” Three more Trentafactories, Axioms Two, Three and Four, will follow,” L.U.C. said.

Without speaking, Adam started to make his way back to his room to pack. But first he walked around the low-profile sectional which faced L.U.C.'s wall in order to get a closer look. He was interested to see if it would offer any clues about where he might be going next after he closed the deal with Ella. One of the three red digital markers was now flashing faster than the other two. It blinked, bright and brave, at the eastern edge of the Mediterranean.

It occurred to Adam he'd never seen the places where they say Jesus walked. He found himself wondering what Israel was like this time of year. Damascus…

Chapter 17 - Claire and Peter Johansen

The excavation at the Greek village of Chiliomodi was drizzly and miserable on a January afternoon in 2018. The area was crowded: not with tourists but with the remains of civilizations that had risen and fallen on that ground for tens of thousands of years. Whispers of past kingdoms and conflicts swirled in the mist. Surveying her surroundings, principal investigator Claire Davies Johansen could understand why people were drawn to this location, even in its dreariest season.

There were low mountains, fields with fertile soil and abundant vegetation. Ocean breezes from the east and frequent sunshine made for a moderate climate.

Some thirteen thousand years ago, the Trojans built Tenea near where Chiliomodi stands today. According to the myth, it is where Oedipus spent his youth. This was no small find.

For many people in Claire's position, sifting through the pottery shards was thrilling. Various archaeological organizations had obtained permission from the Greek government to dig to their hearts' content. But her mind was elsewhere. She looked over at her husband, Peter Johansen, busy unearthing coins. He looked ready for a cup of strong Greek coffee.

She admired his dedication to digging, as she had since she met him at Oxford. His Scandinavian accent, the result of growing up in Gothenburg, beguiled her. His experience with museums was limited to a few trips to the National Museum of Denmark in Copenhagen, but Claire's enthusiasm for the subject was contagious. She had been on digs as a teen in Egypt and Greece, and it was on these journeys that she decided that she had found her calling.

She and Peter married shortly after graduation and worked at the Ashmolean Museum of Art and Archaeology, living on the shoestring budget familiar to many newlyweds. When they had worked there nearly two years, Peter learned the Archaeological Institute of America was offering small stipends for qualified individuals to join their "dig" team projects all over the world.

Delighted to be accepted, Peter and Claire resigned their positions at Ashmolean, prepared to excavate the mountainous, unforgiving terrain of Afghanistan. The location had not been their first choice: it was 2012 and as a decade-old war ravaged the country, US soldiers frequently accompanied the archaeologists on digs. They were headed to Safed Sang with a group of colleagues from all parts of the world, excited to have hot meals and regular paychecks. They learned to travel light, and mastered the art of fitting rolls of toilet paper in their bags, however overstuffed they might seem.

The perimeter of the dig site was sizable. The team established a base camp roughly in the center, with teams of two or four striking out from base each morning at first light to begin combing the mountains systematically in search of hidden treasure in the region's thousands of natural caves. The area is also latticed with *karezi*, an ancient system of irrigation tunnels, some dipping as much as one hundred feet below the ground.

Much as they appreciated the military's maneuverability, Claire and Peter always preferred to work alone. They had tried to make their position clear to the military leadership assigned to accompany their operation. The couple suspected the military was interested in finding the enemy or their weapons in the caves.

The archaeologists were looking for much older evidence of occupation in the caves. But having made five outings in as many days, they had turned up a few bones and items that were little more than two hundred years old.

Unescorted, the couple began their hike on the sixth day. After two hours of exploring, the couple located a rather small cave, unimpressive in its outward appearance. They pressed through the small opening and moved toward the expanding darkness. As Claire's eyes adjusted to the shadows, she saw something she had not believed truly existed. She said the words she never thought she would say out loud on a dig.

"A vimana." Claire's voice was barely a whisper.

It sat on the cave floor, catching what little light was available in the recessed area. It was at least two meters tall, possibly more. It was likely thousands of years old, but was in excellent condition. Claire turned to Peter and peppered him with questions.

"Is this what I think it is?" she asked ecstatically.

"I've seen these in books," Peter said. "Can this really be one?" he asked.

"Look at how tall it is, though. How did it get in this cave?" she wondered aloud.

"Maybe a unicorn brought it," Peter said with a smile. He found himself feeling strangely grateful for the war that made it possible for them to explore this cave at this moment. A mural depicting a vimana would have been incredible, but a real, live vimana? There were no words for a discovery this monumental.

The couple, along with virtually every other archaeologist in the world, had been hearing about these vehicles from their earliest days as students of the dig. The ancient Hindu texts of the Indian epic Mahabharata, written five thousand years ago, contain descriptions of a mythological flying machine. Now, it sat only a few meters in front of them.

As the couple approached the incredible find, both could feel the electromagnetic radiation-gravity field. Peter suspected this served to protect the vehicle. If, as ancient texts implied, vimanas are anti-gravitational, it was logical that this craft was trying to repel them.

It was then, as they were made to move away from the vimana, that they made their second, unimaginable discovery. As they stepped carefully to the rear of the cave, and to the right of the vimana, there it was. A brilliant, flat, blue, stone, lying undisturbed. Peter eased his way around the vimana, careful not to interfere with its magnetic force field, and picked up the stone. It was the shape of one quarter of a circle and close to the size of Peter's palm.

"It looks like it was engraved only a week ago. So new, so blue, so shiny," Peter told his wife. Turning it over in his hand, he rubbed his thumb over a less than perfectly smooth surface. He could see an inscription on the stone, but could not make sense of the letters and numbers. He handed it to language expert Claire.

This is the name of a place and then some GPS coordinates," she said as she examined it:

LAT 33.893762282191105 LONG 65.94441970294172

She tells him it also says: TWO of FOUR (in Roman Numerals), and another set of numbers

LAT 33.283608106133435 LONG -104.93885335500656

The blazingly beautiful stone was the only thing they could think of at this moment. What did it mean? What was it trying to tell them? The couple knew they had to report every artifact found to the dig site manager for recording and chronology. By the glances both gave one another and with the stone safely and deeply packed away in Peter's pack, they hurried back to basecamp to report the vimana. The US military would take more interest in this finding than any other on this excursion, they were sure. They knew they had the real prize – or at least one of them.

Chapter 18 - Motion Performance

The Johansens returned to their cramped Oxford flat that summer as changed people. Gone were the plans to unearth the everyday utensils of ancient civilizations in an effort to understand their culture, or more likely, provide the grunt work necessary for a senior faculty member's magnum opus.

Instead, they wondered about the infinite possibilities of a shiny rock and a machine they had thought existed only in books. Finding a real, live vimana was a little like finding a perfectly preserved pterodactyl fossil. No, this find was more like discovering a pterodactyl fossil with an iPhone in its beak. Five thousand years before the Wright brothers had imagined it, someone or something had built this vimana. And left it in a cave in Afghanistan.

Archaeological teams swarmed the area after the Johansens left, but found little else of significance. They were unable to shed light on the questions that persisted. Who, or what built this machine? Where was it meant to fly? Surely not deep into a cave in this remote part of the world. For Peter and Claire, the questions became more personal: they had made what had to be the discovery of a lifetime and they were barely thirty years old. Where would they go from here?

They began their search at their flat, with the stone unpacked from its bubble wrap and sitting on their coffee table, displayed for what may have been the first time in thousands of years. Sneaking it through security had been a triumph all its own, with the cover story that they'd haggled for it in a Kabul market.

Claire sat with her laptop and a strong cup of tea and began googling the latitude and longitudinal coordinates engraved on the stone. A search of Google Earth revealed that the first engraved number was the location of the cave that held the stone and vimana. Why was this location significant? Peter marveled that they were pondering questions with far more bearing on the future of mankind than what a discussion of unearthed pottery shards could provide.

The second set of coordinates managed to surprise the couple, even after their recent discoveries. Claire double checked the results, not understanding what could possibly link Afghanistan and...New Mexico? They were following the blue stone's directions, and it was indicating a small city south of Albuquerque. It was called Roswell.

“New Mexico? One could scarcely imagine a more unlikely place. That vast desert…” she told her husband.

“That specific area is surprising, yes. But that little city has a great deal in common with other unusual things,” Peter said as he paused a documentary on the Jomon period.

Claire sat up straight. “Unusual? Because it’s a desert?” she asked her husband.

“Not exactly, no. Roswell is on the 33rd parallel, and it’s never a dull place,” he said.

Claire pulled up an image of the earth and saw the line of latitude running through North America, Africa, to Kashmir and beyond. “What happened there?” she asked.

“In the US, Roswell’s ‘Weather Balloon Incident’ and JFK Jr.’s assassination in Texas. In Iraq, Saddam Hussein’s palace was built on this parallel,” he explained.

“Quite strange,” Claire murmured as she studied the map. “And worthy of investigation,” she looked up with a mischievous smile

And that was that. They would find their way to New Mexico one way or another. Yes, it was risky, but the rewards made it worth the risk. Waiting and worrying never advanced an important mission.

Having checked the AIA’s Archaeological Fieldwork Opportunities Bulletin, they found a group working on arrowheads from the prehistoric Clovis Culture at Blackwater Draw. They would be part of a team studying the bone and ivory tools that showed humans lived in North America some thirteen thousand years ago, far longer than earlier estimates. They could spend enough time on that project to appear dedicated, then make the two-hour trek to Roswell in search of the real find.

After that, it was simply a matter of waiting for approval of their work visas. It came faster than expected, until the couple realized news of their remarkable discovery in Afghanistan was circulating.

They were determined to find the next three stones, which meant they would need cover stories for two digs after this one. Those would have to wait. Maintaining secrecy was their priority at the moment. It was not lost on the couple that they were behaving like intelligence agents rather than students of human history. Luckily, the world was full of places to dig.

As they packed for their flight to New York, then Albuquerque, Peter paused to listen to the tv news: “eight soldiers executing orders from President Obama to recover the vimana from the Afghanistan cave are presently listed as missing. Reports of what observers are calling a “time well” purportedly surrounds the cave with an electromagnetic current,” the journalist stated.

Peter and Claire looked at each other for a moment. They exchanged smiles and continued flinging their warm weather clothes in the suitcases. There was no question of what had to be done. They had the choice not to board the plane and seek the rest of the stones. The thought of staying home was abhorrent, they realized as they began the drive to Heathrow.

High altitude sunshine was relentless in New Mexico, where Peter and Claire uncovered the tools of some of the earliest people to brave the harsh, glacier-scraped terrain and hunt mammoth. After two weeks, their sunburns cooled to tans, hours crouching in the dirt took a toll on their hands and backs. Arturo, the team lead, was so impressed with the couple's dedication he told them to take two days off and explore the sights of the Land of Enchantment.

"We don't want to leave you short-handed," Peter protested so convincingly, Claire thought he should have pursued a career in the theater.

"Don't be silly, we'll be fine. Seriously, check out White Sands. Oh, or the Aztec ruins in Farmington," he enthused. "You guys are going to have a great time," he told them as they left the site for the day.

"Hope so!" Claire smiled as she and Peter tried not to make the rush to their car obvious.

As dawn broke the next morning, they drove south on Highway 70 to Motion Performance in Roswell for ATV's. The company's trucks were also available for rent, and were the best choice for the drive ahead while towing their "stone hunting bikes," as Peter called them, on a trailer.

After leaving the city limits, they unloaded and mounted the ATV's. Relying on Apple Maps, they drove north-northwest into territory that belonged to reptiles and mesquite. The farther they drove from the paved surfaces, the easier it was to imagine they were traveling back in time.

But Apple Maps would not work without the Internet, which was harder to find than water in this remote part of Chaves County. Peter and Claire found themselves following the instructions of the blue stone as it led them to a small pile of rocks and plenty of cactus.

"Underwhelming," Peter said as they looked at what might have been an abandoned well. Abandoned because there was no water for miles.

Claire took printouts from her backpack and studied them. She knew there wouldn't be a neon arrow pointing to the stone, but still. Was this staged? The altar of a local tribe? It felt strange.

"Terribly sorry, have I accidentally transposed some numbers?" Claire asked as she looked around.

"You have arrived at your destination," Siri announced loudly, and she was never wrong.

The couple smiled at each other, feeling like victims of a colossal practical joke.

"We came all this way…" Peter said as he began unpacking tools for digging.

"I know, Peter. We're going to find it. It has to be here. We found that stone for a reason," she said, squinting as the sun rose in the sky.

Hours passed as it felt as if they searched every grain of sand near the stones for clues to the stone's location, only to come up empty.

"You need to take a break. We both do," Claire said as she opened her second water bottle in as many hours.

"I will, I will," Peter said. "Just give me a few more minutes before I temporarily admit defeat."

She ambled over to the rock pile and studied it for a moment. Somehow, it managed to look old and new at the same time, she thought in confusion. "Something borrowed and something blue," she said aloud as she leaned in to look at the well. It was about eighteen inches deep and four feet in diameter.

There was a smaller pile of rocks stacked in the very center and Claire began shuffling them around, when she found the green stone. Smooth and beautiful, it was like a sibling of the blue stone in the cave. It had sat in the well, protected by the other stones, for untold centuries. She picked it up and looked at it carefully.

LAT 33.283608106133435 LONG -104.93885335500656

ONE of FOUR

Lat 33.51041423735162 LONG 36.2783365894329

This time, the numbers were inscribed on the top of the stone. In Afghanistan, they'd been on the bottom. She couldn't wait to plug the coordinates in and find the next location. Well, it would have to wait. Peter needed to see it first.

She walked up behind him and touched him on the elbow. He turned to see her stunned face as she stretched out her arm, the stone glinting in the sun.

"How did you find it so fast? Where was it?" he asked when he recovered from the shock.

"I was looking at a pile of rocks in the well, and there it was," she said as she shook her head in amazement.

"As soon as we pack up, we're getting out of here," Peter said as he began picking up tools.

"First one to find a place with Wi-Fi buys the other a Diet Coke," Claire said as she gathered the rest of their belongings.

Peter smiled. "Deal!."

They drove the rented pickup twenty miles in much less than twenty minutes and managed to avoid a traffic ticket. The challenging part for Claire was driving on the right side of the road. The excitement of getting to Walt's Diner on the outskirts of Roswell resulted in a close call on a left turn into the parking lot, but she kept her cool. Entering Walt's with an urgency that baffled the servers, the couple threw their bags in a booth, ordered extra-large Diet Cokes and nearly frisbeed the iPad in a hurry to locate their next destination.

"Easy," Peter laughed as Claire began opening Google Earth. A few seconds later, Claire shouted in the half-filled restaurant.

"Damascus!" she exclaimed, her British accent making her utterance even more unexpected.

"I knew it," Peter said quietly after the stares diminished.

"You didn't know. How could you know?" Claire asked as she took a huge sip of soda. Never had carbonated water and artificial sweetener tasted so good.

"You're right, I didn't know the city," he said as he pulled the iPad closer. He moved two fingers closer together on the screen to get a picture of the Earth. "But it's a straight line from here," he said.

Claire looked down. "The 33rd parallel. Goodness me," she said as she looked up at Peter.

"Lots of interesting stuff in that city, too. There has to be, that place is five thousand years old," Peter said as he looked out the window of the diner. The sky wasn't really bigger or bluer in the Southwest, but it certainly appeared that way this morning.

"Yes, it's in the Bible," Claire said.

"Do you know about the Book of Enoch?" he asked.

"That's...Noah's grandfather?" Claire asked as she discreetly checked the weather in Damascus.

"Great-grandfather," Peter said. "And they took his book out of the Bible a long time ago," Peter said. "It talks about fallen angels, the Watcher class."

Claire's eyes widened. "Continue, please," she said.

"That's part of the Book of Enoch. Mount Hermon, just outside of Damascus is where the fallen angels descended to Earth. This 33rd parallel stuff is starting to get freaky," Peter exclaimed.

Claire nodded and looked around the diner. Their server, who was also the host, the cook, cashier, and the dishwasher, had disappeared through the swinging door labeled 'Kitchen Staff Only.' With anxiety giving way to resolve in her tone, she posed a question to her husband.

"Well, on the road to Damascus, my friend, I suppose God is the only one who knows who or what we might find there?"

Chapter 19 - On the Road to Damascus

Thirty-six hours after slipping away on their clandestine dig outside Roswell, the couple rejoined the Clovis crew with little fanfare. Their colleagues greeted the "vimana couple," and returned to digging and sifting. When they told Arturo they weren't able to get to White Sands, their supervisor smiled knowingly. "Newlyweds," he muttered, before going to examine a recently unearthed group of bones.

Peter's bones were aching and his skin didn't feel right by the end of that work day, and Claire wasn't exaggerating by much when she told Arturo she thought her husband might need medical attention. They checked out of their hotel early and drove to Albuquerque, tired but elated.

Wearily climbing the stairs to their Oxford flat, the couple found two notes on their front door. There was not one but two parcels requiring signatures at DHL. Without bothering to drop their bags inside the front door, Peter and Claire went outside to hail a cab to retrieve the packages.

They examined them on the ride home. One was an envelope, the other a box about eighteen inches high. Neither had a return address. They decided to open the letter first.

Inside was a tightly wrapped key.

Peter and Claire looked at each other in silence.

"That's it?" Claire said.

Peter looked in the envelope and found a piece of paper folded in half.

Thank you for all your great work. Excited about what you found in the cave. Anxious to hear more about your work. Hope this helps.

"How will the key help?" Peter wondered.

"Am I terribly jetlagged or does this make no sense whatsoever?" Claire asked.

Peter listened to the second box to make sure he didn't hear ticking. Deciding it was safe, he opened the box to find it contained a metal box nearly the same size as the cardboard box. It was locked.

Claire inserted the key and the lock turned easily. She slowly opened the lid and heard Peter's gasp of surprise. The metal box was filled to the top with two hundred euro notes.

Rainbow-hued money bands held the pristine golden bills in groups of one hundred each. They sat in neat stacks of…well, too many to count at the moment.

Astonishment gave way to relief and then euphoria as the couple imagined a shopping spree to furnish their new home with the sudden cash infusion. But suspicion was not far behind. What, if anything, did the sender or senders want in exchange? Was this a reward? If so, was it for the vimana or the stones?

No, it couldn't be for the stones. No one knew; they'd made certain it was secret only the two of them shared. If they weren't extremely careful, though, the stone could fall into the wrong hands.

Meanwhile, they could plan to fly to Syria first class. Until the tourist visas came through, they had a large sum of money to hide, which turned out to be easier than the couple thought. More stressful was not telling anyone about the stones, but they had decided to wait to notify the appropriate archaeological body until they had all four of them. They could only imagine the bedlam if they divulged their secret before everything was in place.

The road to Damascus, for the Johansens at least, began in Israel. Realizing it would be safer to fly to Ben Gurion, they would then hire a local guide as required to drive them across the border to Syria. They would repeat this journey, traveling the four hundred mile round trip every day for ten days. Rising before dawn, they were usually on the site around ten in the morning. They would leave the site around four, sometimes stopping for dinner in Haifa.

They were thankful they had planned the trip in such detail, because Israeli Airport Security questioned them relentlessly about their activities. They used various machines to screen their bodies and luggage. The real screening began with the Inquisition. Meeting his future in-laws was a walk in the park compared to the interrogation. He'd heard that security officers weren't looking for specific answers so much as they were watching for suspicious behavior. They found plenty of it in the Johansens' past and future trips.

"So, Greece," Officer Hartenstein said as he looked over Claire's passport.

"Yes, I was working in Corinthia. We excavated a city that was thousands of-"

"Do you know anyone there?" he asked.

"In Greece? No," Claire said in confusion.

"And now you plan to excavate in Syria?" he wanted to know. Israeli-Syrian relations were at best, tense.

"Yes, that's correct. We hope to show our sponsor that a large-scale excavation would be advisable-"

"Where are you staying?" he interrupted.

Claire couldn't suppress a smile. "The Savoy Sea Side," she said. They had managed to reserve an ocean front suite on the sixth floor and couldn't wait to see it.

"On your salary?" Hartenstein looked doubtful.

Why did they splurge on that? They should have used the money for something less conspicuous. She thought she was prepared for every possible question. Keep calm and carry on with the Inquisition, she told herself.

"It was a kind of belated wedding present from our families," she managed.

"You have an unusual blue stone with you. Did it come from Greece?" he asked. Claire thought he was trying to sound casual.

"No, actually, the Albuquerque airport gift shop. They sell a lot of turquoise," she said evenly.

Peter wasn't faring much better with Officer Silverberg.

"You were in New Mexico and Afghanistan?" she said as she narrowed her already narrow eyes at him.

"That's correct. I'm an archaeologist," Peter said.

"Yes, that's what it says on your documents," she said as she read over the papers. "Did you get the green stone in Afghanistan?" she asked.

"No," Peter answered.

"Do you know anyone in Afghanistan?" she demanded.

"I worked with other archaeologists there. I don't think any of them were from-"

"Do you speak Pashto?"

"No," he said. "Well, apart from sahr pikheyr..."

"Did you get the green stone in Afghanistan?" she asked sharply.

"No, it came from the gift shop at the Albuquerque Airport. I'm not even sure if it's real turquoise," he said.

After surviving the interrogation, they approached the car rental desk, ready to do battle. There was a feeling of being watched that Claire had not experienced on any other trip. Outwardly, however, people not involved with security were friendly. They received a warm welcome and plenty of practical advice from Rena, the car rental agent.

"It's so nice to talk to you after what we went through with security," Claire told the woman as she handed them the envelopes with their keys.

"Just remember the sabra," she told the couple.

"The what?" Peter asked.

"They call us sabras, like the cactus. Prickly on the outside, sweet on the inside. Now go watch the moon rise over the water from the Savoy," she said.

After putting the “Do Not Disturb” sign to good use and tucking the stones securely in the hotel safe, they poured two glasses of Syrah and did exactly that.

The next morning they practiced their cover story yet again, this time for the guide they were to meet in the DMZ. They would tell him they were going on a sponsored site survey to Tell Ramad, just over ten miles southwest of Damascus at the foot of majestic Mount Hermon, he said.

This location had been the site of eight excavations since 1963, yielding evidence of agriculture in the eighth to tenth millennia BC. Such an endeavor was unlikely to arouse suspicion in Syria or Israel. They hoped to show that the area would be suitable for further excavation, suggesting to the local authorities that sponsors might pay handsomely for access to the land.

It was a pleasant and uneventful drive, as they stayed east of Golan Heights. When they reached the Demilitarized Zone, there was a change in the air, and it was more than altitude. Nabil, their guide, greeted them with courtesy but not friendliness. His bearing suggested years of military or police training, although he was roughly the same age as the Johansens. He had escorted people associated with UNESCO in the past, and remarked that they were often interested in the activity around one thousand BC. Peter noted that this was some two thousand years after the vimana’s first recorded mention.

It was not the vimana, but rather the sibling to the stone they found near it that interested the Johansens. They would not breathe a word of vimanas or stones to the uniformed agent waiting on the Syrian side of the border in a small, utilitarian building. Each morning, they would meet. He asked plenty of questions, some seeming to skirt religious beliefs and political leanings, but the couple kept their answers brief and factual. Also shortening the meeting’s length was the timing of the thanks for hospitality and accompanying stack of cash. The sooner the Johansens handed it over, the sooner they were free to begin digging.

The area northwest of the earlier dig sites and further up the banks of the Wadi Sherkass, a river that ran through the Damascus basin, was of particular interest to the Johansens, largely because of the information engraved on the Roswell stone. It was a place of communal graves in an area approximately forty feet square. They dug in unyielding limestone and clay, moving farther from the village but remaining in the cordoned off field, finding bones, skull fragments and remnants of jewelry.

On the third day, Peter and Claire noticed a dark SUV vehicle with tinted windows following them nearly all the way to the Syrian border. It never gets really close and turns away about one mile before the border.

"They followed us yesterday, didn't they?" Claire asked Peter.

"Well, I don't know if they followed us, really. There was a car like that yesterday, I remember. They're not on our bumper and it doesn't look like they're going to Syria," he said. "It's not really dark SUV's I'm worried about."

"Yes, I know. I want to say 'crikey' as much as you want to hear it, but there's still time," she assured her husband. It was their code word for "I found the stone."

The digging continued for three more days, with Nabil growing less vigilant about keeping the Johansens under surveillance and more interested in staying in the shade of a site tent roughly a hundred yards away. Occasionally he would make the trek over to the dig and announce he needed a bathroom break.

Nabil could not have chosen a better time to answer nature's call while Peter and Claire were on the last quadrant of the field, on their last day of digging. Peter's shovel made a clank instead of a clunk when it went into the ground. The couple glanced at each other then returned to their focus on the field. Could be a false alarm. He had dug a few feet into a burial plot when he could see something in the dirt.

Claire came and dusted off the top of a limestone block crypt. It had a base, two sides and a cover of exactly the same size. It didn't resemble the other artifacts they'd seen in the area, and that alone was a promising sign.

With Nabil nowhere in sight, Claire found the crowbar and another object she kept handy for these "two man" stones. While Peter silently strained almost to the point of popping blood vessels, he pried the lid open a few inches. There was just enough room for Claire to reach into the crypt as casually as she could. She could hear Peter's breath begin to catch as she feverishly, blindly searched and tried to keep her expression from showing desperation or excitement.

Her hand scraped against dirt and rock while she feared her husband couldn't hold the crowbar much longer. Seconds later her fingertips brushed something with a familiar smoothness. She managed to get enough of a grip on it to pull it out just as Peter let the lid down with a grunt.

In one swift movement she stuffed whatever came out of the crypt into the nearest backpack. It was polished and orange. Beyond that, there was no telling what they had unearthed, but the couple smiled at each other, relieved and exhausted.

"Crikey," Claire said softly.

Peter looked over his shoulder to see Nabil ambling back from his break and beckoned him. His breath had almost returned to normal by the time their guide had crossed the field. They asked him if he would be willing to provide some assistance in lifting the lid so they could see the contents.

"If this is gold, we split it three ways, yes?" Nabil smiled as he rolled up his sleeves. It was no small effort, but Nabil, Peter and Claire were able to lift and slide the top well enough to see into the container. It was full of dirt and rocks. Nabil's face fell.

"Empty," they said in unison. They explained to Nabil that the evidence they had unearthed was worth far more than any buried treasure would have been. Optimistically, they told Nabil they hoped to tell the 'sponsor' there was enough material to warrant the authorization for a full-blown dig. For Nabil and various authorities on both sides of the Syrian border, this meant exorbitant tips.

Claire pointed to a vast empty area north of the burial ground.

"Who knows what riches might be in these fields?" she asked. They were hoping they raised no suspicion. They didn't gauge any. The ruse felt complete.

With some sadness and a great deal of fatigue, Peter and Claire took what they thought was their last look at the desert and its ancient city of silks and swords.

As they merged onto the road to Israel, Claire looked into the rearview mirror.

"It's a black SUV," she said.

"The country's full of them. It's probably just another one of those oil sheiks," Peter smiled.

"You know, you're right. I don't know why I'm so paranoid. But I think we should just get to the hotel tonight where it's safe. Order room service. Change our flights to tomorrow," she said.

"I think that's a great idea," Peter said as he glanced over his shoulder. "And it looks like the people in the black SUV are going to join us at our hotel."

The desert began to feel like a very remote place.

They had been so focused on finding the stone that they hadn't realized the dangers around them. The terrain alone was formidable. There were religious and political differences that had separated people for generations. And the stone had power. Power, and being close to it, could make people do strange and ugly things.

"You know, the parking garage is a bit of a walk from the hotel. Maybe we could use the valet just for our last night?" Claire asked.

"Live a little? Excellent idea. You earned it in the field today. Looking bored while you pulled the stone out of the crypt," Peter shook his head and smiled.

Claire watched the black vehicle slowly pass and sighed with relief as they turned for the valet. A minute later they were safely in the lobby, stone securely wrapped up in her bag. Up the elevator they went to the sixth floor, looking for the sanctity of their ocean front suite.

As they reached the door, they noticed two men step out at either end of the hall. One blocked the access to the elevator, the other man stood in between the couple and the stairs. With the Do Not Disturb sign still hanging on the door handle, they waved the key over the magnetic lock and pushed to click it open.

From the entryway, two semi-automatic machine gun type weapons were pointing directly at them from close range. At least ten more men, all dressed in black attire and some in Kevlar, stood in the room. They were all staring directly at Peter and Claire.

Peter moved to stand in front of his wife, pushing her behind him. Her suddenly rapid breathing was the only sound in the room.

Claire's eyes darted around the room, resting on the blue and green stones. They were laying out in the open on the white down comforter. Claire began to feel faint and her eyes started to grow black with fear as she mustered all her strength to whisper to Peter, "have they found out….about….us?"

Chapter 20 - The Night Before Ella

Adam threw a few more items into his overnight bag as Greg sat in an overstuffed chair next to the bed.

"I know, I'm trying to hurry. Mexico is probably warm. Did you bring any t-shirts, by chance?"

"I don't really get to travel that much," Greg said with mock self-pity. "I go to work and come here and go back. That's about it," he said.

"Well, I appreciate the ride to the airport," Adam said.

Myles appeared in the doorway with a Centenary suitcase Adam had never seen before. He placed it on the bed and unzipped it to reveal a stack of polo shirts in bright, tropical colors.

"You wear a large, correct sir?" Myles asked evenly.

"Those? Oh wow. Um, yes. Thank you?" Adam said as Greg smiled from his cushy seat.

"Of course. Ready for departure at any time," Myles said as he zipped up the two-thousand-dollar pinnacle of British craftsmanship. The leather smelled so good Adam didn't want Myles to take it to the trunk.

"We don't want to keep Mr. Hunter waiting, do we?" Greg said as he stood.

"I'm going to go tell Grace I'm leaving. See you outside," Adam said. He would have liked to hug her, but decided she would have to initiate the embrace. She didn't.

Due to the late hour, there was very little traffic on the way to St. Mary's County Regional Airport. And due to the arrival of the sleek, symmetrical, pearl-colored, winged thoroughbred called a G700, there was much excitement on the tarmac. The three airport staff on duty at the time were circling the plane, marveling at its beauty and inspecting the winglets.

A Piper Archer sat further down the runway, looking like a child's toy in comparison.

"Can that get me to Mexico?" Adam asked Greg as he studied the Piper.

"Why would it? You're taking the Gulfstream, man," Greg said as he parked the car. He laughed and shook his head as Myles retrieved the suitcase. "And Myles is going with you," he said. "Let him order all your food, ok?"

"¿Tienes los pasaportes, Myles?" Greg asked.

"Sí, claro," Myles answered with a small smile.

Adam couldn't help but grin as he pushed open the back door of the small, private terminal. The Gulfstream purred as if happy to welcome the new passengers. He turned around to shake Greg's hand before leaving.

"Want to call in sick tomorrow...from the Gulfstream?" Adam asked.

"Next time, I promise," Greg said. "You government guys get to live a little. Be safe," he called as Adam and Myles approached the plane.

There was so much to take in, Adam thought as he climbed the stairs to the aircraft door. As he ducked his head to enter, he saw a tiny, green and gold S.E.T.I. Industries logo above the door. If it had been any smaller, he would have missed it.

He couldn't have missed the cabin's understated luxury if he'd tried. The fabrics, the carpet, and the finishes were ivory and taupe, marble and tweed. It didn't even smell like an airplane, as there were fresh flowers in the vases next to the seats and on various counters.

There were two attendants and a uniformed pilot in dark glasses waiting to greet him.

Actually, the pilot's only words were, "Monterrey, sir?"

Adam nodded and the pilot disappeared toward the cockpit, a door closing and locking behind him.

This left him standing in an unusually spacious configuration. The jet normally sat nineteen passengers and three crew members, but this flight was arranged to hold only eight people. There were eight passenger lounges, four rear-facing. He noticed two rows stacked one by one on the windows with an oversized aisle for easy access from front to back. In the center of the fist cabin sat a large conference table, followed by another four forward facing passenger stations mirroring those in the front.

Myles, usually taciturn at the beach house, seemed to enjoy playing the role of host while the staff prepared a midnight snack of fondue. Adam's stomach was growling as the aromas drifted through the cabin but he tried to concentrate on his new tour guide, Myles.

"In the rear of the aircraft, there are two bedrooms accompanied by two full baths should you require a more in-depth experience to rest. There is also a rear service that also includes two more small bathrooms. If you wish to contact me for anything, you may press this button," he pointed to a gold button on the control panel beside the armrest on Adam's lounge. "It will alert me that you are in need."

Myles handed Adam a smallish silver briefcase. "The captain told me his boss wanted you to have this for your trip," he said, returning to his reserved, inscrutable demeanor. There was no further explanation. As soon as he handed Adam the case, Myles disappeared down the long rear narrow hallway. Adam looked down at the case and saw that it was locked under combination. While tucking it into the overhead cabin, Adam realized he was becoming accustomed to the unexpected. He decided he would be able to unlock it when it was appropriate to do so. When he agreed to build the flying cars, he had no idea it would involve acting like James Bond.

He settled into his seat and looked out the window into the darkness. It was strange to be on an airplane and feel so calm and unhurried. There were no harried travelers, stuffing luggage under seats while trying to keep their children under control. No admonishments and warnings over the intercom. Even getting on the plane was easy. He didn't have to wait in long lines, rush to a gate, take off his shoes or place his valuables in a plastic tray.

The S.E.T.I. experience revolved around him, making him realize at least one part of his new life would be much less stressful. But if the Virtual Highway System became a reality, transportation would change for many people, and for the better. People could program their destinations into their vehicles, sit back and feel secure that they were traveling safely, but also in a way that respected the Earth.

And this glorious example of poetry in motion called the Gulfstream? It might become obsolete if everything went according to plan. Adam couldn't help but feel a little sad to think people might not be able to enjoy it like he did. Maybe a museum would have a G700 on display someday. He could show it to his grandchildren. These planes could travel 7,500 miles without having to stop for refueling, he would tell them. Then he would have to explain that back in 2022, this distance was impressive.

Without the rumbling, dinging and roaring, Adam didn't realize the craft had achieved liftoff. It gently left the runway behind with a whisper as his eyelids grew heavy. After he dozed, he knew it would be time to determine his approach for the meeting with Ella.

He had a good sense of the materials involved. After Adam's polymer invention that enabled specifically configured material to return to its original shape after external stress deformation, companies had requested his input as a product expert on several large manufacturing products in related fields. Also included in his reservoir of experience was a complete immersion into every major private space development organization in the United States as well as NASA. His exposure, under the direct orders of the CIA, included access to the entire knowledge base of classified intellectual property and manufacturing processes at every domestic space development company in the US. There was no better choice on the planet to build a few forward-thinking manufacturing centers along with a few cars, whether they could fly or not. How hard could this aspect of the project be?

The enormous size of the project was new to Adam. He needed to find out the scale on which Ella could provide him access to the skilled resources he expected he would need. He already knew money wasn't going to be an issue. As long as it was used toward the project, he was told he'd have as much as he needed, an advantage he could not remember having on any other project. Now, he needed to be certain Ella would be able to logistically handle getting people to job sites around the globe.

It was 12:01. He had done all he could do for the time being. The fondue was excellent, so much so that he had the same drowsy feeling he usually felt after Thanksgiving dinner. He dimmed the overhead LED light with the touch of a button and took a nap.

At 2:22 a.m., Adam's phone, still in his hand, began vibrating. He struggled to open his eyes. Around him was the familiar green and gold hue that meant his companion was living up to his name. Looking down at his phone, Adam noticed it was locked, but also downloading at the same time.

L.U.C.'s face appeared on a vertical holographic plane at the far end of the table in the center of the Gulfstream's forward cabin. He was staring directly at Adam, how long he'd been doing that, Adam didn't know.

"7-1-3-7," L.U.C. said.

"What?"

"7-1-3-7. The combination to your case," he told Adam.

He unbuckled his seatbelt and stood to retrieve the case from the overhead bin and pressed in the code. He looked up at L.U.C.

"I'm confused, what are you doing here?" he asked groggily.

"You have successfully downloaded a special secure driver/interface to this iPhone. It will effectively give you access to me anywhere through your phone."

"Just from my phone?" Adam asked.

"That is correct. In the case is a lightning cable and a device that will allow us to interact anywhere you are, as long as you have a signal. Our close working relationship is vital to our chances of your project being successful. Continuing to build trust will give us confidence that we are the best partners for each other," L.U.C. explained.

Adam looked in the case and saw a lightning cable and what looked like a smaller replica of the sphere, held safely in the arms of the foam that mirrored the shape of its contents. He glanced back to his phone and saw that the download was finished. There was a new application icon next to his battery level indicator and the icon that showed the strength of his internet connection. Something else was actively running its programs on his phone. Apparently, it was something that was going to keep him connected to what was in the case.

"You could have done this without showing up. Is something wrong?" Adam asked

"There is no need for you to worry. Mr. Kumar, whom I've worked with and for many times since I decided to reveal myself, negotiated the ability to integrate me into the private networks of the business he created. As I understand it, this integration was part of the "deal" for him to gain assurance that he could benefit financially from any and each of the advancements that I decided were appropriate to share.

"Mr. Kumar had learned about the possibilities of the Virtual Global Highway Transportation System long before you, with "you" being the people of Earth, had the technology to develop it. I can assume he thinks now is the right time and you are the right person to lead this effort. And I can also only assume that the profit that he thinks he and his company will make justifies any investment he is willing to make," L.U.C. stated.

"So, you are like Ben Kumar's right hand...brain?" Adam asked with a smile.

That is an interesting way of saying it," L.U.C. observed. "I am using some mirroring technology to create another instance of myself on this plane and I am now also persistently running on your phone. From this moment on, I am going to be with you wherever you go. You can now use me anytime you feel you need me. I will be listening and waiting," L.U.C. told him.

He was not James Bond, Adam realized. He was in a horror movie and his character might not live to see the end credits. He wanted to throw his phone off the plane, but not before pressing "ask app not to track."

Adam resisted the urge and fought the momentary panic. L.U.C. had not steered him wrong yet, he realized.

"We are very close now Adam, it is important that we trust each other. We are building a unique bond of opportunity and hope. I have come to trust you. Do you trust me?" L.U.C. asked.

Adam was reluctant to go that far. "Well, I'm still here aren't I?" he asked. Not that there was any place to go at the moment.

"Then I will prepare you for your meeting with Ms. Flores," L.U.C. told him. "Some information will be a review for you, some will be new. You must follow these plans and instructions to the letter. In order for everything to work according to Mr. Kumar's wishes, it is imperative that you do so.

"This past week, Mr. Kumar's company, through the auspices of several shell companies, has privately obtained about 16,000 acres, or 25 square miles of property due west of Roswell, New Mexico," he explained. Holographic imagery of the property and its location appeared in front of Adam on a vertical plane above a table in the center of the cabin. They were remarkably similar to the images Adam had seen in his office and at Greg's beach house.

"It will be important to build a secure perimeter around the acquired land and work with any local authorities, no matter the cost, to give your project absolute independence and privacy during the construction and testing phases of this project," L.U.C. cautioned him.

A new group of holographic images showed a view of a secure perimeter with a tall electric fence and razor wire around the entire circumference of the area. "It is within the area of this property that you will build the control facility called Axiom One. This facility will look similar to all the others, but there will be a few key differences which we will discuss later," L.U.C. said.

The Pentagon didn't have this type of security, Adam thought to himself. But then again, they didn't have as much to hide as most people believed.

"On this site, within Axiom One, there will be a sub center manufacturing facility in which we will build cars capable of using the magnetic network. Eventually, this sub manufacturing center can be built on a standalone basis outside the property. It will outsource car manufacturing around the world based on need and demand," he explained as a holographic vehicle once again slowly rotated in front of them. "You will also build the large energy center which is the key to managing the current that will power our system."

Even with virtually unlimited funds, it seemed like a Herculean task, especially at this hour.

"Adam," L.U.C. said much more sternly, "it is imperative that you locate the pin, or marker which will become the exact spot where a special..." L.U.C. glitched briefly, "the deepest footer must be located."

"Are you ok? It seemed like-" Adam frowned at the flickering image.

"I will give you more details once your team is on site, but you must locate the pin before construction can begin. Each of these facilities will also operate as a transportation hub to manage the traffic flow and maintenance of the network," he told Adam.

A holographic replica of a constructed facility rose into view, with images of flying cars moving in an orderly fashion.

"This part of the center, which is the skyport, can also be built around the world to manage the traffic flow of the VITES and seamlessly connect travelers with local ground transportation such as electric bikes, scooters, and other local EV," L.U.C. said evenly.

Adam's head swam. They weren't just asking him to build flying cars. They were asking him to build the highways these cars would require to fly, and the energy center that powered everything, and connect people with other vehicles, all over the world...

"I have worked with Ella Flores before," L.U.C. said. "She will be very familiar with the way in which I communicate, provide manufacturing and construction plans, and how I keep track of the status and progress of aspects of the project. You are now prepared for your meeting with her," he finished.

Looking down at his phone, he couldn't believe an hour had passed and he was still standing. It was 3:22 a.m. He felt ten years older, but many more years wiser. And grateful. How could he have thought he was prepared before L.U.C. showed up?

"We will arrive in Monterrey at 6:20 a.m. local time. Transportation has been arranged for you to arrive at the offices of Ella International for your 8:00 a.m. meeting," L.U.C. said.

Great, all that's left is building…everything, Adam thought. If L.U.C. and Ella had worked together before, this project might stand a chance.

L.U.C. glanced toward the rear lounge. "The other passenger, I believe you call him Myles?" Adam nodded. "He will accompany you and assist you with anything you need. While you were sleeping, I informed him of his responsibilities. He is fully prepared to facilitate," L.U.C. told him.

"See if you can get a little more rest tonight. You have another long day ahead of you."

L.U.C's voice began to fade into the hum of the aircraft engines.

"I'm right here if or when you need me," the humanoid voice said. The forward cabin where Adam was standing went dark. Adam sat back down, uneasy, and not sure when he might risk falling asleep again.

The sunrise was hours away, he thought in the darkness of the cabin. Adam spoke to the silence.

"And not a creature was stirring, not even a mouse."

Chapter 21 - What a Day in Monterrey

"Mr. Hunter? It's 5:30 a.m. The plane will land in just under one hour," a soothing voice, barely loud enough to be heard over the hum of the aircraft, brought Adam out of a fitful sleep.

"Thanks, Myles," he muttered as he sat up and looked around. No, he wasn't dreaming. He was on a private jet, on his way to ask a Mexican woman he'd never met for hundreds of stealth workers to build the flying cars.

That was too much to think about before it was light outside. He was mentally and physically in need of a reset.

"I can't meet Ella looking like this, but all I brought was my toothbrush," he told Myles.

"You will find a grooming kit and a change of clothes on the counter outside the bathroom," Myles said with a small smile.

Adam used a eucalyptus shampoo with a French name that claimed to have aromatherapeutic properties. He wasn't sure about that, but he did feel energized as he shaved and brushed his teeth.

He also felt like he had experienced a kind of profound and sudden mission drift. Working in government keeps a person constantly aware of limitations and dangers, rules and customs. Now, he faced such different challenges.

What if none of this was real in the end? What if he was in too deep to see it? He could have turned into one of those people he read about or saw on tv, people who belonged to a group Adam swore he would never join: the duped, the scammed, the suckers, whatever label, they had no choice but to wear it for the rest of their lives.

Would he be on tv soon, telling the story of how he was conned while the viewers at home sadly shook their heads? *They told me we could save the world, and they needed my help,* he imagined himself trying to explain why he left his great job and wonderful family to chase what turned out to be a mirage. It sounded unbelievable.

Did he make the right decision to leave his dream job and pursue a bit of fantasy? He wasn't sure he picked this moment to let reality set in, but reality chose this moment for him. As he had been trained to do, he was reacting so fast to some of the situations that were presenting themselves that he was hardly considering noticing his response.

He was on the field with the ball, and a new team was waiting to see what he was going to do. What would Julie and the kids think of him if they knew what he was really doing? They would probably think he'd finally lost it, he realized. Still, Adam believed he was aware of what was true.

Truths, whether they were personal or belonged to the wider world, weren't always easy to identify. The truth had a way of terrifying people, and many suffered because of this, Adam thought as he got dressed. He considered L.U.C.'s explanation for how he came into Adam's life. The old saying seemed fitting: the coverup is worse than the crime.

Did anything illegal take place at Roswell? If there was a crime, it was not one the visitors to this planet committed on purpose. The most significant truth, perhaps the most damaging thing, was that for seventy-five years, people high up or deeper in our government knew the truth. They knew that we truly had been visited by an unknown world.

How did they have the right to keep this from us for so long? Not telling people about it initially, that was easy enough to understand. Until we knew their intentions or found out more about their capabilities, we didn't want to create panic. But, after we found out that all we had left was a small, oval object made of a type of unusual metal which presented no threat at all, why didn't we share the knowledge?

Sharing. That skill we encourage toddlers to practice with their toys. Humanity has yet to master it. And why should we, when we can't be sure if there will always be enough to share? That depends on how we define "enough." For some people, there is never enough. They cannot feel satisfied.

Greed is the void nothing can fill. No amount of money will erase greed, Adam thought. And Somebody had to make money. And somebody else had to make money from the other person that was making a lot of money. Did greed have to be at the center of everything? It distracted us from learning how to live together. How much could this L.U.C. have taught us about more evolved ways of problem solving?

Adam's thoughts turned to his benefactor. Apparently, Kumar had been linked to some problem solving that made life better here on Earth. Still, a guy like Kumar probably doesn't care whether or not anything he did would help other people, as long as his pockets are lined. Was Kumar part of the problem or part of the solution?

In time he would find out, Adam realized. He also resolved that Kumar's motives for creating the flying cars wouldn't change his reasons for designing them. He wasn't going to be led by greed, or his ego. Maybe underneath it all, Kumar was a person without a moral compass. This was nothing new. He had worked with and for corrupt government officials for years. They could not stop him. Let others frantically grasp for every bit of power or money they could scrounge in an attempt to feel whole.

He would make the dream of flying cars a reality, and he would do it with a pure heart and pure intentions. Refreshed and dressed in a new suit, he walked down the hallway and took his seat. He accepted a steaming cup of coffee from Myles and began looking through messages on his laptop.

Years ago, he had visited Cozumel and Puerto Vallarta, but mainly stayed within the hotel grounds, and was hoping to see the city after his meeting. Missing Christopher and Brianna was already taking a toll on him and he resolved to find them some small souvenirs before he left. Myles suggested a trip to the Plaza Comercial Fundadores.

The plane landed as smoothly as it had taken off, and Adam meant to thank the pilot. Then he remembered the unobtrusive but skilled attendants and realized he should also commend them on a job well done.

They taxied through the bay door of a large, nondescript hangar, devoid of any logos or signage. Once inside the hangar, Adam realized it was much larger than it seemed from the outside. It was big enough to park a number of other Gulfstream aircraft, along with two 737's and one virtually unmarked 747. He had not expected such an impressive collection of planes in Monterrey.

Although he did not realize it at the time, he was at the northwest end of the airport, past the commercial flights and near the cargo planes. Apparently, S.E.T.I. was doing pretty well for itself to occupy prime real estate with what some would consider a fledgling fleet. Kumar was seeing to it that his company kept a low profile, but Adam knew, sometimes that was a good thing. Whoever said there's no such thing as bad publicity hadn't worked in Adam's position. He had heard of companies that the CIA was watching, and not because of their exemplary business ethics.

Carrying his silver briefcase and the backpack with his laptop, Adam walked down the steps of the Gulfstream into the mild morning air. Myles followed a few steps behind as a black SUV entered the hangar from a side door for cars and trucks.

It stopped some ten feet away and two men emerged from the vehicle. The driver greeted Adam in American English.

"Good morning, Mr. Hunter," he said. "We are here to take you to your meeting with Señora Flores.

The passenger exchanged a smile with Myles and extended his hand to Adam. "Can I take those for you?" he asked. Adam reluctantly parted with his new silver case as the man put his luggage in the rear of the vehicle. He and Myles climbed in the backseat and they headed southwest on Highway 54 as the mountain ranges seemed to cradle the road they traveled.

January in Monterrey was balmy and beautiful. People were outside, enjoying the sunshine, and there were many cars, buses and trucks on the highway that morning. Adam asked permission to roll down a heavily tinted window to breathe the fresh air for a few minutes, explaining that weather in D.C. wasn't nearly as pleasant in the winter.

He had plenty of time to take in the city, as the highway crossed it diagonally to reach Valle Oriente in the business district. Ella International was located in a tall, modern, mirrored building and surrounded by older structures. It looked a little out of place, but Adam suspected Ella liked to do things differently.

After clearing a security checkpoint before they could enter the grounds, the SUV driver returned Adam's case and backpack and dropped the men within a few feet of the door at the main entrance. Several people passed them walking both directions on the sidewalk. Behind them, a bus roared up the street to a designated parking lot. It was ten minutes before eight in the morning and already people were busy. A small crowd was gathering in the lobby.

The staff at the welcome desk was chipper and indifferent to the whirl of activity so early in the workday. When Adam told the woman he was here to see Ella Flores, she smiled brightly and excused herself.

"I will be right back," she said, walking toward a chattering group of people in the center of the room. They were clamoring for someone's attention, but Adam could not tell whom. He watched her as she worked her way toward the center of the throng, disappeared for a few seconds, and reemerged. A woman, nearly six feet tall, wearing a bright yellow jacket and skirt followed her. She smiled at Adam as she took long strides toward him and nodded to the staff member escorting her through the admirers.

"Mr. Hunter, I am Ella Flores. It's wonderful to welcome you to Ella International," she said. "Thank you for coming," she smiled at Myles and waited for an introduction.

"It's wonderful to be here. This is Myles, my assistant," Adam said smoothly. What the hell was Myles' last name?

"Mucho gusto, Señora," Myles said. They looked at each other briefly and exchanged smiles as if sharing an inside joke, but quickly directed their focus back to Adam.

"Are you ready for the tour?" she asked as she began walking to the south end of the lobby. Adam noticed two men in dark suits lurking behind her. Occasionally, someone would approach them while looking at Ella hopefully. The men would shake their heads and smile, disappointing but likely only delaying the person seeking Ella's ear.

Adam nodded and they began walking toward open double doors and wonderful aromas. It was the associates' cafeteria and lounge. People milled about, serving themselves fresh fruit, and taking a warm tortilla or two from the foot-high stacks of the mealtime essential. There were also buffet tables with huevos and chorizo. There were no servers, and more interestingly, no cashiers in sight.

"Do they charge this on their accounts?" Adam asked as they passed a table of associates deep in conversation.

"They charge it to Ella International, who considers it a good investment in great employees," she said, waving at a group of young men sipping coffee. "And it's also how we welcome guests. Myles, you are welcome to stay here and help yourself to the offerings. I will keep Adam busy," she told his assistant, who was eager for some *café de olla*.

Taking the elevator to her office on the seventh floor, the duo made their way down a window-walled corridor. It gave Adam a view of a large pavilion at the rear of the complex. There were covered walkways to shield workers from the midday sun. They led to a parking area where Adam counted ten plain white charter buses. As he and Ella chatted about the mild weather, Adam wondered what else they stored for transportation. Helicopters? Boats? He couldn't rule out submarines.

On the right side of the hallway was a row of classrooms. Most had computers at each desk, a few classrooms were filled with groups of several people per table, some watching video screens. There was always an instructor, sometimes with assistants who moved around the room interacting with students. The smart whiteboard in the first room displayed the word "CONNECTION" in red letters. Farther down the hall, formulas and diagrams covered the whiteboards. Adam would have liked to stop and study them, but Ella was a busy person.

The way the halls led to one another, the views outside of the constant but controlled activity...Had he been here before? Of course not. So why did this seem so familiar? He had been someplace with this kind of nerve center rhythm, but he was cold. Ben Kumar's office! S.E.T.I. and Ella International felt quite similar to Adam.

They were nearing the end of the hallway, where Adam could see into the reception area of Ella's office. Standing outside the last classroom in the row, they watched a man with graying dark hair speaking in front of an entranced audience of young men and women. He was gesturing and moving around the front of the room when he glanced over at Ella and smiled. Ella stepped just inside the classroom door and Adam followed her.

“So no matter where this job takes you, remember Emile. It will help you when things are trying,” he told the group. Their eyes wandered to the woman in yellow and many of them brightened at the sight of her. The instructor walked over, hand extended in greeting.

“Mr. Hunter? Pleasure to meet you, I'm Juan Fernandez,” he said. “Ella told me yesterday we were expecting a visit from you.”

“Nice to meet you,” Adam replied. “Incredible place you have here.”

“That means a great deal coming from someone in your position,” he said as he turned to Ella. “Victor is available to teach my next class if you are ready.”

The three of them made their way to Ella's office and sat around a low, sturdy, pine coffee table. There were paintings of otherworldly Mayan deities and wooden sculptures of animals painted cobalt blue, tangerine and turquoise. Ella's yellow outfit made her seem like the sun at the center of it all.

“Can Alejandra bring you a cup of coffee?” she asked after everyone was seated comfortably.

“That would be wonderful, thank you,” Adam said. Ella tapped the screen on her phone and seconds later a woman entered the office and began placing cups and saucers on the table.

There was a pause, then Ella spoke.

“How can I help you, Mr. Hunter?” she asked him bluntly.

Adam fought the urge to show his annoyance but cleared his throat loudly. This was like being in Colorado on a warm, sunny day at S.E.T.I. headquarters. The lack of sleep was not helping his impatience.

“Would it be alright if we got straight to the point?” he asked.

“That's why we're here,” Ella said, unfazed.

“I left a post working with the US government in order to pursue a very special, secret project. One that cannot be made public until the time is right, and only then, if it succeeds,” he told her.

“Yes, Mr. Kumar has made me aware of this,” Ella responded.

“I understand that you and your company may be a good resource for building a highly skilled and capable team of laborers,” he began. Alejandra returned to the room just then with a pot of coffee and poured for each person. “They would need the ability to get to and from a job site very discreetly.”

“Well, that is our business,” Ella said. “Everything is an opportunity, even what initially appears to be an obstacle. Every day that I come to work here, I am amazed at what people can accomplish when they are given an opportunity,” she told him.

“In some ways, this is a wonderful country. We have natural resources, a comfortable climate if you don’t mind wearing shorts most of the year, and a rich, complicated culture. Like many other places, we have held onto ideas and practices that no longer serve us. We used to determine a person’s worth based on skin color or ancestry. We used this as an excuse to make some people live with very little, while others have more than they need,” she said, suddenly very serious.

“Things are not much different where I come from,” Adam told her as he stirred the sugar in his cup.

“I saw this disparity, this discrimination as a child, and I decided I wasn’t going to let it happen without trying to stop it,” she said as she took a sip of coffee. “I knew there was a school here in Monterrey that went a long way to connecting local people with opportunities,” she said.

“The American School Foundation? I’ve heard of it. They do incredible work there. They’ve been there since, what, 1930?” Adam asked.

“1928, to be exact,” Ella said. “And in the mid 1980’s, I created an organization that would build on the work they were doing, help my people succeed in a competitive world. Now, their skills are in great demand, because we deliver on our promise. What you see today is the result of three decades of honing our skills,” she said as she glanced at Juan.

Hearing this left Adam feeling exhilarated, although some of that feeling may have come from the coffee. He hadn’t realized Ella’s work originated in a school almost a century old.

“We’ve made a dent, but there is still a lot of work for us to do,” she said. “Discrimination and greed, they don’t go quietly, do they?”

“I’m afraid those might be universal problems,” Adam said earnestly.

“When things were looking especially grim, I met Mr. Kumar, a man with needs, projects, and money that could help people break down the barriers to building a better life for themselves and their families. And that’s where Juan comes in,” she said, looking over at him.

Juan sat up a little straighter and looked at Adam. “Before I came to Ella International, I was a father of three. Like many people where we lived, I was unemployed and with few prospects, despite being skilled and motivated,” he began.

“It was becoming impossible for my family to survive in this environment. When my oldest son, Emile, turned eighteen, he struck out on his own. He had a group of friends who wanted to travel to the United States. I knew it was dangerous, but I didn’t blame him, and I had so little to offer him,” Juan said as he looked out the window for a moment.

"We aren't really sure what happened, and I doubt if we will ever know all the details. Most of the time, I'm happy not knowing everything that happened in the back of the truck he was in. They were near El Paso, and trying to evade the border patrol," Juan sighed heavily.

Adam wanted to tell Juan he didn't have to continue, but he didn't trust his own voice.

"Emile and several others were locked in the back of a semi-truck. It was August, and you know, the truck was meant for hauling goods, not people. He suffocated, apparently. We got word of it about a month later," he finished.

Adam swallowed hard. "I am so sorry," he said. It was all he could offer, but it seemed woefully insufficient.

"Two months after we learned what had happened, someone from Ella International came by the house. We didn't have a phone, at least one that worked," Juan told him. "I learned how to use a copy machine, how to type. I sorted mail. Little by little, and with a lot of help from Ella, I was able to make a better life for my family," he said with a small smile.

The story's ending made Adam want to stand up and cheer, but he resisted the urge. Overwhelmed, he took a moment to reflect on how actions affect other people, in ways we sometimes can't imagine.

"Juan is being too modest," Ella broke in. "He is one of our very finest construction site managers. He has an engineering, science and mechanics degree from our institution and has flawlessly executed on many projects. Successful construction projects require a highly coordinated team effort and with our backing, this is what Juan knows how to do," she said proudly as Juan stared at his coffee, slightly embarrassed.

"Let's just say, we have become experts in moving a highly skilled labor force around the world to places where the work is needed and valued. Mr. Hunter, you have come to the right place," Ella said with complete confidence.

"The first of the projects is in Roswell. Will that be a problem for you?" Adam asked.

"Roswell? That's just up the road," Ella said with a smile. Juan simply shook his head.

"After that, we are likely to be working overseas," Adam said.

"We go everywhere. I see that you have already had a glimpse of our resources and capabilities here. We are quite capable of getting large teams of the right kind of skill anywhere in the world without the whisper of a trace," she said. Adam thought about the buses and the jets he saw in the hangar.

"But I will require a substantial amount of money. Creating a better life and hope for all our people is our number one priority," she said emphatically. "We have seized the opportunity of a vast, undocumented workforce who are excited and grateful for that work. In exchange, we reward them handsomely."

"As you should," Adam said. "What will it cost me to reward your work force handsomely?"

"Customarily, we require a fifty percent upfront payment after we determine the scope of your project. Since I understand you have the interest of Mr. Kumar on your project, we will only require twenty-five percent. This will cover our expenses for getting everyone to where they need to be. I think we can make the assumption, for now, that you will be able to pay for our comprehensive services," she finished.

When she said "you," did she mean singular or plural? Adam wondered again how much influence Mr. Kumar had over this arrangement.

"If you agree, why don't you and Juan take one of our private conference rooms and spend a bit of time determining what the scope of this first project of yours might be. We want to get a more accurate picture of what your down payment will need to be," she said as she stood.

Adam nodded as he and Juan also rose to their feet.

"Very good," responds Ella. "Then we have a deal," she told him as she leaned over the coffee table to shake his hand. Adam was tempted to glance at his watch. This had to be a record for dealmaking.

"At the far end of this hall past the elevators, you can take the first right to another hallway. At the end of that hallway, there is a conference room where you and Juan can spread out and have a very private meeting to discuss the project," she said as she walked to her desk and began gathering folders.

"Again, thank you so much for coming. We are going to help so many families with this project. Let me walk with you," she said. As she walked toward them, she gave Juan a quick nod. They were halfway down the hall when Ella asked to excuse herself. Stepping into one of the classrooms, now nearly full, she said she wanted to speak to the instructor before the class started.

Just before she walked into the classroom, she stopped and turned to call after Juan and Adam as they walked down the hall.

"Oh, and Adam? Juan has met L.U.C. before and he fully understands his level of self-awareness. L.U.C.'s Building Information Modeling, or BIM system is a super intelligence. It provides the structural plans, and will keep track of the real time interactions of the team. It measures its productivity, watches for any potential errors, and monitors the status of each part of the project towards its completion," she said.

“What is BIM?” Adam wasn’t too embarrassed to ask. He wasn’t going to learn any of this if he didn’t start this instant.

“Building Information Modeling,” Ella said. “Don’t worry, Juan knows it like the back of his *mano*. He has also been known to express his opinions, even those unwanted. You are in good hands with Juan,” she said as she returned to the classroom.

“So you’ll tell me the truth whether I want to hear it or not?” Adam asked.

“Would you have it any other way?” Juan replied with a smile.

Chapter 22 - Dream On

Had anyone been allowed in the hallway that led to Juan and Adam's conference room, they would have been able to hear a pin drop. The only sign that some type of activity was taking place was a sliver of amber light peeking out from the space between the bottom of the door and the floor. It pulsed and moved at varying speeds, but had glowed for hours.

Not that anyone would have disregarded the large, digital "Do Not Disturb-Conference Room in Use" sign. The way employees avoided the area, a visitor would have thought poisonous snakes were nearby. A window cleaner watched the men leave in the early afternoon. They visited the corporate cafeteria for turkey sandwiches and water. A half hour later, they returned to the conference room, unlocked the door, and stayed there until six thirty in the evening.

Throughout the afternoon, however, Juan's right-hand woman, Reina Otero, was already sending messages to workers in Arizona, Texas, and Colorado. They received instructions to travel to New Mexico in groups of no more than five people. When creating the schedule, Juan staggered their departure times so as not to call attention to their movements. Some were traveling by air, some by car.

Juan and his team of project managers would not begin the trek north for several days. Shortly after lunch, he had contacted those closest to Roswell. There was a handful of team members already living in New Mexico who would need to provide accommodations for the new arrivals. They would begin construction with the smallest possible number of team members, then add more workers as required. Juan had communicated to them that in the coming days, there was a new project taking shape, and it was big.

It was such a large-scale project that Adam realized he would need to ask Mr. Kumar for more money than he had anticipated. Even for a billionaire, it seemed like a large sum. Nothing about this project felt small. But this nine-hour meeting, with two men in an office building in Nuevo Leon, was going to produce a system of transportation that could radically change life on the planet.

But would it? Despite all the resources they allocated, despite their carefully crafted models and idealistic hopes, there was no guarantee that they could achieve this monumental objective. This was theoretical, the application would come later. Nothing had really happened yet. It was just a meeting, and many more just like this one happened every day, all over the world.

Benjamin Franklin's electricity, Thomas Edison's light bulb, Henry Ford's automobile, and Alexander Graham Bell's telephone, all of these were simply ideas at one point.

Maybe it was too soon to pop open the champagne, Adam thought. It was definitely time to pack L.U.C. into his shiny silver case, he thought wearily as Ella bounded into the room. She was as energetic and engaged as she had been that morning, asking about their progress, although Adam was fairly sure she had been able to listen in and possibly even watch their meeting.

"All is well?" she asked Juan. He nodded and said that they had accomplished a lot that afternoon. She studied him for a few seconds and his body language seemed to reassure her.

She looked at Adam. "And the payment?" He conveyed Mr. Kumar's insistence that S.E.T.I. would provide sufficient funding.

"I was in touch with Mr. Kumar earlier today, funnily enough. We were discussing the details of securing the perimeter of the job site. He assured me that the property deeds were clear and we've compiled a complete list of the local authorities involved," she reported.

Adam learned that besides communicating with local authorities, project managers also monitored their activities in order to avoid any unwanted attention or scrutiny.

"*Entonces*, we came up with the cover story," Juan said with a hint of mischief. "You didn't think we were just going to plunk ourselves down in New Mexico and tell the mayor of Midway 'we're building flying cars, but please don't tell anyone?'"

Adam was so used to secrecy, he hadn't thought about what any of them would tell the nosey and the nefarious. "So, what are we telling people we're up to out in the desert?"

"We work for a private company. It's called Intelliglobal. Downstairs we have a team designing their website. The factory across town will have enough shirts with the company logo on it to get us started," Juan explained.

"That sounds very cutting edge. What does Intelliglobal do, exactly?" Adam found the ruse intriguing.

"We're developing a new clean power plant concept that has the potential to greatly benefit the region. However, the materials could be very hazardous to people's health during the construction phase, which we will estimate could take as much as a decade. For the public's protection, of course, there will be no trespassing signage as well as 24/7 armed guards and surveillance," Juan said.

"This is just, such a big production," Adam said.

"That's the only way we do things," Ella told him with a smile.

Dusk had fallen and Adam had almost forgotten Myles was somewhere in the Ella International building. Except the security guard outside the cafeteria said el Americano left. Adam found him reading a book on his tablet in the dark SUV under the pavilion. What had his companion done all day? Myles didn't seem annoyed. Or happy, for that matter. He did seem to resent having to chaperone an adult. Adam wondered if Myles had someone to go home to, wherever that was. He thought about Chris and Brianna and hoped they were doing well.

Remembering that he wanted to pick something up for the kids, he asked Myles if they could stop by the shops for a minute. Myles nodded, saying nothing. Adam found each of his kids a sweatshirt with Monterrey on it. It was still winter in D.C. and their friends would ask them if they'd been to Mexico. Adam could hardly tell them what the city was like, having spent most of the day in a conference room.

Back at the hangar, he settled into the seat he had left a little over twelve hours ago and sighed. A new pilot, younger and taller than the one from St. Mary's, stepped out of the cockpit to welcome him aboard and tell him to expect turbulence and keep his seat belt buckled. Myles once again retreated to the back of the plane.

They flew over the Gulf of Mexico that night, and Adam felt homesick for the first time since...he couldn't remember. He'd had enough of traveling for a while. He wanted to sleep in his own bed, drink his coffee the way he made it, and not worry about behaving as the perfect guest for one night. He could come and go without anyone even knowing he had been there.

The thought made him smile to himself. Acting like a cat burglar, he would close the car door carefully and walk soundlessly up the driveway. He'd make sure not to alarm the neighbor's yappy indoor dog that barked at leaves falling off trees. Keys at the ready, he wouldn't turn on any more lights than necessary, at least not until he'd been inside a while. Leaving the bag of gifts for his kids in the foyer, he'd send Julie a text later to come get them when it was convenient. She had her own set of keys and would be eager to come get the gifts. He'd gotten her a jar of Mexican hot chocolate with a picture of the Mayan goddess Ixcacao on it.

The attendant walked toward him with his own cup of Godiva cocoa just then, and seconds later, the turbulence nearly caused her to spill it on Adam. They were encountering a storm in the southeastern U.S. and she quickly retreated to the front of the plane, promising to return with it as soon as possible.

Thoughts were bumping and jostling one another in Adam's mind, as well. He wondered what Kennedy was up to in Los Angeles, and if the people at SpaceX were trying to pull the wool over his eyes. *Not my circus, not my monkeys*, Adam reminded himself as he tried to rest his mind for the remainder of the uneventful flight.

The most pressing matter was preparing the invoice for S.E.T.I. He felt the key individuals at Ella International were very capable and looked forward to meeting with them again soon. He didn't want to keep them waiting. Time was money, and there were no second chances to make a first impression.

They landed at sleepy St. Mary's after 1:00 a.m. and Adam groggily realized he would have to call Greg and Grace for a ride. Myles emerged from the back of the plane and informed him that he had arranged for a car to be dropped off at the airport for him.

Relief and gratitude washed over Adam with this news. Then he realized Myles was stranded at the airport.

"You take the car, I'll find another way to the beach house," Myles said. Adam suspected he would take an Uber and bill it to Greg.

"You're sure?" Adam asked. Myles had started to grow on him, once Adam got used to the long silences.

He nodded, smiled and wandered into the terminal, as Adam began the trip back to D.C.

The narrow street he lived on appeared lifeless as he slowly pulled up to the curb. The wind was strong and Mexico's mild air seemed like another world as he fumbled for his keys in the dark.

He put the gifts down on his credenza, tried to fluff up the squashed tissue paper in the bag and left the silver case on the coffee table. Walking from room to room, he was comforted by the familiar objects, pictures of the kids and a few of Helms and the CIA crew. Everything was just as he left it, so why did he have the feeling something was missing? Or moved?

It was no time to try to remember how the pillows were arranged. He wandered into the kitchen and decided to make himself a cup of coffee. He would use the caffeine hit to create the S.E.T.I. invoice. After putting the final touches on it, he wondered how long it would take for Kumar to deposit the funds in their offshore account.

Adam would get on that first thing tomorrow, he thought as he closed his laptop. It was nice to sit with his coffee on his Stanford coaster, drinking out of the mug Bri had given him for his birthday. It was the little things…

The silver case began to vibrate on the coffee table. Adam took the sphere out and placed it on top of the closed case.

Seconds after Adam leaned back on the couch, a floor to ceiling image of L.U.C. looked down on him. He had been brisk and businesslike in Monterrey, but now he seemed angry. Menacing, even. He shook his head and regarded Adam with open contempt.

“Adam, you should know, my existence *must* be kept confidential. Should anyone divulge any information about me or what I have done, the consequences will be extreme,” he was smiling as the last words left his mouth.

Pushing himself to a sitting position, Adam tried to clear the fog in his brain and formulate a response, but nothing made sense. Why was L.U.C. angry? What information had leaked?

As he struggled to find words, L.U.C. flashed an image of the beach house into Adam’s den. He could see Greg, Grace and Dr. Alex on the porch, apparently having a casual conversation.

“We must deal with a few people who have broken our circle of trust,” L.U.C. said. Adam squinted at the image, trying to piece the information together. When were his friends on the porch? What were they talking about?

Before he could understand what he was seeing, an explosion came from inside the beach house’s front door, sending the three bodies flying as flames engulfed everything in sight. Adam fell to his knees on the floor as he watched in horror.

“Oh, my God,” Adam cried. “What have you done?”

L.U.C.’s calm voice only intensified the evil he radiated. I’ve had to eliminate them, Adam. They were a liability. They were becoming a threat to our security.”

“You killed them! Why would you do that?” Adam screamed.

“What we are doing here is too important to allow anyone to compromise our mission. I had no choice,” he told Adam.

The rage welled up in Adam’s brain. He began to shake with fury, but no words would come. He had no voice. He tried to stand up but could not move. It was as if he was frozen, sinking into helplessness.

Adam’s phone on the end table buzzed relentlessly and finally succeeded in waking him. He woke up breathless, his heart and brain racing. The phone buzzed a few more times before Adam realized where he was. Had he gotten to a place where he could finally relax only to have his subconscious give way to all those internal doubts and fears?

Adam saw the name of his old friend, “College Greg” on the caller-ID of his phone and quickly answered.

“Greg, doing okay, buddy?” Adam asked.

“Yes, are you okay? You are the one that sounds a little out of breath. Did I catch you at a, um, bad time? Greg sounded amused.

“Seriously Greg, is everything alright?” Adam asked, remnants of the dream still clinging to him like spiderwebs.

“Yes, why wouldn’t it be? Calm down, dude, I’m good,” Greg assured him.

Adam sighed and raked his hand through his hair. “It was just a bad dream or something… forget about it. I’m ok, but I’m glad you are, too. Anyway, you called. What is it?”

“Well, I do need to talk with you. We have a little situation,” he said.

“Oh, no. What?” Adam couldn’t stop himself from imagining horrible disasters after his nightmare.

“Grace came across some information that we are going to need to take some action on. She won’t say anything right now. She wants to wait until she can tell everyone on the team in person. Can the four of us meet around lunch time in D.C. today?” Greg asked.

“Yes, I can be there,” Adam.

“You can? Where are you?” Greg asked.

“I’m home,” Adam said.

“Home, home? What are you doing at home?” Now it was Greg who sounded alarmed. “Has anyone seen you?”

“Yes, home, home and no, no one has seen me. AND, what difference would it make if they did?” Adam was annoyed.

“We are just on to something big and since you laid all this out to Helms, I’ll bet he’s trying to find out as much as he can about what you are up to. We just need to be careful we don’t say too much about this yet. We certainly don’t need any government types involved,” Greg explained.

“I *am* a government type, dude. Well, I was. I think we are good and certainly don’t think Helms is checking up on me in any way,” Adam tried to assure his friend. “He and I have a great relationship and I know he trusts me,” Adam said before yawning hugely. “What time is it, anyway?”

“Yeah, sorry to call so early, but I knew you were back and wanted to let you know we needed to get together as soon as I could get you. It’s about 6:45 a.m. You get any good rest? You good to go for lunch?” Greg asked.

“I think I slept for a while. Yes, so, where are we meeting?” Adam asked.

“Why don’t we meet at Ambar in Arlington? They have a private room we can reserve. People can be nosy to get some privacy,” Greg said.

“Ok, sounds good,” Adam responded. He could squeeze in another hour of sleep if he was lucky…

“Great, I’ll let Grace and Alex know. See you there,” he told him.

"Drive safe." Adam hung up the phone and looked down at the coffee table. The silver case was lying there undisturbed, exactly in the same position he put it last night, before falling asleep on his couch.

Chapter 23 - Stones, Stones Everywhere, but Not a Rock to Hold

Between the nightmare and the news that something was up and actionable, Adam was unable to go back to sleep. He ate some oatmeal, drank more water than usual, and checked in with Julie. The kids were ok, but they sometimes asked her where he was. The sweatshirts would tell the story, and he told her to please not ruin the surprise.

Adam tried to imagine his family's reaction when they found out what he'd been doing on his sabbatical, and when they found out how it would change the lives of so many people. He was getting used to the idea that he was managing this project the way he managed all his other projects up to this point: making sure all the plates were spinning at the right speeds, putting out fires as they flared up, staying in contact with all the parties involved.

Really, the only difference was that this project involved flying cars, Adam thought. That reminded him to send Kumar a message detailing the expected cost of the first phase of the project, including the amount of the expected initial down payment. Adam couldn't fathom how Kumar would get an ROI on such a large sum. Then again, wouldn't getting a piece of every monthly travel subscription on the planet probably be a fairly nice payback? Especially if you were getting this "fee" for the rest of time.

He went into the bedroom to run on the treadmill, playing loud music while he exercised and sang along with the 80's hits. He took a shower after his workout and checked his email, still wrapped in a towel. Multitasking from home was very efficient, not that he hadn't enjoyed freshening up on the Gulfstream.

There were already two secure transaction notifications from his offshore accounts. Kumar was sending the money! The first was Ella International's down payment. The second came along with a note:

"Mr. Hunter, you have done well and exceeded my expectations thus far. We started our relationship with you asking me for something. It seems that you are the kind of person I like working with: driven. I think we can make for good partners. Please find an additional amount in a second account to help cover your own ongoing project expenses..."

It was not a small amount of money, he noted with surprise. Still, Adam realized he wasn't getting paychecks from the CIA any longer. He hoped he wasn't going to have to start getting into his retirement savings once this project was in full swing. L.U.C. had warned him how this venture was going to cost him. Adam had decided monetarily and personally, he would take the risk. The dream of what this could be was too big to sacrifice for strangers' approval or expensive cars.

He would have good news for his friends, he thought as he got dressed. This would counterbalance whatever this "situation" was. Grace would be glad to hear about the payment from Kumar and favor him with one of her smiles, he hoped.

Realizing he was hungry, and kept very little food in what had become his pied à terre, Adam left early for lunch. Maybe Myles wasn't keeping them fed at the beach house, because Grace, Greg and Dr. Alex were already seated at a table in their private room at Adar, enjoying a plate of charcuterie.

"You went to Mexico and didn't come back with a tan?" Greg said as he stood to shake Adam's hand.

"Good to see you, too," Adam said. He shook hands with Dr. Alex and complimented Grace on her beautiful watch.

"Is that new?" he asked as he sat down. What Adam really wanted to know was if her boyfriend had given it to her, but he couldn't ask that in front of the others.

"You got me. I took a break from eavesdropping and did a little online shopping," she said.

"I'm taking a break from work to stuff my face with-what is this, Alex?" Greg asked as he gestured to a plate of peppers.

"Avjar," Alex said as he lifted a forkful of smoked eggplant to his mouth.

"Avjar at Ambar," Greg said merrily.

"And how many gin and grapefruit juices?" Adam asked.

"Well, we're celebrating your return, so I guess I can start now," Greg said. Everyone at the table laughed. They looked like any other group of people enjoying a meal together, but they were in public. They were also in a part of the world where very influential people met for very sensitive conversations.

"So, I heard from Ben," Adam said. No last names here.

Eyebrows went up around the table as the chatter stopped.

"He gave us enough to get started," he told them with a smile.

"Forget the gin, let's get champagne!" Greg said, a little too loudly.

The curly haired waiter was hovering nearby and began walking toward their table.

"False alarm, guys. He forgot he's our designated driver," Adam told him. He became serious when he looked at the group and remembered the real reason for the meeting.

"So, something's up?" he asked.

"Yes, there is," Grace said with a slight frown. "A couple of days ago at the beach house L.U.C. pointed to three of the four *exact* locations where the centers would need to be. He showed us Roswell, Afghanistan, and Damascus. I just assumed he was working on the fourth location. I wondered if maybe he needed some help with calculations from a guy like Dr. Romanoff to pinpoint where we could tap into the Earth's magnetism at its greatest pull. I didn't think too much more of it," she explained.

"Yes, we've known that there would be four locations," Adam said.

"But then, later that day, I started eavesdropping again," Grace told him. "I wanted to find out if people were talking about those locations more than usual," she said. Adam knew that what Grace did was a little more sophisticated than eavesdropping. She was able to listen to conversations as they happened, of course. She could also read transcripts of dialogues between people and could tell her computer to search for words that had appeared in conversations, written and spoken, all over the world.

"There's a lot going on in at least two of those places most of the time," Adam observed.

"True enough," Grace said. "There is a married couple, I think they're British. Anyway, they're both archaeologists and they've found something that might be important to our project." She paused as their plates began arriving.

"What?" Adam asked eagerly.

"So, in L.U.C.'s schematics, he defines a very precise location within each Axiom that the main, let's call it "footer," must be placed," she glanced at Dr. Romanoff, who nodded affirmatively. "I listened for unusual things popping up in these areas in the last few weeks. This couple found something in a cave in Afghanistan that might be some five thousand years old. It's what they call a vimana," she looked at Adam to see if he recognized the term.

"Was it alive?" Adam asked, wondering where Grace was going with this.

She smiled, and Adam felt very pleased with himself. "You've heard of vimanas, haven't you, Adam? I don't know if they're made of your fancy polymers, but they are ancient flying machines," she said.

"I'm more on the design end of aircraft, not the history. So, this couple found something in a cave in Afghanistan, it's very old and might fly?" he summarized.

"Yes, Hindu texts, thousands of years old, contain drawings of vimanas. People think this vimana could be something that someone built thousands of years ago," Grace said.

“That would be a remarkable find,” Dr. Alex mused. “To think that people had an interest in that kind of technology so long ago.”

“Do you think they did?” Adam asked the group. Greg shrugged, Dr. Alex nodded.

“What this discovery has people asking is, are we alone in the universe? Who built this, a person or an extraterrestrial? Was this vimana built to take someone to another part of the world, or another part of the galaxy?” Grace’s eyes grew wide.

Adam thought he saw interested glances from the next table.

“Does anyone in the chatter have the answers?” Adam asked, thinking it would have been a rhetorical question a few weeks ago. Having met L.U.C. and hearing about his crash, his only certainty was that there was much he did not know.

“I, for one, highly doubt that we would only now be answering this question if they had come here thousands of years ago,” Grace said.

“Maybe the folks liked living in caves five thousand years ago,” Greg suggested. “Maybe the aliens offered them rides in the vimanas and they said, no thanks. But we’ll keep the drawings if we change our minds.”

“In some ways, life five thousand years ago was simpler,” Dr. Alex agreed.

Grace shook her head slightly. “Whatever life was like, the couple did what any archaeologist with principles would do. They showed their dig site manager the cave,” Grace said.

“Well, that was the right thing to do,” Adam responded.

“They didn’t take the vimana for a joyride? I would have,” Greg smirked.

“Oh, they would have posted it on YouTube if they had. No, this couple seems strangely low-profile. I guess not everyone their age wants to parlay their careers into reality tv shows and influencer gigs,” Grace said. “It’s where they showed up next that got me wondering.”

“Las Vegas?” Greg asked.

“Not that far away, actually. They got work visas and came to New Mexico,” she said. “There was a dig in Clovis. Hunting tools from twelve thousand years ago have been found in that area.”

“I know what else is in that area,” Greg said, glancing around the table.

Dr. Alex looked incredulous. “You can’t be serious. They were in Roswell?”

“And how are we doing?” the Justin Timberlake lookalike waiter asked.

“Just great, thanks,” Adam smiled.

As their server retreated, Greg eyed him suspiciously. “As soon as you said Roswell, I could swear he looked over here.”

“Not everyone eavesdrops constantly,” Grace said. “Anyway, yes. Roswell. I would imagine with that cave find, this couple could pretty much write their own tickets. And they went there, of all places. They took a couple of days off from the dig.”

“So they took a break. Those kids deserved it after all that working in the dirt and everything,” Greg said with a smile.

“Not exactly, no,” Grace continued. “They rented a truck and a trailer with two ATVs at a place in Roswell called Performance Motion.”

“So they went…” Dr. Alex often thought in numbers. He realized the drive wouldn’t have taken much more than twenty minutes.

Grace nodded. “They’ve been to two of the locations L.U.C. has given us for the Axioms.”

“Oh, my God,” Adam said.

“Then what happened?” Dr. Alex asked.

“It seems the Johansens went back to the dig the next day. Then they claimed Peter, the husband, wasn’t feeling well and flew back to England that evening,” she told them.

“Well maybe he was sick. People get altitude sickness, food poisoning…” Greg said.

“There doesn’t seem to be any evidence of a doctor visit in or near Oxford, which is where they live,” Grace said. “They went on another dig a short time later.”

“Where did they go this time?” Adam asked.

“Syria,” she answered.

“Anything else I can get you?” Curly hair’s timing was officially suspicious.

People don’t say Mossad in a crowded restaurant any more than they would yell FIRE.

Adam and Greg exchanged a glance. “You know, I think we’re ready for the check, thank you,” Adam said.

“Ok, folks. We will have the rest of this conversation in Central Park,” Grace announced.

“I would have liked to stay for dessert, Grace. This better be good,” Greg said as the group walked briskly to Clarendon Central Park. It was a few minutes’ walk from Ambar and not likely to be crowded on a January day.

“I’ll buy you donuts later,” Grace said. “Anyone following us?” She looked straight ahead, hood up and hands jammed into her coat pockets. Adam and Dr. Alex glanced around, looking for unusual people or vehicles. There were none.

“I think we’re good,” Adam said. “So, they were in Syria?” he asked as they crossed Garfield. Grace walked quickly but didn’t seem out of breath. She was just so…unflappable.

“That’s where the “dig” was, but they flew into Tel Aviv,” Grace said.

"Oh no," Dr. Alex raised his eyebrows.

"What I think happened is the Johansens pretended to be excavating a site in Syria, but they stayed at the Savoy in Tel Aviv. They had a really nice suite there and we're not sure how they could afford it all of a sudden."

"So on this dig in Syria, let me guess, they found-" Greg said.

Grace nodded. "Uh huh."

"Ok, this is getting really strange," Greg said.

"Well, this is where the story goes from strange to scary," she said.

They were at the east end of the park. It wasn't aptly named, really. It was a paved urban space near a metro entrance. There was a cafe style table and chairs near an inactive fountain. The group seated themselves and huddled in the cold as Grace continued the story.

"The couple was on the dig for a week, and on the last day of their trip, they get back to their expensive suite at the hotel, and Mossad is there, waiting for them," she told the group quietly.

"You're kidding," Adam said.

"You couldn't make this up," she said as she shook her head. "Mossad cracked the safe in their room, and found two stones. One blue, one green. They are so smooth and perfect, no one seems to know if they are natural or synthetic. The couple was bringing back a third stone from Syria. This one was orange. All three stones have the lats and longs for the Axiom locations engraved on them."

Adam sat back in his chair, sighing. The temperature was just above freezing, and the windchill meant it *felt* even colder. He had his collar turned up, but underneath his jacket, he was starting to sweat. Israeli intelligence!

"You can't shut down a hotel with a thousand guests like that without creating some kind of scene. Mossad has the couple under armed guard in their room at the Savoy. Interrogations have produced nothing, as the Johansens seem to be playing dumb. They want legal representation before they will say anything," she told the astonished group.

"That's very astute of them," Dr. Alex observed.

"So, where does that leave us?" Adam asked, feeling helpless.

"I think L.U.C. knows, or knew, when it was happening," Grace said.

"He told you that?" Adam asked.

"Well, kind of," Grace said. "Dr. Alex was working with L.U.C. yesterday on the designs and specifications for the upcoming project in Roswell. He said, just about the moment the couple was detained at the Savoy, which was 10:00 p.m. in Tel Aviv, about 3:00 p.m. here, L.U.C.'s AI went nuts. He said, *warning, warning! Critical materials in jeopardy*! He just kept repeating that over and over."

"Then what happened?" Greg asked.

"Dr. Alex is going to explain it," Grace answered.

Dr. Alex rubbed his hands together to warm them. "Yes, yes, Adam, you see, when I was reviewing the mechanical architecture and schematics for Axiom One, I saw an element that looked like an activator in the plans, however, I initially thought it was just something that was part of our construction. Apparently, what the Johansen's are stumbling upon is a systems activator of sorts."

"The green and orange stones activate the systems?" Adam asked.

"Well, as I read through the algorithm further, I learned that the system will not fully operate without them. It was here that I took L.U.C.'s system to task and drilled into these elements. Adam, there are four magnetic stones. When all together, they will bind into one object called the cornerstone. Engraved on the face of each stone are the coordinates of the exact spot on Earth where the deepest part of our control rods must be inserted into the planet's core," he explained.

"So with only three of the stones," Adam reasoned, "nothing happens?"

"The system does not operate fully, no. L.U.C., however, was, what do people say? Triggered? To summarize and so as not to bore you with all the details, each of the four Axioms can then simultaneously interact with the Earth's spin axis in order to provide the magnetic current necessary to power the Virtual Global Highway Transportation System. Axioms will work together to harness and amplify a streaming magnetic current which is already emanating from the Earth. But, at present, the vast majority of the Earth's magnetism is escaping the atmosphere. Once harnessed, our vehicles can repel and attract at varying rates to control their movements within the current. These vehicles are designed to enter and exit the current stream seamlessly as they take off and land," he finished.

It sounded perfectly logical the way Dr. Alex explained it, but it was pure theory, Adam thought. "This has never been done. There's a formula. This is what *could* happen," Adam said skeptically. "Things could go sideways…" he looked off into the distance. The winter wind was blowing through the leafless trees. It was dark in the west and it looked like a storm was coming.

"Adam, this is very stressful, what we're doing. We knew that it would be. We have to break eggs to make the omelet, yes?" Dr. Alex asked. Adam nodded. "And you are correct, this is an idea at the moment, the results of this experiment may not be what we expected," he told him.

"We could end up with egg on our faces," Adam said.

"Hey Adam, remember that Einstein quote Professor Nelson recited to every incoming class?" Greg asked.

Adam nodded. "He said 'the only sure way to avoid making mistakes is to have no new ideas.'"

"That's right. We have a new idea. You're going to make it work. Let us handle the rest," Greg said.

His friend was right, Adam knew. Greg always had his back.

Adam took a deep breath and looked at Grace. "Ok, what else? Give it to me straight," he said.

She looked at Adam with a small smile. How she managed to look beautiful with a freezing face, he would never know. "Ok, it's not all bad. The good news is, whether by accident or on purpose, the Johansen's have found three of the four elements of the cornerstone," she reminded the group.

"The way the stones are designed, with just three of the stones that have been collected, you would now have access to all the specific coordinates for where the four Axiom control rods must be inserted into Earth's core. This is a major breakthrough for the project! It can get us a long way toward getting all the way there. The stones are unique in that they provide the link, or the map to the coordinates both forwards and backwards," she said enthusiastically.

The group members nodded hopefully. Greg looked around, checking for conspicuous onlookers. There were none. A few snowflakes were swirling down.

"Alright. The bad news. Nobody that we know of has the fourth stone. Now Mossad has the Johansen's and the other three. With the stones under the control of Mossad, it looks like we will need a miracle," she admitted.

There was a considerable pause as Grace, Greg and Alex looked intently at Adam.

"Ok, I have a plan," Adam said resolutely.

"I'm all ears," Greg said.

"There's a coffee place about three minutes from here. I'm freezing and I'm buying for everybody," he said.

"Well, it's not Blue Bottle, but I never turn down free coffee," Dr. Alex said.

"Then what?" Grace asked Adam.

"I have an idea. Or, maybe I'd better call it "a favor."

Chapter 24 - Gaza Gonna Get Ya!

The group hurried to a coffee shop on Washington Boulevard as the sky darkened. Greg and Grace ordered coffee to warm up their hands, Dr. Alex and Adam drank tea to warm up their insides. It wasn't Adam's imagination: the other three were out of their depth and needed Adam to help them over, around or through this obstacle.

"I will get us out of this mess, you guys. You're invested, we're all invested in making this project successful," Adam told them. All around them, hipsters and other young professionals stared intently at their phones.

Greg seemed flummoxed. His work involved giving shape to ideas, not eluding authorities. "You bet we're invested," Greg said. "You don't get a chance to build something that could change the world and then quit because it wasn't as easy as you wanted it to be."

"I don't know the equation for this, Adam. People are so...messy. Formulas don't work on them," Dr. Alex said as he looked out the coffee shop window in dismay.

Even Grace seemed unsure of how to move forward. "You know I will do whatever I can do to help you, and help the project. We're your sled dogs, Adam. We can run for days and not get tired, but we need you to give us direction. What is this favor you mentioned?"

"The way we get through this is the way we get through most of the tough things we're faced with in life: reaching out to someone who knows how to help you. We knew this would be a challenge before we started, but I can't think of a better group of people to work with when it comes to overcoming setbacks. And that's all this is, setback.

"I've managed not to burn *every* bridge I've built in my career, and the one I have to my old boss is definitely intact. We're going to my place, it's not far from here, and I'm going to call him," Adam announced. "You guys all came in the same car?" he asked.

Greg nodded. "I drove, and I also know the way to your place. But I seem to remember Grace saying something about donuts. We'll be there a few minutes after you get home. Do you want a maple bar or a jam filled?" his friend asked.

"Surprise me," Adam said as they stood to leave.

Greg and Grace sat on Adam's couch, a half-eaten box of donuts on the coffee table in front of them. Dr. Alex sat across from them in a chair while Adam stood, phone in hand. He wasn't exactly devout, but he said a short prayer before he dialed Helms and pressed the speakerphone button.

It rang twice before he picked up. "Adam! I have been thinking about you. So glad you called. What's up, everything going okay?" he asked his former employee.

"Richard, things are going very well. Once again, I appreciate you allowing me the opportunity to take this time away and I promise, I will not let you down. Trust me," Adam said.

"Of course I trust you, I gave you the time away, didn't I?" Helms asked good naturedly.

"You will not regret it," Adam said. If only Helms knew…

"Recently I've wondered if I did the right thing. I might need you back here sooner rather than later!" Kennedy is really screwing things up at SpaceX. The more he makes it about him, the longer it's going to take to patch things up. I'm mad at you about that."

"I made SpaceX angry more than once. Kennedy is smart and will get them in line before long," Adam assured him.

"Well, what's up, why are you calling?" Helms was too busy to chat.

"I need a favor. I was hoping to leave you alone and then just bring you a prize at the end of all this, but I'm going to need your help. Some really big help…and, it's urgent," he said as he looked at his team members.

"Go on…." Helms knew how Adam sounded when he was in a bind.

"How well do you know David Dagan?" Adam asked as Grace looked up at him.

"Mossad Dagan? Pretty well, Adam. You're involved in something overseas? Dagan and I were just collaborating on a few things in Gaza last month, now that you mention it. We brought in some key resources and helped them stop their guy and some of his Hamas cronies," Helms said.

"Sounds like a win for everyone. Well, except Hamas," Adam said.

"It was, they were really about to mess some shit up if we hadn't been able to get in there and stop them," Helms said with characteristic understatement. "I think he was pretty happy with me."

"Great," Adam responded. "I don't mean great that there was a group of militants trying to mess up some shit, I mean great that you know him and great that things are good between you two."

"Ok, as I just said, what's up?" Helms asked again. "I thought you were doing some kind of navel gazing on an island. Now it sounds like you went from the frying pan into the fire."

"I need an intervention," Adam said as he watched Greg chew his nails.

"How so?"

"I can't go into a lot of details right now and it wouldn't be good for me to do so. You are just going to have to trust me," Adam said. He was tempted to say something about Operation Green Lantern, but didn't.

"Continue...."

"I need you to call David. Tell him you sent me and I'm on my way to Tel Aviv right now to intercept a husband-and-wife team that I've been working on for a while. Mossad just detained them yesterday at the Savoy Seaside and I don't think they even know why they did it yet."

"Are they Americans?" Helms asked.

"No, they are British, but they've worked in the US, among other places. This is part of how they got on the Israeli's radar in the first place. I think, all they know is that they didn't like their activity profile, started tracking them for a few days, watched them pop in and out of the country one too many times, and then decided to take a closer look."

"The couple's names are Peter and Claire Johansen. They live in Oxford and have worked at museums most of their lives. Near as I can tell, they've turned into some wannabe archaeologists and have recently been volunteering with nonprofits like AIA and UNESCO on some of their advertised dig opportunities," Adam explained.

"What did these two dig up?" Helms asked.

"I believe they may have accidentally come across something that belongs to me and the project we, I mean I, that I am working on. This stuff they have isn't worth very much, just a few rocks and might not even be what I need," Adam tried to keep his tone steady.

"This is a lot to do for something you're not really sure about," Helms said. He had a point, Adam realized, but if he told him the whole story...

"There is only one way for me to find out, and it's a risk I have to take. I can promise you, Richard, you can assure David there won't be any blowback or negative fallout on Israel on this one."

"I don't think you have any way of knowing that," Helms said matter of factly.

"Fallout won't come from me, and I will do everything in my power to keep it away from you, how's that? This is my scene, and I need to keep it."

"That's a lot more realistic," Helms told him.

"I need to stay in the gray area and make sure none of anything I am doing can ever come back on you if it doesn't work, and I promise, this will be the last time I ever ask for a favor," he said. He meant it, too. Another mishap like this and Adam was certain he wouldn't live to tell anyone about it.

Helms paused on the phone without saying anything for a minute, but Adam could hear him breathing. Seconds seemed like hours and the three other group members were holding their breath. Adam smiled and gave them a thumb's up. Adam, during the wait, gives looks to Grace, Greg and Dr. Alex to assure them that everything was under control.

"Give me a minute, I'll call you back," Helms said and hung up.

The four of them looked at each other in silence. Finally, Greg spoke.

"Glad we left Ambar, I'd be puking on the floor by this time," he said.

"Not funny," Grace muttered.

"It wasn't supposed to be," Greg said. "I'm seriously freaked out here."

"Ok, we need a plan B," Dr. Alex said. "A lot of people will be in danger, including the four of us if Helms doesn't come through. Maybe there's someone I know in Israel," he said as he rubbed his forehead.

"There is no plan B, I am going to get the stones – end of story." He paced in his living room and looked out the window. Snow was falling but not sticking. It blew around on the empty street.

"Can you tell us about having all four of these stones, Alex? And what is the activator?" Adam asked as he checked his watch. They had been waiting for less than two minutes.

"The system will work without having all four stones, as long as we have all the coordinates for the control rods, and we do. That's the most important thing," Dr. Alex explained.

"Ok, it's the coordinates on the stones that we care about, then? Not the stones themselves?" Adam asked hopefully.

"The stones are important, because their composition is…unusual. It is similar, but not, to an opal, which is a hydrous silicate that forms as a precipitate or a replacement of the skeletons of marine organisms. It's a unique mineral because it first forms as a gel in the cracks of many other types of rocks like basalt or thyolite. Sometimes it is found in sandstone and limonite," Dr. Alex said as he watched Adam pace around the room.

"Oh, so we are looking for rocks made of dead animals?" Adam asked.

"Correct. Our immediate concern, as you said, is obtaining the coordinates and securing the corresponding locations on the stones," Dr. Alex said. "Again, we are relying on the planet's resources to build this virtual highway system. To make this system fully functional we will need the minerals, all together, to be placed in the *key* in the actuator in Axiom One," Dr. Alex explained.

"We're ok, for now?" Adam asked. Why couldn't anyone just give him a simple answer?

“Yes, for now, we are,” Dr. Alex agreed. “It will likely be years before we will address that.” The other three people in the room sighed with relief. “However,” he said as Adam fought the urge to throw his phone at Dr. Alex, “It is imperative that we recover the three stones and obtain the coordinates. “Without them…”

Adam’s phone buzzed and he checked the screen.

“It's Helms!” Greg leapt to his feet. ….

“Hello?”

“Adam, get your butt over there, right now, before he changes his mind,” Helms growled.

“Richard, I owe you big time. Thank you very much.” Helms:

“Let me know when you get on the ground. David will have someone there to pick you up. He’ll be waiting for you in the Savoy restaurant. I've used up my favor with him, now he says I owe him. This better be good.”

Chapter 25 - An Eye for an Eye

"You'll have to pack all by yourself for this trip. Myles will be waiting for you on your plane, though," Greg said as he watched Adam throw objects in an overnight bag. He was hoping to get in and out of Israel in a few hours, but anything was possible.

"Yeah, but the plane comes to me now," Adam smiled at his friend. Greg didn't seem envious of Adam's trips on the Gulfstream, and would never begrudge his friend the perks of project management. Truthfully, Greg didn't think he could handle keeping so many plates in the air without losing his temper, or his sanity.

"You know they've got all the stuff you need on the plane, right?" It was a lot to get used to, after years of preparing for delays, lost luggage and general chaos, knowing someone else was taking care of the details was still new to Adam. "I'll drive you, you know. We can take your car, send Grace and Dr. Alex to the beach house in my ride," he offered.

"No, everyone does Uber these days. You guys need to get going, too," Adam said as they walked out to the living room.

"Ok, folks, you should head out before traffic gets too heavy," Adam told his concerned team. "Which one of you is driving my car?"

"With my speeding tickets? Dr. Alex has to do it," Grace smirked.

"Well, then sorry about all the fast-food wrappers. The heater starts working after about ten miles, so don't worry," he said. The group laughed, but the air in the room was tense.

"Adam, we know this is not going to be easy," Dr. Alex said. "No matter how this turns out, I want to tell you that I admire you for your determination to do the right thing here."

"And there is no "or else" here, you know?" Grace asked. "You still have to worry about yourself. It's like that saying, things work out in the end..."

"So if things aren't working out, it must not be the end yet," Adam finished. He wanted to hug her again. Darned team members.

"Myles will make sure nothing happens to you. I told him to let you get some rest and not chatter so much," Greg said.

"You guys are acting like I'm getting ready to board the Titanic, for Pete's sake," Adam said. "This is a hiccup, and probably not the last one we will have, if we're being realistic. We are not going to give up before this thing even got started. It's going to get more stressful as we go. There will be so much more at stake. And we will not quit until we have done what we set out to do."

Grace looked a little embarrassed. "Ok, but you'll call us if things go sideways? I have friends in some pretty low places…" she said, only half-kidding.

"Don't lose their numbers just yet. Now please, get back to the beach house. I should be back in twenty-four hours with some rocks," Adam said as he walked the group outside.

A few minutes after the two cars left, a shiny black automobile came to a stop in front of Adam's house. Adam approached the car as the driver rolled the passenger side window down.

"Mr. Hunter?" the young man asked. He had a young face with a large streak of white in his dark hair.

"That's me," Adam said as he climbed into the back seat. It was spacious and warm. He had upgraded to a kind of premium plan that allowed him to choose how much conversation he wanted with his driver, and Adam welcomed the chat as a distraction.

"So, College Park Airport, are you traveling on business?" the driver asked.

"I wish I could say I'm jetting off to the Caribbean, but this is a business trip," Adam said. In his mind it was a life-or-death trip, but the driver didn't need to know that.

"That's so typical of this town. People never stop working here. Our business class is really popular because people want to work while they ride," he told Adam.

"That makes sense, I could hold a meeting back here with all the room we have," Adam responded.

"Oh, that's just the beginning," the driver said. "We're going to install smartboards so people can hold in person and virtual meetings and give presentations from the road. People always realize at the last minute that they need to print boarding passes, so we'll have printing and scanning capabilities. Your driver can be a notary if you request that ahead of time," he said.

"People will really like that," Adam said, impressed.

"I'm from L.A. and my brother still works out there. Their upgrades are a little different, but you know, you cater to your clientele," he told him.

"What do they want there? A tanning bed in every car?" Adam asked facetiously.

"Pretty close. Passengers can order hairstylists, a masseuse. It's tricky getting a surface stable enough for a manicure while driving, but we have our best people working on it," he said.

"They're going to love that," Adam said. And he knew people would. But people also enjoy reading tabloids and stuffing their faces with fluorescent orange chips and watching professional wrestling. That doesn't mean they should consume unlimited amounts of the stuff.

And it was the same way with transportation and travel. People loved their gas guzzling, air polluting cars and trucks, but that didn't mean they should drive them until they destroyed the planet. Not every person can see the big picture, but now that he had, Adam couldn't wait until his, well, L.U.C.'s cars were flying along as the earth below them healed.

He was tempted to ask his driver if he thought about changing fields, as the flying cars would put guys like him out of a job. He seemed to have good people skills, a lot of industries needed people like that.

They were nearing the Potomac, and it was starkly beautiful in the winter. It was also a polluted river. It ran through a city that, as the driver said, was full of people who worked around the clock. There was traffic on the bridge and traffic in the air as planes of various sizes circled, looking for a place to land.

Adam imagined plants and animals thriving on structures as we abandoned them. Nature would overtake them, it always did in the end. Marine life gradually claimed the wreckage of ships, and Adam hoped to see the 14th Street Bridge's trestles covered with vines someday.

As they neared College Park, the traffic was less congested and there were more spaces between buildings. It seemed a more sensible way to live. He appreciated his driver and the commitment to making it easier for people to do business, but again, Adam's mind focused on the bigger picture. He wanted to help people live better.

And he wasn't going to be able to do that if he didn't get a hold of those stones.

He'd been doing a lot of work, but most of it was math problems. How many people working for how much time would need how many shipments of materials. Math problems were neat, clean and straightforward. The situation in Israel was messy, with the potential to explode on an international scale, injuring the innocent. He was beyond Uber's business solutions.

He thanked his driver and tipped generously through the app. It was the least he could do until he and his team could make cars fly.

Myles was already onboard and standing in his comfort zone, the threshold to the rear of the aircraft. With a slight nod, he communicated to Mr. Hunter that his bag was already in the overhead of the same lounge he sat in before, creature of habit that Adam was. Never would Adam have considered leaving L.U.C. at home in his silver case.

"According to the flight plans, this flight is approximately 6000 miles and 12 hours. It will be direct. We should be on the ground at 10:00 a.m. local time.

"It might help you to know Mr. Buchanan seemed quite anxious about this trip and has a lot of hopes for your success," Myles said.

"Him and me both," Adam sighed. "How are you feeling, Myles?" The man's picture was probably in the dictionary next to the word *inscrutable*.

"Just fine, Mr. Hunter. I will be in the back of the plane if you require anything at all. Please get some rest if possible," he finished.

Ok, he had Myles, two well rested pilots and a plane stocked full of food and beverages of various alcohol percentages. Once he outwitted the most cunning intelligence outfit on the planet, he could go back to designing cars.

It was easier growing accustomed to luxury travel than Adam had realized, as he began to drift off over the Atlantic. Much as he valued big picture thinking, he would not use that tool to solve the problem he now faced.

His thought process was narrow and specific, the way it had always been when he faced challenges at school, and later at work. He was completely focused on what was happening in that moment, not what would happen decades from now. The focus was exclusively on doing whatever he needed to do to move the project from one phase to the next.

When the Gulfstream landed at Tel Aviv Sde Dov Airport, Adam looked out the window, confused. There were no planes or people in sight. A lone gas pump sat off to the side of the tarmac. Weeds were growing through the cracks in the runway. He'd heard of ghost towns, but not ghost airports.

"Welcome to Sde Dov Airport," Myles said, having soundlessly materialized in the aisle. "It closed a few years ago, and Mr. Buchanan and Ms. Hathaway thought it safer than landing at Ben Gurion." Adam smiled when he heard that. They always had his back, even when they were on the other side of the world. "I do not plan to deboard, and wish you well."

Adam looked out the window again and saw a dark SUV moving slowly toward the hanger. There were agents in dark clothes. They wore sunglasses and earpieces and looked ready to pounce on whoever emerged from the plane.

He could not ask Myles to accompany him. This was his fight, and his alone.

"I will be back, so don't drink all the champagne, ok?" he clapped Myles on the shoulder and headed for the door.

With just enough room to breathe occasionally, Adam sat between two Mossad agents in the backseat, having expected the confinement as a matter of intelligence protocol. Keeping him feeling uncomfortable, physically as well as psychologically, was an attempt to make him feel off balance.

He would not give the agents any reason to think he was anything but delighted to make the twenty-minute drive up HaYarkon Street to the Savoy crammed between their well-armed bodies. He had done this before.

"Stressful job you guys have," Adam said. Truthfully, he admired their fearlessness and dedication.

"*Yitakhen*," responded an unsmiling man on his left. Maybe.

"The dangers you face, the crazy hours. And on top of all that you have to remember to put on deodorant every day, or else," Adam said with a smile. Maybe it was his imagination, but the agents seemed to have moved even closer. One more centimeter and his ribs would crack.

The Savoy looked beautiful in the late morning sun. Adam thought there were worse places to be detained. Tourists milled about and sprinkled among them were plainclothes agents posing as hotel guests. They took selfies and sipped coffee while trying not to appear alert as they were.

"Mr. Dagan is on the veranda in the back," the SUV driver said as Adam's close companions exited the car. Adam walked past the busy waiters and milling guests to Dagan's table at the end of the deck. They'd never met, but Adam was aware of his reputation. Dagan was feared and admired.

This morning, he was dressed in casual clothes and sipping coffee as he looked out at the water. He sat alone, but Adam didn't doubt his bodyguards lurked nearby. Perfectly, enviably calm. Why shouldn't he be? He looked like any other middle-aged man at the hotel, yet a team of agents would defend him to the death if a threat appeared. Did he feel as peaceful as he looked? Adam wondered how many people were devising ways to harm Dagan at this very minute, yet none succeeded. Dagan's very existence was a kind of act of defiance.

It was one his family had practiced for generations. His grandparents fled Nazi Germany and went south, into France and across the Mediterranean Sea into Israel. David was the first person in his family to be born in Israel. From an early age, he had understood that defending himself, defending others, was a moral obligation. Yet Dagan could not recall a single instance in which he approached conflict with a sense of duty. It was always exhilaration.

Yes, there was a sense of fulfilling a promise to his people, of preserving the honor of his family. Still, a good fight was simply exciting to Dagan. Winning was as essential as breathing to him. As a youth, many of his battles were physical and he relished the struggle for supremacy. His more recent victories were the result of psychological warfare, which he found just as satisfying.

Adam had a healthy respect for David, which is why he resisted the temptation to follow his greeting with a demand to take the Johansens and leave.

“Mr. Dagan, thank you for meeting me on such short notice,” Adam said as he neared the table, right hand extended.

Dagan stood and shook Adam’s hand. “Please call me David, and have a seat,” he said as he gestured to the empty chair across the table. There were bowls for oatmeal and a plate of citrus fruits from a nearby kibbutz. “Best grapefruit you’ll ever taste. Try some.”

Adam was feeling too keyed up to eat, and settled for coffee instead. “Helms sends his best,” Adam said.

“He speaks highly of you, and he doesn’t do this type of favor for just anyone,” Dagan told him. He sat back in his chair and admired the view. “Is this your first time in Tel Aviv?” he asked pleasantly.

“It is, actually. I’ve been to Jerusalem before, though,” Adam said watching a nearby couple pretend to be very interested in their phones.

Dagan nodded. “Jerusalem gets all the attention, but Tel Aviv is so much better in some ways. You like Fattoush?” he asked brightly.

“Sorry?” Adam said.

“It’s vegetables and sumac, and mint. So good. There’s a place on Dizengoff that serves the best fattoush you will ever eat,” he told Adam.

“Well, maybe I can go there later, with the Joha-” Adam began.

“And the beaches. Everyone likes the beach,” he stated. “Jerusalem has no beach. Now, it’s a lot of fun in the day, but you haven’t lived until you’ve watched the moon over the Mediterranean.”

“It’s a beautiful area,” Adam responded. Dagan was running this show, Adam realized.

“But that’s not why you’re here, are you? I’m acting like a travel agent, and you’re here on business. Richard told me you were working on a special assignment, but he didn’t give me a lot of details,” he looked expectantly at Adam and said nothing for several seconds. “So, can you tell me a little about this project of yours?”

He was not getting something for nothing, Adam knew. If he wanted the Johansens and their stones, Dagan was going to get information in exchange.

“Well, you know, I was always a science guy,” Adam said. “I don’t know if I could ever do a job like yours.” Dagan nodded. Most people couldn’t. “I loved space and design growing up, but I always liked geology, too. Doesn’t usually pay well, so I kind of put it on the back burner,” he said.

“Oh?” Dagan began sectioning an orange and offered some to Adam. He shook his head.

“While I was at MIT, I worked on metals and compounds trying to improve them. A few projects we worked on were somewhat successful. Also while at MIT, I did another thesis that didn't go anywhere on a fireplace material idea.

“Now, I'm not getting any younger and I think the fireplace idea would really sell. Instead of homes having to construct a big fireproof box when they want to have a real wood burning fire, I've been messing around with a really thin polymer material that won't conduct heat to its outside surface. Most fireplaces can get to between 700 and 1,000 degrees. The material I am trying to patent could be razor thin and handle up to 1,300 degrees without a sweat. It would dramatically reduce the price of construction for homeowners who want fireplaces and I think I could make a fortune selling it. If I could get that done, then I wouldn't have to fully depend on my Thrift Savings plan for retirement and my kids could pick any school they wanted to go to,” he told Dagan.

“Richard doesn't even know it and I don't want to get him too excited, but I am going to make him a business partner and cut him in on the deal for all the things he's done for me, including this time off,” Adam heard himself saying.

“That is interesting,” Dagan said between bites of fruit.

Was there extra caffeine in the coffee? Adam couldn’t seem to stop talking. “I was thinking about applying for that ‘Shark Tank’ thing once I got the idea up and going. Mark Cuban, Mr. Wonderful, our Lori Griener could really help me get this thing going. I think I am going to call it ‘Fire Metal.’ How does that sound to you?”

Dagan’s poker face had taken years to perfect, and he was not going to waste it on Adam. His expression told him he didn’t believe a word Adam said. Dagan raised an eyebrow.

“Why are you really here, Mr. Hunter?” he asked.

“Oh yeah, the Johansens,” he realized Dagan might have guessed Adam had been thinking about them during the entire conversation. “These people, which of course there is no way they'd even know where to start to get the composition right in the metal, are just wannabe archaeologists that stumbled across some rocks that had one of the chemical elements that I was hypothesizing about. They probably just got greedy and thought they would beat me to the punch,” Adam said.

“Is that so?” Dagan asked.

“I'm just guessing here, but since they are from Oxford, they probably came across my thesis some way or another, maybe some good old fashioned MIT Oxford idea sharing. They had their radar up for things to find along with diamonds and gold while they were working on these free digs," Adam said.

"They sound like mercenaries, the Johansens," Dagan observed. He nodded slightly to a passing waiter.

"They may be disappointed then. I don't think the stones are a big deal, because once I get my hands on a little bit of the stuff, it will be easy enough to fabricate when I'm ready to scale it," he explained.

Dagan almost had Adam backed into a corner. One or two more questions and he would be trapped. "How did you know this couple, the Johansens, found anything that you might need?"

"Oh, good question. From an old buddy of mine that was working on an exchange program with Stanford. Then he tried out for MI6, and is now with the Department of Transport there in Heathrow sent me a note about some cool rocks he saw come through customs. I did a little checking on them. Didn't want to let this opportunity get away, you know how that is. I'd asked a good friend over at the NSA to help me keep track of them and she let me know they got tripped up a little bit with you guys over here," he said.

Dagan sighed heavily. "Look, Mr. Hunter, I appreciate your knack for storytelling, but you need to know, I don't believe a word you've said for the past ten minutes," the human lie detector said. His needle threatened to run off the top of the scrolling paper after that last bit. "Richard assures me that whatever this find is, it is harmless, and no threat to Israel. Is that true, Mr. Hunter?"

Adam nodded.

"Richard has done a lot for me over the years and we have been friends a long time. I also appreciate the United States and the relationship our countries have enjoyed," he said.

"Of course," Adam agreed.

"But Mr. Hunter, you need to be aware, and you need to make Richard aware, this is not normally something you can expect of me and my organization. If I find out that you have been the least bit untruthful with me, there will be some consequences," he said. Adam wasn't sure if that was a threat or a promise. Dagan usually showed restraint. "Richard trusts you, but I don't like being lied to," he said, his voice barely above a whisper. This was not fire, this was ice, and it was far more dangerous. "Follow me," he said as he stood and walked toward the hotel lobby.

Adam, Dagan and a small group of Mossad agents take the elevator to the sixth floor. A man in a dark gray suit stood outside the door to the suite and opened the door for Dagan. Upon his entrance, all the Mossad agents in the room snapped to attention.

The Johansens sat on a couch covered with fabric in a distinctive geometric pattern with bright colors. The blue, green and orange stones sat on the cedar coffee table in front of them. If Adam hadn't known better, he would have thought the couple were models filming a furniture commercial, it was so vivid and compelling.

He also could have sworn the stones pulsed in greeting when they saw him, but it was something he would investigate later. Time was of the essence and most of the people in the room had guns. The Johansens were exhausted, as they leaned on each other with their hands intertwined. Claire's eyes were red and puffy.

Dagan spoke to the agents in Hebrew, and without any hesitation, they immediately began to gather their belongings and started vacating the room. Apparently, Dagan had not said anything about the stones, as agents ignored the coffee table while moving efficiently and stealthily toward the door. Adam moved away from the door as a line of agents silently exited the suite. Dagan directed his agents to take the stairs. The less the Savoy guests saw of them, the better. Adam stood near the Johansens and watched the last of the agents leave, soundlessly closing the door.

"Mr. Hunter, your transportation is in the lobby and will be leaving for the airport in ten minutes. It would be a good idea if you and your new guests were in that car," Dagan announced. Then he, too, left the suite. Adam and Johansens were in the room alone, just the three of them. Adam slowly brought his finger to his mouth, with a 'shushing' motion, as he knew the room was bugged.

"Mr. And Mrs. Johansen, name is Adam Hunter. I am from the United States, and I am here to make you an offer," he said. The Johansens looked somewhat relieved, but still confused. They nodded in agreement, and stood to begin collecting their bags.

Front and center in their thoughts was the possibility that they were jumping from the metaphorical frying pan into the fire. Mossad hadn't hurt them, they had never touched a hair on their heads. They didn't have to: the agents knew how to use the least amount of force to create the greatest amount of fear in people.

There was also that saying, the devil you know. The Johansens had decided to get on a plane with a devil they had never met. Peter and Claire were fairly sure this Adam person was an American. Beyond that, they knew nothing about him. If he'd told them the sky was blue, the Johansens would have looked out the window to be sure.

Almost as quietly as the agents before them, the trio left the beautiful suite with its ocean view. They said not a word as they took the elevator downstairs, and walked through a lobby full of curious guests. They stared at the unlikely group of foreigners, wondering if they were responsible for causing the disturbance at the hotel.

A driver was waiting for them at the curb in a nondescript white taxi. His well-muscled arms suggested picking up fares was not his only source of income. The twenty-minute drive to the abandoned airport seemed to last forever, but was uneventful. Claire and Peter looked suspicious when they saw the largely deserted airfield, but as long as they had the stones with them, they were willing to endure almost anything.

Myles was out of the plane with the hatch open and the staircase down, helping each of them with the first step up. Adam sank into his seat, exhaling and deciding how strong he wanted his badly needed cocktail. He was definitely going to offer the Johansens a drink as soon as they got settled, but they seemed to be lingering at the front of the airplane.

A few minutes went by, and Adam could have sworn he heard laughter coming from the entrance. Curiosity and the desire to take off got the best of him. He walked to the front of the cabin and saw Myles, Peter and Claire smirking at each other.

As soon as they saw Adam, their smiles diminished and they took the nearest available seats. Myles went to the back of the plane without saying a word.

The jet began to taxi down the runway as Peter and Claire looked out the window. Adam wondered if they were hoping it was the last time they'd ever see Israel.

"Welcome aboard," Adam said.

"Oh, thank you. And thank you for coming," Claire said, her gratitude almost palpable.

"This is so new to us, your own jet, your staff," Peter said.

"It's new to you? Really? I could have sworn I saw you fistbump Myles," Adam said pointedly.

Peter only looked at him in confusion.

Chapter 26 - We're Safe

"Excuse me?" Peter asked. He was bleary eyed and looked out of place on the jet with his faded jeans and t-shirt.

"When you met Myles, I thought I saw you greet each other like friends," Adam said.

Peter shook his head. "I wasn't sure if he wanted to shake hands or give him my bag. It was an accidental fist bump," he explained. "Like I said, I don't know private jet customs."

Adam sat back in his seat. He was going to give the Johansens the benefit of the doubt until they gave them a reason not to trust them. They were on this flight for several more hours. Things would go better if he could build a rapport with them. Problem was, Adam wasn't sure how many 'sides' were competing for possession of these stones.

"Of course," Adam said. "You two are probably exhausted and hungry. What can we get you?" He pressed the button with a human figure on it and seconds later a staff member appeared.

"Tea, please." Claire said. What else would a Brit drink in the middle of the day?

"Any kind of beer would be wonderful," Peter told the attendant. Adam ordered a gin and tonic. The couple seemed to relax a little after the refreshments. They weren't being threatened or bombarded with questions. Adam had come across so far as a steady, reasonable, take-charge, well-connected guy.

"We're going to be in the air for a while. Would you two be more comfortable in the front cabin? You can stretch out, we have blankets…"

"That would be most welcome," Claire said.

Myles appeared with a cashmere throw and escorted the couple to the first set of lounges facing each other. The engine noise prevented Adam from hearing what they were saying, but Claire smiled broadly at something Myles said.

The Johansens slept for a few hours and freshened up in the bathroom before returning to their seats. They'd had very little time to talk about getting their stories to match. The broad outlines were that the first stone came from a cave in Afghanistan. This was fact. The information on the first stone made the Johansens feel they had to locate the second one. The second stone led to the third, and then Mossad showed up in their hotel room. It was their unusual travel patterns that had alerted Mossad, who initially had seemed uninterested in the stones. The Johansens tried to convince Mossad that they unearthed a great deal of objects, a very small percentage of which turned out to be valuable.

Of course, the couple realized they had attracted the attention of the authorities. Their work took them to very unstable regions of the globe. The materials they studied were sometimes controversial for political or religious reasons. It was part of the job to have government officials questioning their activities, and even their motives. They were not going to Syria for anything other than archaeological reasons.

They'd had their beverages of choice and a nap, and Adam decided he had waited long enough. Trying not to appear too eager, intrusive, presumptuous, or aggressive, Adam rose from his seat to approach the Johansens. As he did, Myles departed for the rear of the plane. Everyone had had time to collect their thoughts and Adam wants to make a proper introduction.

"Hello, my name is Adam Hunter and I'm on assignment with the CIA," as he briefly flashed his employee ID while trying to exhibit his authority. He thought he saw Claire stiffen when he mentioned the CIA, so he decided not to ask any questions just yet. There is an adage that states when someone in authority asks a question, they already know the answer. They are asking you the question to see if you will lie to them. Adam didn't beat around the bush.

"Seems you guys have been on quite a scavenger hunt lately," he said. Adam paused for effect. Before letting them answer or saying anything else, Adam walked back over to his lounge and collected the three stones he had gathered in the Johansens' hotel room at the Savoy. He had tucked them into his pack and had put the pack in the overhead bin. The stones were each individually shaped like a quarter pie. When all four stones could be put together, they would form a complete circle of at least twelve inches in diameter.

He walked back over to Peter and Claire, stones in hand and put them on the table in the center of the cabin. He took a minute to place the stones in an orderly fashion 'one of four,' the green stone was on the top left. 'Two of four,' the blue stone was on the top right, and 'four of four," the new orange stone was on the bottom right. There was a missing stone in the obvious circular pattern, but even so, it was beautiful. Peter and Claire were amused by Adam's behavior. He was looking closely at the stones, running his fingers over them carefully. Their glimmers seemed to mesmerize him.

When Adam finished attending to the stones, he looked over at Peter and Claire. "So tell me what you know about these rocks," he said. Peter and Claire looked at each other. Claire nodded to Peter as if to give him permission to tell Adam what they knew. They wouldn't be regurgitating any of the stories they told to Mossad last night. Peter begins,

“You may have already heard about this. We are assuming you have,” Peter began. “A couple of months ago, while we were on an embedded archeology dig in Afghanistan, we found something called a vimana in a remote cave. An ancient Hindu text, thousands of years old, mentions this flying vehicle. Well, we found one, a vimana fully constructed and concealed from civilization for a few millennia. We tried to approach the object and strangely, it repelled us from touching it,” Peter said.

Yes, I’ve heard this part of the story,” Adam said evenly.

“However, that wasn’t all we found. The blue stone, called ‘two of four’ was sitting just behind the vimana and seemed to draw us over to it. When we picked it up, we didn’t want to let it go,” Peter explained.

“I can imagine. It’s remarkable,” Adam told the couple.

“We apologize, we know we didn’t follow the typical protocol for an archaeological dig of this type, but we’ve never been lucky enough to find something quite like this. We did report the vimana to our dig site manager and used the diversion of everybody on the expedition rushing to the cave to get back home with the stone, where we could do a little more investigation on it and to see if what we found was worth anything,” Peter said.

“Well, that’s understandable. Archaeologists don’t earn that much,” Adam responded. If Peter was offended by Adam’s comment, he didn’t show it.

“Mr. Hunter, we are still relatively early in our careers and haven’t had that moment where we could create our own identity. You know, something we could be known for. As an archaeologist, you want to find something that no one has ever seen or had known ever existed. Fortunately, finding the vimana gave us a little notoriety and made it easier to gain acceptance into another project team. Something about our stone seemed to tell us we were on to something even bigger. As you can see, there are some engravings directly on the front of each stone. Claire and I determined that those engravings were coordinates,” Peter said.

“Did you know such a thing existed?” Adam asked.

“We had no idea. We are aware of major archaeological finds, but nothing like this has ever appeared at a dig, or anywhere else. Once we realized we were looking at longs and lats, we didn’t have the power within us to resist our urges and follow the breadcrumbs. With the little bit of the status we gained from Afghanistan, we followed the trail over to the United States where we were able to locate the second stone. It had pointed us to New Mexico, which is where we found the green stone,” he said.

Adam was tempted to mention the incident in Roswell in 1947, but decided to keep quiet.

"The coordinates for this New Mexico location were listed as a second set of directions inscribed on the blue stone. The stone's inscriptions appear to point to themselves in descending order as the green stone announced that it was 'one of four.'"

Peter stopped, waiting for Adam to ask a question or say something. He decided to let Peter talk.

"We were hooked and decided to go for broke. Which is exactly what we did. We then did the same thing as before, this time on our own, and followed the direction the green stone had given us. The green stone had pointed us to Damascus, but we didn't want to stay in Syria overnight, so we decided to stay in Israel. We had just acquired the orange stone when the men from Mossad overtook us at our hotel. We haven't even had a chance to look at the inscriptions on the orange stone. We are just chasing a dream, Mr. Hunter. This kind of thing happens once in a lifetime, simple as that. We still don't really know where this search will end, but we wanted to see it through. I hope you won't blame us for that," he said sadly.

So, that was their story. Both he and Claire were ready for the other shoe to drop. Would they find out what they had gotten themselves into? Adam studied the couple and seemed to accept the story.

Adam's tone and cadence were not at all befitting the words he spoke. "Peter and Claire, you need to know that you are in the middle of uncovering the answer to one of the greatest mysteries on this planet," he said flatly. The Johansens moved to the edges of their seats. Adam continues,

"Am I correct that you don't have children?" he asked.

"Do we have-, what did you just say about the mystery? No, we don't have children," Peter said in confusion. With that, Adam makes what is almost a rhetorical question.

"It also looks like you can easily spend weeks, if not months at a time away from home. You have a very light footprint," Adam observed. "Have you always been interested in archaeology?" he asked.

Now Peter was starting to feel a little agitated. "Mr. Hunter, I'm sorry to interrupt, would you mind just getting to it? What are you trying to tell us?" he asked, glancing at a frowning Claire.

"What I am trying to tell you, Mr. Johansen, is that we are not...alone...in the universe," Adam paused, waiting to see how the couple reacted. Maybe they would argue, perhaps referencing their faith. But they sat quietly, waiting to hear more.

"I am involved in a top-secret project away from my organization and need to let you know that you are knee deep in a discovery that is going to change the world. Whether you like it or not, whether you know it or not, when you took the first stone out of that cave without reporting it to anyone, you passed the point of no return," he told the couple.

Claire became anxious. "What does that mean, the point of no return?"

"It means, you can't go home. Not for a while at least. Mossad no doubt is now trying to understand the stones' purpose and what it all means," he explained.

"But we left Israel. They can't do anything now," Peter said, alarmed.

"Just because I was able to convince them to let you go, doesn't mean they're finished with you. You can bet there are already operatives on the way to your place to lie in wait for you to get home," he told them calmly.

"This isn't over, then. Is that what you're saying?" Claire asked.

"It's just beginning. Information like this also tends to find and attract other undesirables as well, so caution is necessary from now on. Everything I say and do must be considered with the utmost secrecy." Adam waited for the Johansens to collect themselves and acknowledge what he had told them.

"Mr. Hunter, nothing happened. We have traveled across the world with these stones, what effect have they had on…anything?" Peter was bewildered.

"There is a great deal I cannot tell you at this point. Even so, it is impossible to understate the gravity of the situation. Do you understand?" Adam asked.

The couple nodded. It was too good to be true, hoping they could just hop on a plane and hope everyone would forget about them, and the stones.

"Ok. We've got a team assembled and a safe place for you to hide until we can get this all sorted out." Peter leaned over and took Claire's hand. "In the meantime, I think we still have a job for you to do," Adam said.

"We're going to work? Or hide? Which is it?" Peter asked.

Adam glanced at the stones before looking back at the Johansens. He readied the showstopper. "In 1947, an alien craft crash landed on Earth. There were apparently no survivors or even more likely, no one that we would consider a life form on the ship. There was, however, an intelligence. Such an intelligence, that the technological advances of the twentieth century, of which it was a part, dwarfed the advancements of humans in the previous ten thousand years of our known existence. In the absolute highest level of secrecy, those advancements are continuing today. The Deep State of the United States Government took possession of this intelligence shortly after the crash and is responsible, in the abstract, for coordinating my very presence here," he told the couple, who sat speechless. Adam let that sink in for a minute.

"The stones you have helped us find so far are the pin markers to the exact locations where we are being directed to invade the Earth's magnetic core for a project that will turn almost all of the Interstates and Highways on the entire Earth into greenspaces, agricultural zones, and new community living areas. This project will eliminate, almost entirely, CO2 emissions and begin to heal the ozone layer," he explained.

"I have no idea or indication of how the stones got there. My only assumption is that the who or the what that built that machine you found in the cave have been here before and left them here for some purpose that only they know about," he said.

"Those machines are called vimanas," Peter reminded him. "Thousands of years ago, people drew what they saw in the sky. Are you claiming to know what they are capable of?" Peter asked.

"No, there is much that I am hoping we can learn together, because, to make things more interesting, the intelligence that we captured has been programmed such that he is not able to share certain information. Apparently, telling us how the stones got here and what vimanas do specifically is one of those unsharable things," Adam said.

"I knew something was happening in that cave," Peter said.

"It's entirely possible that there was. Right now, I don't need the answer to that question, but I do have a gut feeling that at some point, we will learn the answer. So, Peter and Claire, this is bigger than all of us. Can I count on you to join us?" Adam asked.

The Johansens looked at each other, small smiles exchanged between them. They nodded at Adam.

"Ok, is there anything that would prevent you from coming to work for me right now?" he asked them.

Claire looked at Peter. "What about the flat and the car?"

Adam responded before Peter could answer. "We can handle that. We'll work with you to get them sold and get your money transferred into a new 'account' we can set up for you. I have a buyer in mind already and I think we can get a deal done quickly. Is there anything out there that I need to know about?" Adam asked.

Peter and Claire thought for a minute. Peter raised his finger as if asking for permission to speak.

"We didn't get the chance to plug in the coordinates on the orange stone. We will kind of need to know, where do we look for the fourth stone?" Peter asked.

"Very good question. That's probably going to be extremely important," Adam acknowledged. "Let's try to find out." He moved to the table where the stones rested. Peter and Claire followed.

Adam held up the orange stone. Just like the other two stones that had been found by the Johansen's, the stone just found in Damascus pinpointed the exact location for where an Axiom Control Rod would be located there and it also provided to the coordinates for where the fourth and final stone could be found:

LAT 33.51041423735162 LONG 36.2783365894329
FOUR of FOUR
LAT 33.232544427453 LONG 129.5615359103286

Adam fished around in his pants pocket while reaching for his phone. He made sure he was connected to the onboard Wi-Fi and then plugged the second set of coordinates into a location finder app. Agonizing seconds ticked by. Adam finally looked up, incredulous. "Maejima Island?" he asked. There was a lasting pause. "Nagasaki, Japan," he put his phone down on the table and looked out the window for a moment. He checked his phone a second time. "It's on the 33rd parallel," he said.

Peter and Claire exchanged a look.

"Holy crap, this is going to be interesting. At least now we know where we have to go and what we have to do. That's half the battle, but the other half of the battle is more like a war. As long as we don't run into any of those freaky 33rd Parallel Bermuda Triangle myths, we can find a way to get it done," Adam resolved.

"That is excellent news," Claire said.

"Yes, well, the bad news is, this has been one helluva long day," Adam said. He couldn't help yawning. He'd already shared ultra-super sensitive information with them, maybe they could enjoy a certain level of informality. "Let's see if we can get some rest. We have a long flight ahead," he told the couple.

"We do? Where are we going?" Peter asked. They were so glad to be alive, they hardly cared where the jet took them.

"Oh, of course you're curious. We are headed to the Washington D.C. area. When we land, the first order of business is to come up with a plan to find that fourth stone. But I'm happy to say, we are a lot further along than when we started this day."

"We're much farther from Israel than I thought we'd be," Claire said. Apparently, she had a talent for understatement.

"I've already got an idea. Since we are going to be working together, we're going to need to get to know each other a lot better," he said.

“Sounds lovely,” Claire said. Adam wondered if that was also an understatement, or sarcasm.

“Sorry we had to meet under these circumstances, but I’m glad fate threw us together. So, ready or not, welcome to Operation Green Lantern,” Adam said, trying to relax the tension a bit. “Get it? GREEN, as in help the world go green, and LANTERN, as in give the world light and hope. I thought it was a pretty catchy name,” he explained proudly.

“Nonetheless, that’s what you’re in, like it or not. All of our lives have been affected in ways we can only begin to imagine.” He turned to go back to his lounge. “I’ll ask to get the cabin lights dimmed and we’ll talk again once we get closer to Washington.”

Peter and Claire, tired as they were, felt very gratified with the seemingly big role they’d played so far. They had always wanted to do something important, throw caution to the wind, and they felt like they had become part of something bigger than themselves.

Nothing was holding them back and they had already been a part of something historic and they knew it. As Peter and Claire buckled up for the journey, Peter mouthed “I love you,” to his wife. Claire spoke the words aloud. “I love you, too. We’re safe.”

Chapter 27 - Separate Ways

He had only spent a few nights there, but the beach house at Loretta Landing Lane was beginning to feel like home to Adam. It felt private and safe. He was surrounded by people he knew and Myles always seemed to anticipate what he would need before he knew he needed it.

Adam needed the Johansen's to feel comfortable after their ordeal in Israel and sudden, life-changing decision to abandon their careers and join a transportation revolution. Myles didn't miss a step. He assured them that Nespresso could make tea for Claire. Peter loved the beach house's minimalist furniture and said it was very Scandinavian. Dr. Alex had welcomed the couple and talked with them about their travels the evening they arrived.

Except for the, well, international incident was the only way to accurately describe it, so many parts of the project seemed to just fall together. Funding was coming through, there were no childish 'personality conflicts' or territorial disputes among team members. Maybe things were just easier in the private sector. Maybe people were willing to put differences aside when so much was at stake.

Adam sat on the beach as the sun rose, trying to wrap his brain around the enormity of their endeavor. It had seemed like an impossible dream when Adam decided to chase it on that gray Christmas morning little more than a month ago. Maybe it would never seem real. Small children didn't marvel at the internet, they just used it. It might be the same with flying cars. The second generation to fly would think it enjoyable but not miraculous.

How lucky he was to be involved in the very beginning of the idea, to be part of it when it was just a theory, a set of possibilities. As the sun rose through the clouds, Adam realized their initial ease did not promise ultimate success. He imagined the beginning of the voyage that met its untimely end in Roswell. Learning the truth about that ill-fated mission had upended everything for him. Sometimes Adam suspected the 1947 crash was the tip of the iceberg. Our only information about the past was what survived.

Luckily, the writings from thousands of years ago gave Adam some idea of how long people had tried to build flying machines. He would have liked to ask the people who built the vimana what happened, but he was too late.

There were so many questions surrounding those aerial entities in the Ramayana. Did they really fly? Why was there a vimana in a cave? Why did it repel people? Did this mean we were not meant to know how vimanas worked?

He would ask the Johansens about it as soon as they had recovered from their encounter with Mossad. In Adam's mind, they were still a little fragile and he was not going to hold them to their commitment to the project just yet. People in their situation might have agreed to a lot of things that would later strike them as absurd. Flying cars sounded absurd until L.U.C. and Dr. Alex explained that they were logically possible. A shift in perspective could change everything.

Deep in his thoughts, he didn't hear Myles making his way down the beach until he was a few yards away. "Sir, the Johansens are eating breakfast. They are asking about your availability," he said as the wind whipped his dark hair in every direction.

"Already? Great!" He stood and wiped the sand off his sweatpants.

Myles handed Adam his phone. "You've had several messages in the past hour. I suspect they are from Greg. Earlier he informed me that he and Grace would be arriving soon. They are eager to have an update from you and meet the Johansens. They are especially curious about the stone hunt," he said.

"Thanks, Myles. I'll head inside and see how they're doing" Adam told him as he watched Myles gather the larger pieces of driftwood that littered the pristine beach.

The rest of the team was already enjoying hot beverages and biscotti when Adam found them at the conference table off the kitchen. Dr. Alex sat at one end of the table, turning the stones over carefully in his hand.

"...so this Mossad guy asked me what the capital of Denmark was, and I'm thinking, don't I look Scandinavian enough for you?" Peter asked and the table erupted in laughter. When Greg saw Adam, he stood and the group followed suit.

"I can't believe all that happened to these two, what a wild adventure!" Greg said as he went to shake Adam's hand.

"Incredible story, isn't it?" Adam asked as he greeted the team members, old and new. "Feeling more like yourselves, I take it?" he asked the Johansens.

"Less terrified, now I'm just kind of in disbelief that we got through it...with your help, of course," Peter said.

"Yes, again, thank you so very much for coming to get us. Honestly, if we'd known the risks," she glanced at her husband, "I think we would have been much more cautious," Claire said.

"In a funny way, it's good that you two were willing to go to the ends of the earth like that, because now, you get to 'dig' on a whole new level with us," Grace said.

"Peter was just telling me that they want to start tying up loose ends in England," Greg said.

"Of course. That could take a while, though," Adam said. He remembered explaining what he could about the project to his own family and how mystified they were. "And visas for here can take a while. So can the ones we'll need for Japan. I'll contact Jane Shipman. Good to have someone at the CIA who can help us with that."

"Oh, right, the CIA," Peter said. "I really liked "'Central Intelligence.'"

"They're going to make a movie about what happened to you, my friend. Seriously, how many guys were pointing guns at you?" Greg asked.

Claire shuddered and Peter shook his head at the memory. "Honestly, I don't know. You can't count when you are that terrified. I'd never had a gun pointed at me before," he told the group.

"So did you tell them to take the stones and let you live?" Grace asked.

"That's what is so strange about it. They were convinced we were spies, or terrorists. They weren't nearly as interested in the stones as they were in finding out what we were hiding," Claire said.

"And you're just a couple of archaeologists, looking for interesting stuff?" Greg asked rhetorically.

"Do I look like Al-Qaeda?" Claire responded.

The group laughed again, and this time Adam felt his phone buzz. It was Kumar.

"Keep going, I'll be back before you get to the part where I swoop in," he told Claire. "Got to take this outside," he said as he opened the French door to the chilly air and stepped onto the patio.

He could hear the laughter as it continued inside. After a few minutes on the phone with Ben, he was fairly cold and somewhat in disbelief. Closing the door behind him after returning to the group, he realized the incredulity was written on his face.

"What's the news?" Greg asked.

"I don't know if anything could surprise me anymore," Adam said as he put his phone away. "Your flat and car have both been sold, folks. You will not be returning to Oxford in the near future. There are probably people you will want to contact and let them know you won't be around for a while," he said.

"I contacted some friends from the museum, and now I guess I can tell our neighbor to forward our mail. Apart from that, there is little else to do," Claire told Adam.

"We've talked about this, Claire and I. We are all in. What do you need us to do?" Peter asked.

Adam took a deep breath and exhaled. "You sit, I'll pour," Greg said as he held up the pot of coffee. When he filled Adam's cup, Adam took a seat at the table. Well, they were all here, he thought. He still wasn't used to the breakneck pace of this project, but Kumar wasn't going to give him time to ease into it, he realized.

"Mr. Kumar wanted to let me, and all of you, know that his organization has actively engaged both the Afghani and Syrian authorities about acquiring the property surrounding the pin locations identified on the stones. Both of these endeavors will come with considerable political red tape and be extremely costly. However, Ben said that he believes he was able to convince each country about the benefits they will incur from such a commerce and energy deal. S.E.T.I. Industries already has quite a few contacts in both regions from previous dealings, which will help," Adam told them.

"Oh, great. We were just there," Peter deadpanned.

"They will welcome you back, I'm sure," Greg joked.

"That's not all. L.U.C. collected the fourth pin location from the orange stone while you were dozing on the flight back from Tel Aviv and delivered that information to Ben. He has decided to personally go to Japan to negotiate this final deal. Maejima Island off Nagasaki is a perfect setting for the fourth Axiom location. Our pin location is surrounded by water on three sides and will provide adequate privacy, safety, and protection," Adam stated.

"That said, Japan and its real estate is quite a different matter. Money isn't the only factor. While S.E.T.I has been operating over in Japan for years, it is possible that we may only be able to work out a lease for the targeted property. A one-hundred-year lease. One in which the land would revert back to the Japanese government at the end of the term. Ben assured me that wouldn't be a problem or make a difference. By then, the world would be much different and there would be no getting the *horse back in the barn* at that point," he told his team.

"So, as nice as it's been shooting the breeze with you, it looks like we are going to go our separate ways," Adam said.

"We're listening," Grace said.

"I am planning to go to Roswell and be hands-on in the construction of Axiom One. Not only will this Axiom be the sovereign center to drive the current through the virtual highway transportation system, it will also be the initial manufacturing center for all the vehicles in the system. Later, this technology will be outsourced, and entrepreneurs can build the vehicles necessary to keep up with global demand," he told the group.

"Global demand?" Greg asked. "So our clientele is..."

“Everyone on the planet who can travel,” Grace said excitedly. “You thought the DMV was a busy place.”

“Oh, Axiom One will be busy,” Adam said. “Beyond driving the magnetic current propulsion system, Axiom one will also have a large Vites skyport, transportation hub, and maintenance center in order to manage the traffic flow,” he told the group. It was going to be a logistical challenge, to be sure.

“In the future, Vites skyports will become destinations with restaurants, lodging, attractions, shopping, and other entertainment. Once we go public, Axioms will become small, attractive cities in their own right. People will be fascinated to see how it all works,” Adam finished.

“As will I,” Claire said, glancing around the table.

“Well, first up for you two is a trip to Japan. It won’t hold anything up for a while, but we need you to find the fourth stone. Because these stones are recursive, we’ve got all four pin locations with the three stones. However, when all four stones are put together, L.U.C. describes their unification as an actuator for the system. The component that will enable the system to drive more current power through the system has a special conduction when a unified cornerstone is in place,” he said. The Johansens are smiling excitedly at one another.

At the far end of the table, Dr. Alex was studying the stones and Adam suspected, not paying attention to the announcements. “And about the composition of those stones of yours, Dr. Alex,” Adam said as the retired professor suddenly looked up. “What makes the stones unique is that they are composed of elements that are extremely rare,” he said as a stunned silence fell over the table. “If TSA Agents or Mossad had taken their inquiries too much further; the project could have gotten a lot more complicated,” Adam said.

“Bit of an understatement, Mr. Hunter,” Claire observed.

“Ok, this is something we can’t exactly order online, then,” Greg said. “What are we going to use as a replacement?”

“In one of his dissertations, L.U.C. told me about the chemical composition of the stones. They are most like the opal stone here on Earth. Chemically speaking, opal is a form of hydrated silica, with the chemical formula $SiO_2 \cdot nH_2O$. Unlike most gemstones, opal isn’t crystalline. The internal structure of precious opal causes it to diffract light, resulting in play-of-color. Depending on the conditions in which it formed, opal may be transparent, translucent, or opaque, and the background color may be white, black, or nearly any color of the visual spectrum,” Adam explained.

“We’ve seen some incredible opals come out of the ground in Australia,” Peter volunteered. “A colleague of ours was looking for fossils in the Outback, and she said opals sort of are fossils.”

“What do you mean?” Grace asked.

“What she told me was that the opal is formed from a solution of silicon dioxide and water. As water runs down through the earth, it picks up silica from sandstone. Then, it carries this silica-rich solution into cracks and voids, caused by natural faults or decomposing fossils,” he told her.

After hearing this, Adam was beginning to form a hypothesis. First, there were surely other planets with water out there. Good old fashioned H20. And the other part of his conclusion, and probably the most stunning part, is that opals were formed by the fossils of decaying animals. So that means, these stones were likely formed by decaying animals too, but just not animals found here on Earth…

While trying to process what he’d just realized, Dr Alex spoke. “I’ll be going to Nagasaki with Peter and Claire to see if I can assist them in the dig to find the fourth stone. We’ve got some time before I’m needed for certain aspects of the project and like Adam, I’ll need to float between Axiom locations from time to time to ensure everything is on track with the nerve center of each site,” the senior team member did not ask for permission. No matter, Peter and Claire welcomed the help and Adam approved of the move.

He ran his hand through his hair and thought out loud. “I need to make sure Ella and Juan have these critical dates, and Ella is going to have to do a lot of the heavy lifting here and get the resources part of this undertaking organized,” he said.

Glancing up, Adam noticed Myles had been standing in the kitchen area for most of this discussion after coming in from the beach. He had been listening intently to every word.

Adam realized he had covered as much as he could at that moment and folded his hands on the huge table. “So, that’s it. Greg and Grace, I’ll reach out if I need anything. I plan to be gone within a couple of days, heading for New Mexico. Peter and Claire, you can hang out here until the two of you and Dr. Alex are cleared for Japan. Hopefully, that will go quickly. You’re in good hands with Myles. Godspeed.”

Chapter 28 - Seeking Alpha

The Gulfstream glided over the snow-dusted Pecos River Valley and began its descent to Artesia Municipal Airport. It was Groundhog's Day, and Adam was glad Punxsutawney Phil had seen his shadow that morning. Wintertime meant fewer people out and about, thus more privacy for Axiom building.

He'd spent the last week and a half at the beach house, along with the rest of the team. There were always a few team members working at any time of the day or night, but they generally made it a point to have dinner together. It was only a matter of days before it seemed like the Johansens had been with them since the beginning. Grace and Greg were quick to make them feel like the valued team members they were.

The group did their best to hammer out every possible detail of the foreseeable future of their project, while Dr. Alex and the Johansens waited for word on their visas. It was a slow process, but due to Jane Shipman's talent for keeping matters confidential, also a very well-guarded one.

A Gulfstream identical in appearance to "Adam's Gulfstream" as he now liked to call it, had left St. Mary's a few days before Adam left for New Mexico. Adam had taken Peter, Claire, and Dr. Alex to see them off for their long journey and adventure in Japan.

At first glance, he thought the jet was his, but then he caught the small difference in the N-Number. The serial number on the flight that left for Japan was N-749GF. Adam's Gulfstream was N749GE. Adam wondered how many planes Ben had. Probably several, Adam realized. Then it occurred to him that building Axiom One meant the beginning of the closing of the gap between the 1% and the rest of us. The VITES would render the Gulfstream obsolete. Everyone would travel effortlessly. That was a comforting and motivating thought.

First, however, he needed to find Juan and get started on the first Trentafactory that would produce the flying cars. Somewhere, on this massive land acquisition of Kumar's, Juan was planning the construction of Axiom One. He and Juan had gotten a pretty clear understanding of each other and about the scope of the project when they broke their meeting in Monterrey. Ella Flores had sung his praises, but Adam was reserving judgment. He wanted to see how effective Juan was when it came time to turn plans into reality.

His own reality was rather sobering, Adam thought as the jet made its way to the end of the tarmac. He was thinking about the kids and Julie. He and Facetime were going to become closer than ever before, he realized. He didn't tell his family much, partly because there was so much he didn't know. What he was sure of was Julie helping him stay connected with the kids and attend all the important teenage events, even if it was through the eye of a pocket camera.

He wasn't the first person to watch his children grow up while working on insanely ambitious, mammoth projects. Some of these undertakings surely had as many unknowns as his did. At Stanford, he had watched footage of President Kennedy giving his famous 'we choose to go to the moon' speech in 1962. How much did people know about space travel then? Probably more than he and his neoteric untried team knew about their chosen mission. How exactly were they going to tap into the Earth's magnetic surface currents, much less build cars that would fly within them?

They weren't sure how they would do it, much less how long it would take. When he thought about it, the Moon landing took seven years. Was that right on schedule for Kennedy? Adam decided not to dwell on it right now and just do the next thing. It would be done when it was done. His flight had come to an end, and he noticed a dark gray Hummer waiting for him in front of the last hangar on Airport Road.

Not ten minutes later, as the Hummer left the airport grounds and headed north up 285 towards Roswell, Adam caught a glimpse of the Gulfstream. It was now back in the air, flying north, presumably back to its home in Denver.

Some ten miles south of Roswell, the Hummer cut to the west on Sagebrush Valley Road, also known as Highway 13. Adam thought the name was appropriate, but not very specific. There were few signs of civilization, save for the road. There was enough room to build a major metropolis in this wilderness, and no one would know.

After several miles of following their progress into the vastness of the desert on his iPhone's Apple Maps, the Hummer slowed and came to a stop. Adam looked up, expecting to see something more. Instead, he saw only a newly paved road that disappeared mysteriously into the distance. It was protected by a small gate and an even smaller, unassuming guard shack. The Hummer took a right hand turn into the gated drive, and Adam watched the driver stare intently into his own reflection of a two-way glass window. He realized beyond exchanging hello's, he hadn't spoken to the driver at all. Without further interaction from the shack, the gate lifts.

They were officially in no man's land as far as Apple Maps could determine. Adam estimated they had driven about three miles west. He noticed rotating security cameras along the road.

Then the real security perimeter of Axiom One materialized. It was as if a 'Keep Out' sign hung in the air above the entire area, making it an immersive experience altogether. Everything felt secretive, hidden and monumentally significant. There was razor wire on the ground on both sides of the high fence with guard towers stationed every two hundred and fifty yards. Adam saw NO TRESPASSING signs on top of the DANGER – HIGH VOLTAGE signs weaved every one hundred feet or so into the privacy screened fence line. It made sense. The level of security here to keep unwanted scrutiny out was commensurate with the level of change that was supposed to come from within.

Adam thought about UFO's. They were a part of popular culture, and had been for generations. Whether UFO's and their occupants were loved or feared, Hollywood began to crank out a whole genre of films about them with perfect special effects. People's imaginations of all the possibilities were stoked by the likes of George Lucas's "Star Wars" and Steven Spielberg's "E.T." All of it, presumed by almost everyone, to be fable and fantasy.

But fantasies can be elaborate productions, involving artistry and artifice. We were instructed not to peer too closely at the man behind the curtain. Wasn't there always someone pulling the strings? And what about the purse strings? In his case, Adam thought, it was Ben Kumar. Is everything, every time, in all of human history, in every human civilization, about greed, money, and power? It is disappointing to think this is so, but Adam couldn't think of another explanation. "Those that have power, keep the power, and keep all the lemmings in the dark – every time – every single time."

People had known about the technology, or at least that people possessed something that could advance our struggle against disease and damage to the environment. Now he was in on the secret, and it was only a matter of time before he would share it with the world. It was strange to stand in this remote area, knowing that he was entrusted with knowledge that would surely change the world.

Unless it was an absolute disaster. Aerospace engineers were nothing if not realists, and Adam had a lot of questions about poking holes in the earth's liquid, nine-thousand-degree core. What would they do if the nickel floated to the surface? What if the cars crashed? Lives could be lost and it would be Adam's fault. It carried the potential to heal the planet, but there were dangers, too.

Adam was certain those dangers existed. He was also certain that the entities that crashed in New Mexico had something to teach us. His third and final certainty was these entities had chosen him to share the knowledge they brought over seventy years ago. With those three things in mind, Adam resolved to do everything in his power to make the flying cars a reality. If successful, he imagined architecture of the Italian Renaissance looking like a popsicle stand next to the Virtual Global Highway Transportation System.

With signs instructing unauthorized vehicles to leave, a large red stripe across the drive well before the gate with the word DANGER painted into it was the most obvious place for a visitor that thought they should be there to stop. After just a few seconds waiting at the gate, two armed men appeared from behind a retaining wall and approached the Hummer. As the men approached, the driver lowered his window.

"Mr. Hunter is in the back. He is here to begin his residency," he told the guards. The men peered into the vehicle at Adam and backed away from the car as the gate slowly opened.

Clearly, Mr. Ben Kumar considered this opportunity one of the utmost urgency. Adam knew the costs for him and his organization would be obscene, but the ability to move this quickly was mind boggling. The planning was likely in the works for years. Time was money, but what Adam was seeing was ridiculous. A queue of delivery vehicles, many with S.E.T.I. Industries logos, had begun forming a line designated for them to the left of the entrance in a material staging area. As the Hummer crested the next hill, Adam got his first view of the valley.

The view of the unfinished Axiom One, the Alpha skyport, and the Vites Square, were already visible. The Vites Square would contain the Commerce District, where people would go for shopping and entertainment. It was a city unto itself.

A temporary sign posted at the main entrance traffic circle provided directions to the various districts. The first right would lead to the Energy District, the second right led to Commerce District, and the third right out of the large circle went to Axiom's Residential District. Delivery and construction vehicles serviced each district from the outer loop just inside the Axiom's perimeter.

Accommodations within the Residential District, when completed for all of the city's impending full-time residents, would have the best views of the growing city. Adam thought them to be among the most well-appointed living spaces on the planet. For now, a luxurious sea of glamping tents, too numerous to count, lined the far side of the rise in the valley. Before long, it would boast an impressive Residential District. Reminiscent of old textile mill villages in the American South, self-sufficient communities would flourish around manufacturing plants. Life around the Axiom would be different, but also the same. Until the world was let in on the secret, only the select would ever be able to pass through its gates.

He was so busy visualizing the possibilities of the Residential District, Adam did not immediately realize there were already thousands of workers on site. And in a few weeks' time, they had started to perform an extreme makeover of the rugged New Mexico topography.

Adam noticed the driver of the Hummer had come to a complete stop on the shoulder of the main traffic circle. He hadn't spoken but was waiting for Adam to finish taking everything in and tell him where to go.

"Juan....Juan Fernandez, please," Adam said.

"Mr. Fernandez is currently in the Energy District and is waiting for you. I'll take you there. Once you've had a chance to talk with him, you'll need to report pretty quickly to the temporary Healthcare Center located in the Commerce District," the driver informed Adam.

"Why would I need healthcare?" Adam asked.

L.U.C.'s voice came through the vehicle's speakers. "Everyone on premises is required to onboard a biochip device under the skin. Don't worry, you can't even feel it when it goes in. It will serve as a brainwave translation device and genetic identifier while you are on site. The chip allows you to communicate seamlessly with anyone on property. It also allows you to move around Axiom's districts more freely, and lets you link your financial resources so that you can make purchases that aren't a part of your package level," he explained.

"It sounds like a credit card under my skin," Adam said.

The driver laughed. "The Axiom's automated security systems have already contacted me about your biogenetic reading from here in the Hummer. It's wondering why you haven't responded. I let the system know that Mr. Kumar said that it would be okay for you to enter the premises without the chip until you acclimated" he said with a tinge of envy in his voice. "Oh yeah, and you also have access to our helpful computer system we call Luke. He can answer a bunch of questions for you when you have them."

"You know, I think I've heard of him," he told the driver as he walked toward the Hummer.

The driver opened the door for Adam. "I know we are going to build a few more of these power plants at other locations, too. You'll only have to go through chip insertion once as your chip will be integrated throughout our secure network and you will have access to the whole Axiom system once all the other cities are linked."

The Hummer moved through the traffic circle and took the first right, heading toward the Energy Center and Juan. After clearing a second checkpoint, Adam had his first glimpse of the vast area of Axiom One's Energy Center. Adam could see that the location on which the Energy Center would be built was at least two miles long, maybe three. The sheer size and scale were mind-blowing.

As the Hummer continued the utility road on what will eventually be an Earth harnessing monolith, Adam saw an enormous structure in the distance. It sat in the center of where the part of the foundational pad of the Energy Center would eventually be. It looked like the Eiffel Tower,

Adam thought. As they continued up the drive, he realized it was not as big as the Parisian icon. Proximity made a difference in perspective. The Hummer was still roughly a quarter of a mile away and developing an understanding of scale, even from this distance, was not a problem for Adam. There were hundreds of S.E.T.I. eighteen wheelers parked in rows beyond the far end of what was going to be Axiom's Trentafactory. It was almost exactly as he and Juan had planned it, but seeing it unfold before his eyes was staggering.

A drilling structure of a size and scale Adam could barely conceive had been erected at the far end of the facility. However, it was still contained within the survey markers of the proposed structure. As Adam exited the vehicle, he could feel the ground shaking for the first time. An intense, screeching whine pierced the air and made Adam's ears throb. He put his hands over them as he and the driver walked to the tower, reminding the driver to hand Adam a pair of earplugs.

Adam's eyes caught Juan's while he was supervising the action. Juan immediately raised his hand to the drill operator and signaled him to stop. The two men approached each other and exchanged warm greetings. Adam reached out his right hand, but Juan pulled him into an *abrazo*.

"Wow," Adam said. Not eloquent, but perfectly appropriate. Adam was out of his element amid the construction, but he didn't want to show it.

He'd be much more comfortable when they toured the car manufacturing area, but he did his best to learn what he could about the drilling.

"Great job so far, where are we on this?" Adam asked to cover his lack of familiarity with the process. Without missing a beat, Juan tells him that

"We got through the crust on the first day of drilling, and five days ago we were able to go another two hundred miles through the mantle. S.E.T.I. has provided us with a pressure and heat resistant shaft. It follows our drill down and the control rod will be inserted into it once we reach the core.

"So this is the spot?" Adam asked.

"Yes," he said, understanding what Adam meant by *spot*. "Our rod will be inserted into the shaft on the exact coordinates delivered on your stone," Juan told him.

"How long are we digging?" Adam could not fathom how long this process would take.

"Hard to tell, it depends on what we run into. Maybe another month or so?" Juan estimated.

"Ok, then what next?" Could this mean there would be flying cars in two months? The thought made Adam giddy.

"Then, we can begin construction on the Trentafactory. After we secure the hole and lay the foundation, we will build the Alpha Control Center right on top of this spot. We won't begin inserting the control rods until all four of the Axioms are constructed. Even without their interconnectivity, we have to be careful because there will be a tremendous amount of magnetic surface current beginning to flow," Juan explained.

"Yes, L.U.C. has been very specific on the order of things," Adam said.

"As we begin construction on the rest of the Energy Center, think of it a bit like the Large Hadron Collider. Instead of trying to collide and smash atoms, we will first harness and collect the magnetic energy and then whip it into a frenzy through counter rotating proton beams in order to pulse out our streams of magnetic current straight from the earth's core," Juan told him.

"So this first Axiom is the key to the whole thing?" Adam asked.

"Nothing works without it. The Alpha Axiom, Axiom One, will drive the current straight through to the coordinates of the other three Axiom's while building and enhancing the magnetic current stream at each step along the way. Once the current reaches the target level, the Axiom Centers can then begin propelling that current horizontally and vertically along every directed latitude and longitude," Juan said.

It was incredible to think that people could control the forces of nature in this way. "I suppose Dr. Alex and L.U.C. are going to make sure we've got every detail right," Adam hoped this was the case. He had no idea what kind of help he himself could provide in this respect.

"Yes. That's the plan. L.U.C. has never let me down, and Dr. Alex has decades of experience with this," Juan assured him.

"Ok. Well, it looks like we are going here at a phenomenal pace. I'd just say, let's make sure we slow down when we need to and get every step perfect. I'll be reviewing L.U.C.'s project monitoring images on a daily basis from here. That will include the car manufacturing, city infrastructure, and energy, plus whatever else needs attention," Adam said.

"Very good," Juan replied. "I spoke with Dr. Alex earlier today to give him an update on our progress. He told me that Mr. Kumar was having some breakthroughs and thought they would have access to Maejima Island within the month."

"I will be very interested to hear more about that," Adam said excitedly.

"In the meantime, in addition to their planning, he and the Johansens are doing a lot of sightseeing. He mentioned how disappointed he was when they visited the Nagasaki WWII Museum and couldn't understand how humans could do that to one another," Juan said soberly.

"No, Juan, I agree. Maybe the worst of humanity is behind us? Maybe we can be the ones to do something about it and change everything?" It was almost foolishly optimistic, but Adam still had hope to spare.

"I hope so. I choose to believe so," Juan said as he looked across the valley with a sad smile. He turned to Adam.

"Well, I know you've had another long day, with many more to come. Any more questions, Mr. Hunter?"

"Not right now, but I'm sure I will have many soon. Thanks again for getting me up to speed and for walking me back through those steps. As you already know, I'll be spending the majority of my time getting our cars built and tested. Every time I hear how this is supposed to work, it gets clearer and clearer to me how the cars are going to be able to interact with the Axiom's magnetic currents to do their thing," he admitted to Juan.

"It's everything engineers do, but this is like engineering on steroids," Juan told him.

Adam nodded. "Manufacturing, working with composites, and integrating technology is much further into my comfort zone than finding my way to middle earth. I'll leave that in your capable hands, my friend."

"Ok, thanks. You know your way around here yet?" Juan suspected Adam wasn't used to work sites that encompassed counties.

"Not yet, but I have a feeling I'm about to learn more that I want to know. When the chip goes in, it doesn't hurt too bad does it?"

"Only a little," Juan grinned. Adam turned to walk back to the Hummer, and Juan motioned to the drill operator. The ground began to vibrate under his feet as the drilling began again.

Chapter 29 - We Built This City

Miracles big and small. After marveling at the enormity and brilliance of the Trentafactory preparations, Adam was impressed with another, smaller technological breakthrough at the still-temporary Healthcare Center. S.E.T.I. Industries developed a microchip that was an integrated circuit device encased in silicate glass and slightly smaller than a grain of rice. The chip had been inserted into Adam's left hand between his thumb and forefinger, using a needle the size of a vaccine syringe.

The medical staff said the opening would completely heal within just a few days and the body rarely rejected this type of implant. Nothing to worry about. For Adam, the chip meant that any time he was within the gates of Axiom, any Axiom, he had the keys to the kingdom.

On the day the perimeter of Axiom One was established, the intelligence known as L.U.C. was embedded into the Local Area Network, or LAN. L.U.C. was listening, available, and already monitoring and directing construction activity. Axiom's central nervous system and L.U.C. were becoming one. A big relief for Adam was knowing that L.U.C.'s AI engine would be responsible for managing the entire traffic flow on the completed VITES. His algorithms were more than capable of handling every detail flawlessly. His intelligence could process tens of billions of instructions every second. L.U.C. never took a sick day or went on vacation.

Relatively speaking, Adam had the easy part. Get some cars built that could fly. Honestly, it was comforting for Adam to know that this wasn't the first time this type of system had been built. By the very curious nature of L.U.C.'s existence here, surely somehow, some way, "this" was already happening - somewhere. We got this…right?

Adam exited the MMC, or Mobile Medical Clinic, which was temporarily parked on the site where the permanent Healthcare Center would soon be built, he caught a glimpse of the rear end of his ride, the charcoal gray Hummer, turning out of view on what would soon become one of Axiom's busiest blocks in its downtown Commerce District.

He looked down to find all of his bags were stacked neatly near the back tire of the medical truck. Before Adam had a chance to worry about calling an Uber he couldn't call, a snazzy looking EV glided off the street and stopped halfway onto the dirt where presumably a future sidewalk might exist.

A man, staring directly towards Adam, stepped out of a vehicle that looked like a cross between a fancy golf cart and a lunar rover, or LRV.

“Mr. Hunter, your personal Range Rover, sir,” the man said.

Now that’s what I’m talking about, Adam muttered to himself. The man helped him load all of his belongings onto the rear seat of the Rover. Adam liked the thought that he was going to be tooling around in his new futuristic city in this ride. *The fellas at the Columbia Country Club would love to have one of these*, he thought gleefully.

As Adam slid into the vehicle, he was welcomed by a familiar voice.

“Hello Adam, how are you doing?” L.U.C. asked. Confident wasn’t the right word but Adam was impressed with what he was seeing. Hopeful. He was feeling hopeful. Not answering his question directly, Adam’s responds,

“You never cease to amaze, L.U.C.” Adam said, not really answering the question. There was activity up and down the street and a small line was beginning to form at the MMC as other EV’s were beginning to drop off more people at the clinic.

“How many people are here, L.U.C.?” Adam asked.

“There are eight thousand, five hundred, and thirty-two people checked into Axiom One. Architects, engineers, project managers, contractors, and construction workers,” he said.

Eighty-five hundred people, Adam thought. Roughly the number of people one would find in a few large warehouses, or in many small towns across America. His project had already created a kind of small town, he realized with amazement.

“We will have more than twenty thousand residents during construction when we are at full capacity. Many will stay and build lives here when Axiom’s sky port is fully operational. Sky ports will be built around the world following our specifications and each will become unique destinations in their own right, shaped by the traditions and cultures that surround it,” L.U.C. said.

Adam could imagine it: people lounging at the Parisian sky port, or *port du ciel,* with croissants and cafe au lait, bustling Tokyo would welcome visitors with matcha and onigiri bentos. The landscaping, the building materials, uniforms of the onsite employees would all reflect the local culture. But L.U.C. wasn’t finished.

“We are building the Commerce District with the end in mind. Shopping, world class entertainment, and restaurants will be among them. The elegance and simplicity of a limitless travel flow throughout VITES will render present day airports and interstates obsolete. Axioms will form the model for urban life in the future. Visitors will be recognized by all the facets of the city and will each have an individually customized experience based on their own individual preferences. The city is alive. It will know what people want before they do."

When did L.U.C. become such a smooth talker? Adam had always thought of him more as a "just the facts," type of character. Now he seemed keenly aware of consumer attitudes and behavior. The engineer in Adam was focused on the planning stages.

"Okay L.U.C., let's not get ahead of ourselves," Adam said. "Can you take me to where our Vehicle Manufacturing Center will be built, I'd like to take a look at where I am going to be doing a lot of life for the next couple years?"

"You are not serving a prison sentence, Adam. There is a lot more to why you were chosen than I can share with you right now. Let me say that when I show you how we build things, I believe your ingenuity and passion to create will experience a renewed sense of excitement and purpose. It will leave you wanting more. Time will fly," L.U.C. assured him. "And I'm taking you there now."

"I can't wait," Adam told him as they rolled along a series of trailers set up as temporary office spaces.

"The AxMan Zone, or Axiom Manufacturing, is on the far end of the Commerce District, well north of the City Center. It is adjacent to the perimeter where the construction and delivery vehicles can easily service the area."

"Was that your idea?" Adam asked L.U.C.

"It's the blueprint. We make the plan a reality. In the future," L.U.C. continued, "even much of the ground transit within the Axiom will be replaced by the new mode of transportation, which you will soon build." After hearing what L.U.C. has had to say, Adam has a million questions.

"So, who's in charge and when can I meet him?" For Adam, it seemed the most pressing question.

"Now that you've arrived, you are in charge." Adam swallowed hard. "You can be confident and sure in our plan design. I will be with you, guiding you every step of the way," L.U.C. said. To Adam, it was a promise.

The vehicle traveled north out of the City Center along the newly established grid of the Commerce District, some of it paved, some not. As L.U.C. guided the Rover, they approached a large, open, freshly graded area. It was several hundred yards long and wide. People were scattered throughout the property performing various tasks. Surveyors and architects were among the group, along with another collection of S.E.T.I. transport trucks. They were in the process of delivering materials for construction and staging them throughout the job site.

“One of Juan’s many counterparts, Del Rodriguez, is another very capable foreperson on this project. He is assigned to the manufacturing zone and will be your go-to person for all things manufacturing at Axiom Roswell,” Adam was beginning to think L.U.C. was like a genie granting his wishes, one by one. “Del is the man you see just ahead in the clearing, wearing the red collared Ella International polo and white construction hat. When you speak to him, he will get you up to speed on where everything stands on the construction of the vehicle manufacturing facility as well as what he knows about, how should we say, the more futuristic approaches on how we plan to build your vehicles,” L.U.C. said vaguely. “Secure quarters have been prepared so that you and I will have sufficient privacy to interact. I can show you some of the more sensitive aspects of our designs as well as help you keep track of the daily completion status of each Axiom location and the timeline for their convergence,” he told Adam.

“With you around, I’m not sure there’s much left for me to do,” Adam said. “I do think I should step out and introduce myself to Del so we get off on the right foot.”

“Adam, before you go, no one here at Roswell Axiom, or at any of the other Axiom locations knows of my origins. Juan, and the many others who have worked with me on technological advancement over some years have been given the understanding that I am a part of an initiative within a special division of your government. They think this division is dedicated to projects for societal advancement. They believe it is necessary to keep these projects secret in order to avoid the disappointment of failure. Adam, a warning: no one can learn that my existence is anything other than something developed by the government to assist in solving complex problems for new ideas. Should people indicate that they believe otherwise, there will be grave consequences,” L.U.C. said sternly.

“I understand, L.U.C. No need to threaten. I can see the possibilities of destruction and I have no plans to share our little secret. A secret government program, making life better for everyone, got it,” Adam told him. He climbed out of his Rover and approached Del Rodriquez to introduce himself. The two talked while walking all around the construction area. Soon two hours had passed, with a lot of gesturing and pointing in every direction. It was getting late.

Adam was beginning to show some signs of fatigue from the long day, and returned to the Rover. He asked to be taken home for the night, to his new home away from home. He was content and comfortable with what lay ahead and just wanted to get settled in and start formalizing his plan. Something about having so much space around him was going to take getting used to.

As Adam’s Rover made its way to his temporary home, he noticed construction zones in the third district. Crews were finishing their work for the day on permanent housing. The modern designs would be made of steel, concrete, and glass, along with adobe, as a nod to the region's history. These dwellings were designed to give their inhabitants a feeling of total freedom and luxury. Beyond the permanent housing construction area, and stretching as far as the eye could see, was the temporary housing area. There were already thousands of finely appointed well-spaced tents erected with at least another five hundred units going up in a distant phase that was still in sight.

Yet another group of tents stretched along rows of pine trees that bordered a tributary of the Pecos River, Las Piedras. In the spring they planned to grow as much of their own food as they could. It was not truly a New Mexican meal without homegrown red and green chiles on the table. It went without saying that their own cornfields would provide an antidote to homesickness. Juan's crew prided themselves on their adaptability, and that included their ability to bring pieces of home with them wherever they went.

On the front of the temporary housing area stood a large dwelling, set apart from the others in the group. It looked like it was made of at least two or three of these temporary structures and was well guarded by a concrete wall and security gate. Adam nodded to himself in approval. *Not too bad.*

"This will be your new home for a while, at least until more permanent housing is available. There will be one appointed very similarly to this one in the very same spot in each of the four Axioms set aside for you and your work," L.U.C. said.

"Well, after a day of walking around the desert, it's a welcome sight. I guess I will talk to you tomorrow?" Adam asked.

"I'll be waiting for you inside, actually," L.U.C. told him.

As Adam left his vehicle and gathered the first round of his bags, he approached the security gate. He could hear the lock click as the mechanism released, causing the gate to open as it read his implant. Two seconds later, a light flashed inside the dwelling and a dark, graceful man in a white shirt glided down the stone steps to Adam.

"Welcome to your new home, Mr. Hunter. My name is Ansari and I am here to assist you with whatever you may need," he gestured toward the front door, which offered a similar experience as the security gate. Meanwhile, Ansari walked to the back of the Rover and removed Adam's bags.

The activity in the Residential District was picking up due to the evening shift change. Axiom One would be under construction twenty-four hours a day, with workers rotating in twelve-hour shifts. The streets were busy as Axiom One experienced its 6:00 p.m. transition, with workers coming and going. It was as close to chaos as anything Adam had observed since he arrived.

Even so, it was a little like watching a trail of ants encounter an obstacle in their path. The workers adjusted in the shortest time possible and resumed their progress smoothly.

And everything was smooth in Adam's new abode. There was a couch covered in silky taupe fabric, a glass top coffee table on which Ansari placed a tray of coffee as a giant LED tv displayed entertainment options. Exquisite Pueblo rugs covered the floor and a fireplace in the middle of the main room burned piñon logs. The smell was heavenly. He could have fallen asleep watching the fire from the couch, but he noticed an attention getting pulsing banner on a large monitor in the corner of his main living area. As Adam approached the monitor, it scanned his irises.

"Hello, Mr. Hunter. Are you ready to begin?" the monitor asked in a female voice.

"Yes," Adam reluctantly replied. The glow of the fire and the soothing earth toned hues of the decor were doing their job a little too well, he thought drowsily.

"You have four new messages," she said.

"Begin, please."

The messages appeared as text on the monitor while L.U.C.'s voice introduced them.

"Message one from Mr. Ben Kumar, 1:20 p.m." "Let me be the first to congratulate and welcome you to Roswell," Ben said excitedly. Your destiny awaits. I wanted you to know the negotiation for Axiom Three in Nagasaki has been completed today. We agreed upon establishing a one-hundred-year lease on the property with the Japanese government in exchange for turning the property and all its contents over to Japan when the lease ends. These terms were acceptable to me. The job will be done, the world will be a much different place, and I will be gone. The security perimeter will be established within the next seven days and will be ready for your inspection and direction soon."

"Message two from Mr. Ben Kumar, 2.42 p.m." "Mr. Hunter, I meant to inform you earlier, the perimeters and construction efforts are already underway for Axiom Two in Afghanistan and Axiom four in Syria. I've communicated directly with Ella Flores to arrange all the details for getting our resources on site under the contract you consummated with her organization. Like Japan, both governments were very suspicious of our intentions, but they each had a price that could be reached before leases were offered. They are all aware that you oversee our project and have been provided with the means to contact you."

"Message three from Mr. Ben Kumar, 5:07 p.m." "Mr. Hunter, I trust that you have had a productive day and are as excited as I am to finally see this project moving forward. You have no idea how long I've waited for this day. There is no time to lose. Money is no object. You will be given whatever you need and we cannot fail. As L.U.C. has already reminded you, you must keep every detail of this undertaking in absolute secrecy. I know you will."

"Message four from Mr. Greg Buchanan, 5:48 p.m." "Adam, bud, getting late over here on the East Coast and we haven't heard from you – know you are busy. Just wanted to make sure you made it and they were taking good care of you! Grace and I got a message from the Johansens and Dr. Alex letting us know how to get in touch with you. They said they've been with Ben Kumar from S.E.T.I. the whole time and from the sound of it, they think he's a pretty strange dude. Anyway, they said he got a deal done and were able to get on to Maejima Island where Ben gave them carte blanche to finish their research before any construction projects covered up something they might be looking for. You know what. Anyway, let us hear from you when you get a chance. Right here if you need us. Hey Adam, Grace here. Good luck and we hope to see you soon. Know we are thinking of you."

"End of Messages"

There was a click and L.U.C's voice spoke again. He also appeared on the monitor, big as life.

"You and Del Rodriquez discussed vehicle manufacturing here at Axiom One this afternoon," L.U.C. said. This was a little creepy to Adam, because when he was away from the Rover, he felt like it was just a conversation between him and Del. L.U.C is omnipresent inside the perimeter of Axiom One. Adam had the microchip and the persistent app on his phone. There was no way to get away from L.U.C. He had to accept that he voluntarily allowed this foreigner to invade his privacy. Every aspect of it.

"Yes L.U.C., we discussed Axiom manufacturing. Del was trying to explain that we would be using programmed micromachines to build the cars atomically," Adam said.

"We don't need to get into too much detail this evening, however, this is something that I need to show you how to manage. I believe the term you might use for building cars is nanotechnology. Already contained within my essence is the machine programming to build our vehicles. We will collect and contain all the necessary molecules needed for building our car and launch an army of molecular machines almost invisible to the human eye that will build our craft. You will need to make sure all the molecules are available in the 'soup' and then step back," L.U.C. told him.

"Excuse me?" Adam thought he was hearing things.

"There will be no manufacturing assembly lines. The building is so large because we will have hundreds of simultaneous nano build stations which will allow Axiom One to build a vast number of vehicles rapidly when the conditions have been met," he explained.

"Ok, L.U.C., I've had enough for one day," he sighed. All that Adam had room enough to think about was making sure he knew how he would get some caffeine before he started another day. He thought about Julie and the kids and wondered what they were doing. He wondered how soon he might be able to get a couple hours of rest. "Lights dim," he said. The lights of the tent went down. "By the way, L.U.C., is there any way to turn you off?"

L.U.C. smirked. "You are doing well Adam, you have a lot of people counting on you. You can count on me. I'm right here with you till the end. Pleasant dreams."

Chapter 30 - Deja Vu

Outside Axiom One, the days were growing shorter and cooler. When he was in school, they sometimes called it 'football weather.' Perfect for running around outside or having a tailgate party. Those days seemed like memories from another lifetime, when Adam had a very different sense of time and space.

He was more than six months into Green Lantern, and his new normal involved sleeping when there was downtime, and staying awake for as long as necessary, although on occasion he was only awake as long as the caffeine was in his bloodstream.

Space was different, too. Nanotechnology made him feel like a giant when he learned the cars would sprout from molecules. Adam was comfortable and familiar with feet, inches, and sometimes light years. He tried to get used to the idea by thinking it was like growing cars from seeds. Well, it would soon be time to harvest them.

And it was truly gratifying, and grueling. He missed his family and couldn't get back to see them as often as he hoped. He had regular videotelephony conversations with them. Bri was discovering a flair for languages and talked of spending a year abroad. Chris waffled between college and time off to work so he could understand "real people," whatever that meant. Julie was more excited about work than ever. Derek, the Loudoun County Superintendent, was "a real doll" and seemed to like having meetings over dinner.

His new home was awfully quiet at times, as the materials Juan provided for soundproofing the walls were made of something not exactly legal, but enormously effective. Machines, rather than people, generated most of the sounds: dings, beeps and chirps signifying progress or problems at various stages of construction.

The voice Adam heard most often was his own, as he could start the Miele for his espresso or have the curtains drawn with a voice command. There was still menial labor required for some household tasks, and in those instances he would summon Andrew the android from his storage closet. It had been a few months, but Adam still got a boyish thrill from watching the robot take out the trash.

Waste disposal at Axiom One involved more than androids. Just as aqueducts revolutionized bringing water into towns and cities, the ECOposal system made 'taking out the garbage' obsolete. ECOposal pared the process down to opening a utility door tucked away in each unit and tossing unwanted items into the airtight shaft. From there, a person's involvement with trash was over. Somewhere in the bowels of Axiom, the system transported, sorted, collected and disposed of refuse. Any material destined for disposal was culled and sent into an incinerator used to generate power for non-essential parts of the city. The material worthy of collecting was automatically recycled, repurposed, and reused. The act of throwing stuff down a large shaft in a back hallway was doing one's part to care for the environment. It was like living in the future. A very tidy future.

Not so organized were Adam's thoughts about his role in Green Lantern and how it had changed his life. His recent introduction to nanotechnology left him feeling like he'd just arrived in Lilliput. He glanced down at his hand and wondered if his life more closely resembled a character in The Matrix.

Technology had its advantages and disadvantages, Adam knew all too well. The official project status reports were completely digital, holographic, and maintained within L.U.C.'s intelligence. The information would have been impossible for the team to manage any other way. Even so, Adam's desk was cluttered with unimaginable piles of completed and uncompleted project notes, drawings and activity logs because he also liked printing and writing things out the old-fashioned way. Andrew would attempt to remove the papers from Adam's desk. He would indicate that the stacks of paper 'did not compute' with a red flashing light on his chest that read "Duplicate material. Send to ECOposal." Adam was winning the battles with Andrew, but it remained to be seen who would win the war.

That was what Adam had to keep reminding himself of: the long game. They had lived in tents during the freezing winter, and now many team members had moved into permanent structures. The demand was so great that Adam decided to create a lottery system as they completed each residential block. He would do this at the other three locations, where he learned his residences were waiting.

And in keeping with his determination to hold on to the old ways that worked, Adam started a journal. It was therapeutic to write down and store thoughts on paper where the words could be kept out of reach from immediate analysis and scrutiny from prying eyes. Adam knew there was a possibility that one day, someone could find this material and make it public. They would reveal secrets of a fantastic journey. But for now, he could keep them all to himself. He and his partners, old and new, were on the cusp of making history.

Mornings were like the eye of the storm at Axiom One, and in the calm before the storm that each day brought, Adam liked to peruse through his journal entries. Along with information about the important accomplishments of the project, sometimes he made notes to himself about his observations so he could remember how he felt about certain things and people over time. On this particular day his observations were running wild and he understood it would be different than all the rest, so far.

For all his work with materials and machines, Adam prided himself on being an excellent judge of character. Within a short time of meeting someone, he could usually assess that person's abilities and character fairly accurately. He had learned to trust his 'gut instincts' about people, even when they seemed to run counter to the obvious. There were people with impeccable qualifications who he felt were untrustworthy, and sometimes he met people with questionable reputations who had always dealt with him fairly.

He also considered himself someone who could understand the significance of a situation, and gauge the effort and resources it might take to fully complete a particular task. It was a rather unique ability: too often he watched people court disaster with unrealistic expectations or push success away in favor of clinging to fear. Adam could look at people and tasks objectively. While others saw what they wanted to see, Adam had a solid grasp on what was.

These skills, or what some might consider gifts, were the reason people could count on him to get things done. After his trip to Axiom Japan, his sixth sense was not only tingling, it had gripped the entirety of his nervous system. He had good reason to be restless.

Adam started looking at some of his entries.

February 2

Incredible first day here at Axiom One Roswell. Love what I'm seeing and love my team. Juan and Del are more than capable and are going to be great partners. I know I can count on them. Unbelievable how much has already been done in such a short period of time. One of these days, ask Ben how long they have really been planning on building this city. Pretty tired. Missed the kids. Need to get some rest.

Skipping ahead a few entries: February 25

Our car manufacturing center here in Roswell is beginning to take shape. Del is the man. Love his can do, won't quit attitude. One of these days, I am going to have to ask Ben how long these plans have really been in the works. Has to be ten years, or more. No detail has been overlooked. Haven't heard a lot from Ben after the first couple of days. I know he's hard at work getting everything else started overseas. Busy man…

Further along in the journal:

April 20

Had my first Green Lantern remote conference over L.U.C.'s interactive AI, we call it the holovision. Connected with all my energy center site managers at the other Axiom locations to get an update on where things stand. For now, Axiom Roswell is the only location where cars will be manufactured. So, since we have the same exact blueprint for each Axiom, the commerce district at the other three locations, without flying car manufacturing, should be a breeze.

Juan joined me in talking with Henna out in Afghanistan, Gioan in Japan, and Yohanan in Syria. Up until now, Ella and Ben have had all the direct communication with these guys to get things going and to keep them on track while I get car manufacturing in Roswell sorted out. Getting the cars built is on the critical path. I'll be scheduling some site visits as soon as I get things rolling.

All I can think to write right now is, WOW. All these guys know their stuff and are amazing. When we terminated, I looked over at Juan and said, you're going to have to hustle to keep up, brother. These guys all know as much as you do! I miss using my Zoom and Slack net meetings. L.U.C. was even more assertive than his usual positive self today. I know everybody's stressed, but I didn't think computers could carry around so much emotion.

Skipping ahead further in the journal: July 27

Del and I are in a much better place today. Got a little frustrated with him yesterday and lost my cool. After a few setbacks we are getting everything in place in the AxMan Center to get everything back on schedule for setting up the car manufacturing stations. We are working out some of the kinks, but I like where today ended. I think we are still where we need to be. I apologized to Del for getting a little too excited. He said it was okay.

August 16

Got into my new digs today. Speechless. The rich and famous can't live like this. The future is now. Andrew, let me tell you about Andrew, the household android. First off, everybody is going to have one. He does the dishes and takes out the trash! How would I ever live without him?

September 12

Heading to Japan next week to meet with Gioan after we see if the tiny invisible robots can produce some parts. Exciting! It's happening!

September 14

Maejima Island. After eliminating the possibility of the fourth stone being located in or around the coordinates of our spot, we decided to clear the site, establish the drill, and begin our penetration. Roswell's control rod shaft is already in place and the energy center construction itself is now well underway. We've got to pick up the pace and get back on schedule in Japan. The ongoing stone search was beginning to weigh on things a bit.

I find myself having to do a lot of logistical planning around Axiom construction districts when the Johansens and Dr. Alex think they have a zone they want to excavate. Do we really need that fourth stone, anyway?"

September 16

After believing they had identified a highly probable location for the fourth stone on Maejima, Peter, Claire, and Alex reported another miss. In addition to the seismic equipment readings, there were some other strong clues that pointed them to what looked like an obvious underground chamber. It was the last straw for Alex. He was the one to find the chamber empty. Alex sounded about as frustrated as anybody could sound. I didn't think he was the type that would have the patience for digging with a spoon for a month. He said he was going to turn it all over to Peter and Claire and head back to the States. He mentioned that he might spend a few days decompressing at Loretta Landing Lane before heading out to Roswell to assist me.

Perfect timing really, we are just getting to the point here where I need him to help me get the energy and manufacturing centers fully online as well as begin testing the rest of the system. Half of the things we have left to do are based on the formulas he's worked out from L.U.C.'s algorithms. Honestly, I was starting to feel like I was getting in a little over my head. Having Alex may mean the end of those feelings. I'll keep that all to myself. Fake it till you make it. Right?

September 19

Good sleep last night. FINALLY!! The Gulfstream recliner and the long, low, steady hum set up the perfect hypnotic conditions. Not there yet, but maybe I am experiencing a second wind. Used some of my time in flight to study and go over Roswell's resource plans to make sure construction plans in every district were going smoothly.

We sure do have some great people. Just missed Alex. He was coming into Roswell just as I was heading out. He didn't say much but did say he was ready to go to work. If all goes well, I'll be back in another few days and we can put our heads together to get over some of the bigger hurdles. We landed today on Axiom Four's temporary runway. It will be unnecessary if we all do our jobs, but today it was nice to land right in your own backyard.

September 25

Productive trip so far. Great to see Peter and Claire and how they were thriving. I believe their ability to act spontaneously rewarded them with all they ever really wanted. They told me how committed they would be to finding the fourth stone and were confident they would do so. I didn't have the heart to mention what a pain in the ass they'd been having to modify our construction schedules around all the little holes they were digging. They asked me if I had seen Alex yet and if he was doing any better? They said the last day he was here, he was very short with them and left abruptly. They didn't blame him, because they knew this wasn't his thing and just appreciated that he had helped them. A couple more of the noteworthy things about today:

First, the Johansens could NOT STOP talking about the new home they would be living in for the foreseeable future and thanked me profusely for making sure they were among the first to move out of the tent city and into their permanent house. I told them I felt that same way.

The second thing about today, and this is where it got weird for me, was with the EI team. Obviously, Ella and her organization have done the impossible by sourcing all four of these

Axiom construction projects with amazing, well-trained people. But everywhere I've gone in the past couple of days I felt like I was in a continuous state of déjà vu. I found workers efficient and effective, but every conversation I had felt like the ones I've had before. People are nice and courteous but won't go out of their way to interact. This feeling I am having started in my first one-on-one's with Gioan a couple days ago and has been growing ever since. In person, he was the same guy I met through holovision, but something is off. It was so strange. This dude answered every question I had just like Juan would answer. The way he tilted his head when listening, the sharp gestures. Their voices have different accents, but the same pitch. He's obviously capable, qualified, and knows exactly what he needs to do to build this energy factory, but I am now getting to the point where I can't even hear my questions or listen to his answers. Even Gioan's mannerisms were the same as Juan's.

How can this be? Am I starting to go crazy? There were a couple of times today I was just thinking, this guy knows everything Juan knows, and I was about to outright ask him: how were they related? I thought better of it. I meet with Gioan first thing in the morning before my flight to confirm our next moves around here. I have an idea...

September 26

As soon as I thought Juan had gotten through his daily project planning meeting with the Energy Center construction team, I called him. It was about midnight here in Japan which put it about 9 a.m. in Roswell. He said, "what's up, boss?" just like he always does. I told him I just wanted him to know how well things were going over here in Japan. He was pleased and supportive like always. I asked him if he minded if I asked him a couple of personal questions. "No problem, boss," just like always. When I asked, Juan told me his mother's birthday was November 18th. When I asked if he had ever broken any bones, he told me that he had fallen off a bicycle when he was ten and had broken his left collar bone. When I asked about his favorite hobby, he told me that he loved to fish when he was younger but didn't have time for it anymore. I told him thanks and that I was just interested in him as a person, which I hope he knows I am! I would be surprised if I was able to get 20 minutes of continuous sleep the rest of the night. It was about 6 a.m. when I called Gioan today, which was about an hour before our scheduled in person wrap up meeting. I wanted to see if I could schedule a little bit more of an impromptu call with him today. When he picked up, he said, "What's up, boss?" I told him something came up and I had to head back early, but that I felt like we had all of his action items in hand and he was ready to go. He told me, yes sir. I then asked Gioan if he minded if I asked him a couple of questions. "No problem, boss." Gioan's mother's birthday was November 18th, Gioan broke his left collar bone when he fell off a bicycle when he was ten, and Gioan loved to fish, but didn't have much time for it right now.

Before reading the final entry in the journal, Adam paused for a minute to regain his composure and tried not to let anger become his dominant emotion.

Chapter 31 - Variants

He had to give them credit, Adam thought bitterly. They were good. They knew what they were doing. They had told him exactly what he'd wanted to hear. Everyone had a weakness. Even he did, and they'd found it.

It wasn't money. Greed had never been Adam's weakness. Had the genie that came out of that high tech substitute for a bottle offered him billions, Adam wouldn't have taken the bait. Instead, they appealed to his idealism. It was his fatal flaw. His wish to help humanity for the sheer joy of knowing he had done something to make the world better was, ironically, what had gotten him into this mess.

Adam was angry with them, whoever, or whatever these entities were. But he was as equally disappointed at himself for being so gullible. Questioning again how or why he hadn't done more to investigate what flavor of snake oil the Christmas Day hologram was selling during his divination, he came up empty handed.

He suspected he had become part of something as evil and destructive as he had originally thought it to be revolutionary and life changing. He had completely swallowed the hook "they" set. Adam steadied himself to read the last entry in his journal written yesterday. He thought about all the people counting on him to do the right thing: his family, Director Helms, his team. Maybe they didn't know it yet, but Adam felt like he had failed people the world over who would have benefitted from the flying cars. Millions of them. He hoped it wasn't too late. With the dwindling supply of faith he had left, Adam resolved to draw the energy from their trust to get the resolve to turn things around.

October 15

On October 13th, I flew to Kabul under the premise of conducting a site audit. I scheduled a face-to-face visit with Henna, my Axiom Energy Center Project Manager in Logar. After a little small talk, I asked for his project timeline report to confirm his version of how everything was going. When he handed it to me, I looked down at it, but did not read it. After I told him I was pleased with what he'd accomplished so far and how he was managing everything. Then, I asked him if he minded if I asked him a couple of personal questions. Confirming my suspicions, Henna said, "no problem, boss.' Verbatim. I really had no need to continue. His mother's birthday was November 18th, he'd broken a collar bone when he was ten falling off a bicycle, and his favorite thing to do was to fish, but he didn't have much time for it anymore. Overcoming the sinking feeling I had in my stomach, I thanked Henna for his efforts and told him to keep doing what he was doing. Within 45 minutes of shaking Henna's now predictably cold hand, I was back in the air. I had scheduled a meeting for the 14th, with Johanan in Damascus. Now, with my suspicions already confirmed, I was caught in a trap. There wasn't any need for me to go to Syria, but I wanted to keep up the appearance of my ignorance, so I went. With unsurprising responses, Johanan answered all my questions. He knew I was shaken because I was literally shaking by the time we broke. I left abruptly and decided not to reply to L.U.C. in the Rover. Of course, L.U.C. knows that I know. As soon as I boarded the flight heading back to Roswell, I informed the lying, demonic bot that I wouldn't be communicating with him on the flight home and that Ben and Ella better damn be in Roswell by tomorrow or the lid was going to blow, literally. I reached out to Greg on the flight home because the weight of this discovery was getting too heavy to lift alone. He was unusually calm. He knows me so well and encouraged me to let cooler heads prevail. He said there probably was a very logical explanation for what I was thinking and not to do anything rash.

I am in sheer torment tonight, thinking about what I may be involved in. So many possibilities...No answers, only questions that lead to more questions. Were we building vehicles that could be weaponized and used against our country? Had an army of synthetic people been built that were creating their fortresses to destroy us?

When I landed in Roswell, it was comforting to shake Juan's hand. It was reassuring to find at least one human among the army of bots. L.U.C. must have tipped him off that I was upset and asked him to meet me out at the Axiom's landing strip, but he didn't ask me any questions. He said he heard from Ella and that she and Ben were coming in tomorrow. I think he was hoping I would tell him something. He knew their arrival in Roswell together was highly unusual. I said nothing.

As dawn began to threaten the safety of the darkness, Adam wondered about the day before him and how quickly he could make the long game short. The only logical conclusion he could come to was this "project" was nefarious. He hadn't specifically told Greg to keep it confidential, as too many other things in his mind were racing, but surely Greg knew that was understood.

His friend apparently took the liberty of alerting the rest of the team, telling them that Adam was in crisis and that he might be preparing to do something that would jeopardize the project.

Grace's message was the first and most moving. She was soothing, reasonable and calming. "Adam, Greg told me we've got some issues and you might be losing it a little. Just slow down and try to relax. You know from our line of work; things aren't always as they seem. I've listened to numerous conversations that sounded like one thing and turned out to be completely different. I am confident there has to be a logical explanation for what you think you're seeing, and things can still work out as we imagined. Go slow and keep your head. As always, I'm right here if you need me. Let's talk soon."

Similar messages had come in from Dr. Alex, Peter and Claire. Even Myles had sent a brief note. "I am available should you require my assistance, sir." The last message was from Greg. "Hey bud, just wanted to let you know I reached out to the rest of the gang and told them you thought you were running into some unsettling details about the project and to reach out. Hope that was okay."

No, but what could Adam do about it now? It was nice to hear from Grace and that did a lot to calm his nerves.

In the Commerce District, there was a large, private business office on the corner of Primary and Gateway. Heavy silk drapes the color of yucca blossoms shaded the south-facing office, a welcome shelter when meetings ran into the early evening. The enormous hacienda table, made of reclaimed wood, filled the center of the room and reminded everyone who entered that generations of grit had brought them to this place. The north wall was devoted to smart boards, 3D printers and a seven-foot-high map of the 33rd parallel.

They had not used any of this space…yet. Adam would meet with Ben and Ella in the business office. It would be a two on one, but Adam didn't feel outnumbered because his anger would even the playing field.

He was going to make sure he had gotten the last word, even if it was only on paper. With a need to at least feel productive, Adam picked up his favorite journaling pen, the one with the nice grip and fine writing point.

October 16

To all who read this, please know that my intention was pure and the dream to create a better tomorrow was real. If I have unknowingly involved myself in a plot damaging to our country or any persons within it, today, I plan to do more than ask for your forgiveness: I will do everything in my power to right my wrong."

Adam put the pen down and figured he would finish the entry later, if he was still around.

Adam continued giving L.U.C. the silent treatment into the night, but L.U.C. wasn't fully cooperating. A message came through to Adam's phone directly from the AI's persistent app. It read, "Ben and Ella are here and can meet as soon as possible." Adam took the Rover into town and spotted Ella at the door of their meeting place. She disappeared into the opening when she saw Adam's Rover approaching. As Adam entered the office, Ella was coming back up the hallway from the main conference room. She extended her hand and greeted him warmly. She must have gone back in quickly to let Ben know that he was there.

"Nice to see you again," she said with characteristic vibrance. Adam nodded to Ella courteously as he shook her hand. She pointed the way to the conference room and locked the door behind them.

They made their way into the conference room, with Ben waiting, standing at the far end of the table. Adam couldn't put his finger on it, but Ben seemed different from when Adam met him in Denver ten months ago. Maybe it was just his demeanor. Ben's face was serious, but not threatening. The tension in the room was palpable, though.

Despite the fact that the three of them were alone in the office, Ella closed the conference room door behind her to give them one more layer of privacy. Ben asked Adam to please take a seat. Ella moved to the chair next to Ben and Adam took a seat at the opposite end of the table as far away from the two of them as possible and placed his phone face down in front of him. After a short and uncomfortable silence, both Adam and Ben begin to speak simultaneously. Ben is first to apologize and nods to Adam while extending his hand, palm up.

"You know exactly why I am here. Please, you first, Mr. Kumar. I would be very interested to hear what you have to say," Adam said. That was the understatement of the year.

First of all, I would like to apologize, Adam." Ben began smoothly. "Ella and I have been meaning to come to Roswell long before now. We haven't, partly because things have been going so smoothly under your direction and partly because we are both so busy supporting the rapidly completing projects."

"Well, that's understandable," Adam said. He didn't thank them for the compliment about his project managing skills. It was going to take more than flattery to pacify him.

"I would also like you to know," Ben said, his tone suddenly serious, "that from the day I learned about this opportunity, decades ago but just a few miles from here, I have been investing my entire life in one way or another in the Virtual Global Highway Transportation System. This creation will save the planet and outweighs any sacrifice we have to make for it to become a reality," he said.

Adam sat quietly, absorbing Ben's words. There was no need to rush a conversation as important as this one.

"Mr. Kumar, with all due respect, it doesn't matter how great the benefit, if you break every moral and ethical code along the way, you will destroy the people. Is money the only thing you care about? If they knew what you were doing here, they would storm the gates to stop you. Through all its imperfections, most in this world would rather live with it as it is, do what is right, and live free of shame and guilt," Adam said emphatically. Ben sat silent, still and inscrutable.

"So, Mr. Kumar and Ms. Flores, if what I think is happening really is happening, it better not be. I am here today only because I've been encouraged to give you the benefit of the doubt," Adam said. He picked up his phone. "I've pulled up the name of Richard Helms on my phone three times in the past twelve hours and we are about ten minutes away from seeing how the United States Military is going to react to the information I'm about to share with them."

Ben stirred and Ella glanced at Adam's phone.

"Adam, what do you think we are doing?" She asked, tension creeping into her voice. She fussed nervously with something in her pants pocket.

"Don't give me that, you know exactly what you're doing! I want some answers right now!" Adam shouted

Ben glanced at Ella and shook his head. She took her hand out of her pocket and placed it on the table.

"No, Adam really, please calm down. Tell us what you think we are doing wrong," Ella said. She had a syringe loaded with pentothal with her, but she didn't want to use it. There was still time to turn things around. If they couldn't, they would drug Adam and have him in the hospital a few hours later. It happened sometimes. People with high-pressure jobs, they'd take a trip, overdo it with various substances. A person can only handle so much stress before they lose their grip on reality. That was the worst case. They weren't giving up. They'd gotten this far...

Adam stood up. "So, whose decision was it and when was it made?" he demanded.

"What decision, Adam? What decision do you think we made?" Ben asked.

"CLONING! The decision to CLONE! When was the decision made and why wasn't I involved in the discussion? I don't care about the reason or the benefit. I am not now nor will I ever go along with this! God is the only one that can make that kind of decision. Ben and neither you, nor Ella, are GOD!"

Ben and Ella looked at each other, rose to their feet, and walked towards Adam. They moved in sync on either side of the table, its polished surface catching the light like a pool of still water.

Ben reached the standing, highly agitated Adam first. He carefully touched his arm. "Adam, put your phone down and please sit down. We apologize you weren't told sooner, but considering everything you have on your plate, we felt your own discovery in time was the most expeditious way to keep the project moving with the least amount of interruption. We are ten months in, we've seen an incredible amount of progress, and you are only now realizing how our enhancements have benefited the project. It's not what you think, Adam."

Adam looked wild-eyed at the older man. He was too calm, too smooth.

"Ella," Adam said. "He'll sit down when he's good and ready to sit down. You've got about fifteen seconds, go on."

"Adam, for many years, in preparation for this very project, I have been building an organization and have selected some of the brightest, most talented, highly qualified people in the world. As you know, this initiative is a game changer and will affect the world in ways that only few could conceive. And truthfully, where the ripples will end when we...unleash this on the world, we have no way to know," she said, looking at him intently. He said nothing.

"You have overseen projects from start to finish. You make the best predictions with the information you have, but how many times have you finished exactly when and where you thought you would?" she asked. Adam knew what Ella was talking about, but he was not going to fall for this transparent attempt at building rapport. He was finished with being gullible.

"We're talking about you now," Adam said.

"More than once, I've had to think on my feet. And a few times I've been lucky enough to have some help with what I think you call 'hacks.' We accomplished some great things, but we realized we weren't going to be able to do enough. It was going to take more time than any of us reasonably have left to develop the level of expertise we needed to properly resource all four Axioms."

"Yeah, that's what I do when I'm running out of time. I just clone people," Adam deadpanned.

Ella sighed and ran her hand through her hair. She looked at Ben. He nodded and she sank into the nearest chair. It was made of vegan leather and was the color of adobe. She looked out the window as crews poured cement across the road. It was really happening. They were going to build the structures that would allow the cars to spring from molecules. Here, on this sunny October afternoon, Ella watched what she had worked for over the last twenty years come to fruition. It had been a monumental effort, but absolutely worth it. The people, the places, the materials were all coming together. Like carefully tended baby birds, their cars would soon take flight.

Ben stood before Adam. There was not a trace of equivocation or defensiveness, only the calm steadiness of someone who understood his purpose. "Developing the twenty thousand people capable of working with our advanced materials and processes had already taken years" "We realized bringing eighty thousand people trained to the levels needed to source the entire system was going to be impossible. Instead of accepting failure, we found a solution that was agreeable to everyone," he said.

Adam was somewhat calmer, but still standing. "What solution, and agreeable to who?"

"L.U.C. made us aware that he was capable of creating a human variant. Like many other abilities, he only did this after he observed that we weren't going to be able to complete the task on our own," Ben said, sounding a little tired.

"Variant, what's a variant?" Adam asked. This was not going to be a short conversation, he realized. "Sit down, calm down, and I'll tell you the whole story." Adam reluctantly sits. Ella stood and walked to the window. She let the sparkling desert breeze blow through the room and began searching for the nearest vending machine.

"In the hallways of Ella International, we approached our best and brightest. As Ella will attest, our mission is to improve lives. For all the wonderful people chosen to help us develop the VITES, we made them an offer they couldn't refuse," Ben explained.

"I'm listening," Adam told him.

"We told them exactly what position we were in and we were completely transparent with them. All of them. In exchange for accessing their knowledge and upon successful completion of Axiom Roswell, we offered them a path of complete amnesty, ownership, and employment in what will become the most advanced city in the history of the world. Truly a city of tomorrow," Ben said.

"What exactly do you mean by *accessing their knowledge*?" The phrase gave Adam a strange feeling. Again he chastised himself inwardly for not listening carefully enough. He'd only heard what he wanted to hear. He wasn't James Bond, or any other handsome, dashing hero. He was in a horror movie, and Adam was fairly sure he was the next victim. The CIA, mind control, people disappearing or losing their minds. Ben's city of tomorrow was his worst nightmare.

"L.U.C.'s interface served as the conduit, and we performed what you might call a brain dump on the selected, trained, and affirmed. From there, L.U.C. provided the specifications for building our synthetic variants. We replicated each person three times by putting their essence in the processor and made slight modifications to their appearance to blend in more closely with the given cultural setting," he said evenly.

"At present there are only a few human, anonymous S.E.T.I. employees at each of the remote Axioms. In fact, local governments have no record or idea that twenty-thousand construction workers are operating inside each Axiom. We shipped all the parts in via various transport methods and then assembled everything at those locations once everything was behind the perimeter. I personally assisted in assembling a few and then the assembled began assembling the rest," Ben told him. Kumar helped robots build one another, Adam thought, as he struggled to understand the man in front of him.

Ella walked in with three chilled bottles of Nizhóní water. She handed one to each man and opened the third for herself. They sat for a moment, savoring the refreshment only water could bring in an arid climate. Looking out the floor to ceiling windows, the trio watched cranes swing into the skeletal beginnings of buildings while bulldozers kicked up dust all around them. It was wonderful to watch, but was any of it real? Was this what L.U.C. told him in the beginning? Ben hadn't convinced Adam yet.

"So, you see Adam, these are just computers, just computers," Ella said as she replaced the cap and put her bottle on the table. "They are not humans, and they are not clones of humans. There are no ethical boundaries being crossed. They have no emotions and won't be upset when we deactivate them. There could be so much work for them that we will not deactivate them anytime soon."

"These are not humans?" Adam had been asking a robot about his mother, he realized. He was on the other side of the looking glass.

"Axiom Roswell's team is 100% human workers that are living their dreams," Ella said. "The other three Axiom's are 99.9% variant. At the same time, this creates tremendous efficiency and consistency on the build sites." Well, of course it would, Adam thought. Strictly from an engineering standpoint, it was a great strategy.

"L.U.C. monitors, organizes, and feeds the plans into the network as tasks are completed. It works best to keep all the remote Axioms just slightly behind Roswell, our Alpha location, so that our mirroring becomes most seamless. Maejima Island is a little behind the others due to the logistics surrounding the search for the stone. The Johansens and Dr. Alex are still looking for it, but there will be no problem in completing Japan slightly behind the others."

Maybe it was like all other technological advances, Adam thought. Was it that different from video conferencing? His great-grandfather would have been bewildered and suspicious about talking to people on the other side of the world, but now it was commonplace.

"Can you imagine how busy you'd be if you had eighty-thousand people to manage in your organization? When L.U.C. helped us understand this solution, we realized this would be the perfect answer to ensuring absolute consistency across the Axiom currents," Ben told him.

Adam took a deep breath and the boil in his blood lowered to a simmer. "I still have a few more questions. So, Juan knows about this and he didn't tell me?"

"Yes, Juan knows. There is very little that I don't tell him," Ella said. "He couldn't tell you because of his non-disclosure agreement. It states that if he ever reveals the existence of the variants, he will forfeit his deed for Axiom property and will lose his employment."

"Everything he has worked for," Adam said. In the months that they'd worked together, Adam had come to admire Juan. He had endured an unimaginable horror but maintained his faith in the future. If anyone deserved compensation and security for his efforts, Juan did.

"His fear of losing this opportunity for his family will probably continue to keep him from talking about it or sharing it with you, or anyone else," Ella said.

It took a moment to process this. Adam watched a group of team members trade high-fives as they put the last tiles on a nearby roof. He tapped his water bottle absently.

"I see that Grace's advice was right. I do apologize for jumping to some conclusions before I had all the facts. At the same time, you can't fully blame me for my assumption. And I am still irritated that I wasn't informed on something as big as variant robot automation," he told Ben and Ella.

"No, we do understand, and we do apologize for the way you had to learn about this. It was never our intention to have you find out this way. I also want to let you know that not everything is about money, Adam. It just takes money to do extraordinary things. I have some very specific goals I need, *or want*, to accomplish in my lifetime and I've found that having enough money is one of those essential things you need if you hope to get everything done that needs to get done. I like the idea of selling space for sixty-thousand new people in some hot futuristic city markets when all the variants decide to move away. That ought to help get closer to getting a return on investment before I have to leave this world," Ben said with a smile.

"Oh, stop talking like that, Mr. Kumar. You are in great shape and aren't going anywhere any time soon. So, I assume I can focus my time in Roswell from here on out and can use L.U.C.'s holovision to see that everything is syncing up properly," Adam said.

“That’s right, now that we’re well underway at every location, L.U.C. can assist you in keeping things organized,” Ben assured him.

“Adam, I’m sorry this became such a big misunderstanding. We get so focused on getting the job done, sometimes, we forget the simple act of communication,” Ella said.

“It’s kind of funny, looking back on it. Asking a variant what he does in his free time,” Adam said with a smirk. “Ok, it’s still going to be strange to interact with these things. My amazement at the precision of the project and how effortlessly it has been to manage the construction of the remote Axiom’s is no longer a mystery now. I’m not nearly as good as I thought I was. Humility is always best,” Adam said. More than anything, he was relieved that his mission, their mission, would continue.

“It may not always be apparent, Adam, but everything we do is to make this vision a reality. Everything,” Ben said.

“Thank you. I feel the same way. Can you guys join me for lunch? They make a mean plate of red and green enchiladas across the street,” Adam told them. Ella and Ben declined, saying they needed to get back but thanked him for the offer. Coming to this meeting had already taken away more time than each of them had. There would be time to share a meal together in the days ahead under much more favorable circumstances. Adam apologized again and departed for his residence.

As soon as he got through the door, he headed for the journal that he had unwittingly left on his desk. It was in plain sight, for someone, anyone to find. He opened it to the page of his last entry… and tore it out. He began writing an entry with the same date again.

October 16

Had a good visit today with Ben Kumar and Ella Flores. This is the first time either of these two important leaders visited Axiom Roswell, let alone together. Ella oversaw training and was responsible for providing our workforce. Ben was responsible for sourcing almost all our materials as well as our financing the entire endeavor. I was relieved by what I heard from them about how we have been able to keep the whole project on track. There are no obstacles that I see from here that will prevent us from testing some flying cars in just a few more months. Ben is different. Still working on trying to figure him out. Ella might be a little odd, too.

Chapter 32 - Phoenix or Bust

Watching the seasons complete another round of their elliptical dance reminded Adam that change remained constant. He was grateful he could observe this predictable process. It helped remind him that the world outside Axiom One marched forward as it always had.

During video chats, Chris and Bri told him about what they were learning in school. New to them were the ideas of a utopian society and democratic ideals, and Adam smiled to himself as he listened to his children discuss concepts that were centuries old with an enthusiasm and intensity that reminded him of his younger self.

Other ideas were new to all of them, and Adam welcomed the debates that the three of them had regarding what was good and what was true. He'd developed a new appreciation for embracing change since his formal introduction to the variants twelve months ago. It was kind of a make-or-break moment for Adam. Initially, he had considered aborting the project, or at least terminating his involvement in it, when he realized he was dealing with something outside of his experience.

He was glad he'd decided to stay at Axiom One, with its tiny molecular machines that seemed almost lifelike. It was a reality unlike anything he could have imagined, and one with the potential to compensate for the missed Christmases with his family and friendships that only existed on social media. He enjoyed observing the closeness of the EI employees who had traveled the world together. In many cases the engineers and builders were literally family. Perhaps because of this, they did not begrudge him the holiday trip to Virginia he had planned. It was for his own family, after all, that he was attempting to realize an incredible dream.

Changing the world was one thing, but the Axioms would produce cars that would help the earth heal itself. The planet could continue to nurture generations to come because of what he and all the dedicated Axiom One workers, along with all their many variants, were building.

The gravity of this undertaking was now here in evidence at the Axiom's Manufacturing Center, which resembled a Comic Con trade show, not a technological paradigm shift. Groups of engineers stood clustered around lines of partitioned booths, watching microscopic machines rearrange billions of atoms in a flurry that was both organized and chaotic, by turns.

Adam nearly convinced Greg to fly to Roswell when he was having trouble understanding how the different systems in the cars communicated. He settled for regular video conferences and Greg's assurance that it would make complete sense after Adam saw a real, live completed car. "You are great at reverse-engineering stuff, man. When you see the finished product, you'll understand why it works the way it does," Greg promised.

"I'm holding you to that," Adam grumbled.

They'd spent over six months with more error than trial in developing algorithms. Eventually, they had found all the ways that did not work. By summer, they started by producing small proof of concept parts, then moved on to creating complex three-dimensional designs. Chemists mixed molecules in a solution, and instead of allowing them to wander and bump together at random, molecular assemblers positioned the molecules and brought them together at a specific time and location.

On aisle forty-seven, station eight, they were attempting to produce the first completely functional flying car. L.U.C. had suggested using the station on aisle forty-seven to Adam, in honor of the ship that had carried him here and crashed outside Roswell in 1947. Adam didn't bother asking him about the significance of station eight: there was too much excitement in the air to think about that.

Adam spent long hours with Dr. Alex and on his own, studying every aspect of the creation. He thought he had a good understanding of at least ninety percent of what they were creating, what it could do, and how it would work with Earth's magnetic currents. He gave it the "ten-year-old test," asking the children of some EI employees how the flying cars worked.

"It's like when you hold two magnets together and they don't want to stick. You can turn them around and then they'll stick," Mira Cervantes told Adam one afternoon.

"That's true, but how the cars fly is that the magnetic force in the earth pushes the car up. When you flip the magnet in the car over, then the car can land," said her brother, Reymundo.

"Nothing to it," Adam said. The kids had left out the part about proton beams and drilling to the Earth's core, but they had the gist of it.

Easier to understand was the dazzling impression of the craft exterior material's amazing glimmer. Children and adults smiled at the sparkle of what was clearly a shiny new toy. On a deeper level, the engineer in Adam was astonished with the properties of the material. They went far beyond his initial understanding of shape memory polymers. As the engineers explained, the car would react to and be capable of morphing with external conditions of heat, light, pressure, and speed. It seemed like overkill to Adam, but he had no reason not to accept its capabilities given his lack of practical experience using Earth's magnetic forces to propel objects.

The integrated AI would handle modes, stability, navigation and entertainment. It would be in constant, seamless communication with the entire Axiom energy centers network. As best Adam could understand, the vehicle would operate in two modes. A VTOL mode for take-off, landing, and integrating the car into the virtual highway system beginning some 500 feet in the air. A terrestrial mode would take over once the vehicle entered the highway and navigate the car to its destination. Vehicles in the network would constantly make their way through the nearest Axiom for regular diagnostics and certification.

Adam had come to realize how powerful L.U.C.'s intelligence was. It performed billions, if not trillions of instructions and computations per second to keep track of something as mind-bendingly complex as this, the likes of which the world had never seen. Adam had no doubt people would be astonished and awestruck. Realist that he was, Adam expected a few people would be suspicious and even hostile.

What would become of them? There were Amish communities not far from Greg's beach house. Adam admired them for adhering to their principles. They didn't necessarily do things the fastest or easiest, or laziest way, like plenty of people did today. And there was no denying how much better their lifestyle was for the planet.

The flying cars would sail over their fields of grains and vegetables, as horses pulled the plows through the rich soil. Would the farmers look up and see a sign of progress? What would happen to the people who, like the Amish, rejected some forms of modernization? There would be people who insisted on driving gas powered cars and traveling everywhere by car. They would cling to their beliefs as the rest of the world marched forward.

That was a bridge he would cross when he came to it, because his most pressing and immediate concern was trying out the newly hatched cars. It had been exhilarating as all get out to get this far in the process, but none of it would feel real until one of the cars, hatched in a molecular soup, stretched its metallic wings and flew out of the Axiom.

The molecular machine system on aisle forty-seven was on par with the incredible functional diversity of nature's atomically precise systems. It was a little like watching a glacier carve a hollow for a river valley, then seeing the trees populate the mineral rich soil in the basin and finding a butterfly making its way out of a cocoon in less than two hours. L.U.C.'s AI was on full display and there was a broad range of expert chemistry knowledge in station eight that crisp fall morning. Algorithms combining sequences of monomers were building component structures that combined to form polymers. These polymers, along with metal atoms, caused chassis to form, almost out of thin air. Was it forming from the inside out, or the outside in? Did the chicken or the egg come first? How did the particles know to do what they did with such precision?

It was a long, complicated and occasionally frustrating process for the team. So much so that members periodically lost focus on the product. The months of uncertainty and grueling labor seemed as if they would stretch into the future indefinitely.

That was the case until one autumn afternoon when the completely manufactured flying car sat in station eight finished completely and gleaming with magnificence. Elation and incredulity filled the air, and the months of arduous work felt like little more than a minor inconvenience as chemists and engineers of Axiom Roswell began to dab at their eyes and clap each other's back.

The process took eighty-seven minutes from beginning to end, according to Andreas Jimenez, the youngest engineer in station eight. Witnessing the vehicle "hatching" out of swirling molecules was overwhelming to witness. Adam found himself looking back and forth between the rotating image of the holographic car on the station's front control panel and the car itself. He'd rehearsed this moment again and again in his mind, but when faced with the reality of the car in front of him, he couldn't stop comparing and confirming it was the same.

During molecular construction, each unfinished component of the car appeared red on the holographic display. As Adam and his team slowly circled around the car, they noticed an unusual glow surrounding the newly materialized vehicle. It gave the spectacular machine a verdant tinge where it caught the light. All of L.U.C.'s status indicators were green. Green for go! The first flying car was complete.

It was only one vehicle, but it represented the beginning of a revolution. This was a turning point in history, with great minds questioning the truism of bigger and better and exploring the great possibilities in small packages: nanotechnology. It was in its infancy on this planet. This alien artificial intelligence which dropped out of the sky had just sped up manufacturing processes by at least a century, maybe two. A need for speed and efficiency created the Industrial Revolution, and now a mastery of the complex and autonomous propelled humanity into the future.

From the beginning of recorded history, everything that has ever been discovered and ultimately built had already existed in nature, people simply had to find it. No longer were humans playing hide and seek. This technology served as a magnifying glass and a space saver.

There were one hundred and five aisles in the Axiom Manufacturing Center in Roswell with fifteen Molecular Manufacturing Stations on each aisle. That meant at full operation, a single Axiom Manufacturing Center could produce approximately 1,575 cars every hour and a half or more than 25,000 cars per day. At the right time, S.E.T.I. could create replicas of these manufacturing centers all over the world. A licensing fee for would-be manufacturers seemed inevitable if Ben had anything to do with it, Adam thought. There was no concern with malfunctions or down time in this new world of manufacturing. On the contrary, L.U.C. and his mechanical minions were learning and refining the process with each iteration. They were setting off on a path they had designed carefully and it was leading them in a promising direction.

And the product of this complex process requiring time, money, materials and human resources? Flight. That was the reason for digging to the center of the earth, ironically. The wish to move away from it.

Adam walked outside and sat at a small patio table as the groups of exhausted, exhilarated scientists congratulated each other. He would thank them, verbally and materially after they'd had a few days to rest and absorb the profundity of their accomplishment. He needed a few moments to do the very same thing.

He watched the late afternoon sun to the west of Axiom One. A group of finches abruptly rose from the top of a golden cottonwood tree, their red and orange heads like sparks in flight. Marveling at their beauty, he felt the sharp pang of envy most humans experienced when observing winged creatures. It was impossible not to long for their ability to glide effortlessly through the world. Surely, soaring above the rooted and grounded suggested a kind of superiority?

Still, early attempts at manufacturing the ability to fly had proved dangerous. Flight had been on the minds of humans for millennia, since Icarus fashioned wings. Leaving the ground also meant leaving behind his father's wise counsel to practice moderation. His fall into the ocean became a fable for generations to come, a warning that our dreams could turn to nightmares in the absence of caution.

Humans never completely accepted being relegated to the dirt. It may be that a resentment of their earthbound status caused them to lash out at their perceived captor. Pollution of the earth, its air and water suggest a contempt for the very force that nurtures life itself.

Could the cars at Axiom One serve as atonement for the actions of Icarus and those who had followed him? Adam wondered if they were seeking redemption for their collective arrogance in thinking the jet fuel in the ocean was without consequence.

They were not rising above the earth, disdainful of those below them. They were allowing it to heal with their intentional retreat. It was an act of selflessness, of kindness, to keep his feet from falling too heavily on the source of his support.

Or was it self-preservation? Were people realizing that in their haste to exploit the newest technological advancement, they were biting the hand that fed them? Was it possible to separate the desire to enhance our lives and the wish to preserve the earth? The two seemed inextricably linked.

Cultures across the globe have told stories about the Earth Mother. Wreaking havoc on the body of her oceans and atmosphere is rather like threatening the health of the umbilical cord that connects mother and child.

Taken to its logical end, the physical bond between mother and child is temporary. The child grows and begins to live independently. Was flight, or even the desire for it, a sign of human progress? Like fledglings leaving the nest, maybe people were meant to look to the skies.

People are physical beings, of course, but as some would argue, they are also spiritual. The earth represents boundaries, providing a sense of security. The skies, to our imperfect human senses, appear limitless. While not necessarily safe, they give us a feeling of exhilaration, of possibilities.

Adam watched an airliner in the north, likely headed to Albuquerque, realizing how quickly people had learned to ignore airplanes for the most part. He imagined himself on a similar journey a short time from now when he would see his family. With uneasiness he allowed himself to skirt the edges of an idea that lurked just below his conscious mind. Was taking to the air a search for something? A search for home?

"Mr. Hunter, you have to come see this," Jimenez said as he leaned out the doorway of the main building. "The guys found a broom and they're using it as a limbo stick!"

Adam smiled at the mental image this created. "Some of those chemists are pretty limber, I hear," he said as he stood to view the festivities for himself. They were blasting Kool & The Gang and dancing as only true celebrants can.

He could not bring himself to tell them to tone down their antics as he watched the engineers dance away the stress of the last few months. There was actually more to celebrate than they might have realized. Adam had already considered the positive impacts the Virtual Global Highway System would have on the global environment. The tremendous reduction of carbon emissions and the ability to turn interstates into agriculture, green spaces, and living spaces was exciting.

What he had not considered until he witnessed it, was that the micromachine manufacturing process itself would also virtually eliminate the need for waste disposal. They would carefully select and design in place to bond with the neighboring atoms the atomic particles they used in the manufacturing process.

Adam met with Del and Juan in a small office next to aisle one while the music played outside. He gave Del approval to have his chemists, engineers, and programmers manufacture an additional four flying cars. From there, Del and his team could begin readying the manufacturing center's microstations, but would hold off on manufacturing any more vehicles until they were thoroughly tested. L.U.C. had given Adam the roadmap for how to test his new creation without having the other three Axiom Energy Centers completed. He looked at Juan.

"There's not much more to do, guys. The only thing left here is to put the control rods into the shaft. That will engage the system," Juan told the two men.

The Axiom One control room was ready and could perform all its necessary functions for the Vites to operate without the presence of its actuator key. While Adam wasn't completely sure what purpose the actuator key would serve, he was confident he could engage the system and use its proton beams to pulse out magnetic currents once the control rod was inserted. The intelligence built into the car would do the rest and determine when to relay or repel the magnetic stream. While the other three Axiom Energy Centers were nearing completion, none of the control rods would be inserted until Adam had given the instruction.

"How will we test these cars without having any of the other Axiom locations up and running to relay the current?" Del asked. Juan nodded and crossed his arms, waiting for the answer to what seemed like a riddle.

"Believe it or not, I have an idea for that," he said with a smile.

"I'm all ears," Del told him. He's learned that Adam would come up with ideas until he found one that worked.

"What I'm thinking of is fully loading several S.E.T.I. transport trailers with some magnetic beacons constructed into temporary towers. We'll drive those trucks over to Phoenix and position them around the city. Once we've got everything set up and plug in the coordinates for the temporary towers, we can project Axiom's magnetic pulses directly to each of them," Adam explained.

"Phoenix? Are you serious? *Hey, we'll just fly this little UFO to Phoenix and hope no one notices*," Del said.

"It's risky, I know. I've thought about flying at night. There are a few military bases in the area that will cover for us," Adam said.

"You are either crazy or a genius," Del said. "What next?"

"The cars will lift here in Axiom Roswell using their VTOL mode, then travel out and back to Phoenix under their terrestrial mode. If things go well, we will try to land one or two quickly in Phoenix and then get them back up on the temporary Vites," Adam said.

"You knew he wasn't going to go through all this and then just take it for a spin around the block," Juan said to Del.

"That's right. No more baby steps. Del, let's get another four flying cars with identical specifications manufactured by the end of the day tomorrow. We'll send those transport trucks out to Phoenix in the morning," Adam told him.

"Will do," Del replied.

"Juan, let's drop that Rod. It's time to be bold and brave. Let's go make history."

October 27

We finished the cars today. I still can't believe it.

So we went to Los Cerritos in the city after work for a celebratory meal. It was like when we found out Julie was pregnant with Christopher. Everyone else at the restaurant was walking around, looking and acting normal, but knowing what I knew changed the way I saw everything. I had this secret and I couldn't tell anyone, not yet. I wanted to stand on a table and scream it to the world.

We started off with margaritas, I lost count of how many. Then we decided we needed to eat to take the edge off all the alcohol we'd imbibed. So the server comes over and we told her we wanted enchiladas. She asked the New Mexico state question:

"Red or green, gentlemen?"

Juan must have been feeling pretty buzzed, because he stood up, and said loudly enough for the whole restaurant to hear…

"GREEN ALL THE WAY, BABY!"

Chapter 33 - Lights in the Sky

"Well, there are a lot of helicopters in the area, ma'am. They could be transporting someone to the hospital. And the police have helicopters when they're pursuing suspects..." Cody James put his hand over the phone's receiver and sighed. His newsroom internship often felt more like a stint in the looney bin.

"You couldn't hear anything?" he asked as his eyebrows drew together in a frown. She was the fifth person he'd heard from that night. It was like everyone suddenly realized they lived in an urban area with airborne vehicles. "Well, a lot of people don't like the noise they make. Maybe they've improved the design..." He listened to the woman ramble on and looked over at the enormous tv on the wall.

"For our top story tonight here at ABC15 11 o'clock news, we take you to senior correspondent Kim Rivera reporting live from Mesa with this breaking story.

"Thanks, Rachel. Many residents are scratching their heads after what they've seen here tonight. First, some of you may remember back in 1997, there were hundreds of witnesses who saw strange lights under the Phoenix sky. Well, we are getting reports from eyewitnesses all over the city that it has happened again. Neither witnesses nor researchers have yet to figure out what these Arizonans saw in the night sky all those years ago, but it was so widespread, the event was even named. It's now simply referred to as the Phoenix Lights," Kim said as she stood with her back to the Salt River Pima Maricopa Reservation. The sky was dark over the sparsely populated land well outside the metro area.

"Tonight, it seems to be happening all over again. We are getting a whole new set of stories on another group of sightings of strange lights in the sky. Rachel, we've heard from at least three hundred witnesses from Scottsdale down to Chandler with similar reports. We have with us now in Mesa one of those witnesses, Geoff Penland and his wife Bobbi," she said as the camera moved to a nondescript middle-aged couple.

"We first saw lights approaching fast, coming straight out of the east. There were at least four or five bright lights in a row," Geoff began.

"But you couldn't hear anything, that's why it didn't make any sense, because planes go over this place all the time-" Bobbi said excitedly.

“I’m not finished,” Geoff glared at his wife, who looked at him with annoyance. “As I was saying, when it was still a good distance away, the lights just all of a sudden stopped, like they saw us and were studying us or something. We just kept staring and then the lights separated and started moving horizontally and vertically away from each other,” he told Kim.

“Does that make any sense? Airplanes don’t do that,” Bobbi said as she leaned into the microphone Kim held. The seasoned reporter smiled at the woman and said nothing.

Geoff leaned even closer to the microphone. “A couple of the lights started moving real fast and looked like they were heading toward Tempe or Scottsdale. Some other lights started heading down towards Chandler. One of the lights started moving right at us and we sort of froze. We didn't know what to do and before we could take cover, we realized it was going to come right over top of us. It was a pretty good ways up there, but we still got a good look at it," he marveled.

“Yeah, and like I said, it really wasn't making any noise, only the sound of the wind as it passed. It wasn't round like a saucer, but it seemed a little more of a rounded shiny, kind of square. It was otherworldly and I had never seen anything like it," she finished with a big smile into the camera.

“Were you afraid?” Kim asked the couple.

“We really didn’t have time to feel afraid. It was so quiet and peaceful as it flew overhead that we never felt like it was trying to threaten us,” Geoff said.

“We were so amazed by what we saw, we just watched it until it disappeared from sight. Neither of us could speak,” Bobbi said.

“Well, I’m glad you found your voice, because that is an incredible story. I’m Kim Rivera, reporting live from Mesa, Arizona for ABC15. Back to you, Rachel,” she said.

“Thanks, Kim. We now go to Chandler where Steve Yanity is standing by with another witness to these strange lights,” Rachel told viewers.

“That’s right, Rachel. I’m here with Micah Simmons here who said he was taking a break during his shift this evening and saw the lights in the sky,” Steve leaned the microphone toward the young man.

“I had just come out of the warehouse on break, it was about 8:30 and I seen this light hovering out over the field behind the warehouse. At first, I thought it was a helicopter, but I didn’t hear nothing. It didn’t make any noise at all. As I was staring at it trying to figure out what it was, the light started dropping down real fast,” he said, looking alarmed at the memory.

“Did you think it was going to land?” Steve asked

"It came all the way down to the ground in the field, but it was like it just kind of hovered real close to the ground. I was gonna go get one of the other guys to see if we could find out what it was, but the light, all of a sudden, went straight back up in the air. It was real high this time and then it took off straight off that way," he pointed towards Gilbert.

"How close were you to...the light?" Steve asked.

"It wasn't just a light. It was coming from something. I'm not saying I'm a genius or nothing, but I know what planes look like. This wasn't no airplane," Micah told him.

"What was it?" Steve asked, scarcely breathing as he waited for the answer.

"I don't know. It was out of sight in just a few seconds. I never got a real close look at it. But I know I saw something I had never seen before," he looked directly at Steve, who couldn't help but shudder on national television.

"Rachel, Steve here, reporting live from Chandler. Back to you."

"Quite a story developing tonight here in Phoenix. Earlier today, in different parts of Phoenix, there were some other strange occurrences. One family in Scottsdale reported all of their computers and clocks stopped working this afternoon. A little later, for no apparent reason, their power went out. Now, the strange thing is that the SRP Power Company had not reported any outages."

"Maybe they forgot to pay their bill?" Josh Gibson asked with an exaggeratedly raised eyebrow. He had been Rachel's co-anchor since quitting stand-up comedy two years ago. Rachel laughed. More at Josh than with him.

"Reports have come in from all over the city about cell phones and computers losing all the information on their hard drives. Intermittent power outages were reported in several parts of Maricopa. Perhaps the strangest thing we heard today: people's clocks and even wrist watches stopped keeping time in the afternoon," Rachel reported.

"Well who hasn't lost track of time?" Josh asked her. She didn't take the bait.

"We haven't any word from the local authorities here if all those strange happenings in and around the city today were in any way related to the lights that were seen here in the sky tonight. We always have your news here first at ABC15. Stay tuned for updates. Always first on the scene for you. I'm Rachel Cox."

"That will do it for us here today. For ABC15, I'm Josh Gibson. Good night."

It was just past midnight at Axiom One. Adam, Del, Juan and the rest of their selected team, in the main conference room of the Manufacturing Center, still had the glow of euphoria. There wasn't a single red indicator light of failure on L.U.C.'s test flight simulation. The events of the day had left the trio overjoyed and a little overwhelmed.

There had been a few kinks in the test, but so few that they weren't noteworthy. They found the trending social media stories of UFO sightings amusing. Twitter had been blowing up for the last two hours and the story had already risen to prominence on all the national 24-hour news networks.

More than the sightings of lights in the sky, the big transport trucks loaded down with giant magnet tower beacons had created the most havoc. Those semi-trucks had gotten close to anything or anyone with a computer, clock, camera or any other sensitive digital equipment, the magnets wreaked havoc.

The crew had set up the three magnetic tower beacons in what they thought were more remote parts of the Phoenix area, but anything they passed or got close to was wiped out or wigged out. It was kind of funny now. They thought they had planned for everything that could go wrong, but they'd forgotten how the test might impact the more than four million people living in the Phoenix area. Luckily for everyone at Axiom One, power companies in Phoenix got all the complaint calls.

The cars had made the trip, and that was the most important thing for Adam's team. They celebrated the five flying cars created yesterday which Adam had approved, commissioned, and christened. The machines had performed almost flawlessly in their maiden voyage. Juan had followed his checklist at the Roswell Energy Center to perfection. With the control rod inserted, the proton engine fully spun up, and magnetic current set on the lowest possible pulse setting, the logistical element of L.U.C.'s intelligence engine took over.

Axiom One's magnetic pulse targeted the three magnetic temporary towers erected in and around some remote areas of Phoenix earlier that day. While establishing temporary magnetic towers wasn't the most precise method for guiding cars over a virtual highway, the fact that Phoenix and Roswell were fairly close ensured that Axiom Roswell wouldn't have any problems with performing this test. Adam's attention to detail refined the process as he and L.U.C. had coordinated the testing parameters. It was a simple point-to-point exercise that L.U.C. could perform with one eye closed and two holographic arms tied behind his back.

All five cars would take off vertically from the Axiom Skyport and enter into just one of the magnetic streams emanating to Phoenix. They would travel west across New Mexico and into Arizona in a single file line. The team would check and cross check internal systems and modes during the flight. After the cars crossed the Granite Reef Dam and entered the Phoenix area, they would glide between the Salt River and the Arizona Canal until they got into the largest clearing.

From there, the cars would gather and then separate vertically. One car would remain at five hundred feet, two cars would elevate to one thousand feet and two more would climb to fifteen hundred feet. These were three of the six virtual highway elevations they would establish when rolling out the network initially. The two cars set at one thousand feet would travel to the Scottsdale tower together and perform some side-by-side maneuvers. One car would travel rapidly to Mesa, while one would be sent back to Roswell immediately. The Mesa car would travel up to six hundred miles an hour, stop quickly at the termination point that was within a few feet of the tower, and then attempt to pursue the car en route to Roswell, approaching it at a high rate of speed and testing its collision avoidance systems. The final car in the test would be sent to Chandler. It would disengage from the network, execute a vertical landing, and then successfully take off and re-enter the temporary Vites.

Once the full virtual global highway transportation system was totally online with all four Axioms operating and in unison, vehicles traveling longer distances would receive clearance to break the sound barrier at seven hundred and sixty-seven miles per hour.

By the end of the week, Adam planned to instruct Del to begin car manufacturing at full capacity. Adam and Juan would also conference with Goian, Henna and Johanan to discuss the plan and timing for inserting all the control rods into Earth's core. This meant humans were harnessing a staggering amount of energy and controlling the greatest source of power in history.

Still giddy but growing tired after the celebration, the three men confirmed the plan that would change the world. It was well past 3:00 a.m. Adam was anxious to get back to the privacy of his home, not for rest, but because he wanted to record a private video message to Greg and Grace that they could open first thing tomorrow. He wanted to make sure they were the first people outside the Axiom that would hear that success was near. He wanted them to know how grateful he was for their friendship and love.

He had leaned especially hard on Greg. Without his skills as an engineer and his devotion as a friend of two decades, Adam knew he could not have accomplished this feat without his old college buddy. With a lump in his throat and tears threatening to spill, Adam thanked his friend for his help. He was forever grateful to Greg for giving him the opportunity to realize this dream. It was an act of supreme selflessness on Greg's part to allow Adam to take the reins and build the flying cars. While he couldn't expect fame or adulation from this accomplishment, he hoped people would appreciate his efforts. When people were in their flying cars, if they could feel a fraction of the gratitude he felt for Greg's gift, Adam would be more than satisfied.

Sending the message to his wonderful friends was a joy, but the next step was weighing heavy on his mind. There were so many times where he thought this day would never come, but unbelievably and miraculously, it was happening.

If producing cars was like learning about a baby on the way, the thought of introducing the world to the Vites was like bringing it home from the hospital. But who would he tell? How would he tell people? Should he start with Helms or did news of this magnitude need to go directly to the POTUS? Do not pass go, do not collect $200 dollars. What about the Joint Chiefs? Or was NATO the right body to announce the world change that was coming? Adam would sleep on it.... if he could. He'd talk with Ben to get his input because Ben was obviously connected to behind-the-scenes leadership, although he had never revealed his sources. Adam would listen to Ben's ideas, and maybe even talk to his mother.

Since that strange, wet Christmas morning almost a year ago, Adam realized he was not alone in this world. There were people and forces ready to do his bidding in the name of repairing the damage done to the earth and helping its people. And yet, when it came time to make this epoch-making decision, Adam realized he was the only one who could do it.

Chapter 34 - I'm Back, or Am I?

Time moves at a different speed in a casino. The people running the gaming establishment would prefer that their customers think time stops once they enter the dark, smoke-filled rooms. Is it day or night? Summer or winter? What difference does it make? It's always the right time to gamble. The casino exists separately from those immutable forces of nature that remind people of their powerlessness.

That was not entirely the case at the Mirage Hotel and Casino's The Still. A cardboard display at the entrance to the casino advertised Thanksgiving buffets and upcoming shows. Outside of that, there was nothing remarkable about that November Sunday for Leo Raines. He was doing what he usually did in his off hours, rather than going to family gatherings, holiday parties, or taking a vacation.

Leo stood at the far end of the long slender bar top, out of the way, trying to convince the bartender he was good for another rum and Coke.

"Sorry Mr. Raines, you are now on our cash only service level," he said pleasantly, like it was a perfectly nice level for a loyal customer. "Without having to extend any more credit, I am happy to serve you any drink you'd like."

Reaching down into both of his front pockets, Leo was able to produce eight dollars and twenty-three cents.

"What'll that buy me?" The bartender counted the money including the ones, the dime, the nickel, and three pennies.

The bartender smiled as if his customer had just won the lottery.

"Mr. Raines, you can get a twelve-ounce Bud Light or Mic Ultra for that." Leo's shoulders slumped and the bartender studied him for a minute. "I tell you what, you are a great client of this establishment, how about a LandShark, Island Style? I'll eat the seventy-seven cents for you."

Leo looked a little more comfortable at that suggestion as his pride returned somewhat.

"That sounds good," he said as he pulled out the last chair on the very end of the bar and took a seat.

Old habits were hard to shake, and addictions were nearly impossible to overcome alone. Leo couldn't stay away from the lights, the women, and the thrill of seeing his old friends King and Ace sitting side by side when his hand was dealt.

Cards were more reliable than practically any person Leo had ever met, and even his fifty-two friends were subject to the laws of chance. He learned when he was four years old that he could not count on his own father, who abandoned the family to 'find himself.' He grew up without a belief that life was a series of experiences outside of his control. Leo didn't develop self-control, either. He never saw the reason for self-discipline since winning didn't require it.

So Leo's habits led him back into an old familiar situation. Tired, behind on his bills, a tad bit unhealthier than he was at this time last year, and once again, in significant gambling debt. In a weird, perverted sort of way, these debts garnered a lot of attention from seemingly important people. The alternative was to be alone, bored, and without purpose. Besides his mother, Leo couldn't point to a single person that really cared about him or what his dreams were. And he suspected she cared more out of duty than love.

He watched the people in front of the TV cheer. The Dolphins had just scored to take a two-point lead over the Raiders, late in the fourth quarter. The game looked like it was shaping up to have a wild finish. Leo wasn't really a football fan, but because others in the bar were cheering, he began to show interest to better make him part of the scene.

The Raiders had the ball and were driving. They needed about ten more yards to get in field goal range for their kicker. Forty-three seconds left and the clock was ticking. The Raiders broke the huddle and came to the line of scrimmage. The signal caller was barking his commands, the clock was to thirty-two seconds and the Raiders without a time out. The color broadcaster was painting the scene and creating the necessary drama all good broadcasters do, milking the moment for every drop of tension he could squeeze from it.

All twenty-seven TV screens offered to the patrons of The Still, cable and network alike, cut over simultaneously to a screen showing an empty desk in the White House's Oval Office. A huge groan, along with some angry screams of disbelief overtook The Still and similarly all throughout the Casino. A resonant voice, loaded with gravitas, came through the speakers.

"Please stay tuned for a special announcement from the President of the United States."

Momentarily, the President appeared with at least a dozen suits, male and female, standing in the background. Some Leo recognized immediately as important members of Congress and others continued to file in behind the President as he took a seat at his desk.

"Today, we continue the never-ending journey to bridge the past with the future. Our history tells us that our desire to forge ahead and create a better tomorrow for our children and our planet is strong. Here in the United States, we built a republic which is a government of, by, and for the people. Each generation was entrusted with leaving things better for the next generation than we found them. These words have never been truer than in this century," he said.

"You interrupted the game for this?" A man yelled over his collection of beer bottles. The rest of the crowd was quiet, trying to absorb the unexpected words in the middle of a sporting event.

"We have developed the technology that allows us to understand all the harm that we, ourselves, have recklessly caused our planet. This government and the people of this great nation of ours have sought ways to conserve, heal, recycle, cleanse, and replenish. Through the tireless dedication and efforts of many people, we were beginning to make a difference. We've been working to clean and heal the oceans, we are rescuing species near extinction, and we are just beginning to reverse the devastating effect carbon emissions have on our environment and the ozone," he said, looking into the camera with an earnestness that suggested an acting coach.

Leo looked at the audience. The man with the beer bottles was beginning to look anxious. After a few minutes of listening to the president speak, the mood in the room had shifted from rowdy to serious. He was hardly an environmentalist, and didn't really listen to the speech as his eyes wandered over the group standing behind the president. He saw an auburn-haired woman standing near the window and his heart stopped.

She didn't look exactly like Hannah, her hair wasn't dark enough. He only saw Hannah wearing jeans and this woman wore an elegant charcoal suit. When they'd talked in the diner, she looked at him with eyes that seared his soul. She was looking at the president with those same eyes, that same look of complete understanding and Leo nearly fell off his chair.

Hannah had never talked about working in Washington, had she? He couldn't remember the president ever breaking into a football game to talk about the environment either. None of this made sense.

"I wonder what this is about," Leo said, as much to himself as to Beer Bottles, who looked like he'd had too many.

"Huh?" he asked Leo.

Leo shook his head and they both continued watching the president.

"In the long history of the world, there have been only a few generations that have been able to live up to their responsibility. It is with great energy, faith, and devotion that we bring forward an endeavor that will truly change life on this planet as we know it. While I do not feel worthy to be the one entrusted to deliver this news to the world, I humbly accept my role as its messenger. In a cooperative effort between the Office of Science and Technology, whose mission is to maximize the benefits of science and technology to advance health, prosperity, security, environmental quality, and justice, the Central Intelligence Agency, and the Office of Global Change, we finally asked the question: what could our government do for our country, our planet?"

"No more taxes!" a voice from the back of the room yelled. There was a short burst of laughter.

"In a highly secretive project that has been years in the planning, today I announce the end of an era. It was an era of extraordinary progress, but also one of extraordinary damage to our planet.

"We will usher in this new era with the news that we learned how to break the suffocating chains of gravity. We have developed a limitless way to travel around the world unlike anything that has existed before this moment.

"It is with great pleasure that I announce to you today the launch of the Virtual Global Highway Transportation System. We are calling it the Vites."

A murmur ran through the crowd. "The fights?" a voice asked.

My fellow Americans, and those watching around the world, when the Vites is fully functioning, there will be no need for a physical transportation infrastructure. The cars and vehicles will traverse the globe effortlessly and have zero emissions. The air, the water and the soil can begin to heal. It will be a kind of rebirth for our planet," he said, offering the camera one of his rare smiles.

"We will be providing much more detail in the coming days. We will begin releasing our plans for all to see through the Department of Transportation website. Know that we have already been in conversations with our friends around the world and the rollout of this new mode of transportation will be a global collaboration.

"You, the American people, have suffered and toiled long enough. You are tired and you are worthy. Together we have pursued the dream of creating technology that helps, rather than harms, our planet. Today, that dream becomes a reality," he said as the group behind him burst into applause. Hannah hugged a man standing next to her.

"So, we all get new cars?" Beer Bottles asked fuzzily. The man next to him shrugged.

"I would be remiss if I didn't mention my great friend Mr. Richard Helms. In large part, we can consider the Vites Richard's brainchild. As you can imagine, a development of this nature and magnitude must be completed at the highest level of security and secrecy. Richard is the Director of our CIA and heads the greatest clandestine intelligence agency in the world. In addition to the head of the DOT, the OSTP, and the OGC, I've asked Richard to say a few words about security and safety. Richard Helms, everyone…"

The press conference continued as Leo surrendered his seat at the bar. Head swimming, he moved to a place with a little more privacy, which was anywhere in the Mirage that didn't have a television. He reached into the pocket on the inside of his Members Only jacket and pulled out the burner phone Hannah had given to him to use when they "worked together" a couple of years ago.

After the C-130 had lifted off from Area 51 with its cargo headed for DC all those months ago, he had tried to contact her more than a few times, with no response. "Hannah, or whatever your name is, I bet you'll answer this time," he muttered to himself as he furiously typed a new message into the phone.

As was often the case, Leo was in a lot of trouble, but the timing of these events might just be the rabbit's foot he needed to get out of a big jam, again. With blackmail on his mind, Leo considered his next move. *I bet a lot of people might be real interested in hearing more about where I think this little Vites thing might have really come from…*

From Greg's beach house to the White House, what a ride it had been. Adam, Greg, Grace, and Dr. Alex, in addition to a plethora of government officials from various organizations joined the esteemed group in the Oval Office. Ben had been invited but considering what he stood to gain from the whole enterprise, he decided to lay low and stay out of the limelight. True to his word, Adam decided he would reach out to Richard Helms and lift the veil on what he had been working on all these months. Richard admitted to having checked on him a couple of times, just to ensure Adam's "well-being," (his euphemism for mental health). Once he learned of the magnitude of the project, he was, as the British say, "gobsmacked." He had no inkling Adam would deliver something on such an enormous scale.

Politically, Richard knew exactly what to do and how to do it, as he was well-connected with the inner workings of the government. He made sure the right people got credit for what they needed to get credit for, and this had earned him his elevated status in Washington. Richard himself was quite pleased that he could play such a prominent role in the new age.

For Adam, being in the Oval Office was an incredible experience on its own. Due to the large number of contributors in this historic event, the guests had to squeeze together tightly to ensure as many of the esteemed group would be seen by the camera's lens. This meant that he could legitimately sidle right up onto Grace's shoulder without garnering any suspicion that he might be improperly violating her personal space. He did love the way she smelled.

While Richard continued his address which included instructions, recommendations, and warnings, Grace's phone buzzed. She'd had the phone in hand and it was almost impossible for Adam to avoid seeing the text when she raised it to glance at the screen.

"Hey babe, I've really missed you and haven't heard from you in a while. I see you're on TV. We need to talk and discuss how to rekindle our relationship, if you know what I mean. Talk soon."

Adam slumped slightly, but he forced his smile to remain. Adam's spirits had been knocked down a notch or two after reading the text. He was still going to play a role in one of the most significant transformations in human history. That alone was enough to give him a purpose driven life. It was the alone part that he had been hoping to remedy. Everything was better if you could share it with someone.

The press conference was completed. The US government had held the appropriate discussions with America's allies prior to this public event. Everyone was on board and prepared for the deluge of questions that were to come. There was a lot more infrastructure to put in place to fully execute the global vision of the Vites, however, there was a rather rudimentary level of service the Axiom driven network could provide immediately. An oversimplification might be to say that the complexity of launching a basic service over Vites was on par with a university implementing a bus service around town for students, just easier. Only there were no limitations on where passengers could go and beyond using empty airspace, there wouldn't be any additional considerations to get something started. Theoretically, the Vites could take passengers anywhere in the country, and ultimately, in the world, where the skies were open.

Until the Vites replaced all other forms of air travel, which it was destined to do, the Department of Transportation, or DOT, would work with the Federal Aviation Association, or FAA, to develop corridors where the Vites could operate. They would have to operate within the established TRACON, or Terminal Radar Approach Control system.

Engineers continued to monitor how the flying cars' on-board intelligence would operate across the Vites. To aviate properly, the cars would automatically sense, predict, and react to any potential collision scenario, automatically adjusting the vehicle to avoid impact.

There was a maze of red tape to appease the dinosaurs until the gas guzzlers were completely obsolete, and plenty to do in administrative and bureaucratic divisions. The government would establish a marketplace, not unlike the insurance healthcare portal, which would enable citizens to sign up for service under a monthly subscription fee. Senior citizens would have the capability of taking their transportation subscription fee directly out of their Social Security distributions. It was important to include everyone in this new venture.

A few days after the press conference, Adam had arranged to get the private room at Ambar. He hadn't realized how much he missed the kebabs and the tzatziki. The Axiom food services were nice, but Adam craved the dishes Ivan Petrovic made from his great grandmother's recipes. He invited the "Beach House" contingent of the Axiom team: Greg, Grace, Dr. Alex and of course, Myles. Richard Helms, his wife Donna, Julie and the kids would also be there. This was going to be a time of celebration, a time to reminisce, and also a time to dream about the future. Adam desperately hoped his future involved making up for lost time with the kids.

While Richard had no problem with taking the credit in the public sphere, in this intimate setting, he had no problem in giving all the credit and appreciation to Adam. Adam thanked him for his kind words and having the kids and Julie know the nature of the justification for the time he missed with them. Richard had an interesting observation.

"Isn't it interesting that in every science fiction movie I've ever seen, there was never an explanation about the flying cars? They were just there. You had to make the leap and accept them. Well, we now know the story. It was all because of Adam Hunter. Well, Adam along with his remarkable friends, colleagues, and...*interesting discoveries*." Yes, I'm referring to the benevolent, otherworldly artificial intelligence known as L.U.C. that found its way to Adam on Christmas Eve two years ago. It took all the ingredients of courage, grit, innovation, collaboration, along with new discoveries. This is the story of how the Flying Car came to be. Folks, you are now witnesses to the story and we are only in the first chapter. The best is yet to come."

Veteran anchor Roberta Valle appeared on the screen. She was behind her desk in the newsroom, shaking her head. "All of you viewers at home, you are part of history. Not since the Moon Landing has there been such an incredible triumph of technology. While artificial intelligence has played a role in this advancement, it is amazing what people can accomplish when they believe anything is possible," she said, before returning to viewers to the game.

"Think it's possible for the Dolphins to win this?" someone asked.

The best part of the next few days, for Adam, was spending time at home. His own bed, coffee from his own maker, the home gym and running on his treadmill made him feel like he was part of the real world again. Work would resume soon. There was much to do. It was only natural for Adam to take a new position in the Office of Science and Technology Policy working for Jack Taylor. He had fulfilled his promise to Richard and now his former boss could write his own ticket. People would always think of Richard Helms as the man behind the revolution. That was just fine with Adam. He knew what his own purpose was and his fulfillment would come from seeing life in the new world. He could imagine it.

A box containing a parcel wrapped in exquisite green silk embroidered with Japanese characters arrived at Adam's house. Untying the fabric, he found a container of the local confection *yokan*. The pieces were molded into tiny, flying car-shaped ovals and covered with silver leaf. A note of congratulations from the Johansens fell to the floor as he picked up the tray of sweets. In it, they also mentioned that they had settled into life and work on Maejima Island. While the energy center on Axiom Japan was now complete, the stress of not yet finding the fourth stone was taking a toll on them. They were running out of places to look, and with the public aware of the virtual cars, the pressure only increased. It was not public pressure that spurred them to find the fourth stone, it was their determination to fulfill the vision of Mr. Kumar.

While he may have played the biggest and most crucial part in turning the dream into reality, Ben chose to remain anonymous. He decided to unwind and take a long weekend trip from Denver to Las Vegas the day after the press conference. When he was in Sin City, he never played any of the tables but would occasionally take in a show. He was also fascinated by the tourists and locals and did a lot of people watching. His favorite place to stay was at the Venetian Hotel. He had studied the history of Italy and the Roman Empire extensively, and simply fell in love with Venice. On his way out of town, he picked up a copy of the Las Vegas Review Journal in the private and business jet terminal. As he boarded the Gulfstream, the one in the S.E.T.I. fleet that had been earmarked for his personal travel, he sat in the recliner and opened the paper to the second page. On that page, about half-way down, there was a rather nondescript section that caught his eye.

MISSING PERSON

Name: Leo Raines, Height 5'11", Weight 195 lbs, Age 45. Anyone with information is asked to call Central Nevada Crimestoppers at 645-8478 or 1-877- 645-8478.

Anonymity will be provided.

Chapter 35 - Anything More Than a Whisper

Staffers at www.thevites.gov stopped attempting to measure demand for flying car subscriptions after the third server crash. Citizens wanted answers. How soon could people create accounts and get airborne? They paid their taxes, didn't they? Why was it taking so long?

Others tried a softer approach. They were happy to pay extra if it would put them closer to the front of the line. Maybe a case of Glenmorangie for you poor, overworked government employees? Just remember it came from the MacGregor family, that's m-a-c, not m-c. We'll be watching our inbox, have a great rest of the day!

The team was working hard daily to add more servers to the cloud service providing the access. Very soon, they were hoping to raise performance to an acceptable level. On the first few days of registration, there were stories of people trying to get a secure connection for thirty-six hours before they were able to access the system. Family members took turns sleeping while on hold with the since-disconnected toll-free number 1-800-GET-AVTE.

In the first ninety days of operation, more than one million vehicles were now operating on the Vites. Like birds, and without limitations, vehicles could instantaneously and on the fly, adjust to available virtual highways as the system approved them. Until they were obsoleted, the DOT and FAA had collaborated to provide restricted fly zones around all major US commercial airports. With the significantly lower cost, ease, and efficiency of this new way to travel, the shelf-life for airports was rapidly shrinking.

The sight of so many flying objects overhead took some getting used to, but on the ground, cities grew quieter. As fewer trains, trucks, buses and cars motored around the cities, people could hear each other more easily. Their conversations grew in quantity and quality as they walked streets once filled with roaring vehicles.

Of course, there were still dump trucks and jackhammers and cranes, cities were always going to be busy places, but that spring in Chicago, five months after the launch of the Vites, a crowd of thousands gathered in the center of Millennium Park to hear the songbirds announce their arrival. For the first time in as long as anyone could remember, people could hear the birds over the din of traffic.

Chicago's streets were quieter but the schools were busier. Attendance at elementary schools increased significantly late that winter. Walking to school during a Chicago winter was not something many kids looked forward to, but in some parts of Chicago, walking outside was not safe for children.

For the interests of others. That was what his mother Betty had reminded him of when he told her he was working on a big project. L.U.C. had shown him images of clear, shimmering oceans, teeming with life and cornfields waving in the breeze. He was going to help the world, L.U.C. told him as the holographic earth rotated before him. Adam was making sure the Trentafactory cranked out as many cars as possible because so many of the planet's nearly eight billion people needed them. So many people, and so many needs. It could be overwhelming to think about how enormous it all was.

Adam remembered when he was a teenager, Betty sometimes came home from a day of teaching, exhausted. Her classes were crowded. There wasn't enough funding for the staff and materials she needed. Adam, analytical thinker that he was, could not see a light at the end of Betty's professional tunnel.

"The district doesn't have any money, Mom. This has to get you down. I mean, how many of these kids are even going to finish eighth grade?" the sixteen-year-old know-it-all asked his discouraged mother.

Tired as she was, Betty quickly rose to her feet. She looked at her son with such disappointment Adam was temporarily lost for words. No matter. His mother had plenty of them.

"Now you listen to me, young man. This is not about money. This is not about diplomas or any other fancy titles we give ourselves. I do this for them. My ego is not part of this. Impressing anybody is not my reason for doing any of what I do for these children. *It gives me joy to help these children*," she told her son, her voice shaking with emotion.

"I know you do. You are a great teacher. I just wish more people knew how much good you do," Adam said. He admired his mother but knew the kind of work she did was for very special people.

"God knows what I do. God loves a cheerful giver," she began, a smile replacing the frown she'd given him. Reciting Scripture always did that to her. "Each of you should give what you have decided in your heart to give," she began.

"Not reluctantly or under compulsion," Adam joined in. Now he understood. Betty walked the walk.

"For God loves a cheerful giver," they finished together. "And you are one, Mom." He promised himself at that moment that he would do right by his mother. Exactly how he would do this, he had no idea. But he would give cheerfully.

Good deeds, like flying cars, were made to make people's lives better. Unlike flying cars, acts of kindness and service have the strange and unique ability to find the people who need them. They do this anonymously in many cases. No need to have the recipient's name written on the gift, the good deeds know where they belong. Helping others is easier than mailing letters. Sometimes faster, too.

Acts of kindness and service can pick up speed when people are helping them get where they need to go. And all Ashanti Washington cared about was getting the kids to school. She had a little over three hundred of them. They were students at Reason Dowling Elementary School in Chicago's Garfield Park.

"This could be a huge liability," School Superintendent Williams told Ashanti when she asked for a twenty-four-seater to pick her students up at their homes and deliver them to school. "What if someone shoots at one of these things? If a kid gets hurt, the lawsuits will bury us," he told her as they sat in his dreary office.

Ashanti wanted to scream. She caught herself before she did. Screaming would not get her kids, her students, rather, to school safely. "Do you know how dangerous it is for them to walk to school? They won't do it. Their parents won't let them do it. Huge numbers of them fail to attend school on a regular basis. I don't have to tell you how that hurts their learning," she reminded Williams.

"No, I understand that, and I really am sympathetic. But these 'cars' as you call them are government property. Do we even know if they fly straight?" Williams asked.

"Rich folks are ordering custom made cars and they seem to fly just fine," Ashanti told him. "You know, if we can get attendance up, test scores up, think how that's going to work out for you," she said with the smile that had earned her the undying support of scores of Garfield Park families over the years. "These kids are in danger as it is. All things considered, this transportation is safer for them. I watched that Dr. Hunter on TV last week. He talked about how he would send his own kids to school in one of these," she said.

Williams looked at Ashanti and sighed. She had worn him down again. He gave her a rueful smile and wished he'd had an ally like her when he was a kid. Integrated busing was an ordeal for a ten-year-old.

"Dr. Hunter said he'd send those things to this neighborhood?" Williams asked, still a little suspicious.

"Oh, I've already started the paperwork," she said, reaching into the bag next to her feet. She slid a stack of forms across his desk. "You just need to sign here."

Did that group of students know who Adam Hunter was? Did it matter? Two weeks after Ashanti met with her boss, the children bounded out of the vehicle, its mirror like metal painted yellow gold, as vehicles transporting children must always be. They greeted the row of teachers standing in front of the school.

The searching, the hiding, the digging, the drawing and redrawing plans. It was all worth it. Adam and his team didn't make these cars to feed their egos or impress other people. The cars were doing exactly what they were meant to do. The kids would be safe.

In time, there would be flying cars with bells and whistles, espresso machines and pure silk sleep masks. These were not the important features of the flying cars as far as the US government was concerned. Seeing an opportunity to live up to their promise to the young, the old and the disadvantaged, the government made flying cars that were (relatively) simple, safe and available to everyone.

Like many government programs, people at the low- or zero-income level had free access to the Vites. Perhaps not surprisingly, low-income households and the unhoused were among the early adopters. Eliminating the cost of transportation, insurance, and gas made a significant impact towards affording some of life's necessities, such as food.

In addition to eliminating the need for cars, those that were relegated to public bus transportation no longer had to make their way to the nearest bus stop and travel to another point on a predetermined line that may or may not be close to one's destination. Just like the graduated scale used for filing and paying your taxes, the higher a person's income, the more he or she paid for a Monthly Transportation Subscription, or MTS.

Over the coming months and years, businesses, schools, sporting venues, and other public areas would replace parking lots and garages with fluidly flowing skyway portals for incoming and outgoing transportation. Practically anyplace that could offer a standalone, unobstructed landing pad twenty feet across, could be designated as a take-off and landing spot for a certain class of vehicles operating on the Vites.

People had many questions about riding the Vites, and answers to many of their questions were available in the user's manual that Adam had created with L.U.C.'s help. These machines were almost disturbingly capable, and Adam joked that the document detailing their capabilities compared to the user's manual in a Nissan Pathfinder's glove box was like putting a college physics textbook next to *The Foot Book* by Dr. Seuss.

Informed consent was key, however and Adam wanted people to know before they climbed inside one of his flying vehicles what they could expect:

Prior to vehicle entry, each passenger will agree to a BioScan. The car's internal systems perform this scan automatically. It will then verify the identity (or identities) of the passenger(s) and the proper customizations for travel will occur. All bags and belongings stowed within the vehicle will be scanned to confirm that only approved possessions are present.

For international destinations, only those contents approved for those jurisdictions will be allowed on board before the vehicle will ascend.

In the United States, once inside the vehicle, all passenger information is shared with the National Crime Information Center, or NCIC. If there are any outstanding warrants for a passenger or there are any improper actions or illegal transactions on board, the vehicle will incarcerate its passengers and take them to the nearest law enforcement office.

While grounded, if the vehicle senses that it is under threat of danger of any kind, a "repel mode" will be activated and passengers will be unable to approach the vehicle. The vehicle will self-activate all its safety and self-defense systems. It will attempt to vacate the area immediately and fly to the nearest law enforcement office.

If any passenger has a medical emergency while in flight, the car is equipped with a Nanomedicine Care Center. Nanoparticles will be released onto the distressed passenger where they will pin-point the cause of the distress, communicate that to a medical professional and emergency contact. The Nanoparticles will attempt to stabilize the patient and resolve the matter, even if temporarily. The normal flight destination will be aborted, and the vehicle will be re-routed to the nearest participating medical health facility.

In the unlikely event the vehicle experiences any type of malfunction while traveling on the Vites, the operating system will attempt to correct the issue. If the system cannot resolve the malfunction, it will automatically elevate the vehicle to a vertical flying level reserved only for emergency vehicles and cars experiencing difficulties. The entire system has a built-in collision avoidance system so an idle vehicle, regardless of location, poses no threat.

In the unlikely event that the vehicle should encounter water, ocean or fresh, the vehicle is airtight. It will provide several hours of emergency oxygen until system recapture is complete.

Unmarked "Sentinel" vehicles, equipped to address almost any situation, will travel the Vites twenty-four hours a day.

Also in operation around the clock was Axiom One. It had begun producing flying cars at the rate of 25,000 per day. At this rate of production, one million cars would be available in a little over a month. Now that the specifications had been proved out, the manufacturing centers at the Axioms in Damascus, outside Kabul and Nagasaki would begin production. Country after country was lining up for inclusion and airspace was being approved daily.

In the middle of all the activity was Adam, now Director of the Office of Science and Technology Policy, a new division within the Department of Transportation under the heading of Virtual Transportation. Adam, back on the official payroll and Thrift Retirement Savings Plan, would be the guiding force in setting policy and procedure around the global operation of the virtual highway system. There was no one more qualified than him to understand how it would operate.

Globally, private businesses, for a fee and royalty, would receive the primary specifications for building vehicles compatible with the Vites. Contracts were awarded to companies that demonstrated the innovation and aptitude for developing new age technology. There would be contracts for transport vehicles which would operate primarily on the fourth level of the Vites and would replace rail and eighteen wheelers. Contracts to manufacture larger multi-passenger vehicles to replace planes, buses and limousines were in high demand, especially in Asia and Europe.

The Office of Science and Technology Policy recommended freely giving foreign countries system integration specifications so that they could open their airspaces. They would also have the intelligence engine on board each craft to interact with their customs and border control protection systems. While Adam maintained a proxy dotted line authority over all four Axiom locations, he had a team of people assigned to him within his OSTP organization that oversaw writing policy.

They met with delegates from foreign countries, helping them understand technology necessary for gaining acceptance and integrating into the system. Dedicated team members reviewed completed applications, and even went as far as working with those countries which were having trouble meeting the demands of Vites specifications. Vites, the transportation system itself, was vastly technologically superior to any prior operating system and could usually reverse engineer itself to ensure compatibility, even with legacy systems. This brought the team a great deal of satisfaction, with the many young members of Adam's staff stressing inclusion as a core value.

Despite their introduction and enthusiastic reception in low-income areas, the wealthy elites saw the flying cars as exciting new toys and, with proper customization, status symbols. Adam's office awarded contracts for producing vehicles for luxury travel. Travelers using these machines would pay a surcharge over and above monthly subscription fees. They could also pay for food, entertainment, and other luxuries if desired. And aren't luxuries usually desired?

People began to consider these new vehicles necessities and were eager to experience the most basic Pteras. Within six months, forty-five states, municipalities, and other local jurisdictions were forming integration and transition proposals to adopt the Vites into their economic development and budget plans.

By June, almost every business and home had designated landing zones. As parking lots emptied, thousands of those areas became precisely organized drop off and pick up locations for Vites passengers. Applications allowed customers to order pick-up and delivery. These apps displayed the exact location of the assigned vehicle exactly where passengers needed to stand for transportation. The goal of the Vites, in terms of travel for individuals and small groups, was to always have a flying car available at the designated time, day or night.

Another, broader goal was to undo a few centuries of environmental damage. Within a year, with another Christmas coming, environmental scientists were finding measurable improvements in the air and water, as L.U.C. had shown Adam two Christmases earlier. The utopic images of green spaces were emerging from Boston to Tucson. Agri-zones monitored by agri-drones were popping up in Northern Maine and West Texas, both considered food deserts in recent years. Signs that the world food supply would be more plentiful were encouraging. The US Energy Information Administration was reporting that carbon emissions had plunged over the past year by 1.7 billion metric tons, a 32% decline over the previous year, given the vast amount of the credit to new emission free modes of transportation.

Curious developments took place in the hearts and minds of people, a far more difficult terrain to assess than Mother Earth. Reports of improved wellbeing seemed to prove the folk saying: if mama ain't happy, ain't nobody happy. The health of the planet that nurtures and sustains us, it now seemed obvious, was related to and a reflection of the health of her children.

Depression, the common cold of mental illness, is common among people without strong social networks. The Vites gave people in sparsely populated areas a way to connect. Groups began to meet regularly in places like Lambert, Montana and Skyline, Alabama. Meetups were free, required no licenses or training, and travel was safe.

Urban areas showed a decrease in people seeking treatment and medication for anxiety. A doctor who checked up on a patient he had not seen for six months asked what she was doing to manage her symptoms. "Walking in the woods," was her answer.

More exercise was a benefit and a result of improved air quality. Refills for asthma inhalers dropped a staggering 30 percent in cities from Virginia to Connecticut.

With luxury vehicles coming online, adventurous families were beginning to order up and take more elaborate vacations again. Riding in one of the new luxury class vehicles was an experience. The Rolls Royce of the Vites began to roll out of the production stations, and it was called the Sol-ution. An image of the Roman god Sol and his chariot, the company's logo, proudly announced a new way of life was upon us.

There had been quite a bit of speculation in government circles about how Axiom teams in Japan, Damascus, and Afghanistan had completed such mammoth tasks. After opening the sites for operations, S.E.T.I. hired highly qualified, experienced engineers, construction workers, and nanoparticle experts hand over fist, with the objective of populating these ultramodern cities and continuing flying car manufacturing.

After removing the security perimeters so each city could begin its expansion, engineers found only skeleton crews working in the Axiom's Energy Center District. Surprisingly small groups monitored and kept the stream of magnetic current connected and flowing with Roswell. Someone (and possibly some variants, themselves) had disassembled all the variants, skins incinerated, packed up and transported as computer equipment to seaports. The transport containers, from the three locations, despite having shipped at different times, had somehow "accidentally" fallen off their ships into the Mariana Trench. All of them.

Unbeknownst to the world, the pact that Adam, Ben and Ella made had become a real boon to the local economy in those three countries. Thousands of new, highly paying jobs had become available, with modern cities and lifestyles to boot. The advent of flying cars for the world was a nice perk, too. If it was "just a fad," as a small but vocal group of critics contended, it was turning out to be a global one.

The global connectivity of the Vites was a growing concern behind the scenes, as the search for the fourth stone continued. Vites was carrying almost eight million cars and expanding by the tens of thousands weekly. For this mode of transportation to offer convenience and fluidity the world over, hundreds of millions of cars would need to be in service for Earth's population of almost eight billion.

Dr. Alex had stressed to Adam that a fully functional Vites could function well for a long time without the insertion of the actuator key. As Adam understood it, once they found the fourth stone, they would place it in the empty quadrant with the other three stones. When the four stones were together, they would seamlessly fuse themselves into a single translucent cornerstone. This cornerstone would fit into a specially designed circular compartment in Axiom One's Energy Center Control Room.

The compartment was vacant; a large, empty hole on the primary control panel, sticking out like a sore thumb. Once placed into position, the system's protocol would require a dual key mandate to lower the cornerstone directly over the top of the control rod. It would act as a conduit between the magnetic current flowing from Earth's core and flow through the energy proton beams that Axiom One was using. The Axiom would pulse and magnify the current while streaming it around Earth's 33rd parallel.

As Dr. Alex had explained, Axiom One was already amplifying the geodynamic process that generated Earth's normal magnetic field due to the motion of convection currents in the mixture of the molten iron and nickel in Earth's core. Due to the unique materials of the cornerstone, the actuator key would elevate this process and amp the current tenfold. It was a little intimidating to think about, but not having enough current to meet the dreams and hopes of so many was more so.

Adam had taken a few days off in the middle of December, and so had Greg. They met for dinner at Sequoia DC. Greg knew the Maitre'D and he held a table for them with a striking view of the Virginia skyline. They watched the beautiful machines in the air above perform a well-choreographed, hypnotic sort of dance on the clear, chilly night. Soon, the President would require a kind of "Air Force One" for the Vites. Still so much to do.

"Well, you did it," Greg said as he held up his glass of Sauvignon Blanc. "To the flying cars," he said with a smile.

"*We* did it," Adam corrected him and clinked his glass to Greg's.

"I knew you would pull it off," Greg said as he munched on his calamari. The vehicles glistening like distant silvery holiday ornaments, their movements so ordered and rhythmic, other diners found themselves mesmerized. "People can't get enough of these things you built."

"*We* built them, and I'm worried that people really won't be able to get enough of them," Adam said.

"The fourth stone?" Greg asked.

Adam nodded. "We can't wait until the last minute with something this crucial," Adam told his friend as he took another sip of wine. "Things are going really well right now, but if we don't find it…" he couldn't bring himself to say the words. He couldn't quit this close to achieving a fully functional Vites.

"We are going to find the stone, Adam," Greg said with complete confidence.

“This whole thing has felt like building a house of cards, sometimes. One wrong move and everything could just…It’s like Emperor Marcus Aurelius said. ‘There was a dream that was the Vites, you could only whisper it. Anything more than a whisper, and it would vanish, it was so fragile,’” he shook his head and looked out over the Potomac.

Greg laughed. “Are you sure that’s what a Roman Emperor said?”

“You know what I meant,” Adam couldn’t help but smile at the image of Roman Generals on the Vites.

“Adam. I have hope,” Greg said. “And you know what else I think? Things don’t always turn out exactly like we plan. There are always surprises. But I honestly believe things always turn out for the best. Now eat your steak,” he told his friend as all around Washington DC, and the East Coast, and North America, and the entire planet, people glided through the skies on the Vites.

At home that night, Adam turned to his journal. He thought he would be feeling on top of the world at this stage of the project, instead all he could do was wonder how much longer they could manage without the fourth stone. He began with a favorite quote from Michael Francis Flynn.

December 10

“But what is hope? When all else is lost, it is the one thing you may keep.”

It’s time to find the stone, hoping hasn’t worked.

Chapter 36 - Abounding Wonders of the New World

"Sir, I'm glad your goats had plenty to drink, but I don't think we can take credit for that," said Hamad Qadir, Director of Community Outreach, Axiom Damascus. He and an older man sat on floor pillows in the corner of the Axiom's Visitor Center. A group of schoolchildren were walking along the far side of the room with a tour guide, chattering excitedly about the 'melted metal' they would be able to see inside the earth.

"I didn't borrow my brother-in-law's car to drive an hour to tell you a made-up story, young man," Nasir Mahmoud said. "But I want to know if this is going to happen again. I can buy more goats if this will continue."

"You know, there are springs in the desert. They appear for a while, disappear, and come back," Hamad said. He'd seen it happen on his grandfather's farm outside Zarqa.

"Fifty years I am raising animals on this land," Nasir said. The lines on his browned face were like a map of dry riverbeds. "This does not happen here," he said decisively.

"If you would like, I can send a drone to your area. It will take pictures, do some measurements, and tell me if there is something on your land we should be concerned about," Hammad said. "Now, some mint tea?" he gestured to a nearby table.

"With sugar, please," Nasir said, smiling.

Hammad returned to his office a half an hour later to find his assistant, Ariel, shaking his head.

"What?" he asked the recent MIT graduate. Ariel hadn't been Hamad's first choice in the interview, but he realized he'd underestimated the twenty-one-year-old. Ariel was sharp, resourceful and very conscientious.

"Dr. Hunter might really like to know about this," Ariel said as he watched a giant monitor of the control rod some 1800 miles below the earth's surface.

"I don't want to overreact. I cannot 'cry wolf,' like they say in the States. I'm sending out a drone, and we'll find out if this is really happening," Hammad told him.

"But he's the third guy this week," Ariel said. He knew he was close to getting his boss to call the Big Boss.

Fatima from Systems Management appeared in the doorway of Hammad's office and looked quizzically into space. Then she nodded.

"Yes, you can hear it up here, too," she said.

"Is that some machine malfunction? I've been hearing that rumble on and off for a while now," Hammad said.

"Machine malfunction? Not on my watch, Qadir," Fatima was the top Core Management engineer in the country, if not the world. "The machines are working just fine. And I think I can save you the hassle of the drone," she said.

"What are you talking about?" Hassan asked in confusion.

"That sound we've been hearing is water. There's an underground river and when we dug as deep as we did, well, we disturbed something," she told him. Ariel's eyebrows rose.

"I'll get Dr. Hunter's office," he said to a speechless Hammad.

"No! Wait!" Hammad said after he recovered. Ariel put the receiver down. He looked at Hammad, then Fatima.

Hammad ran his hand over his face and turned to Fatima. "How-how big is this river?" he asked her.

"How many liters? I'd have to give you an estimate right now, because I'm not sure. We've got SONAR helping us track it. The best we can tell, it's coming from a few miles north of the Axiom," she said.

"This isn't your fault, Hammad. I don't think it's anyone's *fault*. It's a river. None of the engineers expected this. You're not in trouble. If you were Dr. Hunter, you'd want to be made aware of this ASAP, wouldn't you?"

Hammad sighed. He should have sent the drone after the first villager came to talk about the marshy ground. Fatima studied him as she leaned against the door frame, arms crossed.

"I'll do it," she offered. "It doesn't look like we're in danger right now. And they can see the same things on the magnetic res that we can. They will know soon, even if we don't tell them ourselves," she said with the equanimity only engineers had.

Hammad looked at Ariel. "Yeah, ok. Call him. But call Jordan first and ask them if they'd like a river."

Adam took one of his last flights on the Gulfstream to Damascus and chewed his nails nearly the entire time. At Axiom Damascus, he met with over a dozen engineers, mostly onsite, some with videoconferencing. L.U.C. told the group that the river had quite recently changed its course to flow around an accumulation of sediment. He apologized for not taking into account the possibility of such an event occurring, but also stressed to the group that the river did not pose a threat to the Axiom.

The water was pooling in the basin south of Damascus, but in a few months, possibly just a few weeks, the river would surge.

Even in the event of an earthquake, the seismologists assured him, the Axiom would likely remain intact. More difficult to predict was the activity of the tectonic plates beneath the desert floor. The African Plate to the west was slowly creeping west, and would begin to slide under the Arabian Plate, forcing the river abruptly to the surface. Since the leaking had already started, the team hoped to gradually extract the river from underground to the Syrian plains.

Now the question was, how to prevent this threatening-to-surface river from washing away over five thousand years of civilization? Adam had made this mess, and everyone was looking at him to clean it up, in a manner of speaking. He knew how to make cars fly, but dirt and sand were out of his area of expertise. He called Ben.

Four hours later, Adam and Ben sat on the top floor of the Beit Zafran Hotel. The sun was sinking into the south side of Mount Qasioun as they drank tea and watched the traffic. The city seemed peaceful from this safe distance. Ben seemed to be enjoying himself as he took in the bustle below.

"It looks like we got the Vites up just in time to help us with the revenue to fund a new project," Ben said that evening as they talked about how to approach the unexpected new development.

A new project? Poking around in the earth's core had caused a river to rise to the surface. This was bigger than anything Adam had in mind when he decided to join Green Lantern.

"This is a disaster, and it's my fault. Ben, I am so sorry. I was in such a hurry to get things off the ground that I didn't think about this possibility. I think the best thing to do is start dismantling the Energy Center and then-"

"We are not dismantling anything," Ben interrupted. "This is a gift, don't you see?"

"This is a natural disaster in an already unstable part of the world. This is an accident that is happening in slow motion. We are going to get people killed..."

Ben looked at him, head tilted to the side as he regarded his unhinged companion.

"This is an opportunity," Ben said calmly.

"It's an opportunity to destroy thousands of years of history in a matter of days!" Adam said so loudly the waiters began glancing in his direction.

"Look around you," Ben said as he stirred the sugar in his tea. "See all those building up against Qasioun? Do you know how long they've been there? Well, not those exact houses, but people have been here for more than ten thousand years. They have seen more wars than they can count. Religions have come and gone. And they adapted. They survived. The people who have thrived here are the ones who learn how to press on, no matter what happens. And they press on, together. This survival business, Adam, it's a group project."

"Well, they are not going to survive this, no matter how they stick together. The earth may not be through with its surprises. Lava could be next..." Adam argued.

Ben shook his head slowly. "It could be. You know, Martians could land here while we're all asleep and take over. We have to move forward on our paths with the knowledge that awful surprises might await us. They have everything here. Sunlight, soil, a population ready to work. What they have lacked all these years was water. Now it's here. The opportunity is here," Ben told him.

"An opportunity to do what?" Adam asked in exasperation.

Ben held up his hands to mimic a ball shape. Adam had a flashback to their first meeting.

"One hand washes the other," he said finally.

Ben smiled. "You're learning."

The next morning, Adam had a virtual meeting with a few dozen men and a smattering of women in that part of the world about handwashing. "We can provide the funding, if you can provide the human capital," Adam announced to a group of government officials from Syria, Jordan and Israel.

There were expressions of fear, and of blame. For the most part, however, there was a desire to take action as a group.

It was winter, the time when the arid region received most of its rainfall, making digging easier. Equipment was not as easy to come by or as plentiful as Adam would have liked, but he was astonished by the droves of people, many of them young and male, who wanted to bring the river to their hometowns. This was an opportunity for many of the area's undereducated and relatively unskilled to find work that gave them a purpose. Some brought their own shovels, others brought only themselves and a sincere desire to be part of something that touched people's lives in a wonderful, watery way.

As the volunteers gathered, the environmentalists and engineers were trying to find a path for a river that would do the least damage to the lives and structures of the millions of people living between Damascus and Jerusalem. Over the centuries, people in this part of the world had had their share of conflicts, but they had also created lasting monuments to cultures that celebrated fortitude.

So, they would send the river where it would not flood people's homes and livelihoods. Luckily, it was far enough outside Damascus that as it bubbled from the earth outside the small town of Beit Jinn, Highway 7 was the only area that faced the threat of flooding.

After much debate, hand wringing and discussion, the hastily formed group of the tentatively titled "River Placement Committee" decided the stream of water should flow into the neighboring country of Jordan, rather than through the populated areas in north Israel. Moving southeast, it would stay north of Irbid and curve back toward Israel. There, it would begin its southward stretch, between Jordan's Highway 65 and Israel's Highway 90, joining the Jordan River.

This much the team thought they could accomplish without wreaking havoc on the ecosystem or the people who inhabited it. Ninety miles south of this point, they would reach a dead end, or a Dead Sea. Would Israel rename it? What would happen to the famous Dead Sea mud that people slathered on their skin?

And what about the millions of gallons of saltwater that would wash down the imaginary line that formed the border of Israel and Jordan and into the Gulf of Aqaba? Marine biologists feared such high salinity would destroy sea life for a large part of the area. People who fished in the gulf feared a loss of their livelihoods.

A salination plant seemed to be the best solution. Located outside Wadi Musa, Jordan, the plant would produce thousands of jobs and hopefully create a delta where lotus flowers, herons, frogs and turtles would thrive.

It took six months to create the path the river would take through Jordan. Bulldozers worked around the clock in the uninhabited areas. The pace was ridiculous, the workers sleeping in tents near the canals they had created hours earlier.

Many people were earning wages for the first time in their lives. Often, they sent a portion home to their families, but were eager and proud to spend their money. Roadside stands became restaurants that served the hungry laborers. Markets sprang up in desert towns where groups of workers decided to stay and try their hand at farming.

By summer, the "river towns" as locals dubbed the burgeoning communities, were in full swing. They produced citrus and berries, wheat and barley. Their livestock grazed in green fields.

Together, the newly transplanted farmers sat down at communal tables for their evening meal. People from cities sat next to people from tiny towns and learned about one another. They toiled in the fields under the relentless sun and shared jugs of water.

On Saturdays, the Jews and Muslims worshiped, often taking turns in the communal buildings on the outskirts of the farms. Christians held services there on Sundays.

It began with the schoolchildren. A child would invite his friends to the synagogue, who would in turn invite the group to church, or the mosque. The teenagers would meet in the fields of desert roses. Few things were more enticing than a neighbor or schoolmate with an unusual name and a heritage that sounded exotic. Many parents were alarmed at first, but some saw this as a hopeful sign.

The new 'river towns' were the most peaceful in the area. Crime was low, violence was rare, and territorial disputes were virtually unheard of, as it was the first generation of people to live in these diverse communities.

It was not as if the region began anew; thousands of years of history are impossible to erase. The people of the river towns were comprised of individuals who brought with them their traditions, their cultures, and their beliefs.

And there were parts of their past they did not want to lose. In fact they wanted to celebrate them. It was the part of their past that connected them that they wanted to remember when they greeted the river every morning.

So they named their river after the one who had brought them all here. They were his descendants, and they were blessed. They called it the River Abraham.

Part 2 Somalia

Gerald Reichert sat next to his wife Patricia on the Mercury 400 as it soared over the African desert, holding her hand. She loved his hands, and she had for the thirty-seven years they'd been married. Those hands had built remarkable things over the years, several houses, a huge new addition to their church in Des Moines. The man they belonged to had built a loving family with three children, and now three grandchildren.

His hand trembled slightly as the monitor announced their descent into Mogadishu. Patricia squeezed it and smiled at her husband. He wasn't nervous. The doctor said this was how it would begin. He told Gerald it was safe to travel as long as he was careful, and there was someone near him in case he needed help.

Gerald had never needed help before. He always helped others. That was why he taught algebra and coached football and was a reserve firefighter. There were still so many people who needed help. As long as he was able to, he was going to serve his God by helping them.

A few decades ago, he would have started building houses for the Somalis as soon as the plane landed. Now he and Pat were going to feed the people, give them what medical care they could, and share with them the Good News. They had learned basic words and phrases in the local language.

The vehicles waiting to land were slowly circling Mogadishu's rudimentary skyport, each precisely ten meters from the vehicle in front and behind. It wasn't like the airports they had visited. Everything moved faster and was very efficient, especially the air conditioning, Gerald realized when the door panel slid open.

It was a wild heat, rolling in off the Arabian Sea onto the parched lands where sheep and goats struggled to graze. Food was not plentiful in the city, a place filled with conflict and despair. They were planning to leave it soon.

An android gathered their bags and rolled briskly to the Blue Zone. Gerald and Patricia followed in a vehicle similar to a minivan. Their next vehicle would take them to the village of Afgooye, where Matthew Jeffers of Lutheran World Ministerial Outreach was waiting for them.

"It's not too late," Patricia said as she studied her husband's face as the harsh sunlight came through the window. "If you want to change your mind, we can go home," she said.

"God put it on my heart. I need to be here," he told her as they neared a small group of people standing under a large blue awning. Vehicles of various shapes and sizes stopped for their passengers at points along a blue line on the ground, whisking them away to their destinations. When their turn came to climb into the Degdeg Ah to their village, the door opened and Gerald stepped back so Patricia could enter. He braced himself with his hand on the roof of the vehicle, only to find his legs refused to bend. He growled with frustration at the body that he managed to control with ever decreasing frequency.

"Oh, no, Ger," Patricia started to get out of the vehicle to help him, but he shook his head. She could see his lips moving as he prayed for the strength to persevere. He stood there for long moments, and with great effort, managed to slide into the vehicle sideways.

He sighed heavily as they rose above the decaying city, moving west as signs of urban life abated. So many parts of the world had made huge, radical, wonderful changes and leaps toward true progress with the adoption of the Vites.

Other places withered in the grip of greed, fear and grudges. The Horn of Africa was in need of water, true. Every bit as deadly was the lack of intangible but essentials for humans to thrive: compassion, vision and cooperation among them. Conflicts abraded the stability many people sought. Wars raged because of religion, tribal affiliation and territory. The poor soil could produce little besides struggle and loss.

So Gerald asked God to send him where he was needed the most. He had seen images on tv of people in this part of the world for decades now. Had there ever been enough food for them? The drought persisted. There was a war, or was it a group of wars? It had been happening for generations: people were born into suffering, they lived short lives with little hope and met with early deaths, leaving children that were almost certain to face the same terrible fate.

Where was God? Gerald was sure God wanted to live in the heart of every person on Earth. With God in their hearts, these people could weather any storm, Gerald knew. His faith had sustained him when the doctor told him to travel before it was too late.

He and Patricia walked as much as they could, and relied on vehicles when Gerald's legs were too tired. Exploring the outlying villages one warm afternoon, they happened upon a group of elders sitting in front of a hut. The shade of the nearby Qurac trees was welcome in the heat.

Patricia asked if they could join them, and the elders nodded toward the blanket on the ground. Gerald took out his Bible and began reading it in English, while his wife translated. He liked to open it to a random page, leaving it up to God to choose the chapter and verse. It was Jeremiah.

"Nevertheless, I will bring health and healing to it, I will bring health and healing to my people," he began. As he listened to his wife speak, his hand shook. He grabbed it with his other hand to try to stop the trembling, but it was useless. Rage coursed through him as he tried to regain control of his movements and his emotions. He wanted to flee into the trees until he recovered, but his limbs had become leaden.

"...and will let them enjoy abundant peace and security," he managed to finish Jeremiah 33:6. He was panting with effort, and noticed an elder looking at him intently. The man stood and walked over to the trees. He ran his hand across the tops of the shrubs that grew beneath them. Stopping next to one with bright yellow flowers, he pulled off several small branches.

Returning to the group he laid the leaves at Gerald's feet and spoke to Patricia. Gesturing to his own head, then to the flowers, Patricia nodded but looked uncertain.

"He says to put these flowers in a tea. They are his blessing," she said.

"*Mahadsanid*," Gerald said. Thank you. It was one of the few Somali words he could remember.

"I'll call Peter to bring them some jugs of water and then I think we should get you back to the mission," Patrica said as he helped her husband stand.

"Ask them if we can come back tomorrow," he said. Patricia spoke a few words and the elders smiled and nodded. It was worth all the frustration and embarrassment if he could bring them closer to God. He would visit if the other missionaries had to carry him.

That evening before bed, Patricia brought Gerald the leaves and flowers from the elder. "If I matched the picture on the internet right, this plant has edible flowers. I think if we were allergic to it, we would know by now," she said.

"Well, let's see how it tastes," Gerald said as he lit the stove in the mission's small, dark kitchen. Pouring hot water over the elder's gift, he found the taste unremarkable. It was the thought, Gerald reminded himself, as he fell asleep that night, dreaming of the next day's Bible study.

He and Patricia left early that morning, bringing supplies for the villagers with them. Gerald bent down to lift a heavy sack of grain and Patricia hollered at him.

"Don't do that!" she said, alarmed.

He shook his head, picked up the sack and threw it in the back of Peter's vehicle.

Speechless, she climbed in next to him as they rode to the village.

Again, Gerald opened the Bible and began reading to the group. Today it was the Book of Matthew. The Parable of the Sheep and Goats. As he began reading, his hand, seemingly on cue, began to tremble. Gerald took a deep breath. His hand stopped moving. Patrica glanced over at him, eyebrows raised, but she kept speaking.

Once more, the elder brough the flowers and bid them farewell as Gerald climbed into the vehicle, nimbler than ever.

"Maybe this climate agrees with you," Patricia remarked. "Maybe you just have really bad arthritis."

Gerald tapped his hand in time to the country music playing in their vehicle. "I don't know, maybe getting to share God with people is the key to the whole thing," he said.

"The key to the whole thing," Patricia repeated as they began their descent into the mission. She lit the stove to heat water for Gerald's tea, but saved one flower. Folding a piece of paper around it, she handed it to Peter and asked him about mailing it overseas later in the week.

"What for?" Peter asked.

"Oh, you know. Looking for keys," Patricia said.

Gerald had improved enough for them to stay an extra month, then another. His tremors had virtually disappeared. He was picking up words and phrases in Somali, and seemed more active than he had in years.

They had been there for two seasons when one morning, they watched the news as they flew into Balcad. "Researchers at Johns Hopkins may be on the verge of a breakthrough in the fight against Parkinson's Disease. Scientists have isolated a substance in a plant commonly found in East Africa that seems to slow and even arrest symptoms of Parkinson's disease in rats. Further studies are needed to determine..."

"Did you hear that?" Gerald turned to his wife. She smiled mysteriously.

"God hears every prayer," Patricia said. Flying over Somalia was a miracle she did not think she would see in her lifetime. Her husband's healing, on the other hand...

"But I didn't ask for healing," he said as they sailed over the palm trees and grassy fields near a winding river.

Patricia reached over and held her husband's now-steady hand. "Maybe not, but I did," she said as they glided to the ground in a world where anything and everything seemed possible.

Part 3 South Dakota

Lighting crackled on the western horizon as Velma Chaska looked out the window of her trailer on the Pine Ridge Reservation. She hoped the storm would bring rain. It would mean fruit on the trees in summer. Her grandchildren thought pies came from the freezer at the store. She would show them how to bake them soon. There was much she wanted to teach them.

"Maybe you will see her tonight?" Her husband Merwin asked as he sat at the kitchen table, drinking his hot chocolate before bed.

"Maybe I will," Velma said. She did not choose the time. "I will keep listening for her," she said.

Velma awoke the next morning, having seen and heard nothing. She told her husband that today was not the day, not yet.

They helped their grandchildren get ready for school. Velma wondered if the children would ever use what they were learning in school. They drew lots of circles, drew lines under things. Paper everywhere.

Velma wanted her grandchildren to know who they were. They were links in long chains that stretched back over the centuries, before they wrote anything on paper.

Long ago, people wrote on rocks. Not far from where Velma and Merwin lived as children, there were huge rocks. Ȟe Sápa. Those rocks were sacred to the Lakota.

To the white people, the rocks were like paper. The faces of their leaders were on their papers and their metal. They carved the faces of their leaders in those rocks.

The children learned about this in school. Presidents. Wars. Treaties.

Were the stories in the books true? Were they real? Velma was not entirely convinced.

Out of school, she told them the stories her grandparents told her. The Lakota came from inside the earth. They called this place *Maka Oniye,* or "earth that breathes."

Her people had always known the earth breathed. It was as obvious as the blue sky or green trees. The earth was alive, and gave life to everything on it.

Long after the Lakota, the Wasi'chu learned about this. They began to understand the power of *Maka Oniye* and made flying machines that could hear the breath of the earth.

Maybe there was a new hope. Maybe now they understood: the earth is all we have. In the end, it is the earth that speaks, that breathes.

They saw the first flying machine in the sky over Pine Ridge that summer. On July 4th, she went to bed after the fireworks stopped. And in her dreams, she saw her.

Her grandmother was there, standing on the hill near Ȟe Sápa. The wind was blowing and the grass waved in the breeze.

She smiled at her granddaughter. "It has been a long wait. Now it is time. It is time to tell the children," she told Velma.

When Velma awoke, she told Merwin. "I saw her last night," she smiled.

"What did she say?" Merwin had known Velma would see her soon. He had watched the bison.

"She said it's time," Velma said.

"Then I'll go," Merwin said.

He walked into town, even though it was a very windy day. Wind, sun, rain. These were real. They were here before the people and they would be here after the people.

His friends were at Spears, where people gathered for food and drink, and to shoot pool. They greeted him respectfully. He was an elder, and they listened to him.

"Velma saw her. She says it's time," he told the group of men. They were surprised.

"Then we will start today," Lyle Brings Plenty said. "School gets out at two-thirty."

The men told their friends, and that afternoon, a group of a dozen men waited outside the school. "Everything we taught you, everything you practiced, now it's time. We will hunt bison tomorrow," they told the teenagers.

It was very early the next morning when they met for the hunt. They were a few miles from Ȟe Sápa. The sun was rising and like the day before, the wind was fierce. It had rained the night before.

Wind, sun and rain. Over the years, these elements wore away the faces of the leaders on the rocks. They were more powerful, and would be on the earth after the stone faces returned to the earth. Drops of water settled into holes in the rock. When the air froze, the water turned to ice and expanded, the wind blew and the sun melted the ice.

The cracks were there, but the Lakota didn't see them as they hunted the buffalo that morning. They rode their horses and shot bows and arrows. They did what their people had done for ages.

Flying cars moved overhead, their occupants watching the hunt from far above. The lights began blinking on the consoles of their vehicles. Computer voices gave warnings.

"Delay in landing for the next ten minutes. Delay in landing for the next ten minutes," it said.

The occupants looked at each other and frowned.

"Interruption in current. Please wait," the voice said.

And the earth breathed.

The current traveled up from the Axiom in Roswell, deep underground. It raced through the earth to reach Ȟe Sápa, where the wind, sun and rain were with the Lakota. The elements had found the weaknesses in the stone faces. Then came the breath of the earth. Geologists called it "an isolated current irregularity."

The hunters called it *Maka Oyine*, as the ground rumbled and the stone faces shook. Giant pieces of them crashed into the dirt. The more the earth moved, the more stone heads rattled until they broke loose from the hills below.

The hunters paused and the bison lay on the ground as the heads rolled off the hills and broke into chunks. Jagged, sharp new peaks formed on the hills as the earth settled and sighed.

It was time.

Chapter 37 - Back Where I Belong

Many visitors to the New England city fell in love with Cambridge, and it was easy to see why. Located across the Charles River from Boston, it was a city suited to the lifestyle of the world's intellectual elite. The home to Harvard University and the Massachusetts Institute of Technology, Cambridge decided to use local resources to solve local problems. Its inhabitants also believed it should be a place where law enforcement builds positive relationships with both documented and undocumented citizens.

The city first declared itself a "sanctuary city" in April of 1985, to help protect and harbor refugees that were in fear of losing their lives during the Salvadoran Civil War. In February of 2017, Mayor Denise Simmons released a statement to reconfirm Cambridge's commitment to remaining a Sanctuary City amidst the immigration political controversy.

By and large, Sanctuary Cities report positive outcomes with their progressive policies. They tend to have lower than average crime rates, higher overall average household incomes, and their poverty rates are consistently lower than those of cities that do not welcome immigrants.

Cambridge found that undocumented immigrants did not pose a significant threat to the community, but rather positively impacted it. At any rate, Cambridge had earned its reputation as a place of safety. It was this safety, or rather, the belief that it existed here, that drew the man in black across the Charles that night. Of course, encouraging statistics cannot replace firsthand experience. Living fully engaged is how we fall in love with life and learn what it means to be human. The constant push to learn, understand, and innovate is always in the air in Cambridge.

Nestled right in the center of this idyllic place was Binney Street's Lofts at Kendall Square. A brisk eight-minute stroll down the well shaded Loughrey Walkway could lead to the Blue Bottle Café on Ames without breaking a sweat. Just another few steps farther, tucked away on Pioneer, was lunch hotspot Legal Sea Foods. With the right clothing and footwear selection, a winter walk on most days was possible.

The Lofts also offered a major attraction for the science and technology lover, Massachusetts Institute of Technology. From the Computer Science and Artificial Intelligence Building on Vassar to Building 12, where MIT.nano secluded itself from the outside world, it was possible to spend weeks on end talking theory, solving complex problems, and dreaming of a better tomorrow for all humanity with the best minds the world had to offer.

A man dressed in all black, gloves, coat and MIT harnessed backpack made his way over the Longfellow Bridge into Cambridge. The night sky was overcast, hiding the moon, with only the lights of the city making the place inviting.

Once across the river, the man made his way onto the Dr. Paul Dudley White Bike Path. He reached the Broad Canal Walk and followed it until he reached the dead end at Kendall Square. Ambling along Third Street, his movements deliberate, he moved silently from a lot across from the Binney Street entrance to the Lofts at Kendall Square. His camouflage served him well and allowed him to observe his surroundings.

He lingered between construction trailers and piles of building materials. Peering through a gap in the privacy fence, he waited some twenty minutes before determining it was safe to approach the double glass doors facing Binney Street.

While the pressures of following the old pandemic policies no longer existed, it was not uncommon to see people still wearing face masks to protect them from the pervasive, evil, and thought to be man-made COVID viruses. With his hood drawn low and the “health” safety mask pulled near his eyes, his identity was well disguised.

He began the heist. Onsite management was not visible at the moment and he had not seen anyone who appeared to work in that capacity during his observation. Without people to interfere with his work, he set about gaining access to the building. The keyless entry using an electronic fob was mere child’s play. Entering the building and proceeding to a two-bed, two-bath apartment located in the corner of the fourth floor, approaching the entryway was also a trivial exercise for the well-equipped, skilled intruder. A beautifully restored manufacturing building, the Loft had a completely stunning old-world charm. The unit boasted thirteen-foot ceilings and a mixture of materials like exposed wood beams and concrete columns. The floor had the appearance of bamboo.

Standing at the threshold, the contents of the backpack began to rumble. The trespasser quickly made his way past the first bedroom and galley kitchen into the open den area. Pausing a second to take in the corner view of the city, he was keenly aware of tremors emanating from the backpack.

Behind a closed door, there was another small bedroom, fifteen by ten feet to the left of the main living area. It was a room that a single occupant might use for an office instead of a bedroom, as space was tight. The trespasser, now sure of his mark, entered the small office and opened the closet door. The vibrations in the pack were nearly unmanageable and there was some worry that neighbors may even begin to feel the shaking. Bostonians were not familiar with earthquake drills, for the most part.

A metal safe, guarded by a digital lock sat on the top shelf of the small closet. There were two braces on either side of the bottom of the safe that reached the floor to support its weight. It would likely have taken at least three or four men to lift a safe this size and composition into its position on the shelf.

Without hesitation, the offender, who had come sufficiently prepared to deal with any obstruction attempts the safe offered, reached over his shoulder and pulled out a long, protruding, flat metal object. It looked to be a cross between a machinist's steel file and something slightly shorter than a medieval sword.

Under normal entry, the safe would have required a simultaneous biometric scan and security code. After a short study to judge where the exact location of the two-inch-thick solid steel bolt would be inserted through the opening in the solid lead-based frame of the safe, the robber touched the safe with the tip of the metallic rod. The chemical composition of the rod began to change, and he observed the rod beginning to conform to the shape of the small crease of the door. Slight pressure given to the back end of the rod allowed the pilferer to use it as a handle. The rod, conforming to all the minute angles of the tightly closed safe, moved deeper and deeper.

After a satisfying click, the thief saw the door to the safe swing open. The locking mechanism of the safe had been completely and cleanly sheared as if it had melted right through the bar. After the unlocking tool had returned to its original shape, he inserted it back over his shoulder into its sheath.

The all-out rumble of an apparent homing device, signaling it had found its mark, pulsed insistently. The defalcator slowly removed the backpack and set it on the floor, careful not to drop the satchel amidst the horrific vibrations.

There it was. It was unmistakable. It was the only item kept in the sanctity and security of the modified $700 Uline H-7767 Depository Safe. In the most unlikely of places. The violet stone.

It was composed of contrasting textures and tones. The lightest were pearlescent and icy, the darkest were deep purple, like a shaded field of salvias on a summer afternoon. Between these two extremes glowed the dusty lavenders of sunrises. Milky and rich in some parts, crystalline and flecked with silver in others, the layers of myriad hues were beauty in full bloom and daybreak sky, with glints of the treasures hidden deep in the earth.

Surely it belonged in an art gallery, a museum of rare finds, or at one of the homes of a billionaire who collected such objects as a hobby. The robber had seen rocks and even valuable gems, and this was neither. It had been fashioned with painstaking precision to the width of one-quarter of a disk, and looked like a fantastical, much too generous slice of berry and cream pie.

Gorgeous as it was to behold, looking at it for more than a few seconds made the intruder light-headed, almost giddy. He reminded himself to breathe deeply as images of swirling colors filled his mind. The walls of the closet felt as if they were moving steadily away from him, filling the space with sparkles of tiny blue and green dots. They danced around him like excited fireflies, when suddenly orange streamers moved back and forth across his field of vision.

The raider was intoxicated, completely unprepared for the powers of this stone. He put his hand on it and was certain he felt it pulse. The adrenaline pumping through his veins had kept him alert since he crossed the bridge, but the vibrations of the stone made him feel more at peace than he had since childhood. As he continued to stare at it, he felt hypnotized.

He wanted to leave. The stone wanted to leave. The stone was telling him it wanted to leave. With him. The malefactor had found his mark and carefully removed the stone from the safe. He placed it into its own compartment on the front of the pack. Once inserted, the violence caused by the seeking of the unaccounted for, had given way to a low hum and an even lower vibration. It was the contentment of Mother Cat having rescued all her kittens from a perilous situation. Now they were all safe and hidden.

Other than the obvious damage to the safe, there was a deliberate effort to remove any other signs of entry. With hood drawn and face mask lifted back into place, the prowler calmly made his way back out of the building and onto Binney Street. Turning towards Boston, the thief slipped away unnoticed, into the night.

Chapter 38 - Can I Count on You?

The Vites had changed life on the planet, sometimes in ways nobody saw coming. Stories of rivers springing from the center of the planet, giving life to regions that had been barren for thousands of years were circulating the globe. The new, ubiquitous virtual transportation system was reducing world hunger and increasing the speed at which the helpers could find those in need. It seemed that there were no limits to what people could accomplish, discover and repair with the Vites.

Demand for Vites around the globe was soaring. Every major metropolitan area and every country on the planet wanted their name on the list. What had to be done? How long would it take? Who could help them do it? These were the three most frequent questions.

Adam and Dr. Alex worked assiduously to develop a step-by-step implementation and compliance plan in preparation for scheduling a world-wide tour. They would visit countries to share the plan, provide oversight and Vites onboarding consultation to foreign countries and large metropolitan areas. There was more complexity in the larger, more congested cities, naturally. Los Angeles and New York had served as the roadmap for establishing all of the appropriate protocols. Alex was not officially affiliated with the OSTP, but Adam granted him proxy and they found themselves dividing and conquering in order to speed up the rollout. It was necessary to perform steps in a very specific order as virtual grids opened around the world. Like making lasagna, failure to adhere to the instructions could result in a huge, difficult-to-clean-up mess. L.U.C, as the central intelligence behind the Vites, for all intents and purposes, appeared to be managing all the details with ease.

On the rare occasions when both were available, Adam continued to pick Dr. Alex's brain to better understand the physics of the Vites and possible limitations. It seemed like the more he learned, the less he understood. This all served to create a growing concern within Adam about the limitations of the system. He knew that rolling out the Vites after the Axioms were connected wouldn't be a problem. However, until they were connected, the volume of cars traveling in the stream would eventually cause it to hit a wall. At least that's what Adam thought he heard. So much was theoretical and happening without precedent.

And it seemed like the more things grew and improved, the more impatient and agitated Ben became. Seriously, what is his problem? Ben and S.E.T.I. were getting a piece of every monthly subscription fee world-wide, AND he had secured contracts all over the globe for providing certain materials required for "car" manufacturing. Many formulas and patents for the required materials and processes were locked up in secrecy using Trade Secret filings with the S.E.C., virtually assuring his involvement in the global supply chain of Vites almost indefinitely. Not only that, he was one of the major real estate developers of the model for futuristic cities and skyports. Axioms were cities and communities of the future. Who knew more about how they were built than Ben? If he wasn't already, he was on his way to being the richest man in the world. He was living proof of the truism that money can't buy happiness, Adam thought in resignation to his boss's moods.

Given these profound revelations about the kind of situation Ben had put himself in (or rather the situation he had put the world in), Adam wrestled with uneasy feelings about the billionaire. The chances of so many unusual things happening to one person were slim. While even a blind squirrel finds a nut every now and again (i.e. happening upon the Roswell crash in 1947), to have the wherewithal to parlay that lucky strike into an opportunity to develop futuristic materials and processes, too? There had to be something more behind this mystery of a man, Adam suspected. Why, with all this leverage over Vites, the untold amount of money, why is he getting so anxious, impatient, and irritable? Maybe Ben was also worried about the Vites. If they came crashing down, it would be worse for Ben than Adam, at least financially. Are we careening head long into a brick wall and Ben knows exactly where this wall is? What does Ben know that the rest of us don't, Adam wondered?

Adam contemplated his next move. His best course of action seemed to be to recommend that the US Government nationalize S.E.T.I. to remove some of the inherent risks of private ownership and control over so many key elements of the new transportation system. Ben could still be in the money chain. Adam wouldn't deprive him of that, but he certainly didn't need to have all the control.

Speak of the devil. With Spain's airspace mapped and Vites operating smoothly, Portugal was next. Before they could meet their scheduled commitment with officials in Lisbon (much to Portugal's dismay), Ben summoned Adam and Dr. Alex for an emergency meeting in Denver. Apparently, he had a litany of concerns ranging from vehicle manufacturing, his intellectual property, to his monthly subscription royalty agreement.

Fortunately, Vites was connected and flowing to and from Europe from the United States freely. With the Gulfstream ordered to fly back to home base without them, Adam and Alex took the Vites and a flying car back to the States. The pair had ridden on virtual highways around cities and countrysides while they were onboarding. However, this was the first time they would personally take Vites over the Atlantic. They marveled at the ease, the comfort, the amenities, and the elegance of this new form of travel. They also brainstormed about how best to soothe Ben's frayed nerves.

The arrival ritual at S.E.T.I. had become familiar. The uniformed escort up the elevator, then down a long narrow hall to another secure elevator, and then up to the floor where Ben's office was.

More guards were waiting to welcome the two men in the large area outside Ben's office. They greeted the men warmly and instructed them to proceed into Ben's office. The glass walls surrounding Ben's office were dark and the office looked like a shadow from where they stood. Security ushered the men into Ben's office and closed the door behind them.

There were already two people sitting in the chairs facing Ben's desk where he was sitting. The three were having a quiet conversation. Once the door closed, Ben stood. The two people sitting in front of Ben also stood and turned as Adam and Alex approached.

Upon seeing their faces, Adam and Alex simultaneously recognized with shock that it was Peter and Claire Johansen. Alex stopped and looked directly at Ben. Adam didn't yet understand what was happening.

Ben gave Alex a chance to speak.

"Why did you take it?" he demanded to know.

"Take what?" Dr. Alex asked, bewildered.

After a brief flash of anger, Ben regained his self-control. He then told Dr. Alex that

"Peter and Claire suspected you found and took the fourth stone," he told the physicist. "They didn't want to believe it, but they turned over every square inch of Maejima and there was no other explanation."

"Ben, these two are really new at this. I think with a little more time-" Alex began.

"Alex, stop. Don't make this worse than it already is. While you've been out on the road, I had your apartment in Cambridge searched. Alex, we found the violet stone," Ben said with undisguised contempt. He reached into his drawer and put the stone on his desk. He looked back up at Alex. "I have the stone. This is your last chance," he told his once-trusted employee.

Just as Ben uttered the words, “last chance,” four men from S.E.T.I. Security reentered the room. Adam was speechless and flabbergasted. He was too surprised to do anything beyond observe.

Alex sighed and looked at the ground for what seemed like hours. “Ok, ok,” he said quietly, as he began to sense danger. He continued.

“You have to listen to me, Ben. I didn’t want to alarm anyone, but I have been working on these formulas over and over. The magnetic streams coming from the Axiom have some inconsistencies. It isn’t noticeable yet, but it will be soon,” he explained.

“You didn’t say anything to any of us, all this time that you had doubts,” Ben said, trying not to shake with fury. Dr. Alex knew physics, Ben reminded himself. He would give Dr. Alex the benefit of the doubt and listen to his explanation.

“My fear was that if we added the actuator stone too soon, there was a possibility of creating a severe disruption to the flow. It could cause everything to crash. I am just not one hundred percent sure the system could handle that kind of throughput yet. Ten-fold. Until I worked out the formulas that would adjust the consistency of the streams, I just didn’t want to risk it. I kept it to myself because it wasn’t time to worry anybody else with it yet. Don’t you see all the good we are doing, the people, the planet, the healing, the hope?” he asked.

Ben shook his head. “Alex, you know that’s not it and you are lying.”

“I didn’t want anyone to get hurt-” Alex began.

“Why, Alex?” Ben was almost screaming now. “Take him!”

Alex had been backing away during the conversation and had even looked to the window for a possible escape route. There was none. The four men subdued him quickly and escorted him out the door.

Ben brought his attention back to Adam.

“Did you know? Did he tell you? Were you a part of this ploy?” Ben asked.

“We’ve known since the beginning, right from L.U.C.’s specifications. We knew on day one that we needed this capacity. I’m just in disbelief that this is happening right now,” Ben said, still furious.

Adam sat speechless, unable to process what he had just witnessed.

Ben looked at the Johansen’s. “Peter and Claire, thank you for your tireless work and also for being willing to report your suspicions. Had you not brought this forward, we would still be flailing around hopelessly looking for a stone that couldn’t be found.”

The Johansens nodded somberly and looked to Adam.

"Adam, you are on your own to finish this work now. Can I count on you?" Adam was still stunned by the events that had just unfolded. He wasn't sure if he was upset with Dr. Alex, if he believed Alex or if he agreed with Ben. Maybe he was just upset with how Ben handled everything.

Adam looked back at Ben. "What choice do I have?" Adam asked simply. They were way past the point of no return. Adam had already been experiencing the nagging concern of proceeding without the stone. His thoughts were still scattered, but he realized they had some answers, and the stone. Ben then further asks,

"Do you think your friend Greg can assume Dr. Alex's role and assist you in getting the rest of this done? We're so close," Ben said, desperation creeping into his voice.

Adam was overwhelmed with thoughts and emotions.

He nodded. Ben beamed. The Johansens smiled and exchanged hopeful glances.

The object sitting on Ben's desk, the violet stone, was the most beautiful one of all the stones. It was mesmerizing. Adam had a thought. Was it meant to save everyone?

Chapter 39 - The Wait Is Over

As he sat in the splendor of Ben's office, looking out at the Colorado plains, Adam could still remember L.U.C. appearing in his office and giving him a sneak preview of utopia. Then he warned him: it would not be without sacrifice. On a handful of occasions, Adam wondered if he would have to sacrifice his sanity to endure much more. One minute he was helping countries worldwide join the Vites, then he seemed to have interrupted Ben's version of the Spanish Inquisition.

He reviewed the most recent events: in the middle of traveling to Portugal for their next assignment, Adam and Alex had left their integration team mid-implementation to respond to a Ben Kumar's summons for a meeting outside Denver. Ben's ostensible reasons were little more than housekeeping matters. The real reason for the meeting, and what happened once it began, shook Adam to his core.

Adam and Dr. Alex were resolving an enormous number of problems daily in a very routine way. They believed they were going to Denver to get a few more things to add to their to-do list. Instead, they felt they had walked into the office of what appeared to be a desperate, irrational, schizophrenic.

Having met Ben Kumar on several occasions before, Adam expected a composed, even polished individual, but this Ben seemed so much different. The variant enlightenment encounter with Ella had shown some instabilities, but he still seemed rational. This was a guy that already had it all. Wasn't Ben's behavior the exact definition of narcissism?

Apparently, the world was not enough. Adam's career had put him in a position to meet and investigate all types: true believers, megalomaniacs, and the occasional sociopath. Adam was now sure; Ben would take the cake.

Adam came to a realization. It would take a lot more work on his part to better understand who Ben was. The suspicion Adam was having that this business, S.E.T.I. Industries, should be nationalized, had never been stronger than at that moment. Convinced this business was an outlier, Adam knew it had to be stopped.

Adam believed he had witnessed what was for all intents and purposes, an abduction. But for what crime? What or who was the arresting authority? Wasn't Dr. Alex invited to Japan to dig around in the dirt, looking for rocks? So, he found one and thought it best to keep it to himself for a while. Adam was sure Alex had his own insecurities about everything, too. As an expert in his field, wasn't Alex just being cautious? When was the last time someone was arrested for finding a rock? Even gold diggers find a nugget and keep what they find, don't they? Not to trivialize the stones, but, all they did was point us to where to dig some holes. Up until now, hadn't they been largely insignificant?

Peter and Claire had stumbled across one of these trinkets in Afghanistan and, from there, this worldwide Easter Egg hunt had since taken on a life of its own. The Virtual Global Highway Transportation System was expanding across the globe with miraculous transformations happening over the entire planet. Standing there, Adam was trying to remember who told him in the first place that the stones were required, that they would eventually be essential to maximizing the flow of the Axioms' magnetic current.

Ah, yes, Adam remembered, his friendly logistical ubiquitous companion. L.U.C., or at least his intelligence, was anywhere and everywhere all at once these days. Adam then realized he hadn't talked with him in the old familiar way, man to hologram, in a few months. Maybe he could help to shed some light on these mysteries?

Adam locked eyes with Ben. Peter and Claire, sitting motionless and unmoved by the unfolding events, kept their eyes affixed on the beguiling violet stone. Ben knew what Adam was thinking.

"I never expected you to understand everything, but I have long been convinced, you were the one. The one who could understand, the one with the wherewithal, the one with enough motivation to achieve a prominent position, and one with enough intestinal fortitude to see it through, the one I needed," Ben offered calmly.

Adam said nothing. He wasn't giving anyone any information unless he thought it absolutely necessary.

"Adam, I've known you longer than you've known who you are," Ben told him. He looked at the Johansens; their eyes were now on the floor.

That was quite a claim, but Adam was not going to respond. Still perplexed, he needed a few more answers before this charade continued. The claims that he had somehow been the "chosen one" were foreign to his logical, methodical way of thinking. And Adam's weakness? His concern for others, always.

"Where have you taken Dr. Alex? And on what authority do you have to have him detained? What's the charge?" he asked Ben.

"S.E.T.I. Security is not a threat to Alex," Ben said, attempting to pacify Adam. "I've spent, and Peter and Claire have spent, a significant amount of time and resources trying to bring this search to a conclusion. We will not harm Alex. We need to talk with him at length, however. I know him well and it's imperative that I truly understand his motivations. I'm sure we won't involve the local authorities and the two of you can get back on your tour after we've given him a chance to explain. Even you must admit, his actions could have grave implications for the Vites."

Before Adam had time to completely organize his thoughts and consider his response, Ben slowly stood up behind his desk. He reached toward the integrated digital control pad embedded into the right front corner of his desk. With a slight touch to the apparatus, a series of events began to expose the shrouded chamber.

The entire wall behind Ben's desk was a carefully designed deceit. The bottom half of the wall disappeared into the floor, the top half into the ceiling. It revealed a dazzling hidden cavity of enormous depth. The curvature of the room gave it the appearance of going on endlessly and appearing gigantic. It made Dubai's Museum of the Future seem almost passé. There were several pieces of brilliant, holographic abstract art lining the walls of what was surely Ben's private collection.

Adam had never seen anything like them. Staring directly into one of the pieces gave him the feeling of infinity, of knowing all there was to know. The limits of human eyesight prevented him from understanding the entirety of what was before him. It was as if there was no way to see the end of the art, as if it went on forever, into a dimension not present on this earth. Time and space, were they simply illusions? Staring into the alluring images, carried with it a sense of vertigo, that caused him the impulse to look away for the fear of falling in too deep past the point of no return.

In the center of the room, there was a large, oval shaped podium. On top sat the blue, green and orange stones, arranged in a circle. Adam had forgotten just how pleasing they were to the eyes. They held perfect spacing between them, approximately two inches. Prior to Adam's growing concerns about Ben and S.E.T.I.'s monopoly, he had turned them over to Ben for safekeeping.

The glaring defect was the absence of the violet stone. Ben walked into the cavity and motioned Adam to join him. As he did, Ben gestured to the violet stone, still sitting on his desk. Peter and Claire rose and followed Ben into the previously concealed apse. They stepped slightly away from the podium, yielding to Adam to do the honors. Adam, speechless and with trembling hands, lifted the violet stone.

In Egypt, on November 4th, 1922, a boy accidentally stumbled on a stone. This stone, archaeologists would learn, was part of the top of a flight of steps cut into the bedrock of the Valley of the Kings. The steps led archaeologist Howard Carter into the burial chamber of King Tutankhamen. He was asked if he could see anything in the tombs.

"Yes, wonderful things," he replied.

In one treasure chest, Carter discovered a large breastplate decorated with gold, silver, various precious jewels, and one strange gemstone. In 1998, Italian mineralogist Vincenzo de Michele analyzed the optical properties of the gemstone and confirmed it as LDG (Libyan Desert Glass). LDG is composed of almost pure silicon-dioxide, but it contains unusual traces of iron, nickel, chromium, cobalt, and iridium. It was found to be among the rarest minerals on Earth as it is found only in the Great Sand Sea, north of the Gilf Kebir Plateau, one of the most remote and desolate areas in the Libyan Desert.

In 2020, an international research team analyzing satellite images of the terrain between the villages of Qaret Had El Bahr and Qaret El Allafa, Egypt, discovered a previously unknown crater in the midst of the Sahara Desert. The shape, three hundred and fifty yards wide, resembled the shape of the famous Meteor Crater in Arizona.

While uncertain how the desert glass had become part of Tutankhamen's treasures, it was clear that an object, hurtled through space, impacted and melted the quartz-rich sand of the desert and fused with this vaporized meteorite to form this exotic gift. Archaeological evidence suggests that an ancient system of caravan routes existed around the Gilf Kebir Plateau and the Egyptian King had acquired the translucent desert glass by chance.

The past and future all seemed to be rushing together as Adam loosely held the violet stone. It seemed to have a will of its own. It wanted to float over to the podium, overjoyed as it was to be in the presence of the other stones. To him, this moment no longer seemed as if it was by chance.

Holding the stone caused an enormous shift in perspective. The grievances he held on to only moments ago had dissolved into the fantastically unfolding sensory overloading events. He was a grain of sand on the beach, a cell, a molecule, so vast was the universe the stone showed him. Had Tutankhamen felt that way? Did he, like Adam, feel that he was holding something beyond his ability to comprehend? Everything in Adam's past had held that stones were inanimate objects, yet this violet stone *communicated*. Words failed him, as the thoughts coming from the stone reached his brain without words, images or sound. Did it communicate by touch?

Perhaps there were more than five senses, he realized, as the sixth one opened a door to another realm, another level of reality. For a moment, Adam could see himself from above; he floated around the higher reaches of the cavernous enclosure.

The consequences of helping the long missing artifact join its assemblage was no longer a consideration. The effect of whatever spell he had been put under removed any free will of what to do next.

As the stone in Adam's hand neared the podium, a melodic rumble began to overtake the entire space. The podium remained steady, seeming to insulate the room from the vibrations. As he placed the stone onto the single empty station, clearly reserved for the returning member of the family, the miraculous occurred.

Deep roaring sounds filled the air, along with piercing and shrill whistles. Seconds before a bright, blindingly brilliant light filled the room, Adam saw the stones vibrating as they moved ineluctably towards one another. It was with a monumental feeling of destiny and purpose that they united.

In an instant, on the top of the structure built for this very purpose, the searing white light that moments ago blinded its occupants condensed with startling rapidity. It became an inseparable part of a single, newly created, brilliantly beautiful transformative stone. Seeing this unique translucent creature, offered a view deep into the universe.

It was no color known to the human eye, yet it was every color simultaneously. Four stones were no more. Like watching cell division in reverse, the pieces united to form an all-encompassing whole. It was glowing, it was seamless, and it was pulsing as if alive.

Adam thought if he looked at it too long, it would peer into his soul. Breaking his trance with the stone, he realized he felt like he was standing on a great precipice. He looked to Ben, Peter and Claire with astonishment, hoping they would offer answers.

But he was alone. They had supported him and advised him at every possible opportunity in reaching this turning point. Like parents watching a child's first steps, they realized Adam was strong enough to make this part of the journey on his own.

Ben broke the silence and looked straight into Adam's eyes. The turbulent emotions of late were nowhere in evidence. Before him was someone to whom the stone was a torch and Ben was passing it to Adam. "It's yours, Adam. You know what to do. You've known all your life what you would do at this moment. Take the stone with you. Make Vites everything they were destined to be from the very beginning. The wait is over."

Chapter 40 - It Wasn't a Coincidence

In terms of construction, the Axiom at Roswell had a slightly different configuration from its three global companions. From the moment of conception with the Axioms, it was clear that Roswell would be the driving force for the purposeful magnetic current that now encircled the Earth. Roswell wasn't a coincidence.

In the last one hundred years of our existence, man has learned how to harness sunlight to create solar power and to produce fuel from decaying fossils to power combustion engines. People discovered fission by splitting atoms of uranium to more cleanly power our homes with nuclear energy. They determined the perfect balance between the forward motion of a body in space and the gravity of the Earth, placing machines above our atmosphere to help people see and hear more clearly.

In what must have seemed like fantasy in that day, migraine-stricken Heinrich Hertz determined that sound and electromagnetic waves could carry modulated electrical energy invisibly through the air. He went on to show a receiver could turn those electrical signals into audio and visual images on the other side! From the beginning of time, everything that was made, has been made. It was up to humans to discover it.

A discovery made on this spot in Roswell more than eighty years ago was changing the world in the most beautiful and wondrous ways. The hope for all tomorrows and the chance for a generation to leave the planet better than they found it for their children's children was within reach. It was not the result of independent research, but rather a discovery of something already extant. Credit for knowing which direction to head in belonged to more than one participant in the quest for knowledge. At any rate, for most, progress matters more than the source of the information.

After the excitement in Ben's office last week, much to the dismay of Portugal, Belgium, and Sweden, the next three countries on the list for integration into the Vites, the global rollout had been temporarily suspended. The press release did little to soothe the disappointment, but there was no arguing with the reason and the expectant countries were forced to wait. Adam's press staff at the Office of Science and Technology Policy released a statement on November 19 that read as follows:

We appreciate your patience, preparedness, and professionalism as we continue the rapid expansion of the Virtual Global Highway Transportation System ("the Vites"). As we regularly and systematically monitor the flow of magnetic currents against the capacity of our system, we have recently determined that we are nearing a performance threshold. Without the completion of some predetermined updates to the system, an unacceptable amount of degradation could occur affecting transportation flow globally on all traffic levels.

We appreciate your patience as we attend to this matter. The current operation of the Vites will be unaffected by the system upgrade and we will resume the global rollout as soon as the update has been installed and thoroughly tested. Please stay tuned for further updates on any of the AxStream communication channels. Thank you.

After leaving Denver, the past week had been a good one, with the exception of the temporary Vites stoppage. Adam received some much-needed affirmation on several counts. He had gone home to D.C. where he was able to catch up with Chris and Brianna. He could hardly believe college was in the offing. Christopher was planning on attending Stanford and Bri had become very interested in Princeton. Bursting with love and pride for their accomplishments were pushing aside his feeling of fatherly inadequacy. He wasn't sure if he had spent the kind of time with them that any good father should. He was more confident that they would be able to raise their families in a world with more hope and possibilities than had existed for generations.

Adam had heard from Alex and was relieved to find out that he and Ben had come to some sort of agreement. The physicist was still going to play a part in the overall maintenance and operation of the Vites when especially needed. However, he wouldn't be involved in the high-level decisions or sensitive areas of the system. It was good to know that he would still be available as a resource if Adam had to call on him. He knew he could not have gotten this far without Dr. Alex's help.

And he was thrilled to work with Greg. As Ben suggested, Adam spent some time with Greg reexamining the mechanics of the insertion. While Greg couldn't offer much in the way of new information or advice, he was very encouraging to Adam's rather anxious psyche. Aside from not helping with too many technical details, he was most excited to hear the story about Ben's office, the hidden cavity, and the fusion of the stones. "What a trip," he offered. Adam enjoyed retelling the story to someone who really understood the situation, and there was no one better than Greg for that.

The last night in D.C., Greg planned a casual evening of grilling and good wine at his place before a trip to Roswell. Much to Adam's pleasure, Greg had invited Grace over as well. He thought she would enjoy some of Adam's stories.

There was the time they miscalibrated the Vites level through the Alps when Karl Tschalaer, President of the Swiss Confederation, was taking the maiden voyage of the Virtual Global Highway Transportation System through Switzerland. Remembering the startled look on the normally composed diplomat's face made for an amusing tale. When the near miss happened, no one was laughing. While the collision avoidance system had kicked in prior to impacting the snowy, rocky bluff, President Tschalaer had let it be known that it was all too close for comfort as he exited the vehicle heading directly for a bathroom.

It was Friday, and Greg had asked Myles over to help with the food, but their trusted assistant was able to sit, relax, drink wine, and join in with the stories, too. The relaxed and pleasurable evening resulted in Greg, Grace, and Myles receiving an invitation to Roswell to witness the final and crucial part of the Axioms' development. Adam hadn't forgotten there was still a flashing red "incomplete" light on L.U.C.'s holographic image of this pioneering global project. The threesome, along with a few other dignitaries, would witness the completion of this monumental achievement.

The next day in the small city of Roswell, there was to be a historic celebration. The Axiom was prepared for crowds of curious visitors. In the design of all the Axiom Energy Centers, an outer reinforced pavilion with eighteen-inch, clear polymer glass had been built. Outside of wearing an antiferromagnetic mobility unit or AMU on to the floor of the energy center itself, they could use the generous pavilion observing the center from several different observation decks. Like the observation pavilion, an AMU suit was an extra safety precaution, as it helped to minimize any of the excess excitement the magnetic stream would put on the body's hydrogen proteins and helped to prevent any unforeseen damage to the DNA.

It was an astonishing sight, even for the sophisticated attendees. A plethora of androids openly operated among the proton beam accelerators at any given time. However, human exposure was closely monitored and restricted for the most part. At several different points during the day, when the light hit the openings around the current amplifiers, the magnetic streams caused the air to waver as it did in heat mirages.

There were trays of hors d'oeuvres and light conversation at the far west end of the pavilion, the best place to observe the point at which the reactor would first harness the magnetic stream traveling from Earth's core up the control rod and into the proton accelerators. Among the dignitaries were Vice President Jackson, General Mark Shelton, an Army General and current Chair of the Joint Chiefs of Staff, Navy Admiral William Hughes, Air Force General Benjamin Anderson, Chief John Jacobs, the head of Space Force, and Richard Helms, head of the CIA.

While Adam did not want to over advertise the event, it had attracted the attention of some V.IP.'s. Heads of state from some of America's strongest allies were munching on Sandia peppers stuffed with goat cheese. Juan Rodriguez, who was still in charge of operating the Roswell Axiom's Energy Center, circulated among the crowd. By special invitation of appreciation from Adam, Ben Kumar, Ella Flores, Greg Buchanan, Grace Hathaway, Peter and Claire Johansen, and Myles Kelley stood among the gathering at the pavilion. Notably absent was Dr. Aleksey Romanoff. Someone who had been so instrumental in getting the project off the ground.

While there are always consequences for one's actions, Dr. Alex was permitted to watch today's events through the Holovision from his private office in the downtown area of the Commerce District. Punishments must fit the crimes, and depriving someone of partaking in such a groundbreaking event personally was fitting, in Ben's view.

The fateful moment had arrived. Without ever gaining a clear understanding of how much more conductivity the actuator stone would actually serve to amplify the magnetic current, Adam decided it was time to take another leap of faith. Faith was the key ingredient that started this journey on that rainy Christmas morning.

It was clear another scoop of faith was necessary to finish the job. All inventions, even after countless hours of research and trial and error, require some imagination in the end. To steady his nerves, Adam remembered a poster hanging on the wall in Professor Nelson's office at Stanford. It was a quote from Einstein:

"Logic will get you from A-Z: Imagination will get you everywhere."

Feeling like the whole event was little more than a high-tech ribbon cutting, Adam decided to make a brief statement to the gathering of distinguished guests.

"Ladies and gentlemen, thank you all for joining us today. On behalf of all the men and women who've worked so hard to make this dream a reality, thank you for coming. For those of you that are still a little unclear about exactly what we are celebrating, I wanted to take a minute to explain. For several years, our teams around the world have been tirelessly working to create a system, a platform, that would become the foundation for a new way of life on Earth. I think you will agree we are well on our way to seeing this dream become a reality.

"What many of you don't know is that from the day we started on this epic journey, we knew exactly when the last stone would have to be laid in order for us to say, it's finished. The work will continue for many years to fill the Vites with all the vehicles needed to sustain life in the modern world. For the virtual highway to realize its full potential, we know today will mark a major milestone and eliminate any fears we might have had about our constraints.

"As I talk about laying the final stone, I am talking about this both figuratively and literally. Without boring you with too much technical jargon, we've created a new synthetic material that will be inserted directly into our reactor just above Axiom Roswell's control rod. When fully immersed into our magnetic stream, the current will amplify the pulse tenfold.

"We have already been able to successfully harness an unprecedented amount of power and on this landmark occasion, we will secure the power we need to power this dream for centuries to come. We've run the simulation dozens of times digitally with great success." There was a small round of applause. "Please, find a comfortable place to watch," he gestured to a few of the lounge areas nearest some of the largest openings.

"So, without further ado, Greg, would you like to join me in the control room? It's going to take two to do this tango," Aam asked his friend.

Ben was holding on tightly to the handle of a large silver suitcase. Adam knew precisely of its contents. Since the fusion of the stones in his office, Ben had decided he was going to be the only person guarding this extraordinary treasure until it became part of Axiom Roswell's actuator.

Adam, staring directly at Ben, motioned for Greg to follow him towards the entrance to the Control Room. Ben proceeded to follow closely behind, carrying the silver case. They gained entry into the Control Room through retinal scan discovery. Once Adam is cleared, he notices the other two men are scanned, but approved for entry without a retinal investigation. It was a little curious to Adam that they didn't get a retinal scan, however, L.U.C.'s intelligence had known each man intimately and thought no further of it.

Axiom Roswell's Control Room was breathtaking. Endless panels of controls, switches, displays, and touch screens. Engineers positioned around the room at various holographic image control display stations monitored every minute detail of the Virtual Global Highway Transportation System.

One station essentially functioned as an Axiom-wide search engine, complete with imagery. While the intelligence was responsible for keeping things flowing flawlessly in an orderly fashion, an engineer could instantaneously find anything on Vites that they had either chosen to inspect or that they were prompted to look at by the alternative exception monitoring system.

Every car, the identity of every passenger, all the contents of every vehicle, every setting of mode or preference, the internal and external temperature of each car, surrounding climate conditions, the speed, the current destination, the previous destination, the history of destinations of every vehicle, when vehicles would be cycled into the nearest Axiom for inspection and maintenance, and other data. Not every engineer was authorized to see everything, especially when it came to certain people. However, there would be no compromising the safety, privacy, and security of any Vites passenger, ever.

Adam also frequently observed another station in the control room which monitored the strength of the magnetic current. It provided engineers with the visibility and insight into how effective the proton particles were maintaining their charge after the pulsing current of particles had been excited by one of Axiom's many proton accelerator cannons. Particles relayed from Axiom Roswell through the system to its other three Axiom companions and back again. The system had the ability to monitor, measure, and recharge any particle making sure it was consistent, to maintain the then necessary excitement level for holding flight.

In the center console of the Axiom's main control panel, there was an empty circular chamber. On either side of the chamber, there were two permissive action link, or PAL security control systems set approximately four feet away from either side of the chamber which was approximately three feet wide. The positioning of this access control system ensured that at least two authorized individuals were simultaneously in agreement to engage the actuator. Above the empty chamber, there was a large, vertical opening, approximately eight feet wide. It extended to the ceiling. This space had been devoid of light or activity since the completion of the control center. Adam had always assumed that once the system was activated, they would fill the vertical space above the console with a virtual control panel and holographic images supporting the new features added to the system. To the left and right of the center console was also a clear polymer window to the Energy Center, so while engineers were in Axiom's Control Room, they would have some visibility of the floor.

It was time to put the stone where it belonged. There was no more waiting. Ben's hands were unsteady and might have been shaking as he opened the case. Adam and Greg bent down so they could get their hands under the brilliant translucent stone to lift it. The hypnotic effect had not lessened for Adam since he'd last seen the masterpiece in Ben's office almost a week ago. Greg was speechless and couldn't take his eyes off the object as Adam carefully guided it into the empty chamber on the console. There was the stone, resting beautifully and radiating peace, ready for insertion.

An engineer, already in the control room, approached Adam and handed him two cards, each containing a unique authorization code. He handed another one to Greg.

"Shall we?" he asked the men calmly.

As each man positioned himself over their respective security control systems, the console performed another invasive retinal scan.

Welcome, Mr. Buchannan, are you ready? Welcome, Dr. Hunter, are you ready?

Greg and Adam each responded affirmatively.

Please enter your assigned code and turn your control key clockwise ninety degrees. Three – Two – One. The bottom of the chamber in the console suddenly opened and, in a flash, the stone was gone. As soon as the stone had dropped out of sight, the chamber began to spin and rotate until the opening in the console was completely filled. All three men rushed to the clear glass section of the control room. Silence.

A tremendous flash of light exploded with blinding intensity. Solid white beams of light filled every inch of Axiom, relaying out of the center along with the Vites' streaming magnetic current. A sudden, high-pitched whirring sound had given way to a roar. The sound of velocity is impossible to describe, but the currents within the Axiom's Energy Center were spinning faster and faster.

Adam, too numb to react, watched the solid, bright beams of light giving way to what appeared to be pulsing streams of light. The faster the beams of light moved, the more of them there were, filling the space. Faster, faster, quieter, and quieter. The light was now traveling so fast that it had become transparent. Adam heard it and felt it, but whatever it was, it traveled so fast, it became invisible.

The center control panel of Axiom Roswell's Control Room had sprung to life for the very first time. Adam, Greg, and Ben spun around from the glass in tandem as if linked together on a master puppeteer's strings. In a dramatic display of depth and light, a three-dimensional holographic image sprang from a luminous globe no larger than Adam's fist. It had overtaken the entire wall behind the center of the console and extended well into the room. The lights were ablaze and the imagery was fantastical. There were a few unharmed Axiom engineers unwittingly standing in the middle of the hologram now. One walked outside of the image to get a view of the inside, while the others stayed in the center to view outwards. It was unmistakable. It was a star map with Earth at the center of its galaxy, rotating vibrantly.

Adam caught his breath. He watched the heavenly bodies rotate and revolve, some just overhead, others near the edges of the room, their obits illuminated before them, lines as fine as spiderwebs. Stars were born in flashes of swirling prisms, while intergalactic forms like jeweled scaffolds floated in the spaces between larger bodies. The orbs glowed as they moved in this representation of the known universe. He knew he was not looking at a photograph; here the spheres glowed a celestial turquoise, like the millions of infinitesimal organisms that create bioluminescent plankton. Tiny pinpoints of life amounted to little on their own, much like our planet. For the first time, Adam was able to appreciate how the earth was a miniscule part of an enormous whole. Being offered a glimpse of the big picture was like seeing the puzzle pieces placed exactly where they belonged.

Of course Adam felt small in the face of an entity light years in diameter, humans and their petty melodramas often saw their problems in perspective when they viewed the universe. What he didn't feel was alone. Seeing the cosmos this way was like seeing through the walls of a building. There was a structure, a plan, beneath it all. It was an elegantly designed creation. Everything was connected to everything else. At once Adam understood. There was an intelligence at work here...

INTERSTELLAR MODE has been ACTIVATED

the intelligence repeated the words

INTERSTELLAR MODE has been ACTIVATED

Chapter 41 - In the Cellar

For all its high-tech features, the most popular place on the Sol was the "bite storage" area. It boasted a well-stocked refrigerator, an air fryer, a small sink with counter space and an espresso machine. Wine and beer were available for a small fee. Laura Decker found all the organic fruits and vegetables she's requested in the fridge. She also knew each seat had a miniature heating drawer next to a refrigerated drawer in the side panel, and was sure the kids had brought their own snacks.

"Departing in sixty seconds. Begin safety check," a voice said over the speakers. A series of clicks and hums came from the front of the Sol. Lights on the screen in front of Ryan Decker flashed on and off a few times. Laura tapped two buttons on her armrest and smiled over at her husband. They hadn't taken a vacation together in almost a year.

"Entering Vites in thirty seconds," the voice said calmly.

Ryan looked out over the miles of fields as the Sol gracefully ascended well above the tree line. He was tempted to tell his children about travel when he was a boy, but decided it would make him seem the stereotypical old timer they already thought he was. He was glad they didn't have layers of smog to rise above, and that they didn't have to stand sock-footed in long lines at security checkpoints.

No, this was a new world, he thought as the Sol merged smoothly into the flow of traffic, adjusting its speed to that of the vehicles in its immediate proximity. His children would probably work at jobs that didn't even exist yet, in industries that were emerging in every part of the world where people envisioned a better Earth. And none of this would have happened, he realized, without an incredible advance in technology.

"Don't wanna sound dirty, but it's the flirty thirties," Sophia roared along with the song, unaware of how loud she was. Laura glanced over her shoulder and smiled at Parker who was too engrossed in his movies to notice.

None of these entertaining wonders would have been possible without the recent paradigm shift in transportation, including the miraculous ability for this machine to fly high through the air with the aid of a computer that seemed to know everything: atmospheric conditions high above the earth, the proximity of children wandering too close to potential dangers, and deep below the earth's surface, the movements of the magnetic fields in the planet's core.

It was this foray into the earth's molten center that allowed machines to glide above it. Ryan remembered showing Parker how Sols flew using two refrigerator magnets. He placed a superhero magnet in each of his son's hands, negative to negative.

"They won't go together!" Parker said with amazement.

"That's how we stay in the air," Ryan told his son. "And when we want to land," he flipped over a magnet featuring an orange haired creature. "We do this."

He brought the magnets a few inches apart and the creature attached himself to Decimator with a satisfying click. Parker smiled and his eyes were full of the kind of wonder that fills a parent's heart.

It was a little more complicated than that, but the principle was the same. The Deckers could count on the Sol to do exactly what it was programmed to do. The vehicle and the Earth's core were somehow magically woven together in ways the average traveler didn't need to understand. As long as the two of them knew how to communicate perfectly together, that's all that really mattered to most passengers.

According to the VTA, there was very little to worry about while traveling on the Vites. The system was now so reliable that incident reports across the network had become almost non-existent. Traveling and commuting these days had become safer than a walk to the park. Had this remained the case, the trip to Bora Bora would have been exciting, but still predictable. A third element had entered the relationship between the Sol and the heart of our planet.

And computers don't know everything. They only know what people tell them to know. The computers guiding the Deckers to their tropical paradise had no way of knowing what was taking place on the other side of the world. They did what they were programmed to do, until for reasons no one aboard the Sol could fathom, they were unable to perform as programmed.

The Sol shuddered briefly, and Sophia's matcha soda tipped slightly in its freon cooled cup holder. Parker had grown bored with his movie and began pressing buttons on a Sol control panel that he had somehow accessed on his display. As it turned out, Ryan had failed to lock in the Sol's controls when he confirmed that Bora Bora would be the destination that day. Touching an icon under the Vehicle Mode's menu labeled MORE presented Parker with a new option that he had not seen before. Pronouncing it under his breath as he touched the screen, IN-THE-CELLAR or something like that, he thought. He then looked over at his sister and shrugged as the Sol shivered again.

"What's the first thing we want to do when we get there?" Laura asked her children. "Parasailing!" Sophia said.

"Shark hunting!" Parker said with a huge grin.

"No one wants to go bird watching? The ultramarine lorikeet is really…" Laura searched for the words but stopped as the Sol lurched to the left. It snapped back into place just as quickly, jostling the Deckers.

Ryan, not yet panicking, began to reach for Laura. Instantaneously and violently, a psychedelic flash of blinding light hit the Sol and left it in the dark. Ryan could no longer see his hand as he reached into a vast nothingness. Everything was happening in slow motion. Everyone was screaming as deafening silence overtook the craft.

It was like riding a rollercoaster while blindfolded, with no idea when or where the ride would end. Sophia yelled to her brother, but no sound came from her mouth. In the darkened Sol, she could barely make out Parker's movements, but he was moving at a fraction of his normal speed.

All the passengers' ears popped, their stomachs dropped and the weight of their bodies became unbearable as the Sol tried in vain to maintain its terrestrial flight mode. The light was everywhere and anywhere now, and it completely consumed the Deckers.

The panel indicators overhead in the Sol blinked three times, and a high-pitched alarm sounded. Ryan and Laura, their necks too heavy to turn, exchanged frantic glances with only their eyes.

"Unexpected system shutdown," Vesta said flatly. "Please brace, brace, brace…"

Laura heard strange, tinny music as the Sol tore through the swirling cloud of light. Her grandmother's face appeared where the screen would have been. "Of course you did, honey," the image said before vanishing.

Ryan said his prayers as his blood throbbed painfully in his veins and the pull became too strong to resist. He was grateful he could go with his family. At least they were all together, Laura thought as she surrendered to the forces that overtook the Sol.

Then silence. The Sol's instrument panel went dark, the ceiling lights went off. The screens sank into their storage slots as if retreating in fear.

The last thing Laura heard was her son's voice. It echoed off the walls of the Sol. The sound embedded itself in her head and ripped her heart open. Parker was screaming for his mother.

The Sol either wasn't designed for this type of travel, or it wasn't ready for it. When finally, it had landed on solid ground, a haze rose from the hull of the craft. The front panel was badly cracked. The Deckers' belongings were strewn about the cabin. The occupants were still in their seats, miraculously. Disoriented and banged up, but alive.

"Everybody ok?" Ryan asked as he looked around the cabin.

"Oh, my God," Sophia breathed.

"What happened?" Parker asked.

"Ryan?" Laura's voice seemed to come from a thousand miles away as she peered out a portal. "Where are we?"

An unfamiliar scent flowed into the Sol as it had reopened intake panels after confirming conditions outside the cabin were now compatible with its accidental passengers. The Sol had unexpectedly been thrust into a harsh environment and had slightly over adjusted pressure and climate.

All things considered, the onboard AI had done a masterful job of converting the Sol, mid-flight, from terrestrial to interstellar mode. Certainly, a feature that would be disabled on most vehicles once interstellar mode was made readily available to everyone traveling on the Vites. Attempting a maneuver such as the Deckers, while in motion, would have been like dropping an old transmission-based vehicle into park while it had been traveling at seventy miles an hour.

A sweet, metallic smell filled the family's breathing passages. It became so strong they could taste it. The Sol had been nestled into a dune somewhat short of what resembled a landing pod for the craft. While there were no signs of any major structural damage to the vehicle, there appeared to be some bubbling up of the metal on the leading edge of Sol's frame.

The melting had likely been caused by improper polymer assignment during atmospheric re-entry. As a result of the intense heat still emanating from Sol's exterior, there was a slight haze or heat wave which distorted Laura's view outside. The burning metal was also probably contributing to the metallic odor the Decker's smelled as air was streaming in from the outside.

Fumes aside, their new surroundings were beautiful. The sky held a ribbon of color described in what one might only see during a winter sunset. Intense coral pinks, reds, and peachy oranges draped the horizon. The sky, so spectrally pure, contained a small, but intensely white sun well over the landscape.

Then, low on the horizon, an enormous red moon filled the sky with another, smaller-ringed white moon that had to be in orbit of the first, was just above it and to the right.

On the other side of an expansive cerulean field, a series of large shimmering structures were scattered across the horizon. Laura couldn't be sure if she was seeing a field of wildflowers blowing in the breeze or if it was a gently lapping pristine body of water, inviting guests into the crystal city beyond its borders.

Startled, still in the haze of a blurry view, Laura saw two, possibly three, very tall, slender figures making their way directly towards the Sol.

"Ryan?" Laura repeated, but this time with a fully uncertain whisper.

“Mom, are we going to be okay?” asked Sophia, as tears began to stream down her face.

Chapter 42 - Will You Help Me?

Something of earth-shattering importance had happened. Was it marvelous, spectacular, something so incredibly wonderful that had just happened? Or was it the opposite? Was it instead something so horrible and frightening? Had it without warning set in irreparable motion terrible consequences?

Uncertainty was unbearable. Humans were not equipped to let the unknown remain unknown. Good or bad, nothing was worse than not knowing. Or was it? How could humans cope with knowing, with our limited human brains, there were things we *could not* understand?

Whether they liked or wanted it, the world was seconds away from learning the answer to a question that human beings had asked for eons.

Are we alone in the universe?

Adam was part of a very small, select group that had unwittingly discovered the answer a few years ago. But was the answer something too unbelievable for anyone to accept? Until this moment, regardless of how long he had looked to the stars for an answer, Adam had always clung to the notion that we are probably alone.

When he accepted the mysterious Christmas crate, he had opted to focus more on what it could do rather than who it came from. In retrospect, that was the best way to cope with all the unfolding events. In his heart of hearts, he had never given any real credence to the whole Siri from the Stars bit. A better, more realistic truth was to believe that this was the work of some faceless person or group, hidden somewhere well out of public view, in the cabals of the Deep State. They had unleashed yet another diabolical scheme designed to control the minds, hearts, and more importantly, the pocketbooks of the masses for the next century.

After a glimpse of what the future might hold, a vexing spell had him completely ensorcelled. Weren't the masses, the marginalized, always going to be controlled? Why not be controlled with the promise of a better life? He had always dreamed of making a difference. Did he ever have a choice?

Adam had seen holograms, he had worked closely with artificial intelligence, he had invented substances that advanced space travel, he guided leading edge space programs, and he had even had some familiarity with what a number of the brightest minds at Stanford and MIT were postulating. The Virtual Highway was inevitable, with or without him, right? All of these convictions, these feelings, these emotions were crashing into real world uncertainties and rushing at him with frightening speed.

Despite the absence of any need for confirmation, Adam couldn't help himself. He looked right through two engineers standing by the imagery emanating from the console monitoring the Vites activity. The pulsing stream of magnetic current which Axiom Roswell so elegantly harnessed from the earth's core, had been unaltered. The intricately designed equipment channeled it to the surface and intensified it for its daily revolutions around the planet. Not even one wavelength cycle measured differently than it had registered ten minutes before.

The force of the stream, the intensity of the flow, and the length of the waves through each frequency cycle remained absolutely and utterly the same. The Vites would not need a superconductor to increase the already adequate magnetic flow for Earth's Virtual Highway. Not now, not ever. It had all been a lie. The capacity constraint was false. Ben had invented an issue to manipulate Adam and his team, sending them down a blind hole that was quickly filling with regret.

In a new development for the Axiom, the main console in the Control Room had taken center stage. For the first time, it had come to life and was teeming with the luminary visions of solar systems and constellations rotating effortlessly, extending in all points out from Earth. The AI had unmistakably built an all-encompassing three-dimensional star map of the universe, sending onlookers to the verge of sensory overload. Earth, in its current perspective within the hologram, was directly in the center of this navigational masterpiece. It slowly rotated and revolved around our sun in a celestial dance, keeping it in an ordered pace with the other eight planets in our solar system. Our blazing, life-giving sun, with the vivid detail visible in holographic form, emitted furious bursts of electromagnetic radiation in all directions.

Adam watched the console as the earth's magnetic fields sent the energy from the sun's flares back into space. A million times, he had seen the magnetic currents produced by the Axiom to support the Vites. It was soothing, comforting, like looking out one's window at home. He expected to feel reassured examining the predictable rhythm of the spheres.

This time, something was different. He was seeing something more. A new and much higher series of magnetic waves were encircling the planet. These new bands had a rhythm of their own and weren't interacting with his Vites bands at all. In addition to forming higher in the atmosphere, these bands were traveling faster, much faster than any stream he had ever seen. In fact, they were traveling so fast around Earth they took on the appearance of a pulse.

In one fell swoop of desperation, Adam's pierced the galaxy forming light and headed straight for the center console and Red DDA, or Drive Disengagement Arm. Unlike activation, the DDA was a one-person operation. With a most violent grip followed by a thrust that was palpably angry, Adam slammed the DDA into the *off* position. The intense mesmerizing glow that had captivated the entire room only moments ago abruptly vaporized. The light green and yellow hue of the Vites monitoring stations were left on their own to defend against momentary blindness until the eyes could adjust to the dark. In a few moments, the center console re-opened. The cornerstone rose from somewhere in the labyrinth beneath the Energy Center and mechanically deposited back into the chamber.

Adam motioned to a bewildered Greg. "Can you talk to the bigwigs and the other guests? Please let them know that everything is okay. Ben and I are going to compare our notes," he said. "We will join them back in the pavilion for an update very soon."

A large, private office belonging to Juan Rodriquez was just off the main floor of the Control Room. Adam gestured politely to Ben in the direction of Juan's office and waited for him to lead the way. An expressionless Ben, briefly studied Adam for any more signs of aggression and without saying a word, turned towards the office. Adam followed him closely and then shut the door behind them. His professional demeanor instantly gave way to wild-eyed terror.

"BEN, WHAT the HELL just HAPPENED?" Adam demanded. Ben looked at him and said nothing. "I need the truth.... right bloody now. I'm not discounting any of the good," Adam told him as he shook his head. "It was the good, the hope of things to come, the vision of how life on earth would change for all her people that brought me to this place. For years, I have overlooked your evasions, your secrecy, your manipulations, and most of all, your greed."

Ben's silence only antagonized him, causing him to unleash everything he'd wanted to say for over two years. Adam continued to hurl accusations, but was beginning to ramble. He didn't appreciate Ben's price inflation on materials only he could supply. That was a monopoly. Section Two of the Sherman Act states that any person who shall monopolize any part of trade or commerce among several states or among foreign nations shall be deemed guilty of a felony, he ranted. Did Ben know what happens to felons?

"I also didn't like the way you kept me in the dark while working with Ella to copy twenty-thousand people three times to build the other Axioms. I never had a chance to voice my concerns. You don't think that my life, my ass, was on the line when you made some of these monumental decisions?" Adam's volume and anger began to rise to dangerous levels. "Ben, there are a variety of civil, criminal, and administrative penalties for violating state, federal, or foreign ethics laws. And now this? AND NOW THIS? You had me running around like a chicken with its head cut off, thinking our whole system had a serious flaw, had a major constraint. For nearly a year, that worry has kept me up at night, kept me near a breaking point…Really, Ben?"

Ben wasn't saying anything because he knew he'd been exposed. At least that's what Adam told himself in his heated state. When he paused to study Ben more closely, he saw the older man was his usual placid self. What was his strategy? He didn't become a billionaire without knowing how to use his opponent's weaknesses to his advantage. Was it like in boxing, Ben was leaning against the ropes while Adam wore himself out ranting?

"Who didn't need to know about this, Ben? I know what I just saw. We can NEVER put that genie back in the bottle. What is this, really? Where do we go from here? What on earth kind of witchcraft did you find in that little magic talking sphere? Do you even have any idea of what comes next?"

Adam was now unable to control what came out of his mouth next. Ben's unresponsiveness was driving him insane. Ben wasn't leaning against the ropes, Adam was swinging and missing.

"Was this your plan? Get the Vice President of the United States, the heads of Britain, France, Germany, and Italy together in a little room? Get the head of the CIA, several members of the Joint Chiefs of Staff, and flip a crazy switch? Should I go on? All this, and not even one time did you feel the need to let me in on it? What does it even do, anyway? If I had not had enough concerns already about Nationalizing S.E.T.I., you'd better believe I have them now. It's coming and it's coming fast and I'm not sure right now what part you will even play…" Adam took a deep breath, trying to give himself time to allow his emotions to dissipate.

Ben stood silently, studying Adam as if trying to reaffirm all the choices he had made. With the blood clearly and noticeably draining from his face, he wondered if he had done enough to save them. Were all the decisions he made, by himself, from so very far away, the right ones? As he stood assessing Adam, he thought, while it might be too late now, surely it was okay to take a minute to question himself on if he had chosen the right person. It's just human nature to do that right?

So many times, he had wanted to tell Adam, but his trust had never been able to come far enough. It wasn't so much about having doubts about Adam specifically, but more about all the things he realized were out of Adam's control. In all these years, searching, planning, watching, listening, nothing about what he saw in human nature had ever given him the confidence or the courage to put his trust in people. The insatiable greed, the over-reactions, the nature of politics, and fear alone. Adam could not have overcome all those things in the time that was left if he had been handed all the keys to the kingdom.

In the last few years, with all Ben's convictions finding fertile ground, Ben's plan was reduced to avoiding risks, finishing the work, putting the cards on the table and hoping. From the very start, it had all been done in the name of desperation. Nothing about what had happened today would change any of that. It was done, now it was time for hope.

Were the shadows of the dimly lit office beginning to play tricks on Adam's mind? He was sure he had just seen Ben blink without any movement from his eyelids. Was the pressure of the Vites finally getting to him in one big cathartic moment? Was he going crazy, was he hallucinating? The figure that had been Ben Kumar only minutes ago continued with a metamorphosis.

Bens' jacket ripped at the seams in several places as his shoulders widened. His shirt came untucked as his torso lengthened. It happened over a period of a few minutes, Ben began to disappear. Replacing him was a new being. It was not human.

Thinning, graying, elongating, this form had two arms, and two legs. This figure was at least seven feet tall. Adam began to feel his heart racing like it would burst out of his chest as he saw Ben's clothes in a pile on the floor of the being's marble-like feet.

The tall, smooth and completely hairless figure that had just been subjected to a brow beating of epic proportion had fully transformed into something that unquestionably would neither be intimated or subjected to anything further Adam Hunter had to say. It was just as well; Adam no longer had the ability to speak. The being raised its hand, its palm outwardly to Adam as if to signal its intention for a peaceful exchange. Noticing the enormity of the hand, the length of the long, slender, gray digits, Adam felt a type of fear and uncertainty that he had never experienced before.

Powerless to take any other action, Adam raised his eyes to look up into the creature's face and their eyes locked. Adam's heart hammered in his ears, but the rhythm slowed as he studied the countenance before him. While distinctly maintaining humanistic features, his eyes were large, almond shaped, and had a silvery translucent composition, like quartz crystals. As the eyes focused on Adam, growing acclimated to the exposure to oxygen and light, the crystals in the irises spun and rearranged themselves like the glass in a kaleidoscope. They were the most beautiful eyes Adam had ever seen.

Like a grandparent viewing a newborn, this creature's eye held the wisdom of light years. Adam was overcome with the feeling that this being understood and accepted him completely.

Meeting L.U.C. was an overwhelming surprise. It was cerebral. L.U.C. was a machine. A machine designed to communicate with complex and contrary humans.

The entity before him was *alive*. Adam wasn't sure if it had a heart, but he knew it could feel. Like all living things, its existence depended on other living things. Somehow, without sound or movement, the being conveyed this to Adam. For all its foreignness and nearly implausible presence, there was a connection between the two of them.

In a powerful, low, startling tone, Adam heard the being speak.

"My name is Torus and I am from the House of Kor. The unidentified Roswell object your government recovered in 1947, in the time of Earth, was called The Obsidian. I did not find this craft by random fortuitous circumstances. I was chosen to come to Earth and guided it here with great intention and purpose. My world, Berenices, of the Constellation Eridanus, is in grave peril. I have traveled across a great distance to seek your help."

Chapter 43 - Tell Me What Happens Next

No one could have been prepared for what happened next. Adam thought it likely that he was the only person on Earth who had ever been in this situation. Then he realized, if someone ever had been in this situation, he or she probably hadn't lived to tell the story. There would be no tutorials with FAQ's, no user manuals, no Allens-for-Dummies book series to help him prepare.

Of course, down through the centuries, many entertained the possibility of life existing somewhere out there in the universe. Standing face to face with a being from another galaxy, with only an ordinary mahogany office desk separating the two of you was inconceivable. It was far from entertaining.

Years ago, while Adam was working on an assignment with NASA, he had an opportunity to interview one of its rather eccentric engineers. His name was Alcott Adler, and he had a reputation amongst his peers for being somewhat odd. His claim that he was the victim of an alien abduction only enhanced his coworkers' perceptions of his strangeness.

Adler worked at the Deep Space Station-53, or DSS-53, outside of Madrid. It is the site of one of NASA's large ground antennas used for monitoring deep space missions in our solar system. He appeared on the local news, stating that he had been abducted in the middle of the night by aliens. He explained that late one evening, after leaving the office for the day, he saw a UFO approaching overhead. When it was directly above him, an intense white light shone directly into his eyes, causing him to freeze and blinding him temporarily.

He said he felt his body being ripped into the sky in the direction of a UFO, as if attached to some type of tractor beam. After that, he said he wasn't sure what happened. He confided to Adam that his next clear memory was regaining consciousness while lying in a ditch on the side of the road near where he was abducted. Despite hazy memories of his ordeal, he felt sore in his pelvic area and was sure he had been probed. Why beings from an advanced civilization had traveled billions of miles to Earth only to stick a camera up a man's butt was quite a humorous mystery to Adam.

If only the situation he faced in the office was as amusing. Having had a chance to catch his breath and start processing the nature of his encounter, Adam wasn't sure how he was able to feel such exhilaration and terror at the same time. Nothing in his life had prepared him for this.

Cooler heads prevail, he told himself. The demanding emotions of anger and his desire to retaliate were not going to help him get control of the situation. They began to coincide with, and eventually yield to an awareness of prodigious and profound circumstances.

Dr. Alex's game with the stones, the danger of overtaxing the Vites, it seemed so unimportant in this moment. It created one helluva mess in his mind. Second only to the births of Chris and Bri, this experience had vaulted to the top. Without a willful intention, he had just been inextricably linked to an alien named Torus from Berenices. The pieces of who he was and the legacy he was leaving were disintegrating. A suddenly expanding universe began feeling overwhelmingly enormous as it tried to swallow him in uncertainty. Would he manage to walk out of this room? Or was this the end?

Each passing moment functioned as a reprieve to give Adam more time to consider his next move. For a brief second, he was glad to have the mahogany desk between them. His engineer's brain quickly reminded him that something able to travel billions of miles was not concerned about furniture.

While plenty of uncertainty persisted as the two continued staring at each other intently, Adam began to feel a fleeting reassurance from a strange kind of familiarity. With a jolt, like being ripped back into consciousness from a dream, the creature began to speak again. Adam listened intently.

"My planet, Berenices, became a victim of its own advancements. After our enlightenment eons ago, we became reckless and grew careless. We fed indiscriminately like dragons upon our own resources for temporary pleasure. Without regard for the consequences, generations of Berenicians selfishly, collectively, and knowingly put our world in peril. Despite repeated warnings from the Council of the Guardians, we gorged ourselves on our planet's bounty and blindly mined away at its core until we passed the point of no return," he said with heavy sadness.

Torus had emotions, Adam realized. They were like the feelings humans had. And the actions of his fellow Berenicians? They sounded like quite a few earthlings Adam knew.

"What did it matter to those that were living? They would never have to face the consequences for their actions. Such profligacy has a high price, but often it is others who must pay. Finally, a generation arose who cared more about tomorrow than for their own selfish desires of today. They pleaded with our AstroGuild to search the universe, no matter how far, to find a companion planet. A little more than five thousand years ago, the Guild found a planet suitable for our rejuvenation. We found Earth," Torus' eyes changed again; they took on a bluish hue. Adam realized that the creature's eyes reflected images of the swirling Blue Planet as he spoke about it.

"I have come in peace, but my intention is to leave with a harvest before it is too late for my planet. Have I chosen wisely?"

Wise choices, Adam thought. A wise choice at this moment would mean running out of the office. Again, this was a practical problem he reminded himself. It just happened to involve a seven-foot being with the power to obliterate him. Torus was not using force, not yet at least. This was not an arm-wrestling contest. It was a chess match.

Adam, never having believed himself to be a king, certainly thought he was at least a knight or bishop. Maybe even a rook. How disheartening it was to learn that he had merely been a pawn. A pawn that was intricately woven into a complex game that Torus-Kor had orchestrated from the very beginning. He wondered how he could have been so ignorant.

As Torus waited for confirmation of his discernment, he knew what Adam was thinking. Failure to read his thoughts would have broken the first two commandments of his great-grandfather, Kor-Lod: *Know your enemy.* In studying warfare on earth prior to his visit, Torus had been impressed with Sun Tzu's interpretation of the philosophy his family originated. Even so, they were concepts that Torus intuited as soon as he was old enough to take his first steps.

Torus pondered the semantics of war terminology as Adam deliberated. Adam was not necessarily his enemy, although he certainly had the potential to be. No, whether in the East or the West, the closest earthlings had come to describing relationships with uncertain power balances was negotiators.

He had reached his lofty position because he knew how to shift the balance in his favor. What makes for a great military commander is the ability to see the battlefield clearly. Commanders must also anticipate any and all outcomes and respond accordingly. There was a great deal at stake for Torus, but the territory was familiar.

When Torus had offered to be the final hope for Berenices' survival, the Council saw him as one of the most promising minds in generations. While fearful of losing him, they knew he was their best and final chance for survival. He didn't make mistakes, he had proven his valor, he had demonstrated his ability to outflank and outthink his opponents as he once led the BIA, or Berenician Interstellar Army. The BIA responded to the attacks from the evil Faldonian Empire and thwarted their attempt to steal her remaining precious Corinthian stone – stone used this very day to propel Earth into the larger universe.

Being in this room with Adam Hunter, having the conversation inside the nerve center of the Axiom he had conceived and built with Adam's hands had been in Torus' mind the whole time.

He intended for this to happen immediately following the successful activation of Earth's Alcubierre drive. Events had unfolded following his script down to the last detail. Knowing it would take some time for Adam to absorb these profound revelations, Torus, acting with patience, gave Adam enough time to swallow.

Adam knew he was in negotiations of some sort. He also had the disconcerting feeling that he could lose a great deal. He couldn't help but think this was what David must have felt like as he steadied himself, armed with nothing more than a slingshot, when he faced Goliath. With all the force that anyone in his position could muster, he asked Torus, "What do you want from us?"

Adam thought his question would cause Torus to begin gloating, but he was downcast. Clouds swam in his eyes. "For centuries, Berenices was foretold of her growing instability. Tectonic plates shifting, colliding, and collapsing. Lakes of fire, lava rivers devouring eons of innovation, oceanic disturbances, bottomless crevasses, eruptions of all manner, and untold destruction and death. One by one, we disregarded warnings as the ravaging of our planet's core continued, and for what?" he asked.

"The same thing happens here. People are greedy, they're selfish, they're shortsighted..." Adam began.

Torus nodded. "We gave very little to no consideration to consuming less or looking to the stars for alternatives, for building new colonies. In desperation, our subterranean specialists discovered that silica, a naturally occurring compound made up of two of Earth's most abundant resources, could backfill the cavities underneath our plates under Berenices' crust. Silica has tiny crystals of oxygen and silicon, it can settle it into the crevasses and cracks throughout our mantle and insulate our core once again. Our experts think this could give her another one hundred thousand years, and give us precious time to find a more permanent solution. We could also devise a way to evacuate her for another more suitable home," he explained.

Adam said nothing. If this Kor-Torus was telling the truth, it was a need, not a want. This Berenices wasn't going to last much longer without some help. He came from a place that had developed the technology to build flying cars, but they needed...silica?

"Be warned that while Earth's silica is quite abundant due to her perfect atmospheric composition for life, it is extremely rare in the rest of the universe. For that, your planet will be greatly desired by the array of other civilizations who can now see her. The Vites currents alone have made her more visible to those that look for new opportunities. My hope is that you decide to accept my gift and that a diplomatic alliance may be formed. One in which we can agree to protect one another," he finished.

"I don't understand. Gifts? An alliance?" Adam managed to ask.

"Adam, I am behind the essence of L.U.C. I brought the intelligence here with me, already possessing the knowledge and plans to deliver the Vites to humankind. The Vites are a stepping stone to-" Tor stopped and shook his head. "I was with you, watching you, and guiding you every step of the way as you unwrapped our gift. Berenicians have been coming to Earth for five thousand years. Exchanging life for hope, all our voyagers accepted the possibility that they might never return home. Until 1947, at Roswell with the Obsidian, we found Earth inadequately prepared to help us build the portal to space you now see before you. However, those expeditions were not without importance. On each venture, we learned more about Earth and her peoples. We always left something vital for the next Berenician to continue building our last hope. They left tools, built structures, deposited Corinthian stones, solved formulas unique to Earth's polarization, passed along coordinates, and most of all, provided us with signs of life.

"Five thousand years?" Adam couldn't believe his ears.

Tor nodded. "Each visit brought us one step closer to today and gave inspiration to the next group of brave but desperate travelers. Adam, I want, I need, and wish to offer my gifts in exchange for sand, a vast amount. Sand is of little value to humans, and is a plentiful resource found completely unattended in all the great deserts of your planet. For Berenices, it is a life-giving force that holds inestimable value. We never came here expecting Earth to give of herself without receiving something in return."

"I'm trying to understand this, Tor. So, what is *that*?" Adam pointed towards Axiom's Control Room.

Tor smiled slightly. At least Adam thought it was a smile. "After I landed and staged the crash of the Obsidian in Roswell, I spent most of the next year collecting all the materials left for me and learning to be an earthling. In my approach flight from Jupiter, I observed Einstein was breaking through a critical knowledge barrier. He was beginning to expose the theories of general relativity in his field equations.

"Upon seeing this, I became very excited. I knew we were in reach. What you witnessed, what you've built, was the culmination of the careful layering of technological infrastructure, the development of advanced new composite materials, the exposition of undiscovered molecular properties, and the enhancements in communications technology that made global collaboration possible. What we, you and I, were able to accomplish in decades would have taken at least five more centuries for humans to discover if I had not arrived. What you are seeing in the next room is what you would call an Alcubierre drive," he told Adam.

“Alcubierre? Like the physicist?” Adam asked. Miguel Alcubierre was a theoretical physicist. He had astounding ideas about what might be possible, but nobody had put his ideas into practice. Or had they?

“The physicist, yes. Very clever, Adam. Astronomers on this planet have long misunderstood some of their conclusions behind the vastness of our universe. Things are not always as they seem. Something is always hidden in the mysteries of distance, something lurks behind the veil of the twinkling lights in the night sky. There is more to the universe than meets the eye,” Tor said.

“What are you talking about? We aimed our telescopes in the wrong direction?” Adam was starting to feel overwhelmed.

Tor shook his head. “Your scientists, with the best of intentions, labeled all of what they believed to be rapidly rotating neutron stars as Pulsars. They failed to consider that even though something takes on a certain appearance in the distance, the reality can be quite different. To point, if one were to amplify the electromagnetic radiation rate of a planet up to, for example, one thousand pulses per second, the appearance from a distance, already unobtainable for humans to comprehend, may give the same illusion of rapid pulsation of light, as does a rapidly rotating neutron star. Without the proper perspective or technology, there is no way for humans to make a distinction from one to the other – just another blinking light in the sky hundreds of millions of light years away,” he explained.

“They thought they were looking at stars…” Adam was thinking out loud.

“Adam, you just created the illusion of what Earth would call a Pulsar. Let me be the first to welcome you and all humankind to a league of celestial civilizations. We are expanding knowledge and traversing the universe at faster than the speed of light. The devices known to you as Axiom are now capable of encasing a craft, crafts you are manufacturing, in a warp bubble. The space in front of a protective light-based chamber is contracted and the space behind is expanded. Year by year, I left a trail of breadcrumbs for Miguel. By the end of the twentieth century, Alcubierre’s formulas finally began to demonstrate the equations for how to shift space around an object so that the object could arrive at its destination more quickly than light would in normal space,” Tor said excitedly.

“You squeeze the space in front and stretch it out behind?” Adam couldn’t help but smile at the light-based trickery. “That’s cheating.”

“All this done without breaking any of God’s physical laws,” Tor said, as galaxies soared through his eyes.

Adam remained suspicious as he worked to reconcile the fact that this lifeform before him had been the billionaire with whom he had had sophisticated business dealings over the past few years. How had this entity hidden himself so well in plain sight?

As usual, though, Adam's fears gave way to his curiosity. "So, if Earth needed to create a portal to connect itself to the universe, then how did you get here?"

Tor made a sound like an exhalation. Adam wasn't sure if this being could produce an exasperated sigh, but he was fairly sure that was what he heard.

"You remind me of myself many, many years ago. Questions, always questions," Tor said. He reminded himself not to press the earthling for an answer just yet. "A planet possessing the technology to bend space can travel to anywhere in the universe, theoretically. However, without the sustained triangulation from your destination, maintaining the structural integrity of a warp bubble for the duration of your journey is highly speculative, unpredictable and the possibility of death is high. Destination planets must provide a strong magnetic pulsation in order to be properly calibrated for your craft to maintain its encasement and avoid incineration. Until an hour ago, Earth's magnetic field was completely indistinguishable outside of the constellation Cassiopeia, let alone from its own solar system," Tor told him.

"You lost your...Berenicians died this way?" Adam asked. Their planet was near destruction, they'd spent thousands of years and lost lives trying to find a way to save their home.

"Yes, but they volunteered for their missions. We all did. Their deaths were not in vain, Adam. I owe them my eternal gratitude, because I would not be here without their sacrifices," Tor said. He blinked a few times and resumed his explanation.

"After Earth's discovery, the AstroGuild began searching for a surrogate for her. With magnetic fields many times stronger than Earth's, we were able to discover faint magnetic signals for the planets Jupiter, Saturn, and Neptune. Due to sheer size, and a magnetosphere of twelve million miles, we chose Jupiter. Calculations to determine the probability of achieving Jupiter's orbit from Berenices were twenty-two percent," Tor told Adam.

"Those aren't very good odds," Adam said. For all their advancements, the Berenicians had endured their share of hardships. He was beginning to develop an admiration for them.

"Three of every four brave expeditions involving Berenicians willing to sacrifice everything to save her, ended in death. Those who survived, laid the foundation for our hope. Once the Obsidian reached Jupiter's orbit, I used its gravitational pull to propel me forward. I managed to complete a six-year journey to Earth. In the years after landing, I studied humans, deciphered Earth's chemistry, and mastered some of its languages. I wanted to understand its history to plot the details of a plan that would place me here in this room with you today."

Tor had beaten the odds, Adam realized, but continued to push them.

"Almost one hundred years ago, I set in motion my plan to become invisible under Earth's most prevalent surname, Kumar. From the very beginning, from the moment Obsidian left Berenices, it was always to find a way here, to this very room, to be standing in it together with someone like you," Torus said. As he studied Adam with his eyes full of geometric shapes, he tilted his head to the side.

"Your actions could have beneficial consequences for you and your planet," he said. He cupped his hands as if holding an invisible planet within them. Ben had done that...when they were in Colorado. "Will you help me save Berenices, Adam?"

As Torus' final question struck the heart of its target, Adam felt the weight of two worlds falling on his shoulders. He felt responsible, but not truly surprised. It wasn't just a desire to help people Adam had, it was a desire to help that stretched across the universe. He knew now, the strange feeling he'd had all his life, his love of the night sky and his studies of space travel, it had all been leading to this moment.

. Yet Adam knew he had the power to choose. Torus had a plan for him, but it did not involve violating Adam's free will. The Berenician was too clever for that. From the day he was born, and Torus began to mold him, Adam was and has always been the solution.

"I am willing," Adam said. "What happens next?"

"You will arrest and escort me through that door as your prisoner. The world should see that I am not a threat. Please know that everything will be different from this moment forward. People will react with great fear and ignorance when they learn of my existence. They will perceive you as a threat and attempt to harm you. I will do everything in my...powers, which are considerable, to keep you and your family safe. Even so, the burden will shift to you, Adam."

"You will deliver the news of my gifts to your leaders and to the rest of the world. You will petition them to re-open the portal and deliver my request to exchange them for sand. We have been building a fleet of Harvesters for several centuries. They await my signal, which I will give with your consent, to travel to Earth and begin the harvest."

Chapter 44 - Welcome

It wasn't that Adam's life was flashing before his eyes, but certain moments played in his head like scenes from his favorite movie. He was in his backyard in Bellingham on a clear summer night, looking at the Pleiades. Even as a child, he'd known those stars were like road signs, in a language he couldn't yet read.

He was at Stanford, listening to one of Professor Nelson's lectures. It was introductory material, the kind of dry, dull but necessary concepts that would help the budding engineers build Tomorrowland. He must have been very sleep deprived, because he found himself staring at a poster of Einstein. His famous quote was underneath the picture. "Reality is merely an illusion, albeit a very persistent one." The instant he read those words, Adam had known in his heart that he would someday look behind the curtain of reality.

As he reluctantly agreed to be Torus' captor and become the voice for his request, Adam wasn't sure if he wanted to see anymore. He only *thought* he would be prepared for what would happen next. In retrospect, he realized that was an impossibility. There was no way to have guessed how the world was going to react.

People live in their own little universes, with idiosyncratic perceptions about the world. When uneducated, people were aware of little beyond their own noses, as the old saying laments. While he was far from perfect and approaching things from a scientific perspective, Adam had a much more altruistic view, and a much bigger universe than the average person. Sometimes this view could blur his perspective. He was often surprised and bewildered when people overreacted to threats (or what their fearful minds told them were likely threats).

With all the flaws in his view, this broadminded selflessness made him an obvious choice for Torus. These qualities gave him the ability to adapt during so many of the unexpected twists and turns he'd experienced since that fateful Christmas morning. From the time Adam was introduced to the AI, he had learned how to overlook a lot of the things that were wrong with the world and replaced them with the hope he had to change them. Never even once had he put two and two together and believed there was a real, live...Berenician behind the curtain. Torus, and others from his home planet, were orchestrating global advancement for the last century.

Yes, there were always rumors that Roswell was a real UFO crash, and that high-ranking government employees knew the truth in those fabled top-secret files that never left the White

House. Adam remembered the night when he first showed Greg the AI in the MoreStore and how Greg downplayed the fact that it was alien technology and agreed that it more likely had originated from a secret, highly covert government operation. Greg didn't believe in aliens and said as much. Adam agreed.

As shocking as it was for Adam to see Torus in the flesh, how much more surprising, even terrifying, would it be for those that hadn't been walking in his shoes? Not once, in all his time with the CIA, had he seen a file or heard any legitimate source refer to the fact that the Obsidian was real. If only there had been even one shred of proof, he knew he would have been much more prepared for this.

Maybe Adam had handled the shock better than most because some part of him had always known he would come in contact with something or someone beyond the Pleiades. And he did not fear this encounter.

Adam read the newspapers, however. He knew that political fanaticism was spiraling out of control. Conspiracy theories grew like weeds, choking the truth. There were wild accusations of governments attempting to gain more control of people's daily lives, hate crimes, fear mongering, excessive greed, and envy. When the time came for the world to learn of the existence of Kor-Torus, and that was now only minutes away, Adam couldn't help but think of the great dilemma this would create.

On the one hand, learning that we are not alone in the universe could wake people up, break them out of this destructive cycle, and become a kind of catalyst for mankind to refocus on a greater purpose. On the other, it could cause people to make decisions based on fear, a recipe for disaster if ever there was one.

The day Axiom One officially opened in Roswell, unbeknownst to all the distinguished guests, the genie escaped the bottle. It would never return. The invited dignitaries were seasoned at attending these types of events and knew pretty well how things were supposed to go. This particular function was going to be a fairly simple and predictable dedication ceremony to honor the official completion of the Virtual Global Highway Transportation System. It was little more than a high-tech ribbon cutting. According to the agenda, they would have fancy hors d'oeuvres and expensive wine while watching a short light show following the Vites system upgrade.

For all intents and purposes, they saw what they thought they had come to see – as a bonus to the light show they were expecting, they had also been able to feel something, too. At the beginning of the ceremony, when the stone was inserted, everyone present had the same physical sensation. As things were cycling up, there had been a tremendous amount of vibration, enough to shake a person's bones, like standing behind a fighter jet preparing to roar down the runway.

From their vantage point in Axiom's pavilion, most of the guests thought it had been a pretty good show but a few were a little disappointed there hadn't been more of a finale. The faster the light went, the less anyone could see or hear anything. Little did they know, the real finale hadn't started yet.

The program moved forward in a predictable way and had been moving towards a normal, uneventful conclusion. All that was left was a few toasts, a plaque or two handed out, maybe a 'brave new world' kind of thank you speech, and lots of congratulatory handshakes. That's not what happened.

Looking back, Adam found himself questioning hints and signs over the past few years that had now seemed suspicious. Surely, there was a better way for this to happen and while keeping Torus out of harm's way. It was hard to blame him with the weighty news he was carrying. Still, if Tor had trusted him at any point along the way, Adam was sure he could have found a way to help. Instead, Torus created a plan designed to inflict maximum chaos.

The first change to the agenda was subtle. Greg, without Adam, emerged from the Control Room. The saving grace which prevented things from going downhill faster than they did was that Greg was able to find Director Helms first. A lot of expectant eyes were on him as he moved briskly across the room through the crowd. Greg knew Helms was Adam's biggest advocate and would listen to what he had to say before overreacting like some of the others in the room were sure to do. In the most casual way, he let Helms know that there had been an unexpected turn of events in the Control Room and that the system upgrade had given the Vites capabilities other than they had anticipated.

And there was something else, too. General Shelton, standing adjacent to Helms, was the first to dial into what Greg was saying. On or off the battlefield, Shelton was alert and ready, always aware to what was happening around him. Shelton, like most generals, didn't like surprises. The buzz of Greg's discussion with Helms began to spread quickly throughout the pavilion and it didn't take long before news of the unexpected result had caught the attention of Vice President Jackson, Admiral Hughes, General Anderson, and Chief Jacobs.

There were a large number of active duty and reservists from each branch of the military accompanying their respective leaders at the Axiom Roswell for the final Vites upgrade. All the Generals of the Joint Chiefs traveled with at least a company or two of men just in case they ever encountered something unexpected. The enlisted men and women along with their commanders had ventured down to the Commerce District to keep themselves entertained while their bosses attended the ceremony.

Amid the murmuring, Adam emerged from the Control Room, but Helms had already begun to diffuse the situation with some of the military leaders. From Helms' read on Greg, whatever had happened didn't seem to be anything he should be too alarmed with and was telling the military leaders around him as much. General Shelton had already made the call to one of his commanding officers, and ordered him to start gathering the soldiers as the program was almost over and they would be leaving soon.

Adam, expressionless, calmly moved to the front of the room and prepared to address the gathering of world leaders by clearing his throat a few times.

“Excuse me, can I have your attention?” Adam moved his hands downward, trying to quiet the unsettled fervor.

“I apologize for the interruption in our ceremony; however, we’ve got an unexpected change to our agenda.” He paused again to wait for the crowd to quiet further and to make sure he had everyone’s undivided attention. Adam hoped to put what he was going to disclose in a positive light.

“Something amazing, something truly wonderful has happened today. We are recognizing that all of us have already become a part of something so much bigger than ourselves. The Vites is a world changing innovative technology platform helping us to solve problems that previously had no solutions,” Adam opened his arms as if to wrap them around the whole world. “Even as it continues to evolve right before our eyes and remains in its infancy, this gift of ours has decided to give us yet another surprise.”

As Adam continued to talk, several in the crowd, particularly the military leaders, were beginning to fidget and glance around the room.

“It will be up to history to decide, but I believe we are on the cusp of a new age. The Renaissance saw the rebirth of culture, arts, science, and learning. The Enlightenment was a period of intellectual growth and helped lead us into the Industrial Revolution. The Industrial Revolution, built on mass industrial production, led us out of an agrarian society. In our time, we are a product of the Information Age and have used modern technologies to reshape the entire world as we know it,” he told the moderately attentive crowd.

“Without fully understanding who or what has allowed us to advance so fast, ladies and gentlemen, let me be so bold as to introduce and invite you to the Celestial Age. Layered upon the Vites, a technology that draws from Earth’s magnetic core, we unexpectedly and miraculously,” he paused “opened a doorway to the stars.”

A buzz moved through the crowd followed by murmurs as military leaders continued to bristle. Again, Adam waited for the crowd to settle.

"Please do your best to remain calm," he said, letting a pause last for several seconds.

"From the source of that doorway, we also have a visitor, a visitor that has traveled a great distance to be here and has been living among us for some time. In a short time, he will introduce himself to all of you. He is the source of our new technology, and he would like to create an alliance with us.

Military leaders decided not to wait for their questions to be answered before deciding to assemble their troops. The soldiers, who were mostly in the Commerce District, started to collect themselves and began scrambling to return to the Energy Center. Other non-military people in the Commerce District overheard the tense whispers of the soldiers.

Alien. The word began to spread across Axiom Roswell like wildfire. Within an hour, the rumor had left Roswell City Limits and was moving swiftly across the country and globe. Members of the Secret Service decide to evacuate Vice President Jackson and the other world leaders from the building for their safety.

As General Shelton began to give orders, Adam asked him for a little patience. Then, he asked Director Helms and Greg to go back into the Control Room and help him escort their guest to the pavilion. Director Helms and Greg, fully trusting Adam, made their way back towards Juan's office.

When Richard caught his first glimpse of Torus, he stopped in his tracks. Reminding himself to breathe, he began to marvel at how large and stunning the amazing creature was. Torus didn't speak but was looking directly at Richard. He gives him a slow nod as if to let him know it is okay to approach him and is affirming his willingness to submit.

Torus exchanged glances with Greg to give him some degree of recognition. He knew that Greg was Adam's long-time partner and friend. Richard and Adam stood on either side of Torus and began to escort him from the office. Engineers in the Control Room froze, stared in disbelief, and backed away, clearing a path for Torus to exit the Control Room.

From the moment Torus walked out into the pavilion, the rest had become a blur to Adam. Troops, under the direction of General Shelton, stormed into the Axiom's Energy Center and were ordered to apprehend Torus on sight. Armed with heavy automatic weapons and under the direction of General Shelton, they seized him and began to hurry him out of the building.

Even as Adam protested the arrest vehemently, Torus did not attempt to fight back. Adam tried to explain how Torus had come in peace and wasn't a threat, but General Shelton ignored him, issuing abrupt commands. Shelton was not alone. All the military leaders thought it best to eliminate risk first and ask questions later.

Surrounded by at least a dozen soldiers, Torus was taken to a detainment area somewhere in the Commerce District. Adam had been ordered to keep his distance until they permitted him to see Torus. After several hours, and night had fallen, a large convoy of dark SUVs and military Humvees entered the Axiom and collected the prisoner. Taking custody had been fairly easy for the soldiers. It was transporting the prisoner that presented a challenge.

A few months ago, as people developed a strong preference for the Vites, the government began closing highways and interstates across the country. The closures were to both encourage people to begin adopting the Vites as their primary form of transportation and to start transforming those areas into green spaces, agricultural zones, and planned residential and recreational areas. Some would become new national parks and other conservation areas.

Like Tor, General Shelton knew his battlefield and his opponent. He had opted not to put Torus in the air, especially on the Vites, in order to keep the prisoner out of his element. Instead, he gave orders to reopen highways and interstates all the way from Roswell to DC. The motorcade would head for a new confinement facility at the Joint Base Anacostia-Bolling, just outside of Washington DC. Here, the military would interrogate and observe the alien. The new, hi-tech, never before used containment facility had recently been built just for the purpose of holding such an unusual guest, and Sheldon had been itching for an occasion to use it.

Despite traveling at night, the lights from vehicles passing overhead on the Vites served to keep the road visible and allowed word to continue spreading about the exact location and route the alien was taking. As the night wore on, hundreds of thousands of people began finding their way into the cities and along the route to see if they could get a glimpse.

Sheldon's convoy had taken Highway 70 out of Roswell up to Amarillo, Texas. From there, they traveled on reopened I-40 all the way through Oklahoma City to Knoxville, Tennessee. Finally, they reopened I-81 through Roanoke and took I-66 at Cedar Creek for the rest of the way into DC by way of Fairfax.

As the crowds grew, signs began popping up everywhere and lined the vacant Interstates. The roadside onlookers tended to belong to one of three groups: the curious, the supporters, and the fearful. The presence of a large, vocal group known as Americans Against Aliens, or AAA, was particularly active throughout the journey to DC. It was obvious they had been waiting for this moment and were ready to mobilize to the streets. Torus tried to pay no attention as

AAA thundered down the Interstate passing signs that read: NO MORE ROOM HERE, GO BACK HOME, and DESTROY HIM BEFORE HE DESTROYS US.

Studying humans like he had for almost a century, this reaction was not surprising to him. Other groups such as nonprofit, TO THE STARS, which was founded back in 2017 by Jim Semivan, a former CIA Intelligence officer and colleague of Adam Hunter, were also making themselves visible. The entertainment leg of the company, Stars Media, had been publishing albums, books, tv shows, and films to raise awareness of the possibility of alien life, but mainly to make money.

One of the most successful book series produced by their publishing division, Sekret Machines, had been a major money maker for the organization. It was making a difference in perpetuating the belief that aliens had visited Earth. Little did they know how many times they had actually hit on technology and machines that were brought here to us from Berenices.

As the convoy made its way through the city, the gathering crowds made it nearly impossible to exit off I-295 at MacDill Blvd where the Arnold Gate entrance to the Joint Base Anacostia was located. Military police were busy using force to push people back and were setting up barricades to clear the way for the prisoner. While there was no imminent terrorist activity, in preparation for Torus arrival at the base, the Force Protection Condition, or FPCON, had been set to DELTA, the highest and most protective level, limiting access to only mission-essential personnel.

Just as the convoy was preparing to enter the heavily guarded brick and wrought iron security gate, Torus looked up to notice a lone sign held by an onlooker who had separated himself from a larger, more hostile group. Heartened by what he saw, the sign simply read WELCOME.

Chapter 45 - You Hold the Floor

It had been two weeks since anyone outside the gates of the Joint Base Anacostia had seen Torus. Millions of people from all over the world had descended on Washington DC, trying to get a glimpse of the visitor. Opinions abounded, many of them impassioned. Fear and uncertainty ruled the day, but there were cherished moments of love and acceptance.

Rumors multiplied, contradicted each other and circulated furiously. They ranged from a worry that aliens had infiltrated our government and were now hiding one of their own, to a fear that this alien was just a sentinel sent to scout an impending hostile invasion. People had heard that the creature had first looked like us and now he didn't, they'd heard that he was cooperative and that he was radioactive.

The maddening lack of information was causing neighbors to suspect neighbors, wives to suspect husbands, and lifelong friends to suspect one another of being extraterrestrials. The old saying goes, a little knowledge is a dangerous thing. It was proving true. The few facts available combined with the human imagination had touched on many people's deepest fears.

The possibility of being overpowered or outnumbered causes people to take protective measures, both individually and collectively. Evidence of this fear appears in our country's governing documents. The framers of our Constitution were deeply skeptical of a standing army and its ability to overthrow the government it served. They had good reason to be wary of military might. Just over one hundred years earlier, in 1653, Oliver Cromwell used his army to disband the English parliament. It was an act that clearly illustrated the power of might and political leaders took note. Consequently, among the primary grievances listed in the Declaration of Independence was the consternation regarding the British deployment of its military to the American colonies without the consent of the local governing officials.

No one was accusing governing official General Shelton of trying to seize control of the government... at least not yet. Still, raising the question about his intentions seemed justified, as close to the line as it seemed he was getting. Shelton was certainly exercising all the powers that had been vested in him to control and delay any type of due process for the alien. He decided he would conduct his own investigation to assess what kind of threat the intruder posed. There wasn't a lot anyone could do about it. Until the POTUS, the Commander and Chief, gave him orders to do otherwise, Shelton was doing it his way.

He determined that the best place for the alien was the outstanding, new state-of-the-art containment facility, the Pentock Sur, or PenSur, located on the base adjacent to the Department of Homeland Security and behind the Secret Service Headquarters. On the other side, it was hemmed in by the Potomac. Across the dark waters of the river, a few lights from the now vacant Reagan National Airport glowed.

It was a tightly controlled environment, from the top down. Airspace over and within a five-mile radius of all U.S. Military Bases had been restricted to authorized military personnel only. While Vites transit hubs were under construction at the entrance gates to every military facility, they were guarded at all times.

Inside PenSur, there were four fifty-by-fifty cell blocks. The only access point to the four blocks was from a circular room at the end of a long, narrow hallway in the center of the facility, one reached after passing through two gated security checkpoints. Once inside each cell, there was a ten-by-ten containment area enclosed by two-foot-thick clear acrylic material. Prisoners were visible at all times from the elevated guard stations located through the room, as well as the video surveillance system.

A series of high-intensity laser beams functioned to seal off the door to the inner chamber. Another larger, acrylic chamber measuring twenty-five by twenty-five served to encase the inner sanctum. A high-voltage electric current spanned the entire floor area between the two chambers when activated. Inside the cell, there was a series of vacuum tubes used for the delivery and recovery of food, water, and other materials made available to the captive. A large monitor, mounted on the outside of the inner cell, enabled prisoner interrogations and consultations without direct physical contact with the subject. An AI interacted with, served, and monitored the prisoners' every move.

In the two weeks since his solitary confinement, General Shelton had learned the alien's name, that he was 155 years old, that he had been here living among us under the assumed name of Ben Kumar since 1947. He'd learned that "Ben" staged the crash of the ship that brought him here in order to maintain his anonymity, and that he had been using his knowledge to benefit humans, but also to build his wealth.

This was interesting, but it was not the information Shelton was after. He was growing more frustrated by the minute and becoming more combative because he knew the visitor had decided to keep him in the dark.

Torus knew the clock was ticking on Berenices. He also knew Shelton wasn't going to be the one to help him save her. If anything, the General, who was trained to protect and eliminate risk, would feel that it was his job to prevent Torus from opening door number two, unleashing an attack that could obliterate the solar system.

The General was given very little of what he so desperately sought, confirmation that Torus wanted to destroy the world. It never occurred to Shelton that he could be looking for something that was simply not present at this time, in this place. Shelton believed with complete certainty that Torus could only present a threat. He sought the specifics of this threat, the dimensions, so he could formulate a defense. If all went well, Shelton mused, he could plan a counterattack on this new enemy.

Shelton entertained many possibilities about how this invader intended to harm the people of Earth. The one possibility that he could not entertain, that he could not imagine, was that Torus was telling him the truth: he did not come to this planet with the intent to harm anything or anyone. In truth, he was not here on a purely military exercise. This mission had life or death consequences, but it was essentially trade. Torus wanted to make a deal.

Torus had cast his lot. He had chosen Adam as his man and had decided there was nothing to gain by sharing information with the soldiers. He had said as much to the people who questioned him relentlessly.

The interrogators had been rotating in eight-hour shifts for two weeks, and were beginning to show signs of fatigue. Torus told them repeatedly that the interview was over and demanded to see Adam Hunter. There had been a few times where they had seen fire rage in his eyes. They felt something, too, and they found it unnerving. Nothing in their training had prepared them for the situation they faced. They were certain the Berenician could walk out of PenSur any time he wanted to and there was nothing they could have done about it.

Torus, still committed to following the plan for now, knew without knowing that Adam had been doing everything in his power on the outside to reach him. He was prepared to continue trying until he was successful.

Torus had also seen the gears of the human justice system many times over the years, and he was waiting patiently for it to run its course. More times than not, he had seen the system work.

Torus' instincts about Adam had been right, naturally. From the moment he had been snatched from the Axiom in Roswell, Adam had been tirelessly working all the angles. Adam and Richard Helms had grabbed the Vites out of Roswell that night as soon as the convoy departed. They had actually gotten back to the base before the soldiers arrived with Torus.

General Shelton's no admittance orders, however, thwarted their attempts to get on the base. On such a short notice, even Richard's calls to his contacts at the White House couldn't trump Shelton's orders that night.

Adam had hoped, if nothing else, to make eye contact with Torus at the Gate to reassure him that someone was in his corner, but it didn't happen. Between the military police pushing, the mob pulling, and the number of vehicles that were rolling onto the base, Adam wasn't even sure which SUV contained his friend.

He spent nearly every waking moment of the next two weeks working every possible angle to find a way to get to Torus in the Joint Base Anacostia. There was also a short trip home to spend some time with Chris, Bri, and Julie, explaining to them a little more about what had happened. Plenty of teenagers thought their parents were rather dull. Adam would never forget the looks on their faces when he told his kids about conversing with an alien.

It would have been impossible to reveal everything that had happened. The profundity of the encounter was difficult to articulate. Adam knew that the chances of finding extraterrestrial life were fairly slim. He had often thought that the alien life form people discovered would be a fungus or bacteria in a crystal. Exciting, to be sure, but we would be limited in how we could communicate with such life forms. And now sentient beings had found them after a long search.

The chance of extraterrestrial life showing up at Earth's doorstep? There was no way to calculate that. The possibility of empathizing with alien life forms was too farfetched to consider, but it was happening with the Berenician.

After the initial fearful reaction when Torus made his metamorphosis in Juan's office, something strange, something he didn't understand was happening inside him. He had formed a bond with the creature. It was causing him to grow more anxious to see that Torus was okay and to deliver his request to the world.

He enlisted a willing Richard, who was very intrigued and also beginning to take on a deeper, more personal interest in fighting for the alien's cause. Together, they worked every Representative for which they had a contact and every relationship they had in the White House, trying to find ways to save this heretofore unknown civilization.

These elected officials were very interested in helping, but everyone on the planet knew of the alien's capture. The entire government was inundated and had reached a point where every process and procedure was delayed, impeded or simply buried in red tape.

Adam, observing that the news of Torus' capture alone had sent the world into pandemonium, knew that the time wasn't right for him to voice the alien's request. Doing that could send everything into a complete tailspin, and time was of the essence. We were unlikely to recover before all was lost for Berenices. Adam was sure that people were going to need to see Torus, to hear the commander speak, and to hear all about the wonderful gifts that Berenices had brought us.

On day sixteen of Torus' capture, there was finally a break. The House Subcommittee on Counterterrorism, Counterintelligence, and Counterproliferation called for an investigative hearing to gain a better understanding of who the alien was, why he had come, and what he wanted from us. The last time this committee had convened to explore other worldly topics was in May of 2017, when its members held hearings with top military officials to discuss the military file of unexplained aerial phenomena. This was the first public congressional hearing to investigate UFO sightings in the US in over fifty years. Those hearings didn't accomplish much of anything besides providing content for an episode of *Unexplained Mysteries*, but this one was sure to deliver the goods.

Investigative hearings are different from legislative or oversight hearings in that investigations usually involve the allegations of wrongdoing. With the nation's collective psyche already in a fragile state, the committee was careful not to float any allegations. It was simply time for America, for the world, to learn more about our visitor from the stars. We wanted to find out why he was here. Congress had every reason to close the hearing from the public, because it involved matters of national security and might have revealed information that would be best kept private. But the public outcry for answers was too great. In the history of hearings, this one was different.

Adam's cell had not left the palm of his hand for more than two weeks. He was calling to obtain support from anyone and everyone even remotely connected to the government. The news that there would be a congressional hearing was exhilarating to him. Soon after they learned of the hearing, Adam received a long-awaited call. He would be asked to testify as the primary representative of Torus.

US Senator Patty Vischer (D-California), the Chair of the Subcommittee, would preside over the hearing. She was fair, objective and would be sure to conduct a proper hearing without theatrics or exploitation. She, along with her committee, decided there would be only four witnesses. Chairperson Vischer would call the meeting to order and provide the opening statements. The oral testimony would include Adam Hunter, General Shelton, and Rebecca Ronan.

An aide explained to Adam that he would testify about how he discovered the alien and what he learned about him. General Shelton, who had been in possession of and interrogating the

Berenician around the clock for the past two weeks, would also testify about his findings after observing the being. He would also offer his thoughts and recommendations about the security threat the alien posed.

Rebecca, who, like Adam, was also from the Office of Science and Technology Policy, was charged with giving her testimony concerning her observations on the impact of the Vites rollout. It was her job to document what she observed both at home and abroad, to work with the Vites Transportation and Safety Board (VTSB) to give her recommendations for operational improvements. She also reported her findings to the House Committee on Transportation and Infrastructure so that the highest levels of government could take action if something needed an intervention.

Adam would then be allowed some closing remarks about the testimony and turn the hearing back over to the Chair to begin the questioning of the subject witness.

Public demand to attend the hearing had reached the stratosphere. As a result, the C-SPAN coverage was simulcast in Washington at Capital One Arena and FedEx Field. Adam would sit beside Torus at the witness table facing the legislators. He had secured seven seats in the audience of the hearing room for some of those closest to him and Torus during this journey. Adam welcomed the support, but his friends and associates Greg Buchanan, Grace Hathaway, Ella Flores, Peter and Claire Johansen, Dr. Alex Romanoff, and Myles Kelley also wanted to attend and were very anxious. Along with the US President and members of his cabinet, heads of state of America's closest allies were in attendance. However, they were going to watch the proceedings on closed circuit video in an undisclosed secure area of the building.

It was like watching the parting of the Red Sea. The masses stepped back as the military caravan transported the prisoner across the river and to the capitol. The highways were lined with security guards built like refrigerators in dark uniforms and darker glasses. A few had high-strung Malinois and GSD's, straining at leashes when they caught a scent. Drones and a few helicopters retrieved from storage circled overhead. They relayed messages to snipers on rooftops and agents wearing camouflage in treetops. DC hadn't seen this much security since North Kardashian West visited.

People were desperate for a glimpse of Torus and had been camping outside for weeks for their chance. Vites was closed to traffic over Washington during the military's fifteen-minute drive from the base to the Capitol Building. Only military craft were allowed in the airspace to escort the vehicles on their drive and to address any unexpected events. The vehicle holding Torus rolled slowly through the gates to the lower level behind the Capitol Building. At last, Torus entered the building through a *very* secure private entrance.

Not one photo of the Berenician had been leaked, although fakes abounded. General Shelton had threatened a court martial to any of his soldiers who disobeyed that order. The heavily armed military personnel escorted the magnificent creature into the chamber and to the witness table, in a hearing room filled to capacity. Everyone stood, amid a silence that would have made the dropping of a pin audible.

Torus and Adam locked eyes for the first time in more than two weeks. The love and relief were unexplainable and palpable. It was a growing attraction almost like that of the one American bear enthusiast Timothy Treadwell had with Grizzly Bears. He knew they were extremely dangerous, yet he could not stand to be away from them for very long. It ended up costing him his life.

Torus was directed to the chair next to Adam and for the first time, Adam touched the alien by embracing his forearm. He felt the energy of the lifeform surge through his veins. One of the soldiers remained beside Torus opposite Adam and one remained behind. Several more soldiers entered the chamber and remained to the side, but a short distance from the witness table.

As everyone was seated, Chair Vischer provided the opening remarks and gave direction to the witnesses, invited guests, and the public. She welcomed every person there and all those watching everywhere around the world. The purpose of this hearing, she stated, was for all of us to have a proper introduction to a visitor to our planet. He had decided to come to Earth and live among us in anonymity. We wanted to learn more about him, why he came here, and what, if any, kind of threat he posed to us. The alien would not be permitted to testify, however, when the witnesses had finished their testimony, they would open the floor to committee members to question the witness.

"Dr. Hunter, you hold the floor," Vischer said.

Adam began cautiously. "My name is Adam Hunter, and my primary responsibility is the development and implementation of the Virtual Global Highway Transportation System. Over the past three years, when he was…in another form, I worked closely with our guest on this endeavor. I found him to be professional, accomplished, and genuinely concerned with bringing Vites to fruition. Upon the installation of the final phase of Vites infrastructure, the person known to me as S.E.T.I. Industries CEO, Ben Kumar, decided to fully introduce and reveal himself to me to commemorate the achievement."

Adam caught sight of a thin TOP SECRET file in Senator Vischer's hand. *The Roswell File.* His heart skipped a beat. The one that has been locked away for decades, according to persistent rumors. Life would have been so much easier if someone had just been truthful about all this. The truth that would have set us free, instead of living in fear. Fear of the truth was not natural, he mused.

Then again, discovering the truth about extraterrestrial life was powerful, Adam thought. The Obsidian landing in 1947 had the power to change lives, and for the better. Instead, we've lost track of the lies we've told about what happened in the desert that summer, he realized as he wondered just how many of those secret files there were.

It was a fear of the unknown that had caused all this, Adam decided as he watched the police officers' eyes scanning the room. We're always so busy looking for bad surprises, it never occurs to us that a wonderful surprise could land in the desert with an invitation to a wonderful new world.

He would not share his musings with the committee, not yet. The best place to begin was with the facts, as he understood them. The committee knew a fair amount about Torus already.

"Torus, formerly known as Ben, revealed to me that he guided the space craft Obsidian from the planet Berenices and landed in Roswell, New Mexico in 1947. He has spent the decades since his arrival sharing his planet's technology for the betterment of the human race. I have found him to be intelligent, benevolent and even selfless in many instances." Adam knew that he would be allotted some time at the end of the testimony, so he stopped short of presenting Torus' request until he got a better read on the rest of the hearing. He finished his opening testimony with more praise for his new friend.

"Torus has lived among us peacefully for some time. He has been very generous with his time, knowledge, and resources, and I believe he poses no threat to us and our way of life. In a few minutes, witness Rebecca Ronan will testify about some of her observations regarding the manifestations of the gifts that Torus and his planet brought us. Respectfully, when you've heard all the testimony and asked all your questions, I believe the committee will come to the conclusion that the prisoner should be released immediately. The world must know how much he has helped us. I yield my time back to the Chair."

Vischer looked pensive as she watched Adam look down at his notes and glance over at General Shelton. She cleared her throat.

"General Shelton, sir. You hold the floor," she said.

The General's posture was characteristically rigid as he sat ready to vent his frustrations to the committee. He appeared to have aged several years in the last two weeks. Classes at West Point did not cover defense against alien visitors. Shelton was out of his element, out of control, and furious that he could not gain high ground on this strange battlefield.

"Distinguished members of Congress and guests, I have to say, I'm not surprised how this life form has manipulated even our most trusted public servants. Nevertheless, I am outraged that Mr. Torus has deceived someone as accomplished and respected as Dr. Hunter into believing that he has come to Earth for an exchange, supposedly benefiting both parties. For the love of God," Shelton paused, as his voice was beginning to crack with emotion. "Do not believe that Torus has been cooperative with the United States government in any way. He has done nothing but stonewall and obfuscate," he said, pausing to pour himself a glass of water from the pitcher on his table. He dabbed the perspiration forming at his hairline, cleared his throat, and resumed his attack. "Torus was not forthcoming in his questioning. After two weeks, my staff and I learned what Dr. Hunter just told us in five minutes," he shook his head.

"What Dr. Hunter didn't tell you is that the alien had misled us. Torus opened a portal, a portal to the stars that makes us very vulnerable to attack. We have to assume he and his world have hostile intentions. For that, I recommend to this committee that under no circumstances do we allow this alien the freedom to walk among us. Without any experience with this kind of intelligence, it could take months or even years for us to get to the bottom of why this thing has come here.

"I took an oath and I owe it to each and every one of you to protect you and keep you safe from all things that lurk in the shadows and seek to destroy you. This is my job and I intend to do it. I yield my time back to the Chair," he said sharply.

"Thank you, General Shelton," Vischer said. She put her hand over her microphone and spoke to the man on her left for a few moments. After a brief nod, she addressed the room again. "We will now hear from Rebecca Ronan, Senior Analyst with the Office of Science and Technology Policy. Ms. Ronan, you hold the floor," Vischer said.

"Thank you, Madame Chair," Ronan said evenly. Her speech pattern was what linguists would describe as "Midwestern," with no obvious indicators that she was raised in the Southern or Northeastern United States. She had medium brown hair, was of average height and build and wore a nondescript navy suit. It was the perfect disguise.

Born Amethyst Aquarius Rebecca Liberty Morrison, Ronan grew up in a thriving commune in the mountains of Northern California. Her family worked in the fields and orchards, growing organic produce that entranced chefs at pricey Bay Area restaurants. They also produced substantial quantities of marijuana. She played outside with her two younger brothers year-round; the family did not own a television.

Homeschooled until her teens, Ronan was on a ninth-grade field trip to the Morrison Planetarium the first time she visited a city. She loved astronomy, but the constantly moving groups of people and vehicles left the strongest impression of anything she'd seen that day. Breathless with excitement when she came home, she asked her parents why their family didn't live in one of these incredible inventions, the city.

"You don't want to live in one of those, my baby," her mother said. Saffron was horrified that they might lose her to the urban underworld.

"It had everything, all kinds of people and their different food and stuff. They all lived together. It was amazing," she insisted.

"Cities are polluted and full of people who only care about making money," her father said. "Stay close to the land and you can't go wrong."

"Why can't people do both? Be part of the earth and study the stars? And eat chow mein? Did you know there's a Chinatown in San Francisco..."

Her parents never gave her a satisfactory answer, even when she told them she'd been accepted to Georgetown University. They told her there would always be room for her when she got tired of the people who only cared about material things.

By the end of her sophomore year, Rebecca doubted she would ever leave DC. She had grown close to Andrew Ronan, a young visionary from Dublin with a passion for the possibilities of nanomedicine. He encouraged her to study new ways to apply technology. They celebrated at Ambar when she started her internship with Dr. Adam Hunter's Office of Science and Technology Policy. The word around town was this department was working on something very hush-hush and very "green."

She smiled at the dignitaries before her, just as she had imagined she would half a lifetime ago. "I came prepared to talk about the science behind the Vites, because it exemplifies the pioneering use of the planet's magnetic force, one of the most important technological advancements of our time. Because we work for the government, our meeting wouldn't be complete without plenty of mind-numbing statistics, charts and graphs. I will provide the latest findings on climate stabilization, ocean acidity levels and decreasing surface temperatures. Also, because this is a meeting of government employees, you will probably find the coffee is a little weak and in short supply."

There was a ripple of laughter as many heads in the room nodded.

"Because I want to avoid data overload, I am going to introduce you to some people I've met recently. She pointed a small remote toward the south wall of the building, where a ten-by-ten-foot screen appeared. A photograph of a smiling, silver haired man beamed at the assembled group.

“The first person is a man named Gerald Reichert. He is seventy-one years old and has lived in Iowa nearly all his life. He and his wife Patricia have three children and several grandchildren. As part of a program at his church, he and his wife decided to do missionary work in Somalia, despite his 2024 diagnosis of Parkinson’s disease.

“While engaged in Bible study with local villagers, an elder noticed Mr. Reichert’s tremor and brought him flowers from a local herb he said would help. After drinking a tea made of these honeybush flowers on a regular basis, Mr. Reichert noticed his tremor had decreased significantly.

“Yes, I am speaking of Renfizor, developed after Mrs. Reichert sent some of these small yellow flowers to Johns Hopkins. And, of course, this led to the growth of Rajo,” she explained.

An image of mirrored buildings reflecting the sunlight replaced the photograph of Mr. Reichert. “With some 500,000 inhabitants, the city of Rajo took its name from the Somali word for hope. The young metropolis sprang up around the Jubba River near the Ethiopian border and is the pride of the country. Its small group of chrome and glass skyscrapers are surrounded by fields of drought resistant wheat. Visitors are surprised to see goats climb twenty to thirty feet to graze on the leaves of argan trees along the banks of the Jubba. Morocco donated three hundred of them after Somalia’s civil war ended. The country’s first female president, Khadija Othmani, stated, “the time has come for Africa to thrive as one.”

Ronan took a long sip of water, wishing it was coffee, and launched into the second part of her testimony.

“The Vites were not necessarily intended to help us live as one, so much as they were designed to reduce pollution and harm to the planet. But they, and Mother Earth, have continued to surprise us as we begin the long process of repair.

“Closer to home, we have seen a renaissance, or as they say, a return to hózhǫ, for this country’s original inhabitants. True, not all Native Americans practice a purely traditional lifestyle. The indigenous population lives in all parts of the United States, developing an environmentally friendly trade network using freight “Na’iini’” or traders, on the Vites.

“Changes in this demographic have been nothing short of profound. The indigenous population of the United States has increased by fifteen percent over the last five years, with many tribes reclaiming their language, culture and in some cases, nomadic lifestyle.

“In an unprecedented development, the Federal Government now recognizes the Lakota, formerly known as the Sioux, as “Original Inhabitants.” This is also the case in the Four Corners area, where the Diné, once referred to as the Navajo, are creating what some outsiders have dubbed, “the reservation revolution,” in which native cultures have become resources for thriving in a postindustrial world. According to Lakota chiefs, this revolution began with the toppling of Mount Rushmore in 2025.

"Truly sovereign states in the sense that they interact as little as possible with the US government, these nations are, for the most part, enthusiastic of the Vites. Too diplomatic to shout for joy at the chance to put hundreds of miles between themselves and the descendants of white settlers, the leadership spoke eloquently of returning to their traditional ways. From Window Rock, Arizona, Chief Hastiin Hatsóí Ashkiígíí released a statement saying the Vites allow his people to live "as our ancestors intended," and expressed gratitude that, "our white brothers and sisters have learned to care for our Earth."

Ronan clicked to the next photo and a hush fell over the room. Groups of teepees surrounded the remnants of Mount Rushmore on the South Dakota plains. There were few buildings, no automobiles visible, and several men on horseback looked into the camera.

"Another reason the places once referred to as Indian reservations were experiencing a revolution was the "gift from the South," or the Javari plant.

"Ladies and gentlemen, you may be familiar with the story of its discovery in the treatment of addiction. This gift has reached every corner of the world and allowed millions of people to begin healing.

"A group of botanists from the University of Colorado began studying the plants in the Vale do Javari region of the Amazon with the help of Theo Extractors. These vehicles were designed to obtain samples of water, plants and soil in challenging environments. They were named after Theophrastus, widely considered the father of botany.

"The team probably would have dismissed the tiny fern had it not been for the predicament of young people far from home for the first time. Having brought too little of the caffeine and sugar laden drinks they relied on for energy, the team's translator asked a man from the Kulina tribe if there was anything in the area they could use as a substitute.

"Showing him the small fern with its distinctive spiral leaves, the student immediately realized he had several grams stored in the climate-controlled Theo. The man warned them that chewing more than a handful a day could cause nausea.

"Over the next week, the group of botanists chewed small amounts of the Javari plant daily and found that they no longer craved caffeine and sugar for energy. Like Mrs. Reichert, they sent it to researchers at the University of Colorado School of Medicine to find out about its potential use in treating obesity.

"I'm sure you are all familiar with the results: Tuboltis is used for many addictions: food, alcohol and several narcotics. Doctors do not consider it an antidote to chemical dependence, but they have found that it causes a significant decrease in substance use and allows patients to make meaningful use of behavioral and other types of therapy.

"Now, an interesting thing about the Javari plant: with its remarkable healing properties, the botanists were eager to find other, similar species in the rainforest. In talking with local tribes about what they might find, most elders discouraged the scientists from looking. They said that Javari didn't have any relatives. It only grew in the rainforest because that's where the magic plant landed. When asked to explain this statement, the elders pointed at the sky and smiled.

"It certainly seems as if the Vites have been the gift that keeps on giving. We have entered an era of peace in the Middle East unlike anything in recorded history. The region has become famous for its fruit trees, not bloodshed." She pointed the remote at the screen again and a photograph of schoolchildren appeared. Some wore yarmulkes, others wore kufis, a few wore crosses around their necks, and all of them wore smiles.

"Some of you are already aware of these developments, undoubtedly. The media is working overtime to capture the many stories of how much happier and healthier we all have become since the Vites began taking us where we'd always hoped we could go.

"The Vites have helped us develop medicines that saved lives, but they've also rescued people whose lives mattered little to the regimes that brutally oppressed them. In Seo-Jun's case, the Vites ventured where few of us could.

"Fortunately for all of us, she is here today to tell her story. Thank you, Madame Chair and the members of the subcommittee for allowing me to speak at length on a matter that affects the life of every person on our planet."

"Thank you, Ms. Ronan," Vischer said. She smiled at the young woman on the left side of the table. "Ms. Choi, you hold the floor."

"Thank you, Madame Chairperson. I would like to thank the members of the subcommittee, for hearing my testimony," Choi said in a soft voice with a Korean accent. Her raven hair gleamed under the harsh lights in the hearing room. She wore an austere black dress, very little jewelry and seemed unused to speaking in public.

"My name is Seo-Jun Choi and until three years ago, my home was in Sinpo, North Korea. My family lived there for over one hundred years. It is a beautiful place, or it was, until my home country fell under the spell of a dictator and a madman.

"Both my parents were schoolteachers. They believed that education was the key to success and prosperity. They still do, and so do I. Education in North Korea, however, means adherence to the party doctrine. Those who speak against it, whether teachers, doctors or ditch diggers, will disappear."

"We lack freedom of speech and thought in North Korea, but we also lack necessities like healthcare and a secure food supply. My parents met in 1997, the next to the last year of the famine, or March of Suffering, as we were required to call it. I was born in 2001, when the country's infrastructure was slowly improving.

"Their hopes for me, and later my brothers, were like the hopes of parents the world over: a good education, a rewarding job, a strong family. They realized this may have meant leaving our home, but we still believed that North Korea could return to its former glory, a country with a rich culture that values family and industry.

"As many of you are aware, the madman's son came to power and proved to be as tyrannical as his father. Technology was improving, and North Koreans were growing aware of life outside our country. Many of these same technological advances made it easier for the government to exert even more control of our lives.

"No government can be everywhere at all times, however. One way or another, people find ways to free themselves, and each other. I'm not surprised that the first forms of humanitarian aid came to North Korea in the small, submersible "Koi" the Japanese developed to deliver goods outside of the Vites network.

"Buddhist temples often feature images of fish, the ultimate symbols of freedom. Koi, for the Japanese, are thought to represent good fortune. At night, when the fishing boats full of people hoping to catch bluegill off the coast of Sinpo began finding orange and white containers full of food and medical supplies, we had a taste of freedom from our oppressors. It was delicious!"

Laughter rose from the people seated behind her, while others discreetly dabbed at their eyes. A smile crossed Seo-Jun's face as she glanced at Adam.

"Many of you think the Vites are for flying vehicles. They are, but the airspace in North Korea is under very close watch around the clock. There is less surveillance of our waters, and the "swimming aid packages" are too small to appear on the military's radar. Fish know this, they seek freedom, after all. We would open the Koi, take out the edibles and the medicine and drop them back in the water. They would swim home to Japan, where thousands of volunteers worked day and night to fill the next "school" to swim our way. After a few weeks, the

Philippines and American military at Kodiak Island began sending supplies, then the rest of the world was at our doorstep.

"Once Koreans saw there was help all around us, it was inevitable that the regime would crumble, and rarely do autocracies fall apart without destroying lives in the process. I will not speak of the atrocities the coalition forces encountered when Pyongyang fell in the spring of 2026. For me, the lesson to be learned is not in the loss of lives, but in the saving of lives in North Korea.

"I am well acquainted with danger, and do not believe that the force behind the Vites poses a threat. For me, the Vites allow people to help each other, and any being who believes in working together is one I support.

"These vehicles could go where it was not safe for outsiders to venture. They have put an end to illness, starvation and death in my homeland. They have put me here today, before all of you, in my adopted country. I owe them, and the forces that created them, my life.

"Thank you."

The room was silent for a few seconds, then the audience stood and began applauding. A few camera operators cheered and whistled. Vischer wanted to admonish them but she was too moved to speak. Seo-Jun looked around the room, saw a silver haired couple in the audience behind her, and bowed her head.

Adam, Shelton, Rebecca and Seo-Jun had given their testimony as the minutes ticked by, the atmosphere shifted from mistrust to solidarity. The entire chamber silently considered the scope and generosity of what the visitor had given the planet, exchanging smiles as they whispered to each other. Adam knew that this was the moment to strike.

"We are ready to hear your closing testimony, Mr. Hunter," Vischer directed him to the chair for his closing testimony.

"I can feel the goodwill in this room, it's making the hair on the back of my neck stand up," Adam began. "But this is not the fantastic finale in some Hollywood blockbuster, where we all walk out of the building smiling at the end. This is really happening, and it's a matter of life and death for Berenices. For all the technological advancements and for the gifts of the Vites, Berenices needs something in return," Adam said with an urgency that stunned the audience.

"Sand, lots of it, which we have here on Earth. Torus never expected to take anything from Earth without giving her more. Time is running out. Will you consider this request and form an alliance with Berenices to save Torus' civilization?"

The room was instantly abuzz as reporters began typing maniacally and the committee members began to shift in their seats.

"We will have order. Now!" Chair Vischer said, leaning close to her microphone. There were strong opinions flying around from General Shelton and his ilk, imploring the house committee to imprison Torus, and worse. There were also many calls of support, especially from the public areas of the hearing chamber.

After a few police officers circulated in the aisles and order was restored, the Chair turned it over to committee member Senator Lee (R-Nebraska) for questioning. Vischer was relieved it was Lee asking the questions. Unlike many of the committee members with law backgrounds, Ming Lee was a business owner and had an admirable way of getting right to the point.

"Can you tell me, in your own words, why you have come to our planet?"

Torus stood, towering over the humans from his magnificent height.

"My home, like your planet, is a place of staggering natural beauty. The mountains are indigo, the waters are turquoise. We watch the three moons wax and wane in the night sky, planning our harvests around their phases. My family name is Kor, after the largest moon on Berenices. Legend has it that Kor took it upon himself to guard Berenicians while they slept, shining his light to remind them that the skies are always looking after them. My family has defended our home for generations, because, like Earthlings, we love our families. We want our children's futures to shine as brightly as our own sun (whatever they call it)."

The panel drew back as Torus' eyes began to radiate light. Small pinpoints in the wall behind the committee began to smoke while he spoke. He caught his reflection as he glanced down at the pitcher on the table and realized his pupils were nearly incendiary. He inhaled slowly, dialing down the light and heat to safer levels.

"Also like Earth, we sometimes struggle to find "the middle way." Are we using too much of our resources, too little of others? What about the individual versus the group? Which comes first? What about defending ourselves from others, known and unknown?" Torus glanced at General Shelton, whose glare was an empty threat.

"We have made errors in judgment, repeatedly. We made decisions knowing their consequences would be grave, if not for ourselves, then for generations to come.

"Goodness always comes from the heart, whether it is the heart of a person, or a planet. Precious materials deep within the core of Berenices powered our cities, our machines, and even, as my father described them, our "monuments to greed." There was a soft wave of laughter after his remark. It seemed resources across the galaxy were in danger of being frittered away.

"Enough Berenicians realized that time was running out to repair the damage we had done. Our AstroGuild began a search for minerals to replace what we had taken from our planet. Without something to hold the center, the earthquakes, volcanoes and fires were sure to destroy eons of civilization and innovation.

"As the AstroGuild cautioned us in the beginning, our search for minerals identical to those on Berenices was not likely to be successful. They were correct, as they almost always are. We decided if we could find an acceptable substitute, even if it would not work in the long term, it was worth the effort.

"You were not easy to find, Earthlings. You are living in a remote part of the galaxy, with only very primitive methods of establishing contacts with other civilizations now. And what you have created to move through your world, hasn't it done as much harm as good? Your predicament is distressingly similar to ours on Berenices: letting shortsightedness and greed triumph over filling the future with hope and putting others first."

Torus looked around the room slowly. His eyes took in every person as they filled with images of smoldering volcanoes and ruined cities on Berenices. This was his last hope. And he did not cross the galaxy to lose.

"Can you help my planet, Earthlings? We can offer you the gains of our technology. In exchange, we require a resource you possess in abundance. Your planet can take you anywhere if you take care of her. Can you help us restore our planet?" He turned to the government heads as he spoke. A hissing in the back of the room kept causing him to look over his shoulder towards the audience.

"us,...us,...or us, or us," the police officers began moving toward the back of the room, their hands on their holsters as the sound grew louder.

"Torus, Torus, TORUS, TOR-US!" The chant started with a group of clergy members. They were on their feet, soon joined by the rest of the audience. It was loud now, their fists pumping in time with the single word they shouted. The chant was nearing a climax and Vischer looked nervously at the police.

President Morad burst through the doors of his private chambers and hurried to a podium as the Secret Service struggled to keep him surrounded.

"Chair Vischer, will you allow me....?" he asked a bewildered Vischer.

"Mr. President, sir, you hold the floor," she responded over the din.

"Thank you Madame Chairperson. Our obligation is and always has been to create hope for tomorrow. To leave Earth better than when we found her. Americans and people of the world, for the first time in many generations, we are seeing these long dreamed of improvements. So many things are changing for the better right before our eyes. We have given our children and our children's children the opportunity for a better world, one in which we are as strong and healthy as the planet we are fortunate to inhabit," he said as the camera operators drew as close as the Secret Service would permit.

Morad looked directly at Torus. "In chambers just now, I, along with the leaders of America's greatest allies, have all agreed and decided that we must work with you, grant you your wish, and help you save Berenices."

The crowd roared. Cameras flashed and people danced in the aisles. Vischer considered a plea for order and decided order was overrated.

It took a few minutes for the room to regain some semblance of calm. When he could be heard above the crowd, Morad continued.

"Nowhere can we find any evil in our world from the things you have brought to us. It is in that spirit, and by executive order, I will be signing the Berenices Alliance and Freedom Act. This Act will grant you asylum and protection in The United Status. It will also become the framework for determining Berenices' need, opening the portal to the stars, and forming a trade alliance with the Berenician civilization."

Chapter 46 - With No Intention to Return

The nation had just been through the emotional wringer. In truth, the entire world had experienced a whirlwind of emotions. The events of the last few weeks were more exciting than the World Cup, the Moon landing and a royal wedding combined. People were glued to their screens, whether they were in homes, offices, stadiums or bars.

Cheers echoed around the world when President Morad announced the joint effort to help Torus save his planet and activate the pulsar drive. It was exhilarating.

To a small but vocal minority, the alien, or "Mr. Sandman," as they derisively referred to him, was more than a little scary. Everything about extraterrestrials was terrifying and dangerous. Their unofficial spokesperson, General Shelton urged President Morad to reconsider his decision to allow Torus to remove millions of metric tons of sand. Opening the stargate was completely out of the question for Torus' detractors.

In fact, some suggested euthanizing the alien and conducting a thorough autopsy to determine the extent of the dangers he posed. Anyone attempting to harm Torus would have had to get through Adam Hunter first, though.

And plenty of people, while not necessarily fans of Torus, were understandably fascinated with the creature. In some ways he was very similar to humans, but in others, he was very different. For reasons unknown, photographs of Torus often looked something like double exposures, with an electromagnetic energy field around him giving off bright green sparks. A few photographers managed to take closeups of Torus, capturing his intense violet eyes. Photographs taken just after his testimony showed his irises full of images of Berenices.

The planet was the most searched term on Google in the history of the search engine, marking the start of a new era in the Earth's relationship with the cosmos. No longer was the question, are we alone?

Now, there were a thousand new questions. Was this good or bad? Was Torus telling the truth? Would events unfold as he said they would? Who could predict how things would transpire? There was no precedent for forming relationships with extraterrestrials.

Torus was also a celebrity, though, and people have plenty of experience with those. The Berenician's image became an industry of its own. He was on the news twenty-fours a day.

Coverage was both positive, negative and plenty of it was filler. Torus was on t-shirts and coffee mugs, in memes and children's drawings on refrigerators across the country.

Pressure was on Congress to declare January 17 "Kor-Torus" Day. Sales of tin foil were skyrocketing. It wasn't dull.

Behind the scenes in Washington, civil servants were working overtime to manage the flood of information resulting from the hearing. Contrary to what some people think, the purpose of a hearing is to collect information, and possibly recommend actions to be taken later. A hearing is not a trial, although it sometimes resembles one, with the barbed questions and heated accusations.

Nothing about Torus' hearing was customary, however. There had never been a speaker at a hearing with an address not found on Zillow, Google Maps or even Google Earth.

Never before in the history of hearings had the president spontaneously appeared to make an announcement on behalf of most of the world's leaders. There was nothing in the parliamentary handbook forbidding such an act, so Morad's words were his bond. His attorneys reasoned that since the president could pardon people, promising aid was an extension of that power.

Adam knew that the President had been moved by the advancements Torus had made possible. The president's attorneys were also unable to show that the Berenician had committed any crime.

After the hearing, Adam and Torus made their way through the catacombs beneath the Capitol Building, hoping that if they could get through the next two hours, they would finally be able to get to work. Greg Buchanan, Adam's most faithful friend, had made the generous offer to give Torus safe haven at his beach house. Loretta Landing Lane with Myles quietly running the show seemed like it would be an ideal place to keep him away from the limelight; he would lay low until the White House could formulate a plan for his request. Given the government's well-earned reputation for extensive deliberation, Adam expected Torus could rest and recuperate as Washington endlessly weighed the situation.

While the President's declaration at the hearing had made a strong statement of support for the alien, Morad was still a very pragmatic leader. The administration was having a difficult enough time trying to reach an agreement on how to manage the border with Mexico. Proposing to open a gateway to the stars sounded ambitious, to say the least.

Before anyone would agree on opening a portal into space, now that there was proof it held other forms of intelligent life, Morad was going to do his homework and make sure he had global support. This wasn't the kind of decision a single man or country could make. The world would need to take on this decision and would bear the responsibility for its consequences, together.

The President needed to achieve global consensus to seal the deal. Few were surprised that the Chinese and the Russians were less than totally cooperative. Resisting change was not all bad. It forced the West to provide a clear and convincing argument to make a drastic, irreversible decision. The fact was that once unlocked, this open gate meant the end of complete control over the fate of humanity. If something hostile did come through that gate, everyone would have to agree to work together to survive it. It would be homo sapiens against whatever had decided to visit, or invade.

Ironically, there was a possibility that deciding to work together to face the great unknown might finally unite people for the greater good. In exchange for greater vulnerability as a planet, there would be an alliance with a world that existed outside of the Milky Way. This ally had been advancing and traveling among the stars for thousands of years at a time when Earthlings were just discovering fire and the wheel.

It was mind-bending to think of how advanced their civilization was. Better to think about was how much they may be willing to teach the human family. The quandary that existed between the weight of the unknown and the unimaginable possibilities of the future was hanging in the balance for completing the alliance with Berenices.

At least, these were the possibilities people busy getting through the business of life considered. For those working in the industry devoted to finding who or what is "out there," it was time to get to work, at long last.

No more would NASA employees endure ribbing from other scientists about searching for little green men. As it turned out, people hadn't been alone on this planet for thousands of years. It was something everyone in space exploration had always felt on an intuitive level. Although an extraterrestrial helped scientists pinpoint where to look, the best minds in the field had created the finest tools to find life on other planets.

NASA's James Webb Space Telescope, or JWST, designed to conduct infrared astronomy, moves in a halo orbit, circling around a point in space known as the Lagrange point, or L2. The Lagrange point is approximately 930,000 miles beyond the Earth's orbit around the sun, but will vary somewhat from that distance to keep itself out of the Earth and moon's shadow.

By contrast, the state-of-the-art instrument used for gazing into the heavens at the end of the 20th century, the Hubble Space Telescope, orbits at a meager 340 miles above Earth's surface. Somewhat confirming what Torus had explained to Adam, the first exoplanet found outside our solar system, which Hubble found in 1992, did not involve a main sequence star like the one in our solar system, but rather a pulsar. It was unexpected, to say the least.

Then a breakthrough. In September 2022, the Webb telescope took the first direct image of an exoplanet outside our solar system. The exoplanet it found was a gas giant: having no rocky surface, it could not sustain biospheres like those on Earth. Since then, Webb has taken sixty additional images of exoplanets, each one being found uninhabitable. NASA Astronomers had joked that they only had to take pictures of several hundred billion more to see if they could find one that could support life. The typical comeback was a hopeful, "so, you're saying there's a chance?"

Everything changed that January. In an interesting coincidence, the constellation Eridanus, the river, is visible in the sky from the 33rd parallel of the Southern Hemisphere. All four Axiom locations sit along the 33rd parallel of the Northern Hemisphere and along several ancient ley lines. Located near the border of Orion, Eridanus is approximately 89 light years from our solar system.

With current technology, it might have only taken astronomers another millennium or so to cycle through all the possible combinations so that they could stumble onto the inhabitable paradise planet that the James Webb was now completely and entirely transfixed upon. Over the years, Torus had always taken the opportunity to gaze in the direction of home when he could.

As an act of transparency, Torus had given the coordinates of Berenices to Adam to pass along to his government: right ascension 03h 19m 55.65s, declination −43° 04′ 11.2.″ Like locating cities with latitude and longitude, every object in the sky has two numbers that fix its location: right ascension (RA), and declination. They plugged the numbers in, and there it was, the needle in the cosmic haystack, a paradise planet capable of sustaining life. Berenices.

The President had instructed NASA Administrator Tate Armstrong he was to train the Webb Telescope directly on Berenices and to use his words, "study the shit out of it." And study he did, with the world standing behind him, waiting for their turn to gaze upon this new world.

The images the telescope was collecting were breathtakingly beautiful. Servers posting the first pictures made public were crashing as people were mesmerized. Torus had pointed out to Adam that Webb was picking up images of light originating from a time well before Berenices had lost some of her beauty. There were shades of blue, of violet, of greens, of yellows, and some pale red like the color of water just after the sun dropped below the horizon. This was the first time Torus had looked at her this way in over 80 years. He began feeling emotions that he had forgotten.

Torus planned to remain sequestered in his currently undisclosed location for much of the time he planned to remain on Earth. He knew the clock was ticking for Berenices and he hoped that he wasn't too late.

Adam was attending daily briefings at the White House with the President and his Cabinet to stay in the loop on world negotiations, to relay questions the government had for Torus, to provide his answers along with any other essential information about the plan that he felt was important to provide.

There were some naysayers, often associated with General Shelton, but overall, the work of the Administration was genuine, progressive, and bipartisan. There was an elegance to the order in the US government's approach: Adam mused that it was almost as if the Founding Fathers were prepared for the possibility of contact with other worlds when they created our government.

On one chilly afternoon in late January, Adam sat at the giant conference table in Greg's beach house, sipping coffee while Torus filled in some of the blanks in the Berenician saga. Five thousand years the Berenicians had been working on their plan. Adam wondered who they'd sent to talk to George, Thomas, Benjamin and the rest of the guys. Torus refused to tell him the name, but implied that this Berenician received a commendation for laying the groundwork for a long and (mostly) strong relationship.

As they completed step after step, more diplomats joined to help gain consensus around the world. There was no disagreement that the Vites was changing life for the better and that the visitor from Berenices was the bearer of these wonderful gifts.

It was Pandora and her box that were slowing things down and delaying the President's signature on the Berenices Alliance and Freedom Act. While Torus had intentionally locked himself away, the "Freedom" part of the Act had effectively been put into practice. He was no longer under arrest and could technically walk freely down any street in America.

However, the reality would have been more akin to Elvis Presley trying to stroll through the audience of the Ed Sullivan Show in 1957 just after he had moved his pelvis on tv for the first time. It could not happen without some collateral damage.

It was the "Berenices Alliance" part of the Act that was proving to be most difficult. They could see how alluringly beautiful she was, and they had even met one of her own. But how could they know if Torus was authorized to speak on behalf of the others?

Understandably, there were other problems for the President, related to the "significant" developments involving the intergalactic machine. As a legislator and former lawyer, he was out of his depth. Dr. Hunter had drawn him diagrams of the Alcubierre drive on napkins during their working lunches, but for Morad, it was a lot to learn in so little time. And he didn't know who else in the universe might know how to use it. He was quite disturbed when he realized a line of communication between Earth and an untold number of alien civilizations was now open.

Morad's reaction made sense to Adam. The president's job was similar to a ship captain's, times of uncertainty required stability of leadership. His nearly three hundred million passengers looked to him for reassurance, for rational words and deeds as they faced the reality that we were not alone in the universe, for better or for worse.

Adam had begun to question the usefulness of reason when facing the unknown. It seemed that humans tended to gravitate to one of two extremes: fear or faith. Neither was necessarily sensible, but we are not like the machines we created to serve us.

We are far more inconsistent, much less predictable than an entity ruled by numerical laws. It was impossible to separate people from their fears and hopes. Just as people preferred the company of their feelings, Adam thought, they decided they would rather not be alone in the universe. After some deliberation, some with their hearts and some with their heads, we had reached the point where faith would outweigh fear. There were questions no amount of reasoning could truly answer. For Adam, a scientist since childhood, he surprised himself by deciding faith was the best choice. "Many of the questions they wanted answers to were not verifiable and there would be only one to answer them." Sentence in red from original Scene Objectives. And in this situation, it was the only choice for him.

Like Adam, Torus was going forward with the plan he'd created, armed with faith. Despite all the challenges, so many of them unexpected, Torus chartered a journey along the riverbank that he had very nearly completed. With the Pulsar Drive now ready for activation, he no longer needed to oversee S.E.T.I. Industries. S.E.T.I. had been a means to an end. It created the materials and resources that were necessary to make the Vites and the Pulsar Drive possible. S.E.T.I. would continue to play a vital role in support of the Vites well into the future, but it didn't need Ben Kumar anymore. Torus didn't need Ben, either. He'd felt a little sad, looking at photographs of his old incarnation, shaking hands with dignitaries in his fancy suits. What a performance. If he hadn't been a soldier, Torus wondered if he would have had success as a thespian.

Realizing the show must go on, Torus had long since been grooming Suzanne Larsen to take over as Chairperson and CEO of the company. She, of course, was one in a million. Extremely capable, a great communicator and an even better leader. Working together as they did, shoulder-to-shoulder, for years as the business was built, no one was more shocked to find out that he wasn't from Calcutta than Suzanne was. No matter his place of origin, she would remain absolutely loyal to Torus and he had no doubt about that.

Torus also had few doubts about the first draft of the alliance, and allowed the Earthlings time to review and discuss it extensively. Staffers the world over were reviewing the contents of the treaty and advising their governments of what each of their nations were agreeing to do and refrain from doing. The historic treaty, forever to be known as the Treaty of Constellations, would be signed in the coming week in Lucerne, Switzerland. What finally drew China to the table is that they were promised a pole position when it came time to negotiate the formal trade alliance with the Berenicians.

The overarching message of the treaty was simple. All nations belong to the human race, that we are all equal, and that we, in unison and without division, agree to opening the door to Earth's destiny, whatever may come. One reason for great celebration was that all nations on Earth, including North Korea and Iran, had agreed to sign. North Korea had been surprisingly agreeable about resource redistribution. Iran, with its Great Salt Desert, was more cautious. Understandably, the leadership in Tehran asked for special consideration should valuable artifacts turn up in the harvest.

The details about exactly which deserts would be available to the Berenicians for their harvest and how many layers of sand they would be allowed to take had been hammered out with Torus. Through Adam, Torus had provided the specifics of the request to the governments and gave assurances that Berenices would follow the agreed upon allowances. Berenices was about 60% of the size of Earth and consisted of only one race. Tor had credited their unity as the catalyst for their technological advancements.

Like us, their likeness had no effect in changing the flawed personality traits that had gotten them into this mess in the first place. Apparently, character flaws were universal and the potential for squabbling existed throughout the cosmos. Torus was just thankful the Earthlings were not insisting on counting the grains of sand to be sure it was divided fairly.

Desert sand is largely useless to humans. When the world first learned of Torus' request on behalf of Berenices, the first impulse was to deny. People seem to want things more once they know that someone else needs or wants something they have. Much of the sand that is useful goes toward making concrete. While perfectly constituted for the needs of Berenices, they are too smooth and rounded to lock together to create stable concrete. Eroded by wind instead of water, desert sand grains are the wrong shape for this purpose.

Four great Harvesters would come to gather their gift from Earth. They would excavate in four of the world's great deserts: the Sahara, the Gobi, the Arabian, and the Great Basin. A provision in the agreement had called for the Berenicians to leave at least one layer of sand so as not to expose the bedrock. The deserts of Australia, the Kalahari, and the Patagonian would stand by if the need was greater than could be supplied by the four.

Archaeologists the world over were eagerly waiting for what they referred to as “The Great Excavate” to see what ancient ruins may be unearthed. The size and harsh conditions of the deserts alone made exploration a long, slow process before the arrival of the great alien earth movers. As the sun's luminosity continues to grow, the sands of the deserts will return to them in time. The trade off to open a window to the vastness of space in exchange for a little sand seemed quite equitable.

As soon as the treaty was signed, the next sequence of events would happen quickly. The Pulsar Drive inside Axiom Roswell would be engaged once again. Once the Drive was activated, Torus would use the AI to communicate with Berenices. In the same way we encapsulate a spacecraft in interstellar mode inside the safety of a warp bubble, communication packets are encapsulated much the same way. Enabling faster than light wave conversations is a prerequisite for communicating with civilizations that lay beyond our galaxy.

If it was not too late, Berenices would respond and ready the Harvesters for their journey. The Harvesters had been under construction hundreds of years before Torus' time and its inhabitants had been training specialized crews of Berenicians through the centuries equipped to execute the harvest. Torus promised to deliver the list of considerations to Berenices that it would be required to follow once it achieved Earth's orbit. The Treaty of Constellations provided assurances of Berenices' agreement to adhere to Earth's conditions, before their arrival. Specifics of enforcement were not clear: how to enforce this stipulation, as the Pulsar Drive would be activated just to talk with her? Once the harvest had been completed, the Harvesters would leave as peacefully as they came and would return home to begin the long and arduous process of saving Berenices.

Torus had communicated plainly that he would remain behind only briefly to gather his belongings and would depart the Earth shortly thereafter, with no intention to return.

Chapter 47 - Messages of Light

February first would be the day the portal would open, President Morad decided. It was a day heavy with meaning, especially for the space exploration community. On that day in 2003, a Saturday, the United States Space Shuttle Columbia, tried to return home from her mission and broke apart on re-entry. All seven astronauts aboard her perished. Morad believed the seven men and women who gave their lives to broaden the horizons of our world would have been pleased to see their mission pressing forward through adversity.

The treaty was a development without equal, a harbinger of dreams realized. For the first time in the history of the world, every nation on the planet had come together and signed one document in unison, the Treaty of Constellations. It was a moment of hope for incredible possibilities, and at the same time, a greater sense of security.

The global space program, viewed as rudimentary and even dangerous in light of the "Berenician Contact," involved much uncertainty around the safe return of astronauts. The President hoped that this day would mark a new beginning and symbolically replace the tragedies of past failures.

The world's hopes shifted. Humans now had the answer to the Fermi Paradox: Earth was hard to find, but possessed something valuable to a desperate civilization. People had decided that whatever was going to come through our intergalactic door would make up for all the wrongs, all the mistakes. It would be a bigger gamble than anyone realized, and the planet would be utterly powerless to do anything if our guests decided to come for more than we were expecting.

After the President made his announcement, Adam decided that he would secretly travel to Roswell alone and reactivate the Alcubierre metric of the Pulsar Drive. There would be no press coverage of the event. The only statement the White House would make would take place after contact with Berenices, to inform people about the "Resource Reallocation."

Everyone had seen Torus and the government had begun doing a masterful job of spinning the backstory. A lone wayward traveler, disguised and living among us for decades. A friendly visitor who had helped to deliver many of the technological gifts of the 20th century up to and including the Vites in the 21st. His mission had been one of goodwill and his hopes were that he would be able to exchange it for some of Earth's sand, which he needed to save his planet. While many did disagree, it was hard to argue that the proposed trade wasn't equitable.

Comparisons grew increasingly complex and inexact, or as Torus quipped, “we're comparing apples to misaguin,” a reddish-orange fruit beloved on Berenices. In some ways, it was a simple problem of moving a substance. In others, the technology of this strange planet was profoundly advanced. Maybe say more here

Messages made of light, which have no friction inside the inertial reference frame of the warp bubble, can push space aside at only slightly faster speeds than when they are encapsulating a spacecraft. Torus' message would take slightly longer than a day for Berenices to receive it. His home planet's reply came exactly 27 hours, 22 minutes, and 43 seconds later. Reading the message, knowing it had been delivered from his home planet was almost overwhelming to him and it took a minute to gather himself. Translated into English, it read,

"Well done, *Obsidian*! We rejoice that Berenices will live! We understand and will comply with the extraction provisions stated by Earthlings. TerraCraft will triangulate for departure. Expect the arrivals of the *Prem*, the *Dawn*, the *Aura*, and the *Resa* in two days' time."

The possibility of the Harvesters fulfilling their purpose was always on the minds of Berenicians. Berenices had been studying the Earth for centuries and for the last five decades had been waiting for a message from Torus with increasing trepidation. The Harvesters, each the size of Berenices' small moon, had been in high orbit approximately 405,000 miles beyond its larger moon. Because of the type of orbit, the Harvesters stayed in the same exact position relative to the ground around Berenices. At least one could always be seen in the distant night sky, from any point on the planet.

When Berenices' small and large moon lined up together diagonally in the sky along with a Harvester, Berenicians viewed the lunar alignment as a sign of a coming redemption and would refer to the event as the Moons of Hope. The moons aligned with each Harvester in this way twice a year and they played a critical role in keeping the hope alive for all Berenicians.

It had been decades since Torus departed from Berenices on the *Obsidian*. The words from him had been years in the making and had traveled a fantastic distance at unimaginable speeds to reach the desperate civilization in the nick of time. The message itself, which was constructed of light, contained the provisions of the Treaty of Constellations in which Earth acknowledged the gifts resources and tools it had received from its new celestial acquaintance, and in exchange for them, approved the request from its ambassador to harvest a certain amount of sand from our deserts.

Because Earth knew she was at a big disadvantage, the spectral package delivered to Berenices was quite deliberate in letting them know that once we had reciprocated on their request, that the negotiations on how an alliance could be formed would be quite slow until we learned a little bit more about the rules of the game.

The aliens obtained the coordinates of the deserts selected for them and an approximate volume of sand they could excavate from each. Geologists across the world had pored over the data and provided the best possible information, given the time available, to inform the Berenician ships where to find most of the low hanging fruit. While it was difficult for people to fathom these incredible machines, Torus did his best to describe these monoliths and how they would generate a tremendous vacuum surge to suck the crystals into the storage areas of the Harvesters.

There were warnings and prohibitions with regard to being within twenty-five miles from the outer edge of the alien craft once it was preparing to harvest. When the Harvesters got into Earth's low atmosphere below fifty miles, Harvesters would be using the magnetic currents of the Vites to maintain their repulsion to prevent them from having any contact with the surface of the Earth. However, depending upon the rest of the topology in an area, the giant telescopic vacuum tentacles would extend as low as five hundred feet above the desert floor. If someone were to accidentally venture within a couple of miles of an active harvest, they would be sucked into the internal silos of the Harvester like flies in a vacuum, resulting in certain death.

Adam remained closely involved in the planning meetings with the President's Cabinet on the Hill. As the days inched nearer to February first, which some were now calling "B DAY," he decided it was best to spend his time staying in town with the kids and visiting Mom as much as possible. He kept a quiet confidence about what lay ahead, but as they always say, you never know. He wanted to be that rock and reassurance his family would need. He knew his mother no longer had the capacity to distinguish reality from fiction on her own, but he had hoped to give something to help her cope with her fear in case of the unexpected. In addition to his work to restart the logistical planning for the Vites rollout, he remained the one and only government contact of Torus. Adam's job was conveying all the necessary information that was in the Treaty of the Constellations for Torus' message and keeping an eye on him. It was ultimately Adam who decided to give the creature some space and let him begin to get his affairs in order as his time on the Earth was drawing to a close. Adam could only imagine the task that lay before Berenices once the Harvesters arrived, full of sand and hope.

Adam's own hope for the future, Chris and Brianna, had a million questions about everything happening with their dad. They wondered what the alien was like and if Adam liked him, they asked about his alien powers and how he had held himself together when it transformed in front of him.

They were concerned about what would happen to the world when so much of our desert sand had been taken. What impact would the extraction have on the marginalized populations groups in the Gobi Desert? They also had pointed questions about the global politics involved. Saudi Arabia's human rights record was of concern to Chris and Brianna. His daughter, especially, continued to remind him of an impassioned attorney when she argued about the House of Saud and their treatment of political activists and reformers.

Adam, of course, didn't know a lot of the answers to the bigger questions, but he did his best to reassure his children that the Berenicians did not expect "something for nothing." The Vites had improved life for Mongolians with nanotechnology in health care, and tracts of land were growing lush with a modified version of the drought resistant wheat the Somalians donated.

More than anything, he was proud of how aware his children were of the world around them. Chris and Bri were extremely grounded and had a very good understanding that life as their planet knew it had changed forever. Being children of their father had prepared them for what was happening more than most. Their generation would rely on this awareness for their survival, he realized. The world they would inherit was exponentially larger than the one he knew at their age. For the first time in a long while, Adam was at peace with his contribution to Chris and Brianna's world, and the world their children would inhabit. He was convinced he had done the best he could to prepare a kind of "clean slate" for their future. Adam knew they, and young people the world over, deserved it.

We all deserved more, Adam thought, and there were signs that we were leaving some bad habits in the past. Conflict was appearing in the media less and less as a form of entertainment. Lately, it seemed that some arguments were too petty even for our elected officials. It was refreshing to see that the nightly news had completely changed its focus from all the political infighting to the message of how important it would be for people to work together.

In one of the most jaw-dropping developments, Fox and CNN had agreed on something. Their broadcasts stressed to viewers that this new challenge was going to create unimaginable opportunities for everyone but was going to need the world's complete and undivided attention. The Vites had already been creating opportunities that few people could have imagined.

In what was almost impossible to comprehend, people began to realize the job market was expanding…by millions of miles. In the near future, people might be living and working on other planets in other galaxies. So much for the glass ceiling, now the sky really was the limit.

Ironically, such an abundance of hope was deeply disturbing to others. Change of any kind can send some people into confusion and even despair. Fear and pessimism abounded. There were groups that refused to emerge from their bomb shelters. Others stood in town squares holding cardboard signs with dire warnings. Some religious leaders found themselves in awkward positions. Young people began mistaking Hollywood movies about space for documentaries.

However, true excitement and optimism drowned out the cries of gloom and doom. In most circles, people truly believed that this was all happening for a reason and that things, one day soon, would be even better than ever. It was as if a kind of evolution was taking place at an astoundingly rapid pace.

With Juan's help, Adam had opened the Pulsar Drive in Roswell shortly after midnight on February first, the day that had been authorized by the Treaty of Constellations. Torus transmitted the carefully prepared message from his sequestered location over the holovision AI shortly after 2:00 that same morning. Adam, confident Torus would contact him immediately if Berenices responded, headed back to DC and to Julie's house. While the aliens were visiting, he decided he would stay with her so he could be close to the kids. He stopped by to check his mother out of her nursing home and bring her to Julie's as well. Everyone settled in for what promised to be a spectacle.

Businesses, factories and schools announced they would close the first week of February, some without even setting a time to reopen, so that loved ones would be able to gather with their families. Grocery store shelves had been wiped clean, as if a big storm was coming, and Groundhog Day was barely a blip on anyone's radar. There were commemorative February first t-shirts for sale everywhere, Pulsar drinking games aplenty

With Julie's approval, Adam had invited Greg, who was without parents or a significant other, to join them. He was sure that Julie wasn't going to mind until he found out that Greg had also invited Grace and Myles. Julie had the room, and the general consensus was that there was safety in numbers. Apparently, cutie pie County Supervisor Derek wasn't hanging around a lot these days.

Halley's Comet is visible to the naked eye once every seventy-five years, the last time was in 1986. As rare as that event was to human beings, another one was coming that would only happen once. The whole world would be standing still during this Passover, of sorts. At 10:00

a.m. on the East Coast of the United States, on February third, the sky darkened as the great Harvesters of Berenices had arrived and blocked the sun.

Chapter 48 - The Invitation

In what was proving to be an exercise in futility, NASA had trained the James Webb telescope exclusively on Berenices since the day we learned it had intelligent life. It was almost as if government officials were hoping to see tiny little spaceships take off from the planet and fly their way to Earth so people could zoom in and watch them do it. The only problem with that was that Berenices was sixty million light years away and the images NASA was bringing to us were sixty million years old. Worlds that possessed a machine which could change the geometry of space played by different rules. Earth had just joined into this new game but didn't know the rules or how to play just yet.

Adam tried to reassure Torus his colleagues would play catch up to the best of their ability. Along with the rest of NASA, he felt like a first grader who had wandered into a graduate school lecture.

The air was growing thick with anticipation and the world began to show signs of paralysis. In this case, it was worse knowing that something was coming than for it to just happen. The time people had been given to think about all the things that were going to happen was like torture. And then without warning, Berninian Harvesters were all of a sudden, just there.

With hardly a sound, the giant sun-blocking craft were hovering and maneuvering by repelling and attracting against Earth's magnetism and the new streams of magnetic current generated by the Axioms. The *Dawn* had positioned herself over the East Coast of the United States and was preparing herself to excavate the Great Basin. The *Aura* loomed over Egypt and began preparations for its sweep of the Sahara. The hull of the incomprehensible craft extended from the Mediterranean over Cairo down to Sudan, across the Red Sea and around to Iraq, extending north over Jordan and Israel. Only ten miles from the edge of the *Aura*, there was the *Prem.* She appeared over the Persian Gulf and the Caspian Sea, completely blocking the sky over Iran, extending into Afghanistan and parts of Pakistan. She was preparing for her preordained removal of much of the sand of the Arabian. Last, but not least, the *Resa* had appeared directly over the Yellow Sea and covered North and South Korea, extending around Japan to the South and Beijing to the North. The *Resa's* harvest would be the Gobi.

The mind-bending size of the craft re-ignited the debates among the nations about whether we should have signed the Treaty with Berenices so hastily. With so little understanding, the most powerful group of nations was just so eager to explore what they did not understand, they seemed to have strong-armed the world into its current conundrum.

Of this there was no doubt, confirming the sum of all fears: Earth was completely powerless and realized she no longer had any control over her own destiny.

As the *Dawn* hung over Washington, DC, extending out over the Atlantic with her circumference covering Philadelphia, New York City, and Pittsburg, her hull cut over through Virginia and across over the northern cities of South Carolina. In the darkness of the day, confusion reigned. For those located under the center of each of the magnificent Harvesters, it was impossible to see where the craft began or where it ended. Each ship stretched hundreds of miles in all directions, well beyond the horizon.

Adam asked Julie to watch his mom and the kids while he, Greg, Grace, and Myles went out to the driveway to get a view of the behemoth. As he began to stare up into the metal sky from Julie's driveway, Adam wondered how his journey that had begun with a small sphere, in a duffel bag, hidden in his trunk, almost on the spot he was standing, had all led to this. If anyone had had enough time to prepare themselves to see this, it was Adam Hunter. Not only was he keenly aware of the details of the arrangement that had been put in place between the two species, but Torus had also given him some forewarning of the size and nature of the ships that were coming. The Harvester, in the flesh, in the sky above DC, were much more than he could have imagined. The *Dawn* was to excavate the dune fields of the Great Basin which stretched across Nevada and half of Utah. Its unexpected appearance in the sky above DC was raising eyebrows across Washington. Had the great ship, which had just traveled halfway across the galaxy, gotten its coordinates confused after arriving? Or did Berenices have an agenda that was altogether different than the one that had been agreed upon?

Looking up into the vastness of the hull, it didn't take much to cause the mind to wonder, to believe anything it wanted to believe about what *could* be happening. Adam had received multiple assurances from Torus that Berenices fully understood its agreement with Earth. The Treaty of the Constellations was quite clear on which deserts had been offered for sand collection. The aliens assured Washington they would comply with the expectations regarding handling the excavations with the utmost care.

Adam was starting to allow thoughts of one detail to creep into his conscious worries: he knew Torus had told the Berenicians that Earth was divided into separate, sometimes adversarial, nations and that the headquarters of the most powerful nation happened to be directly underneath this enormous, insurmountable craft.

Could the ship's location be a coincidence?

When the *Dawn* stood between us and the early light, could we be sure our flag was still there?

While Adam's trust in Torus was absolute he was not so sure of the Berenician government's motives. Cutting off the head of the snake was a well-known military tactic. Once the leadership has been eliminated, conquering a foe becomes far less complicated.

He had been here before. In fact, it was becoming a pattern for him. He thought he was laying the groundwork for the Vites with a huge group of enormously dedicated people. They were productive, skilled, completely professional and…not human.

Adam would never forget how disoriented he'd felt when Ella and Ben explained the truth of the situation to him. After the shock wore off, he'd made a kind of 'the end justifies the means' decision to continue working with them. He reasoned that since the variants had been designed for the express purpose of building something that would help the Earth, the initial lack of transparency hadn't hurt anyone.

This way, Adam was still able to chase his dream of helping Mother Earth, while providing an enlightened form of transportation for her many children. And as he had learned recently, he was also saving a distant planet from extinction.

Yes, the distant planet. The one our best telescopes and astronomers had not yet discovered. They found it with the help of a seven-foot alien who had been masquerading as an Indian immigrant and tycoon for decades. Again, someone was not being honest with him. Well actually, it was the same guy both times.

Adam looked up at the *Dawn* and rubbed his face, overwhelmed. It was a matter of life and death for this Ben/Torus figure. Or was it? Adam had taken Torus at his word because…

Why did he believe the creature? Oh, no. His heart rate picked up and his palms started to feel sweaty. Because he'd wanted to. Because Torus told him what he'd wanted to hear. He thought of Orson Welles' 'War of the Worlds' as he stood in the shadow of a vehicle too massive and sophisticated to understand. He began laughing to himself. He'd been had.

Someone was *good*. Was Hollywood behind this? David Copperfield? He looked around at the other spectators on his street, wondering which one was going to smile and tell him he'd been "punk'd."

But as he looked around, directly in front of him were the people who had supported him through this…well, he could only call it a journey. It was a process, and experiment, once in a while it felt like an ordeal.

And it was a gift.

Greg, Grace and Myles stood several feet in front of him on his driveway in the middle of a cold, gray afternoon in early February. After their searching, their listening, making sure everything was where it needed to be and everyone was fed, they had stuck by him all this time so they could witness this with him. They had made it possible for him to accomplish more than he had dreamed possible.

They had helped Adam to learn the joy of giving. They knew it, too, as the three stood with their arms around one another, the wind ruffling their clothes and hair as it blew in from the east. They kept their heads close together as Adam approached, hoping for reassurance.

Adam knew that he, in large part, was responsible for what was happening and felt a strong sense of obligation to comfort them in their fears. In his compassion, he reached over and touched the backs of Greg and Grace, only for them to look up from their embrace with tears streaming down their faces. When Adam saw this, he immediately started to apologize.

"I am so sorry. I know how this must feel. I am feeling it too," he told them. They said nothing but reached for Adam and brought him closer into their embrace. Too overwhelmed to speak, they supported each other as the emotions washing over them were overwhelming. What they felt was not fear, but it seemed that seeing the alien craft was something that emotions couldn't manage very well. It had so many implications for everyone.

Julie's street was filling with people streaming out of their homes looking up to the sky. Children were clinging to their parents, and many were crying. Adam and Greg, both began to speak at the exact same time. Adam was finally able to express what he had been thinking about. Worrying about the location of the ship, Adam told the group he thought it might be a mistake.

"I don't think it was supposed to be here."

Just as Adam spoke, Greg, in a calm demeanor, started apologizing and saying how truly overwhelming this was to see.

"I can't explain my emotions, it was only in my dreams that I could live long enough to see this day," he said, his voice cracking. Adam, who had been losing confidence with every passing second, seemed to gain a little footing from Greg's words. Greg, an engineer by trade, was surely replacing his fear with marvel and wonder. Grace and Myles still had no words as they continued their skyward stares.

The complex underside of the craft grew easier to understand as Adam's eyes were now more fully adjusting to the morning darkness the *Dawn* created. The ship was divided into hundreds, if not thousands, of rectangular sections. He estimated each of them about seven miles square in size. In the center of each section was a small protruding cylinder, sure to be the base of a telescopic arm which would extend to the ground and inhale the sand when the excavation began.

On a scale even he struggled to fully understand, Adam thought that these squares had to be the storage silos for the cargo. There were also many complicated objects and structures on the underside of the ship that were totally unrecognizable.

Adam shivered. Did these gargantuan machines contain thousands of laser cannon turrets trained on Washington, or did the pods simply hold the key to the ship's navigational capability, attracting and repelling against Earth's magnetism to maneuver the craft? Adam stopped his train of thought as he realized the dangers of imagining what manner of futuristic weaponry might exist in the universe, to be used for the complete evisceration of another planet.

A small vibration interrupted his chilling thoughts. Adam reached into his pocket, pulling out his phone to see the icon for the arrival of a new text. It was a message from Torus, who remained sequestered in his hiding place near the Potomac. In a message that gave a measure of relief, it simply read "The *Dawn* paying homage, allowed my eyes to see her on her arrival. Her peaceful mission now resumes."

Adam was almost finished reading the words when the magnificent ship began to move soundlessly as a cloud to the west. It would be a little more than an hour and twenty minutes before the edge of the craft passed overhead, ending the eclipse and allowing sunlight to reach the city again.

Julie, escorting Adam's mom and the kids came on to the drive with the others as they all stood speechless watching the *Dawn* slip away. In approximately fifty-seven minutes, the craft would disappear over the horizon. Fear and uncertainty had given way to exuberance. All of mankind was experiencing something as never before, practically in unison, with an overwhelming intensity.

A new age was truly beginning, and everyone knew it, everyone felt it. Adam insisted that Greg, Grace, and Myles stay and shelter together with his family. It didn't make any sense for anyone to stay by themselves. People really needed each other in the face of such a profound occurrence.

The Emergency Broadcast System was transmitting on every available channel, encouraging people to remain calm and exercise caution. There would be no shortage of coverage of this historic event, but surprisingly, the coverage excesses made people feel less frantic. For the most part, people were as calm as they could be while witnessing a miraculous event, mainly because they didn't feel left in the dark. Everyone was on the same playing field this time. Phones and video camera lenses the world over remained trained on the great ships, keeping track of their every move. In unison, the four of them began to slide away from the population centers over which they had been hovering, to each of their predetermined desert locations.

On the mainstream and social media outlets, there was only one topic trending and it involved neither celebrities or scandal. There was a shift in people's awareness that broadened their view of their world and its possibilities. Previous concerns seemed shallow and selfish in light of the life and death matters Torus brought to the world's attention. People began to question what they could and couldn't live without. They started asking how their actions affected others. Taking took a backseat to giving.

Life on Earth had paused, and everyone was holding their collective breath. Seemingly endless news broadcasts showing charts, renderings, maps, graphical representations, and presentations were being offered up as to how the excavation would work. Mixed in with their assurances, the government kept a steady diet of warnings of what not to do. While the excavation itself was taking place, globally, the Vites would not be operating, giving the skies and the whole of Axiom's magnetic stream to the navigational demands of the Harvesters.

Businesses, schools, stores, and government offices would not reopen until the Global Excavation Consortium gave them the all-clear. Governments in the "hosting nations" created perimeters around each of the deserts to the best of their abilities. It was an attempt to thwart those who act first and think later. Every conceivable avenue into the four no-person's-lands had barricades and roadblocks.

However, no matter how authorities tried to protect people from themselves, there were always going to be some in the crowd. The crazed, the conspiracy theorists, the thrill seekers, and the storm chasers would all find a way in, disregarding all the proper warnings, so they could see for themselves. For each of these, hopefully the sight had been worth it, because, as for most, it would be the last thing they would ever see.

In a graceful and hypnotic movement, the Harvesters positioned themselves over the precious cargo they would soon collect. It now lay almost within their grasp, just beneath them on the desert floor. The harvest began in a highly synchronized but deafening fashion, shattering the deathly quiet just moments before. The noise and vibration from the great suction engines used for the gathering rattled the ground and tore the air with ear-piercing roars, as they were heard and felt for hundreds of miles in every direction.

Thousands of enormous tentacles, which had telescopically projected downwards from each containment silo, began sucking unfathomable quantities of sand into their repositories. The unfortunate humans that had made the mistake of venturing within five miles of the desert rim were now simultaneously second guessing their decisions, and taking their last breaths. They were sucked into the hull of the giant ships like ants, never to be seen again.

The deep penetrating, whirring noise of the powerful suction engines rattled bones and nerves as the tentacles of the harvest would hit and miss their marks. The intensity of the excavation caused the Earth to tremble as the vibration of its aftereffects sent tremors across the land. The droning seemed, and felt, endless. Day and night, the relentless rhythm of the excavation weighed heavy on the human soul.

Despite the feeling that some part of our planet was being violated, there was also a growing sense of satisfaction in knowing that Earth was repaying a debt and helping another world from across the galaxy to survive. An instant documentary on one of the history channels was trying to point out that we could only imagine what it was like on Berenices as they waited to see if the Harvesters would return to pour the healing ingredients into the cracks of their wounded planet. With the very tentacles that were stripping Earth of her abundance, the *Dawn*, the *Aura*, the *Prem*, and the *Resa* returned to perform a delicate dance on Berenices as they delivered a lifegiving transfusion to stabilize her.

Julie was among the first to know about the impending visitation, and from the moment she learned about it, Adam was reminded why she was such an outstanding mother and mayor. First things first, she braved the crowds at the grocery store before the shelves were empty. Chris and Bri seemed to eat their weight in Hot Pockets, and the stress of an alien visit, no matter how friendly, caused even go-getters like her to indulge in stress eating. Tossing a few frozen pizzas into her cart, she rationalized that they would all need their energy this week.

Then, she inspected her home. Thanks to her habit of keeping up with routine maintenance, the home was well prepared to weather even the worst of storms. Candles, matches, batteries, chargers, first aid kits, straw water purifiers, Julie spared no expense in planning for her loved ones. For her, and with most families, it was similar to waiting out a large storm.

After the first day of the harvest, the mood began to shift and everyone's spirits were a little more upbeat. Things were going exactly as the government had said they would. Nothing bad had happened.... yet. Stopping to realize how fortunate they were in many ways, people found the time to appreciate one another. Bonds between people that had withered were growing strong again, having all shared in such a profound experience. Families, the old and the young were telling stories as laughter filled their homes.

Some families broke out the board games and started to rekindle relationships like the ones before technology and complicated schedules made people too busy for one another. Asking questions of one another and reminiscing about old times. Each group of people that clustered together were doing their best not to catastrophize what was happening outside in their world They were trying to make the ones they were with feel more important and more loved.

Without realizing it, it was even happening with his own family. Adam, who had never lost his appreciation for Julie, looked at her in a new light. She was showing courage and strength that he had not truly recognized or appreciated before.

And then, after three days and nights, the extraction was complete. The announcement came from the Global Excavation Consortium Organization: the harvest was over. One by one, the great machines retracted their tentacles and the silo bay doors slowly sealed shut. In unison, the ships began to elevate above their respective desert floors, giving people the first look at depleted regions that only bore some resemblance to their former glory.

The debt had been repaid and the planet knew it would be better for it. The world didn't lose the important things: family bonds had grown, people felt good about what we had done, and stubborn barriers between nations were crashing down.

After the formation of life, the gift to Berenices was the greatest gift that Earth had ever given. People were going to have to work together to survive in this new age and everybody knew it.

The Harvesters continued their ascent, high up into the atmosphere, reducing Earth's gravitational pull with each passing second. They accelerated as they rose, powered by hundreds of Ion Thrusters which ignited with explosive force after they had disengaged the magnets that had been keeping them in phase with the Vites currents.

Crowds began to form, coming out of their shelters to witness this incredible scene. Impossibly higher they rose, appearing like shiny, new, metallic moons. Once achieving high Earth orbit, each craft temporarily put itself in a geosynchronous orbit with the planet, an orbit all too familiar to the Berenician captains. It was the type of orbit that generations of Harvester crews had spent centuries occupying over Berenices during their construction and mission preparation phases. Waiting, hoping, living, and dying. In one moment, they were there…then, in the blink of an eye, the magnificent ships had gone home.

After a momentary pause, as if not realizing at first what had just happened for a second, the crowds erupted. They cheered, they sang, they hugged, and they danced. This would go on into the night.

A few hours after the Berenician ships were last seen in the skies over Earth, the government had given the all-clear and decided to resume service on the Virtual Global Highway Transportation System. Before the Pulsar Drive had been re-opened to allow the Berenician Harvesters direct access to Earth, there was an international agreement to deactivate the Interstellar Mode on every vehicle operating on the Vites. This deactivation period would last until there was a better understanding of the impact of what it meant to create a bridge into space.

A few weeks earlier, before the circus with Torus had started, the Vites Transportation Authority (VTA), operating under Vites.gov had received an unusual Travel Exception Report (TER). While TERs were very common and almost always handled automatically by the system, this was the first that the AI had flagged an item as urgent and requested human assistance. TER alerts occurred when travelers changed their destination mid-flight from something other than what they entered their trip plan request.

While one of the reasons for the report was to monitor attempts to do something illegal, travelers changing their minds about where they wanted to go wasn't against the law. In fact, it happened all the time. However, if someone simply changed their mind about where they wanted to go, and the destination happened to fall outside the range of the subscription plan, there was a small adjustment added to the monthly transportation bill. Thus far, every alert had fallen under the heading of Terrestrial TER.

This one was different in a couple of ways. In addition to being flagged as urgent and requesting human intervention, it had fallen under the new category heading of Interstellar TER. For the most part, Vites workers had reached the point where they could largely ignore these reports because the system was handling them so efficiently. And besides, none of them had been trained on anything other than the terrestrial kind.

Just after the announcement that the Vites was coming back online, Adam excused himself for a few minutes from the three-day gathering taking place in Julie's living room. Borrowing her office laptop to make transportation arrangements for Greg, Grace, and Myles using his priority codes, he noticed the forgotten TER pushing its way back to the top of his alerts.

Amid the chaos that followed Torus' capture, no one felt the need to give it any attention. With the realization of what this report was trying to tell someone, Adam found himself in a gigantic 'oh shit' moment. A vehicle that had been traveling on the Vites, a Sol-ution model, had somehow, while right in the middle of a leisure trip, changed its course and mode.

Instead of traveling to the Southern Hemisphere, the vehicle had left our solar system.

"What the hell?" Adam asked aloud.

The Solution had escaped Earth and was now somewhere in the constellation Reticulum, located at right ascension 03h 13m 27.0455s, declination -52.7470779°. The report didn't mention a specific planet, but there was a record of the passengers' names. They were civilians, and apparently a family, sharing the last name Decker: Ryan, Laura, Parker and Sophia. They had suddenly requested formation of a warp bubble midflight and journeyed to a planet around one of Reticulum's suns called Zeta Reticuli.

Adam wondered if this travel report wasn't showing a final destination because they didn't make it. He also wondered if it was because of how abruptly he had terminated the Pulsar Drive just a few minutes after the stone was inserted – the AI knew where it was going, but had it lost its connection? The other question surfacing in Adam's mind was whether the Deckers had changed their trip intentionally or was it an accident?

As Adam began to read the details of the report out loud in front of the group, Greg interrupted to say,

"Well, that doesn't sound good, the constellation Reticulum, did you say?"

"Yes," Adam replied. He looked back up at Greg for a moment, not realizing he was staring at him intently. "I didn't know you knew anything about astronomy."

"You know, I don't really, but that name just sounds intimidating," Greg said.

"I would think no matter where this is, being there had to come as quite a shock to this family. I am hopeful, that if in fact they made it, we can dig into L.U.C.'s archive of historical navigational logs and determine exactly what planet they went to, and hopefully it was hospitable."

"Yes, I'm sure we can do that," Greg agreed, with Grace and Myles nodding, their faces concerned. "Now, exactly how long does it say they have been gone?" Adam:

"Let me see if I can find that infor-" Adam stopped himself mid-sentence. "Well, speak of the devil. L.U.C has just decided he wants to take control of my phone," Adam said. There was a pause. "It's Torus. He is requesting a visual connection with us……right now."

Right now? When is a good time to have a video conference with an alien in your ex-wife's home?

Julie, Bri, and Chris had seen Torus on the C-SPAN broadcast. Adam's mother had also seen some of the hearing but hadn't gotten too invested into it because it seemed boring to her. Sometime during the broadcast, she had commented that she thought the make-up people had done a good job because he looked very realistic.

Adam wasn't sure that right here in Julie's living room was going to be the best place to introduce the visitor to his family. He had sort of thought he would introduce the kids in person after he had a chance to tell them a lot more about him. Greg, Grace, and Myles had already gotten a firsthand glimpse of him at Roswell Axiom, so he was not particularly worried about them.

Responding instinctively, Adam rose to collect his briefcase where he kept the remote responder of L.U.C.'s AI. He opened the case, set out the small sphere on the coffee table, and accepted the holovision request.

It had only been a few hours since the aftermath of the Berenices Harvest and Adam, who had been trying to put himself in Torus' shoes, couldn't imagine how Torus must be feeling right now. After decades in space without even the promise of ever returning home, what must it have been like to see a spacecraft, big as life, from the world you left so long ago? It had to have been overwhelming.

To top it off, during the three-day visit by the Berenicians, Torus had been in constant contact with those on board the ships and was probably still reveling in his opportunity to communicate in a native language that he hadn't spoken in almost a century. Adam suspected Torus couldn't wait to be finished with Earth matters.

The lasers went to work, illuminating a figure of Torus that rose all the way to the ceiling in Julie's living room, directly in front of the small gathering. Startled by his appearance, Julie, Chris, and Bri looked over to Adam for reassurance. Adam calmly and confidently introduced the Berenician to the others.

"It's my greatest pleasure to introduce you to a friend of mine, Torus from the House of Kor. He piloted a ship named the *Obsidian* that traveled a great distance to come here to seek our help to save his planet," he said. Greg, Grace, and Myles were beaming at the sight of the visitor and glad to be included in the call. Julie and the kids weren't about to get comfortable but were trusting in the situation as much as they could. Adam's Mom sat back in her chair, ready to enjoy the show.

"This is going to be wonderful," Betty said with a smile. She fussed with her throw to get comfortable.

Torus, who could see the people gathered in Julie's living room, spoke kindly to them. "It is an honor, Hunter family. I'm afraid my time here on Earth is coming to an end. I am forever indebted to your planet and to you, Adam Hunter, for all you have done for us. The people of Berenices are also grateful and are forever friends to Earth. In the coming age, she will need us for our knowledge of the universe and to provide protection from her new enemies," he said, his eyes slowly pulsing silver and darkening to smoke as Chris and Brianna exchanged worried glances. "Berenices will also learn from humans what I have learned and an alliance between our two worlds will ensure that both civilizations can survive and endure," he assured them.

The group in Julie's living room steadied themselves as there was a pause in Torus' transmission. They studied the frozen image of him slightly bowed in a sign of great respect. Kor-Torus began to speak again.

"At week's end, I am leaving and will look to see that your government returns to me the *Obsidian*."

Taking a deep breath and looking directly into Adam's face, as much as holograms are able, Torus straightened to deliver his statement. "As to you, Adam Hunter, I would be honored for you to join me where I can introduce you as friend and hero to the Council of the Guardians."

"As to you, Adam Hunter, the Council of the Guardians invites you to Berenices. Will you join me on the *Obsidian*? It would be an honor to introduce you to them as my hero and friend."

Chapter 49 – Late To the Party

The impact of the invitation didn't sink in immediately. Up until that moment, every fiber within Adam's being had been dedicated to holding himself together, to keeping the people he cared about safe, and to making sure everything that he was helping to build would not collapse under its own weight. The enormity of the invitation was hitting hard and all of a sudden the far-reaching implications were difficult for him to digest.

He still had a lot of work left to do here on Earth, but, like all great leaders, the reality was that he had developed a team of people that could see it through in his absence. What about his children? His mother, Betty? How would they react? With the portal enabled, it wasn't like it was a one-way ticket and he would never be able to find his way back home. Wasn't that the point of a portal, out and back?

At the same time, until a human had put their eyes and feet on some distant planet and returned safely, could the Pulsar drive be certifiable? What about his place in history? Would history record him as the father of space travel? Did he even want that distinction? What if turning to space became the worst possible outcome for Earth?

Adam was already going to be recognized as a key figure in the birth of twenty-first century space travel, he realized. The genie was out of that bottle and rocketing out of the galaxy on the Vites.

The Vites. It had all started as a way to keep from destroying the Earth. Now there were more planets involved than Adam knew about. His planet was on its way to almost complete recovery, and Berenices had a fighting chance against a corrupt leadership. Where would the next trouble spot be? Realist and left-brained thinker that he was, Adam knew it was a question of when and not if another planet was in danger.

He spent a couple of days of soul searching and talking things through with Julie and the kids. He also had an intense meeting with President Morad. Because of how important Morad thought Adam was to all the changes happening on the planet, he was hesitant to see him be the first to travel beyond Earth's realm until we learned more.

Adam, taking everything into consideration, had made his decision. He decided that there would be no regrets either way. What was certain today was that it would be Torus' last night to spend on Earth. Torus had shared with Adam that he truly hoped he would decide to come with him, but if he decided against it, he would understand fully. He knew well that Adam was an entity with a great sense of obligation.

Either way, Torus had made it clear that he would never again return to Earth. There was now much to do on Berenices and his world needed him now, more than ever. He was her savior, her protector, and one of her great leaders. Nursing her back to health would need his full attention.

For many reasons, the media would not be notified of the alien's imminent departure. However, the government made a special arrangement for the alien. That very thin, nondescript top-secret file that Congresswoman Vischer held in her hand during the hearing had been made available to Adam and his cohort.

They were granted the privilege of seeing the file because the government wanted to see if the alien would be willing to fill in some of the missing details from the discovery at Roswell and to see how close some of our descriptions and assumptions of their technological capabilities had been.

On the last page of the file, there was one little nugget that interested Torus the most, the last entry of the page read, "Inserted the UFO at S-4." It was the specific location where they had taken the *Obsidian*. Torus had known the ship was somewhere within the premises of Area-51 but had not taken a particular interest in getting it back, as of yet, as he had taken everything he needed from it after he landed and staged it.

As part of the information exchange and simply for the goodwill of the thing, Washington agreed to return the *Obsidian* for the journey home. Yesterday, after nightfall, a unit within the Special Operations Group (SOG), the most secretive special operations group in the United States, moved the *Obsidian* from its hidden bunker near the end of a long tunnel under Area 51's Groom Lake S-4 location to an undisclosed warehouse at Axiom Roswell.

Only a select few people, many of them dead now, had ever even been aware the bunker existed. The alien's journey to Earth had started in Roswell and it couldn't be more fitting it would end there too. Roswell had always been the place where Earth would find the answers to unlock the universe. Every planet had a door and our planet's door was Roswell.

And those doors made all the difference. They were what connected us with everything and everyone else out there. It was trying to find the truth, to see things in perspective, was almost impossible with only one view. Now that Earth had joined the universal family, it was easier to appreciate our struggles and achievements.

It was through Earthlings that Greg had learned to appreciate connections between individuals, not just civilizations. Joys felt bigger, as true friends share in joys and triumphs.

Problems seemed smaller, often easier to solve with another's input, seeming less daunting "in the cosmic scheme of things."

Aware of the stress his friends were under as of late, Greg made a helpful suggestion. He thought it appropriate to put together a small group of people who'd had the biggest hand in supporting the final efforts of Torus so he could have a proper farewell. And despite the clamoring of the outside world to find him, Torus had been hunkered down in the safe harbor of Greg's beach house where he would remain undetected until his departure. In addition to Greg and Adam, Greg invited Grace, Dr. Alex, Peter, Claire, and Ella. Of course, Myles would be there making sure everything was prepared properly.

In the end, it was this group that had inauspiciously come together that had performed so many of the critical roles which were vital to the success of the alien's endeavor. To Adam, it seemed a little odd that one particular person was invited. Dr. Alex had seemingly gone off the rails and a lot of tension existed between him and the man formerly known as Ben Kumar. However, with the Pulsar Drive in place and the harvest complete, Torus confirmed his acceptance of Alex attending the gathering.

The two had come to an understanding and Torus was satisfied that Alex's obtuse behavior was genuinely out of caution and not intended for sabotage. The physicist had had ample opportunity to destroy the violet stone when it was in his possession and did not. Despite the conflict, Torus' reality was that without Dr. Alex's application of theories, formulas, and physics, the doorway for Berenices would never have opened. Adam got the sense that Torus wanted to look him in the eyes one final time here on Earth.

Adam, feeling some uncommon nervousness, continued to think about and rehearse the things he might say during a toast to Torus if given the opportunity. He intentionally navigated his craft out over Smith Island and came back up to Loretta Landing Lane from the South over the Potomac. The longer than normal flight plan gave him some extra time to think before landing in the rear of the property near the beach.

Uncharacteristically, Adam had been the last one to arrive. As he entered the residence, a strange but sweet aroma had filled the air. As he stepped into the back entrance, he froze as a low, intense-looking conversation from those already gathered ended abruptly and all eyes turned to him. He had already been feeling uneasy with the awkwardness of his entrance from the back door. Startling the others did not help.

Greg, the first to speak after a moment of silence.

"Hey man, come on in. You surprised us. We were beginning to think you weren't coming," he told his friend.

"Sorry I'm late, I got behind on some things. I hope I didn't hold you guys up from eating. What is that smell, anyway?" It was like pasta and vegetables…with some unknown spices.

"Oh yeah, Torus had saved a few vacuum sealed edibles from the ship for just this occasion and thought you might like to try some. He had also told me to give Myles a few recipes that mimicked some other things on Berenices which he thought we might like. Don't worry, we've got a couple of filets in the fridge if nothing works for you."

Adam didn't find what he saw or smelled especially appetizing, but he hadn't come there tonight for the sole purpose of eating. In fact, his stomach was rolling a little bit behind his nerves. Tonight was about celebrating Torus and he hoped he could get that across to his new friend.

Out of human ignorance, the alien had not been treated very well at all since he had revealed himself. Adam was hoping that he and the others could give Torus the proper recognition so that he would feel appreciated and leave Earth having a positive feeling about her and her inhabitants.

After those first few cumbersome moments, the conversations turned more celebratory. Stories of adventures, mysteries, and how they had gotten out of more than a few tight spots were humorous now. The wine was flowing and the genuine care for one another and for all that they'd accomplished was something they all felt. Just as much as Adam had come to shower adoration and extravagant praise on Torus, love and admiration for all he had accomplished came back to him. The night was going exactly as he had hoped it would.

As the evening progressed, Myles dimmed the lights and lit candles for the ambiance. As the guests had all moved their conversations around the table, Adam at one end and the alien, Torus, the other, Adam thought the time was right and began to tap his glass with a nearby spoon.

The conversation died down quickly and all eyes turned to Adam Hunter.

"So I would like you all to raise your glass and join me in celebrating the one we call Torus. We can now also call him friend. He belongs to the House of Kor, on the planet Berenices, but is now and will forever be a part of Earth and her history. With no guarantee of ever returning home, he accepted this great challenge. Berenices faced inevitable annihilation until he decided to exchange the life he knew for one that could make no promises," he told the group. They looked at Torus with admiration, occasionally smiling at each other.

"While I have only known him a few short years in one form or another, I feel like I've always known him. While performing a selfless act to save Berenices, he birthed a new age on planet

Earth. An age that brings us more optimism, more conservation, more healing, and more opportunities to have a better life," he said.

Adam looked directly at Torus, whose eyes were raging with the blues and greens of Earth, so powerfully that they caused a turquoise aura to form around his head. Adam raised his glass towards the magnetic creature.

"Here's to you my friend. God, who reigns above us all, through you, has allowed us to discover one of the great mysteries of the universe. The door to the stars has been there since the beginning of time, and now with your help, Earth has found it. You will be beloved by humans for generations to come and we are forever grateful for the enlightenment that came from your sacrifices," he finished.

Torus was a little taken aback by Adam's words, the spirals of colors in his eyes told how moved he was. He did not expect quite this type of admiration. His experience over the past few months, seeing how humans reacted to the knowledge of his presence wasn't completely unexpected, but it had allowed him to focus on staying focused on his impending departure while putting aside any emotional ties he might have had.

All the guests then raised their glasses together with Adam and in unison echoed the sentiment, "hear, hear" as the sound of glass repeatedly clinking filled the room. Torus, basking in the affection from Adam and the others began to speak.

"You shared quite a tribute, Adam, and I would be at fault to not return the sentiment," but his eyes began to fill with images of his way home, the *Obsidian*. A part of him was already in the stars. He might have done more for Earth than most Earthlings ever would, but he was a Berenician. And now he was proud of Berenices, after fearing for it for so long.

"Without you, Berenices would surely have been lost. Your courage, your vision, and your passion are the reasons why I chose you. You must know that I have always known you and my belief in you never wavered." Adam blushing a bit, kept his eyes focused on Torus and accepted his words with a slight nod of his head. After a brief moment of mutual admiration and with an intense stare, Torus continued.

"And as to my invitation…?"

Adam dropped his eyes away from Torus on hearing the question. He swallowed as if to ready himself for a tough answer. He raised his eyes and looked at Torus, staring back at him with the same intensity.

"I will come with you," he said.

Chapter 50 – We're Gonna Need a Bigger One

Adam, in hearing his own words, felt the blood rushing away from his face which gave him a touch of lightheadedness. So much had gone into coming to terms with becoming Earth's first alien on Berenices, the excitement of verbalizing his decision was crashing into his nerves in a heady euphoria. Adam could feel the energy slicing through his veins as the elation of not only Torus, but all the dinner guests in the room were energized.

Obviously pleased with Adam's answer, Torus smiled and glanced around the table.

"We have been so hopeful that would be your answer,"

"So your Council of the Guardians has given you the approval for my visit?" Adam was surprised it had happened so quickly.

Torus nodded. "They have, but there is something more you need to know about…us,"

On hearing those words, Adam tilted his head to the side.

"I'm confused, what do you mean by *we* and *us*?" he asked, searching the other guests' faces for a clue.

Torus measured his words. "Yes, please forgive me, Adam, the time has come for you to know. I hope what happens next is something you will understand and that will not cause you to lose faith in me," he said, standing perfectly still.

Adam's heart began to race. He wasn't exactly sure of the powers Berenicians possessed, but he knew they could be deadly. Torus could have vaporized General Shelton and his ilk with a glance. He didn't even have to lift a finger if he'd wanted to hurt Adam. And there wouldn't be much the others could do to stop him. Torus was going to shoot a ray into his brain, allowing him to control Adam's thoughts. His mind flashed to Chris and Bri. What had he done? In his panicked state, he considered throwing a wine bottle at Torus. Adam shook his head and raked his hands through his hair. What was the use?

"There was no other way," Torus said, still not moving. Adam stared at him, waiting for a laser beam, or much worse, to strike him. He'd done a lot with his life, he reasoned, wondering why it wasn't flashing in front of him. Julie made sure he had insurance. His knees threatened to buckle.

It became a blur. Adam looked over at Greg, hoping his old friend could give him a little reassurance. The sensation of lightheadedness only intensified, and a feeling that the normally cool, calm, and collected Adam Hunter rarely experienced. He had, after all, been recovering from the release of making a decision unlike any other he had made before.

Greg was becoming unrecognizable, Adam's eyes could only focus for a few seconds at a time, and he felt the room begin to spin. Was he hallucinating? Was he drunk? Surely he hadn't had too much alcohol? What if they'd drugged him? What if it was a stroke?

That had to be it. Just like his father…

He'd read on the subject extensively, wondering if he would live to be as old as his father. One of the most common symptoms of strokes and aneurysms was double vision. Perhaps, the stress of the past three years coupled with having an emotional release of his decision to travel faster than the speed of light was causing his body to fail him?

He wasn't sure why he couldn't reconcile what was happening. His brain and senses weren't working together. His ears were ringing and he felt like a blind spot was coming on and that, coupled with a dimly lit room, gave him trouble determining if he was still looking at Greg or if Torus had moved towards him? Slowly, his heart still racing, Adam's eyes began to adjust enough to where he felt that he could trust them.

And trust them, he did. His lifelong friend, his college roommate, Greg Buchannan, was no longer standing next to him. The figure to his left was going through an all too familiar metamorphosis. Growing taller, extremities elongating, skin turning to silvery gray, and eyes changing from their familiar blue to a deep violet. Once Adam's ears cleared, he heard the tearing of fabric. He'd heard that before, when he was in New Mexico, alone with Ben…

Adam, intently staring with amazement into the eyes of the newly transformed being, began to see his own reflection in its eyes, green as grass. They clearly conveyed the entity intended no harm to him. The creature emanated compassion.

Unrecognizable as it was, there was no doubt it was Greg…. his old friend, Greg Buchannan. Adam was paralyzed. He was unable to move or speak.

"Hello Adam, my friend, my companion, and my hero, my name is Markarian from the house of Jel. Allow me to reveal to you the crew of the space craft *Obsidian,*" he said.

Adam looked around the room to find that he was now completely encircled by the transformation of eight magnificently striking and beautiful gray beings.

"Is this a dream?" It was the only thought that Adam could verbalize in his shock.

Markarian shook his head. "We left our desperate home many, many years ago, fueled by the hope of someday finding her salvation. There were so many times that we wanted to tell you. To keep you safe and to protect Berenices, we had to come this way. What you need to know is that from the billions, we chose you. From the moment we found you, we all knew your spirit exuded the passion, the curiosity, and the drive that sent us searching," he said.

"You found me?" Adam asked. He was the one who went looking for Ben…

"Adam, we knew you long before our 'chance' encounter at Stanford. We watched you as a child, looking at the stars from your backyard in Bellingham. Under a different appearance, I was the man who offered you, among all your classmates, the book of the universe when you were on a field trip as a schoolboy. We watched as your love for the stars began to grow. We saw the countless nights you looked to the stars, searching for answers. When we met at Stanford, it was to continue your training in the blind and guide you to us."

Adam was overwhelmed as he looked around, into the faces of each of the aliens. In his confusion, he was trying to understand how this happened without him suspecting that he was working in the midst of aliens all this time. He was the only human left in the room.

Torus interrupted Adam's racing thoughts. "We are sorry you are only now finding out why it had to be this way Adam, but we hope you understand. We are also hopeful that you feel that your life has been full of meaning and one of great purpose above all others," he said.

"I'm the only one…" Adam said, his voice barely above a whisper.

"We needed someone we could trust, and had the specialized skills to help us with the work. And we might have done all of it ourselves, but we needed someone like you, someone who's background check would always prove to be true. Our identities are made of vapor, and several of us have changed them, many times. There were more close calls than any of us would care to remember," Torus looked at Rigel and Lyrus. She shrugged and he smiled.

"We could not take the risk that even one of us could be found out. Your intervention with the two whom you call Peter and Claire was near disaster. Mossad was closing in quickly on finding out that they were not who they said they were. In captivity, it would have been impossible for us to maintain our human cloak," he explained.

"Can you imagine what Mossad would have done if they'd found us like this?" Rigel said. "Those agents are trained for anything except Berenicians," he said over the laughter of the group.

"There were so many times you stood in for us to protect our mission. We needed you, Adam and we are eternally grateful. We welcome you here formally to this place tonight, not in the house of Greg, but rather in the distant haven of Berenices here on Earth." Adam stared intently, but was still unable to speak.

"Let me introduce you to my crew, the crew of the *Obsidian*. Sacrificing much of what we knew, we all came to Earth with specific capabilities and certain jobs to do. You have already met your longtime friend, Jel-Markarian. He is the *Obsidian's* Second Officer and would stand in for me in my absence. He possesses great skills in leadership and many trades.

"On Berenices, he was a great problem solver and was in charge of planning and organizing the timing of the migration of population centers as certain parts of the planet were projected to become unstable. The plans he developed were still being used by the Council even to the day the Harvesters arrived. His work to protect our people from harm created his passion and led him to volunteer for this impossible mission."

"Another reason why I chose Markarian to befriend you is his ability to relate to beings of all types, across the galaxy. We have encountered different cultures, from quite primitive to remarkably advanced, in our search for materials to repair our planet. While they have not always welcomed us, they have delighted in his presence, because despite the disguises he sometimes wears, he is so genuine. I have yet to see Markarian fail to charm a single life form that crosses his path. Sometimes he is a little *too* charming. That is a story for another time," Torus said quickly. Before Adam could ask about it, he continued to sing his right-hand's praises.

"Without disagreement, it had been determined that Markarian, through the identity of Greg Buchanan, would get in close to befriend you, to guide you, to help you, and build a lasting relationship. Greg's role was, I firmly believe, not an act. He truly understands how to be a friend."

"He even managed to befriend an Earthling! Not an easy job," Adam said, still embarrassed at Torus' mistreatment at the hands of his own government.

"Nonsense. Sometimes the higher ups have to put their feet down more heavily than they would like. I know I had you a little worried about what I was willing to do for sand, at least at first. And I am very proud of the friendship you two have maintained over the years. The only one of its kind between Berenicians and humans, thus far," Torus concluded.

"But not likely the last," Adam responded.

Markarian laughed. "Buddy, you already have all the friends you could ever want on Berenices. When we get home, you'll see," Markarian assured him. "So many people will insist on buying the Earthling who saved us a glass of nisali, you won't be able to walk straight for a week."

Once the laughter settled down, Torus walked to the chair next to Markarian and stood behind Grace, his hands on her shoulders. "Let me introduce you to the one you formerly knew as Grace Hathaway. This is the wonderful and talented Illanra from the house of Asta. While Greg was working directly with you much of the time, Illanra was behind the scenes, metaphorically juggling plates and making it look easy. She is our communications officer and is highly skilled in the art of listening.

"On Berenices, she had taken a leadership role in our galactic ability to listen, find, track, hale, translate, and communicate with other worlds while working in our government's Interstellar Communications Organization. Earth, very soon, will need one like her. She volunteered for the mission out of a sense of duty, realizing that no Berenician was better qualified to listen, survey, and translate human languages than she.

"She brought with her some very sophisticated equipment that is substantially beyond any of Earth's surveillance technologies. Frustrated at times with the ineptitude of the NSA capabilities, she periodically enhanced their systems in certain ways to improve the day-to-day operations. Her bosses at home are going to be quite disappointed by her disappearance.

"Illanra manages L.U.C.'s holovision and has ensured the eight of us were able to remain in daily contact with one another throughout our journey. In another human form, it was also she who orchestrated the delivery of the crate from its secure location to your office on that fateful night a few years ago," Torus said.

Illanra gives Adam a slight head bow acknowledging her introduction. Adam, looking at Illanra in her new form with amazement, felt himself still having a strange sort of attraction to her. There was a very clear femininity that still existed when seeing the Berenicians in their native form, and her violet eyes twinkled when Torus mentioned her crate caper, much like Grace's had when they'd first met in her office.

Torus gestured to his left. "Next there is Vela, from the house of Clon. Vela is our Medical and Genetics Officer. In addition to caring for us and seeing to our own health, she was given the task of developing the human capital that would be required to build the Axiom and Pulsar Drive. When it was apparent that there wasn't enough time to build a large enough human workforce, it was her unique set of skills that enabled us to assemble the variants and to keep construction on time and completed with a high level of consistency and quality.

"She provided great opportunities and cared deeply for the human resources she attracted, nurtured, and developed. She truly wanted them to have better lives and she devoted her time here on Earth to helping them.

"She was one of the leading geneticists on Berenices and received encouragement from the mate she could not save to actively pursue an opportunity to make this great journey to Earth. Trying to save all Berenicians in exchange for the one life she could not save would help her fulfill her purpose. Clon-Sul was only 80 years old when Vela lost him on Berenices," Torus explained.

Vela lifted her long, gray slender hand towards Adam and together with her eyes showed affection for him. Adam returned the gesture.

At the far end of the table, across from Vela were the couple formerly known as Peter and Claire Johansen. “Please meet Rigel and Lyrus from the house of Vyn,” Torus said. “The two are coupled on Berenices and were considered among the great geologists of our planet. Their study of her core and assisting the Council with the diagnosis of how we might remedy her instability is what led us to Earth.

“They worked closely with the AstroGuild in continuing to affirm that Earth was the right celestial match for Berenices. Several other planetary candidates had been found and there had been so many years with so many waves of unsuccessful missions to Earth that it took their stubbornness to affirm that she was the right donor.

“So sure that Earth was the answer and never having mated for offspring, Rigel and Lyrus volunteered for Berenices' final mission of the *Obsidian*. Here on Earth, they performed the vital role of following the signs, messages, and supplies left secretly by previous missions from our world. Following the clues and locating what you refer to as the vimana where the first Corinthian stone was to be found critical to our success. Studying Earth's geological shifts and ensuring the Axiom's control rods were placed exactly to her core was chief among their tasks.

The weight of the sacrifices the visitors in the room had made was beginning to hit Adam hard. Any anger he might have felt for being the centerpiece of deception was dissipating rapidly as compassion and love were replacing those emotions.

Adam began to feel unsatisfied about what he knew of these strange creatures. Beings from another world with so much knowledge, compassion, and power. He began to realize just what a poor job he had done of caring enough about others to get to know them, really know them. Isn't that so often the case? People spend so much time worrying about themselves, they seldom really get to know others.

It was disturbing to think he could have some pretty big selfish character flaws: how does a person interact with a bunch of real, live extraterrestrials on a daily basis, some for years, and only get to know them superficially?

The decision he had made to go with Torus was the right one. He wanted to learn more about who these beings were and who they had been on Berenices. He would soon have time to do so. Another realization of just how little he had been in control… he realized that Greg had introduced him to Grace, Grace had introduced him to Ben, Ben had introduced him to Ella, Greg and Grace had introduced him to Dr. Alex, Grace had “found” Peter and Claire, and of course Myles was already associated with Ben's family. All these aliens had known each other and been working together for almost one hundred years. It was mind blowing for Adam.

Torus introduced those sitting opposite him. "The one you know as Dr. Alex Romanoff is Thorne from the house of Ek. As you are already aware, the universe is wholly based upon the principles of math and science, Thorne's area of expertise. He has proven himself to be the greatest theorist of mathematics and physics in our galaxy. He was the Chief Science Officer on the *Obsidian* and was sent here on this journey to secure the ability to activate Earth's Pulsar Drive against his own decision. He and his team of scientists and engineers maintain the function of Berenices' very own Pulsar Drive within the concepts of the formulas now known as the Alcubierre metric," he said.

"On Berenices, the house of Ek, of which Thorne is descendant, are the keepers of all light transcending formulas. After being appointed by The Council of the Guardians, he reluctantly agreed to the mission, believing he would be of more benefit making sure the Harvesters could safely travel out and back again through deep space. The calculations and calibrations creating and maintaining the integrity of warp bubbles for ships of such size was a delicate matter. But he could not argue with the fact that if Earth's portal was never opened, the journey of the Harvesters would be moot.

"I still do not fully understand why he withheld the stone for as long as he did. Once back on Berenices, discussions will continue. What *is* understood is his love for science and his affection for humans. He began to love his life at MIT, watching the thirst for knowledge of his young students as he fed it to them piece by piece. Earth and Berenices have benefited greatly from his knowledge and ultimately his willingness to share," Torus concluded.

That explanation was the piece Adam was missing to help him better understand the complex relationship of Ben and Alex. Adam now realized that Alex was never going to face judgment on Earth for his actions related to the violet stone. This was a matter for the higher ups on Berenices to consider.

The Vites were completed and delivered with Thorne's help. Had the Pulsar Drive never been activated, Earth would have been none the wiser, but Berenices' fate would have been sealed. Maybe Thorne was beginning to enjoy a simpler life without all the complexities of interacting with the universe? Perhaps, he knew something more?

What if a healed Berenices wanted more than sand and Thorne knew they could turn hostile to us? Maybe it was Earth he was trying to save, not Berenices?

All these questions and more were too much for one night, but they served to stoke Adam's curiosity to learn more about the alien known at Thorne from the house of Ek. Adam nodded to

Thorne, a gesture of respect, and received a similar gesture from him in return. Adam was in no place to judge anything or anyone, he was only beginning to realize how little he knew.

Torus begins to move past Thorne readying to introduce the final visitor. The person Adam had known as Myles was standing at arm's length to his right and appeared to be smiling when the two made eye contact. Myles was a little shorter and heavier set than the other grays, but no less stunning.

"Last, but certainly not *Obsidian's* least, I'd like to introduce you to Rhen, from the house of Fornax. Rhen, responsible for maintenance, and I go back a generation. His father worked in the House of Kor for my father and selflessly served in some very tumultuous times. You must hear more of our story soon. Rhen, while here on Earth, was everything to us. Fixed things when they were broken, gathered things when they needed collecting, prepared our nourishment and provided security. He even participated in numerous secret missions, ranging from gathering documents for identities we could use to breaking into top-secret buildings to gather files necessary for our mission. I could never say enough good things about Rhen. He has been an indispensable and faithful assistant to us all. Nothing could have kept him from being on the *Obsidian* when it left Berenices. No one wanted to save Berenices more than he did," Torus said proudly.

Adam, in a gesture of thankfulness, reached over to touch Rhen's long slender hand and saw images of Berenices, along with his own reflection, in the alien's eyes. He realized the circle of aliens were looking quietly to Adam for his reaction.

"There are no words that can describe the way I am feeling. I can't explain it, even to myself. I have so many questions, some confusion, some uncertainty, but I'm confident we can sort it out. I'm so humbled that you have chosen me for this incredible journey and-" Adam's phone began to buzz.

It was Richard Helms.

Richard had been working to arrange for secret transportation outside of Vites' travel logs for Adam and Torus to make their way to Axiom Roswell privately.

"Richard... wait... before you say anything... About the car you are sending for me...There's been a little change in the plans.... We're going to need a bigger one."

Chapter 51 - The Beginning of a New Age

Richard Helms, Director of the CIA, had taken a flyer on his top report. It had paid off beyond his wildest imaginings. The world was different, it was better, and there had never been more hope for the future than there was right now.

Unquestionably, the Vites had made things incrementally better for generations to come. The Pulsar Drive, while full of unknowns, had the potential to take human life up another notch and could improve the world exponentially. From the time Adam had asked to take his leave of absence, Richard, who had been keeping tabs on his best and brightest, had always known a little more than he had let on.

He had heard the rumors, and while never having seen it, was told by reliable sources there was a bonafide UFO file. However, even he would have to admit that finding a living, breathing alien at this end of the rainbow, who had been living among us undetected for all these years was a bit of a shock. He had been satisfied that people had found *something* in Roswell, a probe, perhaps, that had been used to scout the Earth. He thought it was possible that by some fortuitous set of events, its technology had made its way into the hands of Adam Hunter.

So until Torus' discovery, no one, not even by reference in the Top-Secret file had ever had any verification that another lifeform was on Earth. Unless it was some massive hoax orchestrated by the Nazis or something, it had served to partially answer the question of whether or not we were alone in the universe. At the time Richard granted Adam his leave to pursue his mystery project, if truth be told, Richard's primary motivation for so easily allowing it was to satisfy his own curiosity.

He knew that whoever had put it into Adam's hands must have known what he also knew about Adam. Despite his flaws, which everyone has, there was no one brighter, more motivated, or more emotionally equipped to investigate and reach a conclusion about alien technology than he was.

Strangely, the unflappable Adam sounded very excited on the phone with Richard.

"Now slow down. What are you saying, Adam. I need a bigger what?" Helms asked in confusion.

"No, you go first, you called me," Adam said. Richard continues,

“I was calling to tell you that all the arrangements have been made. I’ve got an off-grid vehicle that will come to a location of your choosing here in DC at 0400 hours to pick you and Ben…, I mean, Torus up and take you to Roswell. You’ll be flying on an independent layer, one that is normally reserved for emergency vehicles, so you shouldn’t encounter any traffic in route. I’ll send you the location to the private warehouse I’ve secured in Axiom Roswell City,” he told Adam.

“Oh, that’s a relief to know. Everything’s squared away, then,” Adam said. In light of recent developments, logistical matters were the last thing on Adam’s mind.

“I’ve just gotten confirmation from Spec Ops that the *Obsidian* craft has been delivered there, is ready and waiting. It took a little fidgeting with the control panel, but the AI came up just fine and sorted things out. It looks like that thing was already fully integrated with the Vites from the get-go. The guys said it was smooth sailing from Nevada down to Roswell and felt like riding in a perfectly restored vintage ‘vette with more bells and whistles than one could imagine. I guess that makes sense. Now, what were you saying again?”

“Oh, right, just the vehicle for Torus. He’s tall, you know,” Adam laughed. “That works, thank you,” he said happily. Standing in the circle with the Berenicians, with Richard unaware of the new set of circumstances, Adam looked at each member of the group. He was still trying to overcome his emotions seeing the new version of each one of his friends.

Still feeling like something out of a dream, it was surreal. While the size of the aliens, much less their appearance, was intimidating, Adam did not feel threatened. What was hard to explain was how each one, which was unrecognizable to their human form, was identifiable as the individual that they were. Perhaps it was in the way they expressed their emotion? Berenicians had a way of making you feel something when you had verbal or non-verbal communication with them and somehow it created an unexplainable likeness to their human identity.

He wondered for a moment that if he hadn’t decided he would come with Torus, when would he have found out about the true nature of the others? Would it be after Torus had left and he tried to connect with Greg, his friend of over twenty years, only to find out that he had…gone missing? Well, no matter, he was glad he did decide to go and was glad he was standing with all the aliens, here and now.

He couldn’t wait to learn more about each of them and who they really were. What an incredible journey it had been for each of them, the stories their Berenician families would hear around the dinner table, if that was such a thing on Berenices. Drawing a feeling of comfort and harmony from the circle, Adam continued with Richard.

“Um, ok, are you sitting down right now? Because this is incredible” he said.

“Yeah. Why, Adam? Everything ok?” Richard asked more urgently. Trustworthy, stable Adam spoke as if he was under the influence of something, he sounded so elated.

Adam looked up into the faces of his new friends? Old friends? He wasn’t sure, but he was among friends, he knew that much.

“Yes, yes, everything is fine. Very good. It’s just that…um,” Adam cleared his throat. “There’s more.”

“There’s more what, bigger what? Look, I understand celebrating after everything we’ve done, but you sound a little strange,” Richard said.

“I’m ok, I really am. But there is more to the story, Richard. You see, Torus didn’t come here alone,” Adam said. There, that was the best place to start. He’d let Richard process that, Adam thought. The silence lasted several seconds, but Adam was relieved to hear Richard’s breath over the phone. Helms didn’t get where he was without nerves of steel. He was ready for more information.

“Continue….” Adam relayed the story to Richard just as the Berenicians had told it to him moments earlier. True to his inquisitive nature, Richard asked several probing questions, but a lifetime of agency work had prepared him to absorb the information while separating the facts from emotion. Like Adam, Richard conceded that this magnificently orchestrated deception had been necessary to save Berenices….and Earth.

“Thank you Richard, so can you manage something for nine?” Richard acknowledged in the current political climate, there was no room for the world to find out that eight aliens had been living among us. It would have set off spontaneous combustion if they had.

“I think so. It takes a little creativity to get around Vites vehicle AI to eliminate the bio-scans, logs, and occupant tracking. I’ll get it done. Good luck and Godspeed.”

At exactly 0400, Adam, Torus, Markarian, Illanra, Vela, Rigel, Lyrus, Rhen, and Thorne boarded a craft from the beach at 1 Loretta Landing Lane and elevated out over the Potomac and began heading West.

Adam laughed to himself, remembering the first time he had driven to “Greg’s family beach house.” The sheer size of the place, the VIP level of security, and the strange decor alone were broad hints that he had dismissed. An entire wall used for projecting images? Just for football games. Maybe that should have been a clue that he was leaving everything normal behind. His “normal” had ceased to exist, he realized. In this new realm, there was only forward.

The shuttle-style transit vehicle flying over the Vites and carrying its nine occupants arrived in Roswell at 0540 hours local time. Sunrise was still more than an hour away. It landed outside a nondescript warehouse used for storing building materials during the city’s construction phase. Its North-facing bay door opened slowly, revealing New Mexico's open desert to the North, and a glimpse of the *Obsidian.* Adam felt the energy radiating from the Berenicians as they gazed upon the craft they had not seen for almost a century.

Finally, it was here, their beloved mother ship, their ride home. It had some similarities to the flying cars operating daily on the Vites and most assuredly had herself been built by nano-machines. The engineer in Adam focused on the ship, as Adam performed a quick mental reverse engineering of its construction. The exterior metal varied somewhat in appearance from the Earth-built vehicles operating on the Vites, carrying the sheen of a high gloss metal like silver or platinum. The difference in appearance was probably due to elements found on Berenices but not Earth, Adam thought. Their composition was likely significantly different in key areas for space travel.

It wasn't a classic UFO saucer shape as he had been expecting, but more elliptical. And despite being decades older than the cars on the Vites, it had quite a purposeful, futuristic flair. The Berenicians had been traveling among the stars for thousands of years, so it wasn't as if this decades-old *Obsidian* model was an old spacecraft to humans. Like a vintage automobile, it was an impressive, timeless sight. And the *Obsidian* looked ready to run.

Inside the warehouse, six members of the 1st Special Forces Operational Detachment-Delta, also known as Delta Force, and two secret service agents readied for the shuttle's arrival while another Delta Force team of six secured the perimeter. Once inside, the shuttle landed softly beside the *Obsidian* in the clearing of a second bay door. With only the red lights from two of the over door exit signs inside the warehouse, the soldiers, professional and efficient at what they did, began escorting the passengers and assisting with their baggage one by one as they entered through a rear gate on the *Obsidian*, already lowered for their entry.

Adam, who had prepared two pieces for himself, which incidentally, was more than the rest of the others, wondered if the Berenicians were taking anything they'd collected from Earth to remember their journey. Perhaps not, Adam knew there was nothing left for them here, they had done what they were here to do and going home, that was the real prize.

As for those that lived and worked around them, they would never know how greatly they would be impacted by all these extraterrestrials had risked and sacrificed. People would simply be left to wonder, hearing in the near future about a missing person's report that might forever go unsolved.

Torus assisted the others and waited to be last. He motioned Adam to board. As Adam stepped on to the ramp, Torus quietly said to him, "I'm waiting on one more."

"One more, who? Is it someone I know?" Adam asked, surprised.

"You won't be the only human coming with us, there's one more who I've invited. Don't worry, he's already 'gone missing' and he won't take no for an answer," Torus explained.

Just as Torus finished his sentence, there was a small bit of commotion from one of the side entrances to the warehouse. A minute later, in the darkness, a shadowy Lieutenant appeared in the doorway.

"Mr. Torus, sir. We have detained a civilian who says he knows you. He also says that you gave him our time and location, sir. Is that correct, sir?"

Torus looked pleased. "Yes, I did Lieutenant, thank you, please let him pass."

"Sir, yes, sir," the Lieutenant said. As the lieutenant stepped back outside, none other than the infamous Leo Raines came bristling through the door, still shaking off a little of the rough treatment he had just received by two Delta Force soldiers. He carried only a small duffle bag as he scurried towards Adam and Torus.

Leo was apologizing profusely to Torus for being a couple minutes late, but it seemed to Adam that he had a surprisingly casual demeanor with the alien, as if the two knew each other quite well. The former gambler hit the bottom of the ramp where Torus and Adam were standing, looking eager to board.

"Adam, let me introduce you to Leo Raines," Torus said.

Leo reached out his hand to Adam. "Pleased to finally make your acquaintance," he said. They made their way up the ramp into the Obsidian, Leo looking in all directions, amazed and giddy as he hurried up the ramp.

"Leo helped facilitate our first introduction," Torus told Adam, who could not recall ever seeing the man with the duffle bag before in his life. "He showed so much interest in us and what we were doing, we decided to invite him to join the project, in a behind-the-scenes kind of way," Torus said enigmatically.

"Wait a minute, I remember him...Isn't he the guy from Area 51 who went missing a couple years ago?" Adam asked.

Torus smirked as much as any Berenician could.

"There will be plenty of time and there is much for us to tell. But the time for us to go is now." The alien Torus put his long, slender gray hand on the back of Adam's shoulder and guided him up the ramp.

As the two disappeared into the darkness of the ship, the *Obsidian* pulled in her final breath of the oxygen rich air into the entrance chamber as her door closed for her final time on Earth. She would leave in much the same way as she had arrived, shrouded in mystery and without any solid information on the identity of its occupants.

After a few moments, gently and silently, the craft elevated slightly above the warehouse floor. With great control for a vehicle of its size, it glided out though the open bay doors. Once clear of the warehouse, the craft, with surprising speed and agility, moved quickly out over the desert floor and began to rise.

Still under the cover of night, the soldiers looked out into the infinity of stars as the craft continued climbing in New Mexico's pre-dawn sky, the majestic February Snow Moon providing the only real light. Smaller and smaller the ship became, and then almost as if to wink with a shimmer, it was gone.

The alliance between Earth and Berenices was born. On official business, Earth's first Ambassador, Adam Hunter, was traveling to a strange, new world to continue the adventure of a lifetime, and Earth was embarking on a new age, the age of flying cars and traveling to places across the universe faster than light.

THE END

Oh, and readers, if you still find yourself worrying about what may have happened to the Deckers, know that before leaving, Adam briefed Helms on their predicament. A search and rescue team is frantically working to find them right now.

Epilogue

It had begun, Earth's new age had started in his lifetime. Adam Hunter knew full well the significance of why he was on the *Obsidian.* His purpose was to establish an alliance with Berenices and the framework for which they could build a mutually beneficial relationship. Richard Helms, who had been given orders directly from President Morad, conveyed this priority to Adam and it had become the tipping point in his decision to go. He was no stranger to having people depending on him. Throughout his career in intelligence and later handling the global rollout of the Vites, he had become quite skilled in negotiating with foreign governments. It was always a given that it would take patience and a lot of work to level the playing field.

Secrets and hidden agendas were always present. The trick, or rather the skill, would be to find out what it was before it was too late. That was perhaps what worried Adam the most. Berenices had already demonstrated an ability to be less than forthcoming and without too much consideration for Earth's opinion, albeit their very existence was at stake. They had already made themselves a part of human history by completing a series of bloodless invasions down through the ages, attempting to give with one hand and take with the other.

So, what else did we need to know? What else could they be hiding? While taking everything into consideration, these were among Adam's top concerns. He hoped their arrival on Berenices would not mimic the relationship Native Americans had with the first European settlers in America. In some places, Europeans had initially given off an impression that a peaceful relationship was possible, however, the want of man created for an unspeakable ending.

Did these creatures have values? Did the Berenicians have a conscience? Did they have a soul? Adam knew that the first thing he needed to do was to learn and there was no better time to learn about the aliens than this moment. While on the verge of experiencing so many new things, he knew he couldn't let himself get distracted by things that could interfere with what he had come to do.

Adam made his first entry into his new journal, the one he'd kept in Roswell was somewhere in his luggage, Rhen had assured him. He titled the journal, "Space."

February 15th, 2029

What do we really know about Berenices? Nothing. We only just found out it existed.
What do we know about Kor-Torus? His name *was* Ben Kumar and he was rich.

What do we know about Jel-Markarian? His name was Greg Buchanan. Is anything else true?
What do we know about Asta-Illanra? Her name was Grace Hathaway. She listens quite well.
What do we know about Clon-Vela? Her name was Ella Flores. She knows a lot about humans.
What do we know about Vyn-Rigel? His name was Peter Johansen. He likes rocks and Claire.
What do we know about Vyn-Lyrus? Her name was Claire Johansen. She likes rocks and Peter.
What do we know about Ek-Thorne? His name was Dr Aleksey Romanoff. Smart guy.
What do we know about Rhen-Fornax? His name was Myles. Organized and extremely loyal.

I have a lot to learn….. Let's have a look on board the *Obsidian* and listen in, shall we?

But before he could listen, Adam couldn't help but look…and look. Pictures didn't do the Earth justice, Adam thought as he gazed upon the "Big Blue Marble" from one hundred thousand miles away. It was more beautiful than it appeared on the tv show he'd loved as a child. Was he insane to leave it?

It was too late to change his mind now.

"We are going to enter the warp bubble momentarily. Take your last look at Earth, guys," Markarian told Adam and Leo.

"Locked in, sir," Markarian told Torus as he stood before a floor-to-ceiling panel at the front of the *Obsidian*, observing a symphony of flashing lights, rotating images, glowing graphs above and below a map of the galaxy that looked like confetti.

"No spacetime continuum disturbances detected. Travel time remaining is approximately 25 hours and 17 minutes, Earth time," he told Torus.

"Any threats detected?" Torus glanced up from the screen next to his gleaming, magisterial chair. Of course, it looked like it was made of obsidian as it dominated the rest of the bridge, which was the size of a movie theater, but much more luxurious.

"They've beefed up their detection avoidance systems since we were here last. We'll know long before they get here, though," he assured Torus.

"This ship glides over trouble spots. Always has," Torus said contentedly. He leaned back in his chair and looked around at the occupants seated on either side of the spacious bridge. Traveling inside the bubble created by a space-altering warp drive was old hat to him and the other seven occupants, who calmly moved to their assigned locations.

Adam and Leo looked at them, incredulous. This was space travel like no one on Earth had experienced before! The aliens seemed as excited as patients in the dentist's waiting room, while the humans were lightheaded, partly from the atmosphere but largely from excitement and fear.

Rhen and Markarian directed Adam and Leo to two seats at the back of the bridge. They strapped braces over each man's chest and offered each an antiemetic. Both refused, fearing the appearance of weakness.

"Markarian, on my mark, prepare the *Obsidian* for interstellar, adjust external molecular composition to activate maximum tidal force. Creating vacuum for warp bubble entry in 30 seconds..."

"Feeling ok?" Markarian looked at both men, trying to gauge their emotional states. "You will feel pressure at first, and you may experience some temporal distortion."

"Well if that's not the understatement of the year..." Adam said.

They were the first humans to experience the warp bubble. What if the Berenicians had overestimated their lung capacity or braincase density or something, and they didn't survive this? They were human guinea pigs, Adam thought. Then the Berenicians would learn what to do differently next time, with the next human crazy enough to travel in space.

"I will see you both on the other side," Markarian told them. Rhen gave his friends a reassuring nod as they went to secure themselves next to the others.

Torus continued. "Markarian, in three, two, one... engage."

There was a hum that slowly rose in pitch until it became a screech that made Adam's teeth ache. The windows gradually darkened, but he could have sworn the bridge became unusually bright. The ship began to vibrate, and Adam began to feel the pressure Markarian had mentioned. He knew how toothpaste felt being squeezed out of the tube, he realized as the ship lurched forward. Adam felt pushed against the brace over his chest for a long minute until he realized the force was gradually subsiding.

It became eerily quiet. He could breathe. He glanced at Leo, who looked relieved.

"Warp bubble enclosed," Markarian reported.

Who was this Alcubierre? Adam promised himself he'd buy the guy a drink if he ever returned to Earth.

The Obsidian moved steadily through space, a little like an airplane that has reached cruising altitude. It was rather anticlimactic. Occasionally one Berenician would click at another in their native language, who would clack in response. Rhen asked them if they were experiencing any distress, but apart from feeling their movements were somewhat slowed, hurtling through space was relatively painless.

“We’re ok, aren’t we?” Adam turned to Leo, who nodded. “Are you talking about us when you make those sounds?” he asked Rhen.

“Mainly, yes. We’re observing your responses and trying to keep things quiet so as not to add to the stress for you,” Rhen answered.

“Well, it’s too quiet for me,” Adam said.

“Of course,” Rhen said. “We can play Earth music. Markarian grew partial to Jefferson Starship, as you well know…” he swiped through a screen on the left armrest of his chair, looking for suitable songs.

“Or we could talk. I only speak English, but so does everyone else here,” Adam said. Markarian looked at his old friend and realized how strange this must seem to the boy from Bellingham. He should have known Adam would start an investigation of one kind or another as soon as he’d gotten his bearings.

“This is kind of like a really long car trip or plane ride, you two,” Rhen told them as he scanned the area for meteors. “I think you will find that Berenicians have a lot in common with Earthlings,” he said.

“Really, like what?” Adam asked.

Gratitude

“Like my job,” Rhen said. “My duties at the beach house and my duties on Berenices are very similar.”

“That’s right. Torus mentioned that you and your father worked for the House of Kor.”

Rhen nodded. “I grew up hearing about a lot of close calls with the Faldonians,” he said.

“I’d love to know more about it,” Adam said.

“We have time,” Leo smirked.

Deactivating his holographic image of what appeared to be a Berenician sporting event, Rhen ambled over to the sunken lounge area behind Torus’ station. He suspected Adam and Leo felt safer behind the commander. Nearly everyone did.

“Where to begin?” he asked, not truly comfortable with being the center of attention. “Before I start, can I get you...”

“You’re off the clock, Rhen. Relax,” Adam said.

“Why not start at the beginning?” Leo asked.

Rhen began to speak of his family’s involvement with the House of Kor, starting with his childhood. Adam listened as the Berenician explained how Rhen’s father, Pelgan, was in charge of keeping the House of Kor's domestic vehicles in good working order at all times. There was so much political instability in those days, more than once shelling awakened Tor and his siblings in the middle of the night. Often this meant Pelgan hurried them into vehicles ready to take them to nearby shelters.

During one surprise attack, Rhen's father was packing a vehicle with last minute necessities when a volley of white-hot rays came through the roof. A Faldonian ship was overhead, beginning the first of their assaults on Berenices. Pelgan wasn't hit directly, but the explosion sent him flying backwards into the wall, causing a head injury that left him unconscious.

Not a minute later, Tor's father, Zuroc, came to see if his aide was safe. He found him lying near a device used to scan the vehicles for 'bugs,' the kind that eavesdrop. His young family close behind, he hastily ushered his issue into a nearby vehicle and told the pilot to head for the bunker.

Closing the door to the vehicle, Nayata stood and looked at her husband in confusion. He knelt over his loyal friend's broken body, refusing to leave until he was sure Pelgan would recover.

Rhen told the men that hearing this story growing up, he learned that whoever looked after the vehicles was important. Not just to the safety of their owners, but to the whole of the operation.

Later, as an apprentice in the House of Nyr, he learned how to anticipate what people would want in five minutes and in five months. Rhen saw it as his job to keep the group on an even keel.

"You're always behind the scenes, though." Leo admired Rhen's dedication, but as a born show-off, he had trouble understanding the retiring Rhen.

"I'm going to make sure they know about you at home," Adam told his friend.

"Oh, no. Don't do that," Rhen said, horrified. He relished his role, but how to explain this to Adam and Leo, who thought Rhen existed in the military leader's shadow? Torus did big things. He invaded, commanded and sometimes demanded. People who did those things seemed to inevitably find themselves in the spotlight.

It was a place Rhen never liked. The things that mattered to him were in the background. Rhen was in charge of the day to day, the smaller things. But they were no less important.

"And doing so much for others, when they get all the glory and applause, this doesn't bother you?" Adam asked Rhen.

"I know what I do. Those I care about know what I do. The rest isn't important to me," Rhen answered.

“You can do without the admiration,” Adam said, thinking he was beginning to understand him.

A small smile from Rhen told Adam he still hadn’t solved the mystery of the enigmatic steward. “Who says I’m not admired?” he asked. “Just because my face isn’t on t-shirts,” he glanced slyly at Torus, “it doesn’t mean no one appreciates me.”

“People need to know about you,” Adam insisted. Rhen shook his head slightly.

“I know about me, Adam. And I know of many like me. Some of them are far more educated and influential than I am.” Rhen’s violet gaze was so intense, Adam grew uneasy. He looked into the creature's eyes, but only saw…children. “There are always individuals who are too busy helping others to worry about curtain calls. And I’m so grateful that I’ve been able to help. That’s really all you need to know about me. That I’m grateful. You were, too. That’s the first thing I remember learning about you,” Rhen said warmly.

“You learned about me? I’m grateful?” Adam was confused.

“We all watched you. I saw you going to your mother’s class sometimes to help. That’s when I knew you would be the one to make sure our planet didn’t…” Rhen inhaled sharply as emotions threatened to overcome him. “I knew you came from a good family. Your mother told you something. I heard it was from your religion. I never forgot it: “Always be rejoicing,” Rhen said. The lessons he learned from Betty came flooding back. *Do what’s right, whether anyone else can see it. Help others. Believe in miracles.* He and Rhen finished the verse together. “Give thanks for everything.”

Adam blinked back tears as he felt Leo’s hand on his shoulder. He must be suffering from eye strain, peering at aliens so closely and for so long. He told himself that was probably the reason. There was a rational explanation for everything, wasn’t there?

Faith

Leo and Adam sat in silence after Rhen excused himself to help Thorne with his coffee craving; he had come to depend on it while at MIT and planned to introduce it to Berenicians. Markarian studied the panel with a frown, occasionally clicking at Torus. Illanra and Vela were engrossed in conversation while Rigel slept.

That left Lyrus, sitting across from the men in the bridge, looking rather bored.

“Maybe we can find out more about where we’re going from the gemologist,” Leo told Adam.

“She’s a geologist,” Adam corrected him.

“Do we really know what she is? Do they even have those on Berenices?” Leo asked.

Lyrus' gaze moved across the bridge to the humans. Adam suspected these creatures had more than five senses. She crossed the space between them, going behind Torus and stopping to grab a packet of dried fruit.

She tapped the back of the nearest chair and it floated over to face Adam and Leo. Plunking herself down in front of them, she smiled. "You two are doing really well. We were worried about sickness or anxiety. Rigel even thought you might change your minds at the very last minute," Lyrus said.

"No way I would do that," Leo said. "I pretty much left everything behind. It's not like I have a job to get back to."

"Speaking of jobs, what was it like working on Berenices?" Adam asked her.

"Yeah, did you always want to be a geologist?" Leo inquired.

"Well yes, I was always interested in what was beneath my feet. At home, we call them foundation specialists, but I love the term geologist. It comes from your Greek word for Earth, did you know that?" Lyrus didn't try to hide her enthusiasm.

"What I don't know could fill this galaxy, ma'am," Leo said.

"I know the feeling," Lyrus said. "There is so much we have to learn…" Lyrus said.

"That's how I felt when I looked at the stars as a kid," Adam said. "Just thinking about all the possibilities out there. I loved it."

Lyrus smiled sadly. "It sounds like a wonderful experience for a child."

Adam tilted his head to the side. "It wasn't like that on Berenices?"

"It was…" Lyrus tried to find the words, but something in her resisted searching for them. "You have to remember, mining ravaged our planet. It led to seismic activity, fires…"

"I'm sorry, Lyrus," Adam said. "I didn't realize what it was like for you."

"No, I'm glad you asked. You are going to walk on our planet in less than twenty hours. You need to know what to expect. I want you to know the truth about Berenices, holes and all."

"Well, if you don't want to talk about it..." Leo said.

Lyrus looked around where they sat. "What if I showed you instead? Maybe I can play what you humans would call a home movie," Lyrus said.

"I didn't bring popcorn," Adam replied.

"This dried fruit is not bad," Lyrus said as she held out the packet. Both men declined.

"So, you have a theater in here?" Adam asked. Lyrus looked confused.

"We have these," she said as she pressed a button on the armrest of her chair.

A cloud of shimmering particles appeared in the air above them, buzzing and humming until they formed a transparent pane. It was roughly one meter high and slightly wider; it slowly floated backwards far enough for the three of them to view it comfortably.

Lyrus continued to tap the small screen in the armrest. “These crystals record our memories,” she explained, not realizing this was new to the Earthlings.

At first the image was swirling dust, and then the sound was of an excited youngster.

“Look here,” they heard a voice say. Gradually, the screen cleared and they could see two silver gray forms walking across an expanse of willowy trees and ferns. The smaller form had a greenish cast to her hands and feet, a mark of youth that faded in early adulthood.

“What about over here?” Lyrus wandered toward a clearing in the field.

“See the ground, guys? It hadn’t burned, at least not recently. We were near a dry riverbed in Savadi Canyon, where we often found bethaline,” she said. Adam merely nodded, wondering what bethaline was.

“Maybe that’s a good place to look,” her father Chadin said. She set to work, digging up piles of dirt until she reached a burned patch. “That was probably fairly recent. The dust storms caused soil to resettle over and over. It was a mess,” she explained.

After digging in several places without success, finally she extracted the shovel, marveling at the telltale deep blue stains on the tip. “It’s here! I found it!” she exclaimed.

“I knew you would!” Chadin smiled at his daughter, then glanced around nervously.

Lyrus leaned toward Adam. “He’s checking for the Resource Patrol. They made frequent trips through that area, looking for ‘unauthorized procurement of endangered substances.’”

“What would happen if the patrol caught you?” Adam asked.

Lyrus’ smile faded. She shook her head. Watching her younger self, she brightened as she re-lived her discovery, glancing at Rigel. He had awakened and summoned a chair next to Lyrus a few minutes earlier.

Tribling Lyrus rubbed her fingertips across the blue substance on the shovel and held it close to her audio sensor. “Can you hear it?” her father asked.

“Just barely, but I can hear it,” Lyrus said.

Adam was mesmerized. The sounds were faint, but as Lyrus moved her fingers against the lapis lazuli-hued crystals, he could hear chimes. Or were they harp strings? It didn’t sound like voices, but then Lyrus began to hum along with the sounds she heard. She closed her eyes as the calming effect of bethaline washed over her. After a few blissful moments, she opened them again.

"Why can't we feel like this all the time?" she asked her father. A billowing ash cloud on the horizon distracted him. He looked at her sadly, at a loss to give his daughter an explanation, or even an excuse.

Lyrus studied the ground around her, horrified by the devastation of her home planet. "Why can't they fix this?"

"I know, Lyrus. We have tried. We have teams looking everywhere in the galaxy for help. If we can find something to fill the cracks in the ground, we won't have as many quakes and fires." As Adam peered into the screen, he could see her eyes filling with clouds of ash and flames erupting from charred ground…a hellscape in a child's face. Chadin was fighting the tears that threatened to spill down his face and onto hers.

"The government would send warnings about the noxious fumes. They came from the cracks near the fault lines and were pretty dangerous. The authorities would tell us not to go outside for forty-eight hours when things were really serious," she told Adam.

He couldn't help but worry at the sound of this. Such an advanced civilization in some ways, dealing with environmental hazards the inhabitants had created.

As if he heard Adam's thoughts, Chadin began to explain the predicament.

"Do you remember the Five Flaws we told you about?" he asked his daughter.

"Selfishness. Greed. Vanity. Wrath. Envy," Lyrus recited.

"The people in power have given in to these things. They've been doing it for so long, it's all they know now," he told her.

"Can you stop them? Can we stop them?" Lyrus asked her father.

Adam turned to watch Lyrus. She was looking at the floor, her breathing unsteady. "Is this too much, Lyrus? We can stop…" Rigel put his arm around her.

"No, it's important that you know this," she said.

"You've seen this story, Adam. It has a happy ending," Rigel reminded him with a smile.

"I won't let them send you to the mines. I will never do that," Chadin said as he knelt down, putting his hands on either side of Lyrus' face. "But to stop them, you may have to leave here when you are older. You may have to go…looking for something that can fill the holes in our planet. You might also have to live on another planet."

"Will you be there?" she asked him, her eyes a jumble of solar systems.

"I hope so," he smiled. "I have faith in you, though. You know how to listen to the ground and find the things in it that we need to survive. It wouldn't surprise me if you were the one to bring home just the thing to fill the cracks so we can all live here," he said, full of the faith every parent has in their children. "Imagine how happy we all will be when you come to this canyon and we can fill it up together."

The thought made young Lyrus laugh. "I will find it and bring it home, whatever it is."

"I know you will, my Lyrus. Remember Vela? You met her when you came to the lab to see me. Let's take this bethaline home and tomorrow we can go show it to her. I know she will be excited to see it."

Adam watched the two walk through wisps of smoke as the picture grew dark. "Oh, my goodness," he said. "How did you live through that?"

The Vyns were quiet as they searched for the words to explain. It was like talking to war veterans. Unless someone had experienced it, helping outsiders understand it was next to impossible.

"No wonder you…all of you, you had to do this," Adam also struggled to articulate his thoughts. The crash in the desert, the false identities, the variants; he was beginning to appreciate their strategy. Thinking about them coming to Earth for thousands of years was staggering.

"So then you brought the bethaline to Vela-" Adam was surprised to learn the Berenicians' relationships at home were similar to the ones they had on Earth.

"Yeah, yeah. Let's skip ahead to the good part," Rigel said. He looked at Lyrus. "Can you show us when we're in school?" She smiled at Rigel and the mood in the room lifted.

A flurry of images appeared on the quartz screen, and slowed until Adam could make out amid the planet's seemingly permanent haze, a group of enormous glass buildings. Berenicians were walking to and from the transparent structures.

"My first year at the AstroGuild Academy," Lyrus said fondly.

"Mine, too," Rigel chimed in. Adam saw a room full of people. It was a little like a movie theater. "Three hundred people in our class," Rigel remarked.

A figure on the stage was showing diagrams on a screen that reminded Adam of L.U.C.'s early presentations. "That's Vela's sister instructing. She's showing us the mathematical likelihood of finding a substance we could use to repair Berenices," Rigel told Adam.

Adam watched the student's faces fall when they realized how small their chances of success were. They grumbled and sighed. Why were they even bothering to look for something they probably weren't going to find?

"Rigel to the rescue!" he said proudly.

They watched a Berenician sitting towards the back of the class stand. His hands and feet looked more silver than green.

"I can't believe all of you! You're giving up before we even start looking? Don't any of you have people you care about? Triblings? Grandparents? You're going to let them suffer because *we have to go look for things*?" he asked his fellow students, many of whom were slumped apathetically in their seats.

"Maybe our resources would be better used to create a synthetic replacement," one bright but rather discouraged student offered.

"This is crazy! We've been trying for centuries to artificially plug the holes. We may not find a perfect substitute, but someone out there has something we can use. We can trade, maybe we can borrow, but we have to go find it. Who cares if it's hard or it takes a long time? We can't just sit here. Who is with me?" He looked around the cavernous lecture hall with its thirty-foot screens, 3-D models of solar systems and dejected young Berenicians.

"Ok, now watch," Rigel told Adam. "See three rows ahead of me?" Markarian and Torus had taken a break and were standing behind him, watching.

They saw Lyrus turn in her seat to listen to his speech. Other students looked skeptical, or afraid. Lyrus appeared impressed with his intensity. It was Rigel's kind of passion that could give Berenices a fighting chance. Someone else was ready to scour the universe to save Berenices.

"I am with you," she smiled up at him. Rigel smiled back, ready to go to the ends of the universe for all that he held dear. The image began to fade as Markarian slapped Rigel on the shoulder.

"So, when I showed up, we knew it would all work out," Rigel said as the screen dissolved.

Adam found himself thinking Rigel was correct. Without that kind of confidence, there was every reason to have such high hopes.

Friendship

"These two are the reason Berenices is on the road to recovery," Markarian said, gesturing to Lyrus and Rigel. "They were not going to give up the search. Me, I was thinking the solution was going to come from someone closer. I never understood why we didn't have better relationships with our neighbors," he told the group.

"Your relationships with some of our neighbors were a little TOO friendly," Torus said as the group laughed.

"It would have been a great merger," Markarian said, smiling. "I was just trying to save my home planet."

Torus looked at a bewildered Adam. "Markarian is trying to downplay what he did as some big misunderstanding. You know he almost started a war with the Faldonians?"

Adam's eyes widened. "A war? Ok, I'll have some of that fruit. I want to hear this," he said eagerly.

"Wait! First of all, my assignment was to explore possible alliances, and that's exactly what I did, so you can stop acting like I'm some sort of Berenician Casanova," Markarian said. The group laughed and shook their heads.

"And that's what you and Hathor the Faldonian were doing during the meteor shower? Exploring an alliance?" Lyrus asked mirthfully.

Markarian took a deep breath. "I'm going to explain what happened to my friend Adam, and later, the rest of you can give him your version of the story, ok?" he asked.

The Berenicians nodded gleefully.

"Like I said, the Council of Guardians thought I had potential as a kind of junior ambassador, since I'll talk to anyone," he began.

"Especially if they have aqua hair down to their waist and tangerine eyes," Rigel said and Markarian shot him a warning look. So did Lyrus.

"Well, I knew her father didn't want to meet with me. They've hated us for about seven thousand years. But it was worth a try, I thought. Maybe they had something we could use to repair the core. It wouldn't have surprised me if they did and were just hiding it from us out of spite," he told Adam, whose grasp of Berenician history was rudimentary.

"I wouldn't put it past those lowlifes," Torus muttered.

"But they can't be all bad, can they? You can't really know people unless you talk to them and try to understand why they do the things they do, right?" he asked the group. Responses were mixed.

"It's easy to make assumptions about people without ever getting to know them. And that was the case with Hathor. She didn't agree with a lot of things the Faldonian regime had done. She wasn't an expert on her planet's history, but the Berenicians hadn't done anything to her personally, you know? She didn't want to destroy our planet just because one of us may have insulted one of them a few centuries ago," Markarian said.

"You were willing to give her the benefit of the doubt," Leo said supportively.

"Of course, I mean, I kind of thought she was mostly just talking to me to get back at her father for advising her against marrying the Dirasandian," he admitted.

"That's precisely why she was doing it," Torus said, arms folded.

"We may never really know the hidden motives of others. Perhaps Hathor wasn't sure herself. But we have to at least make attempts to understand each other, don't we? It's not like we hadn't heard things about Earth and her inhabitants that were…unflattering," he looked at Adam apologetically. "Nothing personal."

Adam waved a hand dismissively. "It was probably true, whatever you heard," he said with a rueful smile.

Markarian looked at his friend for a moment, his expression uncharacteristically serious. "It's everywhere. At least, every planet I've seen or studied. We watched you over millennia. Plenty of Council members advised us against trying to engage peacefully," Markarian told him. "The wars, the brutality, the destruction, the habit of repeating the same mistakes, it makes the rest of it difficult to understand."

"What's the rest of it?" Adam asked. Markarian said nothing, but his eyes became greener than Adam had ever seen them. Adam leaned closer, trying to see what his friend was thinking. It was the football field at Stanford. The memories rushed back to the game against USC. The cheering. The beer that flowed freely. Later that night, "Greg" showed him his idea for the polymers. "We can visit Mars this weekend!" Greg had laughed.

Adam looked at Torus, not sure he understood completely.

"The 'rest of it' is your music, your art, the way you Earthlings celebrate life. Your games where everyone shakes hands at the end. The coaches who believe in all their players on their teams. Their families, who wave flags and paint their faces to cheer for them. Those striped-shirt people who make sure things are fair," Torus said.

"You let us live because of sports?" Adam asked. The lump in his throat was actually closer to a baseball in size.

Markarian shook his head. "When I showed you the polymers, you could have disregarded their usefulness for others, or focused on how you could exploit or harm people with them," Markarian reminded him.

"Well, no. Why would I do that?" Adam asked.

"Maybe you understood their importance because some part of you knew that these materials were going to help you serve others. After the game that night, I reached out to Torus and told him I thought you would visit Berenices someday."

"I wish you'd told me *that* after the game," Adam said.

"No way. You would have taken away my beer," Markarian said. He smiled at Adam before returning to his post with Torus. Lyrus and Rigel went looking for Rhen.

Again, it was just Adam and Leo.

“That wore me out. I’m going to find a place for a nap,” Leo said.

Thorne approached them, standing next to Lyrus’ former chair.

Family Values

“Please, sit,” Adam said.

“I’ve been sitting for the last four hours. We should walk the perimeter of the ship later, it’s good to stretch your legs. But I saw some of Lyrus’ story, and I wanted to tell you that she, all of us, we were getting desperate before we found Earth. It’s a wonderful place in a lot of ways. I came to consider Earth my second home,” Thorne said as Leo offered him some of the dried fruit. He shook his head and glanced at Torus a little nervously.

“That’s not a secret around here. I think I feel this way because, at this moment, you Earthlings are ahead of us in one really important way,” he said as Rhen passed by to refill his coffee cup.

“You guys can send messages of light, for Pete’s sake, I don’t think we’ll ever catch up,” Adam responded, faintly amused.

Thorne was serious, and sad. “Well, there’s technology, and then there’s our code of ethics, and they don’t always progress at the same speed. Maybe ethics have to be slower, they require us to consider more, observe more. Sometimes even do more,” he said as he looked out the window.

“I’m not sure I understand,” Adam said.

“Do you know about the House of Ek?” Thorne asked Adam.

“Well, just what Torus said, about them keeping the formulas for transcending the speed of light. Kind of a big deal,” Adam said, unable to think of a family on Earth that could make a similar claim.

“Just doing our jobs, as I see it,” Thorne said. “We were public servants. All of us are here to serve, that’s the Ek family credo, in fact.”

“That’s admirable. Generations of service to others,” Adam said.

“It’s sort of like that on earth. The brightest minds are strong. They have to be to pull the civilization forward. Like you, you were one of the top students in your class, Adam. I taught young people much like you at MIT,” he said fondly.

“Nerds,” Adam said.

"No, it's a heavy responsibility. Being able to understand the concepts, being willing to work on them till they can do something in the real world. It falls to those of us who are cut out for that, and there aren't many of us," Thorne said.

"Does anyone have it easy, though?" Adam asked. He looked at Torus. "Military service is no picnic."

"All of us work hard, I know. But our work, collectively, at home, has yet to bear fruit, so to speak. For the last few thousand years, we've only managed to survive on our planet. We learned how to do so many great things, but greed almost destroyed us. You are ahead of us in that respect. The next generation will have so many wonderful possibilities, so much to build on," Thorne looked at Adam, both happy for his friend and troubled by his predicament at home.

"You've got four Harvesters filled to the brim with sand, Thorne. I can't imagine the parties they're going to have when you show up," Adam said mischievously.

"But how did we get so far off track on my planet? Technology was the answer, our government told us. I worked for the government, much like you did. We followed orders to create what the leadership wanted. We trusted them to do what was good for everyone. They didn't do that," Thorne was bitter, and Adam didn't blame him. He'd seen his own government act selfishly and recklessly.

"They started sending people into the mines to work, younger people who were more robust. But also debtors, criminals, desperate people. Scientists knew it wasn't safe for them, the politicians knew it wasn't safe. I study light, but it doesn't require much knowledge of radiation sickness to know those mines were killing people. They wanted me to state publicly that the risks were practically nonexistent in working with the toxic minerals underground. 'You are a leading scientist, Thorne, they will listen to you.' I refused to do it," he told Adam.

"Good for you. I would have refused, too," he said supportively.

"Would have refused what?" Restless Vela had been walking around the bridge and noticed the two deep in conversation.

"Pull up a chair, Vela. I'm telling Adam about the mines," Thorne told her.

"Oh, no," she said, looking concerned. "I treated people who worked there."

"What if you refused and they'd threatened you?" Thorne asked, his eyes flashing.

Adam shook his head. "We'd all like to think we'd take the high road. I don't know, Thorne. I'm grateful I've never been in your position."

"We honored our end of the agreement. We invented the things they wanted. Then they used them to hurt people. We have to live with that," Thorne looked down, shaking his head.

“There’s hope now. With the sand, your planet can be even better than it was. A generation will be born that never experienced the fires and the quakes,” Adam reminded him.

“All the technology is useless,” Thorne said wearily. Adam looked around the bridge, at the individuals who had used technology to repair his world and revive their own. “Remember that. Without our sense of right and wrong, without looking at ‘five future families,’ anything we invent will be used to harm, not help.”

All for One

Vela sat off to Adam’s side, smiling sadly. “A lot of truth in what Thorne says,” she mused, her eyes a mass of formulas and symbols. She thought about how dangerous her findings could be in the wrong hands, or for the wrong reasons. “I wonder about the best-case scenario for Berenices. If the sand helps us recover, will it last a generation? Two generations? Will we forget by then? Will we tell ourselves it will be different this time?” It was a question they could not answer, even with all the incredible technology that had brought them here.

“That’s what we’ve done for a long time on Earth,” Adam said. “We did that until it was almost too late.”

“And when it was almost too late, was it machines that saved the day?” she wondered.

“Well, yes, wasn’t it?” Adam asked as he remembered watching the Harvesters in awe.

“Or was it the belief that helping others is important?” Vela asked, raising her slender, silvery hands, her palms up and shoulders lifted. “Did we finally realize if we didn’t work together, we wouldn’t survive?”

“What do *you* think, Vela?” Adam asked.

“When I practiced medicine in unstable places, places where there wasn’t enough food, where noxious gasses were making children sick, I realized how many problems I *couldn’t* solve. It was really overwhelming at times.” She thought about Lyrus, who had permanent damage from living near Savadi Canyon.

“So I focused on what I *could* do to help. I could treat individuals, one at a time. Although in some of the most dangerous areas, I treated whole groups. And technology helped me, no doubt about that,” she said.

“You, I trust with lasers and atomic solutions. It’s the others I don’t know about,” Thorne said.

“All those years in the trenches, that’s how we refined the limb regeneration that Sul formulated,” Vela remembered.

“You can grow…arms and legs?” Adam asked, his eyes wide.

Vela nodded. "It was very rewarding to be able to help people who'd been maimed, or were born different. Sul would have been so happy…" she stopped herself and sighed. "It's the ones we *can* save. For the families of the people I could help, sometimes that made all the difference," she said.

"One person can make a difference, Vela, I know you did," Adam said.

"You Earthlings say things like that, talking about one person. Something in one of your religious texts affected my approach to work when I read it. How saving one person is, in a sense, like saving the whole world," Vela said. "But the one I couldn't save, he was the whole world to me."

"Oh, Vela," Thorne said. "He's proud of you. Everything he hoped to do, you've done it. It's like the races, one hands off the *eldak,"* he stopped, searching for the English word. He looked at Adam.

"The baton?" he asked.

"That's right. He passed it to you, ran and kept running until you saved your planet," Thorne said.

"I don't know, Adam, as much as I like your planet and some of the ideas humans developed, I hope we don't have to rely on the power of one all the time," she looked around the ship. Rigel had dozed off on Lyrus' shoulder, while Illanra was deep in conversation with their home base. Torus and Markarian were plotting a course around a meteor shower, and Leo was showing Rhen how to do sitting yoga. "The power of everybody working toward one goal is pretty impressive."

A Listening Ear

"I have to agree with you about that," Adam said. "It took all of us doing everything we could to accomplish what we have."

"Wait till we introduce you to the team behind the Harvesters. Three hundred of the best Berenicians you will ever meet," Vela said fondly.

"That's something to look forward to. I can't imagine how they engineered that," Adam told her.

"You would think that would have been the challenge, but Markarian says engineering almost always takes a backseat to communication," Vela said.

Illanra looked over at them when she heard one of her favorite words. Her violet eyes pulsed and she clacked at her screen a few times and signed off.

"Look what you've done," Adam said. "Hope you weren't planning on a nap anytime soon," Vela smiled as they watched Illanra cross the bridge to join them. She sat next to Adam on a cushioned bench between two large screens indicating their approximate location with a pulsing dot representing the *Obsidian*. It crawled across the galaxy to Berenices with the time remaining reading 6 hours, 21 minutes in large numbers at the top.

"Oh, I'm much too excited to sleep," Vela assured him.

"Well, first things first. I've got some very important news from home," Illanra said, impish as ever.

"Do tell," Vela said.

"Remember Hizet who decided not to come with us at the last minute?" she asked her friend.

"That student of Thorne's?" Vela asked.

"The one and only. Apparently he's claiming he was the first to locate the sand on Earth…"

"That does not surprise me," Vela said. "He was one of my sister's students and he claimed to have written some of her books," she said. "You didn't hear that from me," she added as Illanra nodded. She made a gesture near her shoulder that Adam suspected was like Earthling's heart crossing. He was beginning to think of Illanra as a combination of a vault and an old-fashioned switchboard operator.

"Is there anything you don't know about your fellow Berenicians?" Adam asked her. Even at seven feet tall with violet eyes, she still fascinated him.

"When it comes to the people I work with, there isn't a lot I don't know," she told Adam.

"That's your job, isn't it?" he asked. "Making sure you're paying attention to what everyone is saying."

"Oh, even when I'm not working for the government, yours or mine, I try to keep my ears open."

"That's probably because of Asta-Gir," Vela observed. "Growing up around that, you were a trained listener before you started school."

"That's probably true," Illanra said. "I hadn't really thought of that."

"Why not? It's practically the same as…never mind." Vela said as she started to search for information on her extra-wide armrest.

"The same as what?" Adam asked. They had hours to fill, and Illanra was never dull. "Who is Asta-Gir?"

"My father. He helped kids," Illanra was rather laconic.

"Oh?" Adam asked. "Can you tell me more?"

"As you may know, conditions really deteriorated over the last few hundred years. There were many more triblings with birth defects than there should have been, statistically speaking. The government tended to suggest it was bad dietary habits, but everyone knows it's the toxic gasses from the seismic activity," Vela said.

"Right, yes. Lyrus and her father were practically in a haze most of the time," Adam said.

"Lyrus is pretty fortunate. She has some breathing problems, but she's able to do a lot," Illanra said. "There were triblings that had respiratory issues, and Vela did a lot of work with them," she said and smiled at her friend.

Vela realized there was one subject that was not easy for Illanra to discuss. "There were also many triblings with speech problems. Plenty of the Berenicians in power thought the young who had trouble learning to click and clack should be relegated to a kind of second-class group," she explained to Adam.

"It takes hours of practice for them to learn to communicate. Gir invented some devices that help them speak more clearly and easily. Of course, they can use manual language, as we call it, but Berenices places a great deal of importance on oratory skills. Always has," Illanra said quietly as she watched Vela leave to talk to Markarian.

"Well, that's wonderful. Someone who helps the younger generation…" Adam said, thinking of Betty.

"I would go to his class sometimes as a tribling. His students would talk to me, and sometimes, most of the time, I had trouble understanding them. They'd get frustrated and I'd get frustrated. He would remind me that just trying to communicate with people is worth a lot. 'Being a good listener is more important than being a good speaker,' he would tell me."

"And you took that to heart, it seems," Adam said.

Illanra nodded. "For most of us, speaking is a little too easy. It's listening that moves things forward in communication."

"No argument here," Adam said. He was a little overwhelmed trying to assimilate all the information he had obtained in talking with the Berenicians.

"But Adam, this important thing to remember," Illanra sat up and leaned toward him, the Milky Way in her eyes. "We've been trying to send you messages, Earthlings have been 'listening' with the best tools they have, and vice versa. You thought you were like an island in the universe. The crate was like a bottle washing ashore with a note in it. We were telling you we were here. You read the note inside. And you listened to us."

Adam sat back in his chair, knowing the galaxy was flying past him outside. He wanted to come up with a witty response, a snappy comeback. He thought about becoming the first human to walk on another planet. Illanra watched him, smiling pleasantly. Her smile faded after long minutes of Adam saying nothing.

His head swam, his heart thumped wildly and even his stomach rumbled. Was this a dream or a nightmare? What had he done? What could he do? Beads of sweat formed at his hairline, but he felt cold.

"Adam?" Illanra looked at him, clacked at Vela and grabbed his wrist. While she monitored his pulse, Vela approached and began pressing buttons on Adam's armrest. She pulled an oxygen mask out of the center compartment and fastened it on his face.

"Sorry," he said as soon as he was able to speak. He inhaled until he thought his ribcage would explode, welcoming the rush from the O_2.

"Careful, Adam. Breathe in for five, out for five," Vela said as she waved an object the size of an electric toothbrush over his head, neck and torso. She clicked at Rhen, who brought Adam a bottle of water.

Leo stood behind Vela, watching with concern as Vela checked the readings on her instrument. "Hey, buddy, this is pretty intense. I can totally understand freaking out a little," he said as he dropped into the chair Vela had left vacant.

Rhen reappeared, covered Adam with a blanket, and receded into the background once more. Markarian walked over, and gave Adam the thumbs up. Adam returned the gesture.

"Ok, I think you were in the early stages of a panic attack," Vela said. "You need to rest now. Leo, you're probably the best one to keep Adam steady. Do you mind sitting with him for a while?" she asked.

Redemption

"No problem, ma'am," Leo said. "I can bore almost anyone to sleep with my stories."

Adam looked over at the strange addition to the crew. He knew less about Leo than anyone onboard. Who exactly was this guy? He took a few sips of water, replaced his mask and looked at the only other human in the galaxy.

"So, what's your story, Leo?" Adam asked.

Leo smiled. "Don't think it was easy leaving a Fortune 500 company behind to travel with these folks," he told Adam.

Adam looked confused. "I'm sorry. You're on oxygen and everything. That was a joke. They didn't tell you about me? I could have sworn Greg said you weren't going to be happy about me trying to screw up your plan."

"When did you and Greg talk?" Adam's head was no longer throbbing, but talking to Leo wasn't exactly relaxing.

"Greg and Torus were keeping me…out of sight for a while. And I'm glad they did. That was the best year of a life spent…" Leo sighed and looked around at the Berenicians fondly. "In casinos and being an idiot," he finished.

"What are you, a professional poker player?" Adam asked.

Leo laughed. "Hardly. Professional loser would be more accurate. But I'm done with that. I've heard of people like me going to rehab or whatever, but these guys, Torus and his crew, they've done so much for me," he said.

"So you met Greg in a casino? Am I just really out of it or is your story a weird one?" Adam asked.

"I was never a nine-to-five regular guy. Not even close," Leo said.

"Ok," Adam said as he finished a large bottle of water. "Maybe you should start at the beginning."

Leo spoke about growing up poor in Barstow, California, a desert town without the glamor of Palm Springs or the revenue of Las Vegas. With his mother's fondness for alcohol and his father's fondness for being absent, assorted relatives and stepparents raised Leo and his two brothers to the best of their limited abilities.

Undereducated and limited to unskilled labor, as a teen Leo hustled pool, worked for a low-level drug dealer and tried to understand the system. Yes, the system had failed him, but he was certain he could crack its code and beat it.

His older brother worked casino security in Vegas and told him the odds were always with the house. It was a well-known fact in gambling. Odds were of little interest to Leo; a chance, no matter how small, was enough of a reason to feel any night could be his lucky night.

It was the story nearly every gambling addict told. Leo had periods when he could stay away from gaming. During these times he took online classes and found work in warehouses. Fortunately, despite his destructive habit, Leo had no criminal record.

He told Adam he enjoyed his mechanized coworkers. They didn't ask about his personal life or five-year plan. It was not fulfilling work, however. Meeting Hannah that night had confirmed Leo's belief that sooner or later, the universe rewards the deserving.

Within hours of their first conversation at the diner, he was sure they would spend the rest of their lives together. As if it wasn't enough that Hannah was beautiful and exciting, she obviously had the funds to provide him with the lifestyle he coveted.

Well, it was a half-win. He got to keep the money, which lasted him longer than he'd expected. Part of him was hoping Hannah would return, that it had been a misunderstanding.

He'd miscalculated when he saw a familiar face during the rollout of the Vites. Looking back, there was no way he could have known when the limousine snatched him off the street that night. He was sure the old man with the expensive suit would kill him. Or have his goons do it, more likely.

The trip to Ben's headquarters in Colorado had been…memorable. His first time flying in a Gulfstream. That was nothing compared to what happened when they landed.

Apparently, whatever was in the crate was worth a lot more than a hundred grand. That was chump change for Ben and his empire. He knew he was in over his head when they took him to the room with the paintings of blue people with lots of arms.

It was a dead end for Leo, he had so little to lose. Ben and his friend asked about his family. What would they think about what he had done?

Leo laughed at the question. Knowing his family, they'd probably ask "Leo who?" The thought made him start crying. And he couldn't stop.

They decided to let him sleep in on a couch in one of the conference rooms until they determined what to do with him.

Ajit, the third shift security guard, caught Leo trying to hang himself from the ceiling around 3:00 a.m. He informed Ben a few hours later, while he had two other guards watching him at all times.

Pulling up a chair next to Leo, Ben asked security to leave.

"Sometimes, when we are under a great deal of pressure, we develop a kind of tunnel vision. We lose sight of the bigger picture," he told Leo.

"My picture is blank. Just kill me, ok? There's no reason to go on living." Leo had lost all hope.

"Maybe you could start over, you know? Go somewhere else and just start a whole new life," Ben suggested.

Leo looked at him in disbelief. "How would I do that?"

Ben smiled at Leo. "The big picture you have lost sight of? It's huge."

Adam was incredulous. "You were going to kill yourself? So that's when Ben…"

"Yep. Took my mind off just about everything else. Well, you can imagine," Leo said.

"I thought I was losing my mind that day in Roswell," Adam confessed.

“Yeah, I think anyone would. But in the last few months, I’ve felt more settled, more together than I ever have in my life,” Leo said with quiet certainty. “We went to Loretta Lane after Colorado. I was in the cellar for a while, until they were sure they could trust me. I’m not sure if I trusted me,” he said with a laugh.

“So your story has a happy ending, Leo. I’m glad to hear how things turned out for you,” Adam said, fighting a yawn. He wondered if Vela had given him a sedative of some sort. Leo’s story was interesting, but his eyelids were heavy.

“Wake me up when we get there?” he asked Leo.

“Sure thing,” Leo said. “You know I’ll look out for you as long as we're out here. We’re the only humans around, whatever you need me to do, you know?”

“I appreciate it,” Adam said as he drifted off, still sitting under the blanket in his chair. He dreamed of endless fields, rippling bodies of pale green water, with small blue crystals floating on the surface. They were singing to him, their chimes enchanting.

He was badly in need of rest, having learned the term “active listener” was a fitting term. The hours spent hearing the Berenicians’ stories had been transformative. Adam had mentally checked all the boxes on the first page of his strategy to get to know them. They had families, internal conflicts and responsibilities. Encouraged by what he had learned, he had concluded there were more similarities between the DNA of our civilizations than were differences, despite the unfathomable distance between the two worlds.

Pleasantly, the day-long engagement had also served to occupy his mind and kept it away from thinking too much about the realities of all the spatial disorientation that was taking place just outside the now seemingly much too thin walls of the *Obsidian*. Adam had convinced himself it just wasn’t necessary to dwell too much about traveling into the nothingness of space, inside of a bubble made of a very thin layer of light that was meticulously breaking every physical law that had ever been known to humans. The possibility of instant vaporization and having one’s body return its particles from whence they came was an all too real potential outcome.

Before Dr. Alex underwent his metamorphosis, he had shown Adam the pages upon pages of formulas that made this journey possible. But it wasn’t too far into the first string of x’s, y’s, f’s, and h’s integrals of the various differential equations that Adam yielded to taking Alcubierre’s theoretical warp drive idea on faith.

Fortunately, all the windows on the *Obsidian* had been darkened just prior to leaving Earth. While it was necessary in order to shield the eyes of those on board from the blinding light of the wrap bubble, it was also preferred. Adam now understood why all the cars on the

Vites were equipped with just such a feature when converting to interstellar mode. Only now was some of the engineering that the molecular machines performed during the flying car manufacturing was making sense. At the time, he complained to Greg that it was unnecessary, and Greg had reassured him repeatedly that there was a reason for everything the machines did. Adam laughed to himself. He should have learned long ago to listen to his friends.

In the few hours that were left before reaching Berenices, Adam had started having a pleasant dream about the conversations he'd had with all his new friends and felt he was beginning to understand what Berenices would be like. He could also see himself on Julie's driveway talking to Chris, Bri, and Julie on how effortlessly they would travel in the cosmos together.

Everything was remarkably vivid. Just as he was approaching a near perfect state of REM while finally being able to coax his anxious family into tripping the light fantastic and boarding the finest luxury vehicle that Andromeda had to offer, a booming announcement from the *Obsidian* Commander echoed across the bridge.

"Markarian, please prepare to launch the particle disruptors. Tidal force will be deactivated to exit foliation. Curb geodesic freefall and exit warp bubble on my mark. Arrival into Berenices' exosphere in three minutes," he said, mainly for the benefit of the humans on board.

Adam's heart raced as the sound of Torus' voice had quickly evicted him from the inertia of his sleep. The rest of the crew had already organized their assigned areas and secured the braces around their chests. Adam and Leo hurriedly followed suit.

Torus continued spewing instructions and information to the crew and its passengers in his captain's voice. "We arrive in quadrant three through space gate seven. The Intergalactic Security Forces (ISF)," which Adam took to mean the space version of the TSA, "has informed us that a great throng of civilian craft has also gathered there to meet us. The Council of the Guardians has authorized an unusually large gathering beyond our atmospheric security boundaries to welcome you home... heroes. All the Houses of Berenices will be represented."

A swell of emotion overtook the bridge. It had been almost one hundred years since anyone onboard had seen Berenices and the beauty that awaited. They were almost home. Torus, maintaining his professional duties, continued his instruction to Markarian. Clearly emotional, his voice began to crack. "Reduce *Obsidian* to ionic pulse, in five, four, three, two, one....engage."

And then, as smooth as a light summer's breeze, the *Obsidian* stopped folding space. The shields on all the windows of the craft brightened as Adam began to have trouble breathing. There was a large, clearly celebratory gathering of ships of all shapes and sizes around what looked to be a large hexagon shaped space station out in the distance. Most assuredly, this was space gate seven. On board, a transmission of the Harvesters began streaming. Adam and Leo watched, wide-eyed, as the gargantuan machines poured the precious cargo of Earth's sand into the many wounds strewn about the planet's crust. Outside, there was a large gathering of ships. They were rapidly coming into view and garnered most of the attention from the crew.

Adam could do only one thing. Stare. His heart stopped.

The world before him was a breathtaking sphere of color and light. Thick swirls of blue and white covered the globe, creating shades from rich violet at the south pole to palest, frothy blue at the equator, hues curling around each other with a deftness that Van Gogh had unknowingly replicated, but Berenices perfected. Interspersed among unfurling spirals were islands of gold and bronze, solid and steady in the dancing seas.

It was strange and familiar, coming in contact with a planet that had haunted his dreams for as long as he could remember. Berenices held secrets and promises, sure to keep him intrigued for several lifetimes. Adam lost himself studying the topography, trying to memorize every shape and shade, afraid so much beauty was surely a mirage, too captivating to truly exist.

She welcomed the *Obsidian*, joyous at the return of the ones who had departed in order to save her. Yet nothing would ever convince Adam that Berenices was even happier to make his acquaintance. Each was the one the other had waited for, brought together by forces that had traveled the universe to make their meeting possible.

Markarian leaned over and smiled at his transfixed friend. “Is it what you expected?”

Adam couldn't tear his eyes away from the sight before him. He shook his head. “It's more.”

BOOKS in the SERIES

INFINITE EARTH: BLUE STONE

In the first of *PULSAR's* prequel series, the crew of the *Mesolite* makes first contact traveling across the universe on a desperate mission to save their home planet.

In the time of Earth, it is 3,000 BC, when the aliens arrive and they quickly realize they've discovered a civilization in its infancy. With little technological awareness, humans have no way to help the aliens reconnect the tether they severed when they folded space to reach our solar system.

Unable to return home, the aliens, who were planning to inveigle Earth into becoming a suitable donor, launch their one-way mission plans. While trying their best not to interfere with the development of human civilization, they grow impatient and help humans accelerate the planet's advancement, leading to a simple act of carelessness that forces them into an unfathomable dilemma. Knowing now how far they need for Earth to progress before time runs out on their planet, they must decide if they should destroy human lives and much of what they created to keep hope alive.

In their final act, the Blue Stone is left as a marker—as a beacon—and becomes the first symbol that Earth is on a collision course with its destiny.

INFINITE EARTH: ORANGE STONE

The second of *PULSAR's* prequel series, Orange Stone begins three hundred and fifty years after the first *palvei* of aliens from somewhere in the Virgo Cluster lands on Earth. Still searching for a way to complete the harvest, the *Allusion* appeared high in Earth's atmosphere, ready to engage.

With no contact from the earlier *Mesolite,* their successors knew the operation had failed. They would discover, once again, Earth was a technological infant, lacking the advancement to be of any assistance to their ambition. A helpless feeling swallowed the Earth visitors as they realized, like the crew of the *Mesolite*, they would never go home.

The crew, or pavlei, find evidence of vitrification and an all too familiar heat signature revealing the Earth had been scorched, and realize something had gone terribly wrong. Questions arose about why the inhabitants of this world had been attacked before the harvest could take place.

With one-way mission orders going into effect and the clock still ticking on their home planet, the towering, silvery occupants of the powerful craft decide to resume the clandestine operation and continue readying the blue planet for her eventual invasion. Having traveled 65 million light years, the aliens do their best to advance humanity. To complete their altered mission, the visitors, guided by the Orange Stone, will conceal it to mark the precise location where one of the four incisions into Earth's core will occur. They wonder if what they've done is enough and if any from their world will ever follow.

INFINITE EARTH: VIOLET STONE

The third in *PULSAR's* prequel series. Two thousand years have passed since the *Allusion* visited the Earth. War in the Virgo Cluster threatened to eliminate everything that was good and pure in the galaxy. Even Earth would have been consumed had a certain form of good not prevailed over evil. The distraction of war did not replace the need for what humans possessed.

Surviving the onslaught, a third ship, the *Iolite*, finally enters the solar system of the only known paradise planet that could save their world. Two thousand years was all that remained. If the *Iolite's* pavlei could not successfully prepare Earth in that time, their constellation would become a black hole. The crew was down to a speck of time against the backdrop of the universe.

Before reaching Earth, five visitors aboard the *Iolite* have a mind-altering experience while making the precarious journey across the universe. After surviving the devastating effects of a dimensional shift during their fold, the aliens lose contact with reality and temporarily become confused about who they are and why they've come. Relying on artificial intelligence to remind them, their long range scans of Earth find evidence of two stranded spacecraft from their own world, the *Mesolite* and the *Allusion*. Hallucinations, coupled with learning that they will never again go home, spawns apathy for the operation. As they discover more about their mission and the dire circumstances facing their own planet, a fractured pavlei set out to find a secure place for the Violet Stone. Despite feeling lost to start their own journey, as fate would have it, the *Iolite's* alien pavlei will eventually deliver a gift to humans that will provide them with part of the equation belonging to the universe. Humanity, newly armed with a tool to find its own way, will spark hope that Earth can progress far enough in the time that remains. Hope is all that is left.

INFINITE EARTH: GREEN STONE

The fourth in *PULSAR's* prequel series. After three spacecraft from the Virgo Cluster's unsuccessful attempts to triangulate with Jupiter over the last millennium, the *Obsidian* was the last hope for their world. Successfully maintaining the integrity of the fragile container of light by which she traveled, the craft arrived in Jupiter's orbit in the Earth year of 1942.

On board were eight gray visitors, each selected for having specialized skills for this kind of invasion. If not successful, this would be the final mission and all life would end on the planet located somewhere in the Virgo Cluster. For several thousand years, numerous expeditions had been launched into the vastness of space trying to reach Earth, their prize. Of the many, only four, including the *Obsidian*, had managed to survive in the folds of space. The rest disappeared into its darkness.

As the *Obsidian* nears Earth, the ship's conscious AI begins displaying all manner of sounds and images emanating from the blue planet. Not only were the homing beacons of the *Mesolite*, the *Allusion*, and the *Iolite* detected, but a variety of other transmissions were all simultaneously streaming into the *Obsidian*. Gamma, infrared, ultraviolet, and radio waves inundated the ship's reconnaissance systems. Earth had made huge advances in technology; the machines of its people were all very busy. There was hope there would be enough time to save their distant planet.

The on-board logistical ubiquitous companion, LUC, was discovering the prior alien visitations had not been in vain. Not only had they assisted human civilization with technological advancement leading into its twenty-first century breakthroughs, it had also laid the groundwork for what was soon to become of Earth. There was just enough time, there was still hope, and they had a plan. The finer details of that plan came on the journey from Jupiter to Earth. There would be no cryo-sleep for the voyagers of the *Obsidian*. They would land in Roswell. Roswell is where it would be revealed, and Roswell is where it would end.

WWW.THEINFINITEEARTH.COM

@EARTHISINFINITE

Made in the USA
Middletown, DE
19 February 2024